"Mr. Butor writes well, an[...] what he wants to achieve [...] so disinclined to dramatiz[...] gifts are those of a lyrical p[...] elist—a sort of urban Words..... who has lost faith in tranquil recollection."

New York Times

"Judging by this novel the experience [of working in Manchester] has marked him for life, for *Passing Time* is not so much a hymn, as a whole oratorio of hate. The mood suggests Kafka at his most paranoid; the method harks back to Virginia Woolf but here the stream-of-consciousness has become a turbid flood, the dark Irwell, mazy as the Ganges delta."

The Guardian

"Butor's most accessible work in English. Sentences last whole paragraphs, with their Claude Simon-like sub-clauses and meanderings—personally I rather like that kind of writing."

ADRIAN TAHOURDIN – *TLS*

"Without doubt the most formidably intellectual of all the fabrications of the *nouveau roman*."

JOHN STURROCK – *The French New Novel*

"This is at once complex, brooding, and compelling, exciting; a book that demands attention and draws its reader completely onto the fictive journey. The city is so forensically evoked it takes solid form in the imagination. What an achievement, to make such a comment on societal structures and the stratification we humans impose on our existence in a book that's also a proper page-turner."

DONAL RYAN – author of *The Spinning Heart*

"*Passing Time* is as revelatory as Butor's critical writing on time and space: here is a model for the metaphysical noir tradition that has borne such rich fruit in the quest narratives of tortured detectives seeking to escape labyrinths of their own making. It's about time this Manchester root of the *nouveau roman* was given fresh attention. Respect to Pariah for breathing new life into this almost forgotten classic."

"A fascinating hybrid: vivid & disorientating, cartographic & discombobulating. It is reminiscent of Italo Svevo's *A Life*, but this sort of post-industrial ode to the admin worker is also entirely original. It moves simultaneously on separate tracks, speaking of the life of the bewildered, and might even be a reclamation of selfhood in an alien place. As an anatomy of a place and a life at a particular juncture in time, it is unique, and feels like a unique post-industrial (Manchester) novel. A remarkable work, a brilliant brilliant re-discovery."

"A meditation on Britain's imperial and industrial decline, a search for lost time, a dizzyingly self-reflexive detective story: in reading Michel Butor's *Passing Time*, we are reminded of the fact that the best English experimental novel of the 1950s was written in France. Jean Stewart's translation is unbowed by Butor's labyrinthine sentences, while also offering its own sense of the language-world of Bleston, the imagined northern city in which the novel is set."

"The long, and often lyrical sentences consistently produce an incantatory, even hallucinatory effect, essential to Butor's purpose. To those readers who have lived in one of the cities of the industrial north, the novel will have special appeal."

"In *Passing Time* and *A Change of Heart*, Butor's heroes display great energy in their effort to resist the leveling power of the capitalist city and bourgeois life."

·PASSING TIME·

Michel Butor

Translated by Jean Stewart

P
A
R
I
A
H

First published as
L'Emploi du temps
Copyright 1956 Les Éditions de Minuit
7, rue Bernard-Palissy
75006 Paris

Passing Time
Copyright 2021 The Jean Stewart Estate
English Language Translation Copyright 1960 Jean Stewart

ALL RIGHTS RESERVED
Published by PARIAH PRESS 2021

PARIAH PRESS
pariahpress.com
pariah@pariahpress.com

British Library Cataloguing in Publication Data
Butor, Michel
Passing Time
ISBN 978-0-9930378-7-0 paperback

Cover art by Steven Cherry

Text designed and typeset in Linotype Granjon by Tetragon, London

Printed by CPI Group (UK) Ltd.

Thank you:
Danny Moran, Catherine Annabel, Julien Van Anholt, Salomé Dacquin, Andrew Biswell

I
First Steps

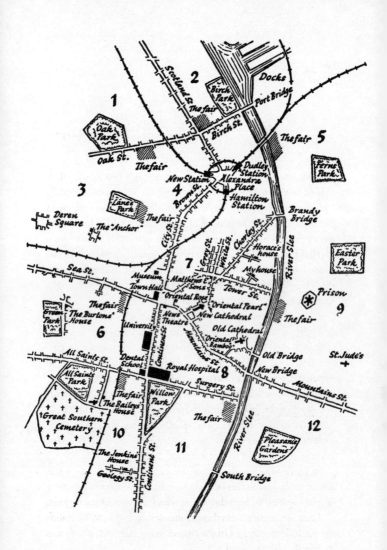

I

Thursday, May 1st

S uddenly there were a lot of lights.

And then I was in the town: my year's stay there, more than half of which has now elapsed, began at that moment, while I gradually struggled free of drowsiness, sitting there alone in the corner of the compartment, facing the engine, beside the dark windowpane covered on the outside with raindrops, a myriad tiny mirrors each reflecting a quivering particle of the feeble light that drizzled down from the grimy ceiling, while the thick blanket of noise that for hours past, almost unremittingly, had enfolded me began to thin at last, to break up.

Outside there were drifts of dark mist and cast iron pillars going by, slowing down, and between them lamps with enamelled reflectors dating, no doubt, from the days of paraffin lighting; and then white letters, regularly spaced, against tall red rectangles spelt out: BLESTON HAMILTON STATION.

There were only three or four passengers in my coach, for this was not the fast through train which I ought to have taken and on which I was to have been met; I had missed that by a few minutes at Euston, which was why I'd had to wait indefinitely at some junction for this mail-train.

If I had foreseen the extreme inconvenience of such a late arrival in a place like this I should have had no hesitation in putting off my journey 'til next day and sending apologies by telegram.

I can remember everything quite clearly, I remember standing up and smoothing out the creases in my raincoat, which was then still sand-coloured.

3

I feel sure I could recognise with absolute accuracy the place where my single heavy suitcase lay in the rack and the place where I let it drop between the seats and through the door.

For my vision was still like clear water; since then, every day has clouded it further with a sprinkling of ash.

I stepped onto the almost deserted platform, and I realised that these last few jolts had wrenched off the old leather handle of my case, and that I should have to endure the extra strain of holding my thumb carefully pressed over the torn place and my fingers clenched.

I waited, standing upright with my legs slightly apart to steady myself on this unfamiliar ground, and stared about me; on my left, the red metal plating of the carriage I had just left, with its thick door swinging to, and on my right other lines, with a few glints of hard light on the rails; farther off other coaches standing motionless and unlighted under the same huge vaulted roof of metal and glass, the scars in which I could guess at through the haze; and opposite me, above the barrier which the ticket-collector was just preparing to close behind me, the great luminous clock face showing two o'clock.

Then I took a deep breath, and the air tasted bitter, acid, sooty, as heavy as if each droplet of its fog were laden with iron filings.

I felt a gust of wind brush my nostrils and cheeks, its touch as rough and sticky as a damp blanket.

I sniffed the air, I tasted it, knowing I was now condemned to breathe it for a whole year, and I realised that it was laden with those insidious fumes which for the past seven months have been choking me, submerging me in that terrible apathy from which I have only just roused myself.

I remember I was seized with sudden panic (and this showed foresight: what I dreaded was precisely this sort of madness, this darkening of consciousness), and for one endless second I was overwhelmed by an absurd wish to draw back, to give it all up, to escape; but a huge gulf now separated me from the events of that morning and the faces I knew best, a gulf that had grown

4

inordinately wide while I was crossing it, so that now I could not plumb its depth and that its other bank, incredibly far away, only appeared to me as a faintly jagged skyline on which no detail could be discerned.

Friday, May 2nd

I picked up my case and began to walk on this unfamiliar ground, in this alien air, amongst the motionless trains.

The ticket-collector locked the gate and went off.

I was hungry, but in the great hall the words "Bar" and "Restaurant" flaunted themselves above closed iron shutters.

I wanted a smoke, and felt in my jacket pocket; but my packet of *Gauloises* was empty and there was nothing else there.

And yet that was where I had stowed away, a few minutes or a few hours ago, I'd forgotten exactly when, that letter from the head of Matthews & Sons giving the address of the hotel at which a room was being kept for me.

I had read it over once more in the train, and so it could not possibly be in my case, which I hadn't opened during the whole journey; but after hunting through my clothes in vain, I had to make sure and rummaged among my shirts, in vain.

It must have fallen down in the railway carriage, where I could not possibly look for it now, but that did not worry me, since I was sure I could easily find some provisional shelter in the immediate neighbourhood.

The taxi-driver, seeing in me his last hope of a fare that night, asked where I wanted to be taken (that must have been what he was saying), but I could not recognise the words he spoke, nor could I utter a word of thanks in reply. I heard myself give a sort of mumble.

He stared at me, shaking his head, and as I walked silently away from the station, keeping straight ahead, I saw his black car circle round the terrace, drive down the parapeted slope and disappear along the deserted street below.

The tall street-lamps cast an orange glow on the unlighted shop signs, the high shutterless housefronts in which all the windows were dark and all the shops shut, and there was no sign of any hotel. I came to a place where a gap between houses showed an open space where double-decker buses were starting up.

The few people I met seemed to be hurrying as if there were only a few minutes left before some rigid curfew.

I realise now that the broad street I had taken on the left was Brown Street; on the map I have bought from Ann Bailey I can retrace all my wanderings of that night; but during those bewildered minutes I did not even look for a name at the street corner, because the inscriptions I longed to see were "Hotel", "Boarding-house", "Bed and Breakfast": those inscriptions which I have since seen on going past those houses by daylight, in bright enamel letters on first or second-floor windows, but which were then so completely hidden in the gloom of the small hours.

I went back to the square, which had emptied meanwhile; I wandered slowly through some of the lanes at the back of the houses, stopping every few yards to put down my heavy case and change hands; then as the fog was turning into rain, I decided to go back to the station and wait for morning there.

When I reached the top of the slope, I was surprised by the breadth of the façade; true, I had not looked closely at it before, but had I really gone under that portico? Hadn't there been a glass porch? And how could I have failed to notice that tower?

When I went in, it was only too plain that I had gone astray during my brief wanderings; I had come to another station, Bleston New Station, just as empty as the first.

My feet were aching, I was soaked, my hands were blistered; I decided to stay where I was.

I read over various doors: Enquiries: Tickets: Bar: Station-Master: Assistant Station-Master: Parcels Office: First-class waiting-room (I turned the door-handle in vain): Second-class waiting-room (I was equally unsuccessful): Third-class waiting-room (there was a light inside).

I went in; I saw two men asleep on wooden seats, two very dirty men, one stretched out on his side with a hat over his face, the other lying on his back, his knees up, his head thrown back, his mouth open, showing almost toothless gums, with a fortnight's growth of beard and a scab on his right cheekbone, while his right hand with two fingers missing dangled to the ground.

A third man, sitting by the fireless chimney-piece, an older man, with bowed back and arms folded on his stomach, looked me up and down, glanced towards his two companions as though to warn me, and then with a jerk of his chin showed me an empty place, which I cleaned in cursory fashion before laying my case on it and sitting down beside it, leaning my elbow on the lid.

A quarter of an hour later, as a heavy footfall was heard approaching, the man who was awake closed his eyes.

I saw the handle turn slowly; the hinges began to creak; through the crack of the door appeared the blue-black helmet and then the face of a policeman. He seemed satisfied at finding all quiet and turned out the light; the hinges creaked once more; the latch clicked gently.

Soon after, against my will, I fell asleep.

2

Monday, May 5th

An ache in my right side woke me up; I was trying to turn over; my hand was rubbing against a rough surface; I felt as though I were covered with frozen mud.

When I sat up all my muscles seemed to creak, all my joints were stiff; I had to flex them one by one.

When I opened my eyes a grey light, like lye-water, was flowing through the room; I heard the regular breathing of the three tramps.

I checked the contents of my pockets (there was the whistle of a train), I picked up from the floor a long piece of string which was lying among some torn paper and mended my handle after a fashion, then I went out as noiselessly as I could and made my way towards the bar, which was open at last.

There were about a dozen people sitting there drinking out of white earthenware cups without saucers, at little round tables scattered about near a fireplace just like that in the waiting room except that lumps of coal were burning in the grate.

Three or four other people stood waiting, leaning on the counter behind which two women were busy with great urns.

I studied the price list over the shelves laden with glittering bottles, and then went up and asked for a large glass of rum.

"What did you say, Sir?"

She was at least forty, dried-up, bony, with nervous gestures, and there must have been a good many grey hairs behind her little starched cap.

"A glass of rum."

I wanted to say "if you'd be so kind", to make my request politely, but I already had the greatest difficulty in finding the few indispensable nouns, and I pronounced them so badly that I was conscious of it myself, to my distress.

"Rum?"

"Yes."

"Oh no Sir, sorry."

"But…"

She turned to another customer who was holding out a cup which she filled with tea.

Against the wall I could see the curving labels that displayed maps of Jamaica, negroes' faces, sugar-cane plantations.

"A glass of whisky then."

"Oh no Sir, I'm very sorry. Tea, orangeade?"

Her fellow-worker by her side, an older woman, about sixty, was gazing at me with disapproving curiosity.

"Nothing else?"

"Mineral water, soda, coffee, soup…"

"No spirits?"

"No spirits, Sir, it's no use keeping on asking, not before half-past eleven."

"Tea, then."

I went in front of the fire to drink it, in my steaming raincoat (which was still sand-coloured then). When I laid down the empty cup on one of the tables I noticed that I had left finger-prints on it; I had passed my hands over my rough cheeks and felt ashamed of having appeared before the waitress in such a state; I was nearly as filthy as the men in whose company I had slept.

I went down to the lavatory to wash; shaving was out of the question and there was no soap, but this preliminary clean-up was a great relief.

My shirt was clinging to my skin, and in the mirror where I could barely recognise myself I saw grey streaks on the collar and the black smuts that were still dropping out of my hair.

Wednesday, May 7th

I got rid of my case at the left-luggage office; then, tightening my belt and digging my hands into my pockets, I set out in search of a barber's.

The big clock outside showed half-past six; the rain had stopped; a few black taxis were parked alongside the entrance; a few porters, in shirt-sleeves, were pushing packing-cases on trolleys and loading them on to a lorry; a few travellers were hurrying off, in dark coats and tight bowlers, with umbrellas over their arms.

I turned round to study the façade, with its tower on my right, and on the long red rectangle the inscription in white letters: BLESTON NEW STATION.

I kept saying to myself as I went down the slope: "It wasn't here that I arrived but at Hamilton Station, this is the first time I've walked in this direction…" but I could hardly believe it, I confused the two buildings in my mind, and could not picture their respective positions.

There seemed to be something fake about the houses, which, still lifeless, rose ever higher around me.

Above the square stretched a wide October sky with a low, pale sun, faintly pink, while clouds raced by like herds of wet-furred tundra animals and on the pavements the wind raised eddies of bus tickets, straws, shavings and dead leaves.

In the middle of the square the great double-decker buses had begun massing again.

On two iron plates fastened on to a corner-stone I made out: New Station Street, Alexandra Place, and opposite, on an arrow pointing to the right, projecting halfway up a lamppost: Hamilton Station.

I tried to reconstruct roughly my last night's journey, and identified Brown Street, along which I had so fruitlessly wandered.

Some two hundred yards on I noticed the thick two-storey bridge that spans it, which darkness and fog had previously concealed from me; a train was passing over it; presently, walking round the three sides of Alexandra Place, I saw other bridges like it, at equal distances, over each of the streets leading out of the Place except those that led directly to the stations, and as all these arches looked like so many gates in an enclosure I fancied I must be in the heart of Bleston.

At the junction of the two longer sides I passed under the architrave upheld by four squat Doric columns, so thickly coated with black that they seemed like the trunks of fir trees left standing after a forest fire has destroyed their upper branches; then, at the top of the third slope, on which the new bricks on the façade of Dudley Station were still red, I went into the main hall, where the clock showed seven.

How slowly the minutes passed! How slowly they would go on passing until I could call at Matthews & Sons' office, which would not be open before nine—until things would at last be restored to their anticipated order!

I was forced to wait for nearly an hour, drinking one cup of tea after another, until the shops opened on the Place and I found a barber to remove my filthy beard, and nearly an hour more after that slumped on a bench near the bus station, running through my first packet of English cigarettes.

When I heard nine strike I went up to collect my case from the left-luggage office at New Station; by now the portico was disgorging a dense silent crowd and a long string of taxis moved steadily past.

I flung myself into one of these, giving the address of Matthews & Sons which I knew by heart, having written it on so many envelopes while fixing up my journey here.

The driver, who naturally enough had failed to understand me, started off at once so as not to hold up the traffic, then opened the communicating pane and shouted questions at me over his shoulder.

I had to tell him several times: "Sixty-two White Street", trying to improve my pronunciation, while we moved slowly down the slope; then he closed the pane, turned right, turned again, and we dived into Brown Street under the bridge.

I watched streets and houses go by, posters, red lights at crossings, huge buses past which we sped, and I was wondering at the length of the journey when I suddenly became aware that we had stopped and that he was getting out to open the door for me.

I glanced at the meter and paid him generously to avoid any argument, then I stood for several minutes on the pavement beside my case, looking at the brass plates on either side of the wide-open doors, three on each side, all obviously newly polished save for one already caked with verdigris, inscribed in relief with the names of the various firms and the floors they occupied, and more particularly at that of Matthews & Sons on the left at eye-level, between Bloomfield Ltd. and Habersmith & Co., and staring up above the number, 62, at the five rows of windows dwindling as they soared towards the cloudy sky, and the six cornices strung together by a drainpipe.

Friday, May 9th

I went up to the first landing slowly, clinging to the banister because of the weight of my case, and trying to remember the scant English I knew; repeating various polite formulae to myself.

Tensely apprehensive of not understanding, I rang, and the door opened of itself, disclosing the big room in which I now work every day of the week.

Only one of the nine gentlemen bent over their papers or their typewriters raised his head and addressed me as though I were a customer.

"Can I help you, Sir?"

"I should like to see Mr. Matthews, I am Jacques Revel, I…"

"Oh yes, the Frenchman; have you had a good journey? Pleased to meet you, Monsieur Revel, I'm Ardwick. Wait here for a moment; I'll find out if Mr. Matthews can see you."

I stood looking at the tenth table by the end window, that unoccupied table which presumably was going to be mine.

"Monsieur Revel?"

A bouncing, dumpy little man, red-faced, in a high stiff collar, led me into his office.

"Delighted to see you, Monsieur Revel, I am John Matthews, John Matthews junior as they say. You must excuse my father; he doesn't want to be disturbed just now. Do you like your hotel? James Jenkins went to meet you at the station…"

"I took another train; I only arrived this morning… I'm very sorry."

"It doesn't matter, Monsieur Revel, it doesn't matter at all, but you should have let us know. You must be very tired. Jenkins! Will you take Monsieur Revel to the Anchor, when you've introduced him to his new colleagues, of course. Have a good rest, Monsieur Revel, get settled in and be here at nine o'clock tomorrow morning."

Then James Jenkins, closing the door behind me, led me round to each table in turn, and I heard those eight names which I only began to memorise several days later: Blythe, Greystone, Ward, Dalton, Cape, Slade, Moseley and Ardwick, the names of the eight men whom since then I save seen every day of the week in the same place.

"Is that all your luggage, Monsieur Revel?"

I felt heartened by his gentle voice, with its note of shy gaiety.

I saw his hand close over the handle of my suitcase, his thumb carefully concealing the piece of white string that fastened it; his light blue eye winked at me; I felt myself blushing with shame and almost tottering.

"Of course you're going to the Anchor; old Matthews always sends newcomers there; it's become almost proverbial among us. He used to live quite close to it and as nobody has ever complained he's never seen the need to make a change. You'll see, the district is quite pleasant, there's even a cinema just next door;

I suppose it'll suit you all right, at least for a few days. We'll get there in a quarter of an hour with the car."

We drove on; the rain had begun to fall; the windscreen wipers were flicking to and fro through the streaming water; James went on talking in his quiet voice, telling me that this black Morris belonged to Matthews & Sons but that he had charge of it because there was a garage available in his mother's house; I was incapable of answering him and, before long, incapable of following what he said.

We stopped in front of a porch with small pillars thickly coated with white paint, above which the inn sign, a large gilt anchor, was swinging.

At the reception desk James talked at great length to a young woman with excessively blonde hair, wearing unpleasant horn-rimmed glasses, while I awaited the result of this conversation, too fast for me to follow, looking at each of them in turn and smiling to keep myself in countenance.

At last James Jenkins turned to me slowly and said, articulating very clearly like a conscientious interpreter: "The room reserved for you is on the third-floor. They haven't any other. You don't mind?"

I nodded my acceptance; I wrote my name and my passport number in the register, on the page headed Tuesday, October 2nd, and then James insisted on carrying up my case and deposited it in the small room, on the small bed.

"Jenkins", it was the first time I had called him by his name and it was to be several months before I used his Christian name, "excuse my bad pronunciation: I should like to know if the man who sat at the tenth table before me was a Frenchman?"

"No, Monsieur Revel, there have been no foreigners at Matthews & Sons since the war, and before then I was not with the firm, you see. You're the first I have met."

"Is it possible to have meals in this hotel?"

"No, Monsieur Revel, only breakfast. But there's a restaurant not far off, the young lady will show you."

"Thank you, Jenkins; goodbye 'til tomorrow, Jenkins."

There was no table; the window looked on to a brick wall at the end of a yard.

I said to myself as I undressed in the third-floor bathroom: "I cannot stay here, I must not stay here, I shall be done for if I stay here. Tomorrow I shall go and search for a better lodging."

When I went to bed that morning my watch said half-past ten, when I got up in the afternoon, six o'clock.

In the nearby snack bar I gulped down ham sandwiches and cups of tea.

Oh, on that second night at Bleston, how slow real sleep was to come!

3

Monday, May 12th

As my alarm clock rang, as I threw off my bedclothes in the wan light that crept through the thin curtains, as the cool lather frothed on my chin I kept muttering to myself: "Matthews and Sons, nine o'clock, sixty-two White Street", and gradually this became a question: "How am I to get there?" I carefully prepared my words to ask the young lady downstairs.

She leaned back in her chair, tapping her teeth with her pencil.

"White Street, did you say? What part of the town is it in?"

"I don't know exactly; near the centre, I believe."

"If it's not too far from the Old Cathedral, the best thing is to take a number seventeen bus. The stop's quite close by, second turning on the right. Ask the conductor, he may know."

The conductor told me: "Best get off at Tower Street."

I climbed to the upper deck and watched the cars gliding beneath me like river fish.

"Tower Street, Sir, Tower Street!"

I stood between tall buildings with brass plates on them, in front of which people were hurrying to work, and I stopped one of these as a clock was striking nine.

"Excuse me, White Street?"

"But you're in it, Sir!"

Then I recognised the door, the first after the crossroads, the number sixty-two, the six cornices, the drainpipe, the three steps up and then the staircase.

"Good morning, Monsieur Revel," John Matthews junior broke off his conversation with Ardwick to greet me, "did you have a good night? Everything alright? Today you will please file the letters. You'll find everything laid out on your desk, in the corner by the window. If you need anything explained ask Jenkins."

I sat down at my place; to my left I could see, through the windows, the upper stories, skylights, slate roofs, chimneys and lightning-conductors of the Vigilant Insurance Company; in front of me, in a swivel-chair that creaked with his every movement, sat Blythe (I still don't know his first name, I never have any dealings with him) and on my right James Jenkins: the whole set-up that has remained unchanged these seven months and more.

That morning old John Matthews, whom I had not seen before, made his appearance in the room, looking like his son's skeleton covered with shrivelled skin; on catching sight of me he rapped out: "That you, Revel? All right, don't disturb yourself."

At half-past twelve I took part in the general exodus, surprised to see Ardwick and Greystone remain seated at their desks as if nothing were happening.

"They won't go out to lunch 'til we come back," James explained to me. "We never close between nine and six."

I followed him into a second-rate café in Tower Street, a windowless basement.

"There are cheaper places, but they're self-service ones, and I think it's pleasanter here."

There was a little soup, a little fried fish, a few hard potatoes, a bottle of red sauce for seasoning, a small roll the size of a tennis ball, and to end up with a sponge cake which lived up to its name, covered with the inevitable custard, faded-daffodil-colour, that leaves a gluey taste in your mouth.

"If you're still hungry I can ask for biscuits and cheese."

How I missed his gentle considerate voice that evening, when I went back to the basement for lack of energy to hunt for anything better!

How dull the meal tasted (it was always identical, save for a few insignificant variations, the soup greener or browner, some currants or jam in the sweet) unenlivened by the questions he put to me, speaking so distinctly and waiting with such indulgent patience for my stammered replies!

It was thanks to him that I soon learnt to cope with my duties at Matthews & Sons, and he is the only one of my colleagues with whom I have had any relations other than purely professional ones, for although I have often lunched at the same table as Dalton and Cape at their favourite restaurant the Lancaster (which has the enormous advantage over James's, the Burlington, of serving drinks) they have never tried to get me to talk; they never sought to discover, all through that month of October, whether I were able to fit a meaning to their sparse remarks, which I now know consisted of "nice soft rain this morning", "old Matthews is in a rage", "you seem pretty peckish", or else "Bradford are leading again this year". And yet how obvious it was that I was straining to understand and to make myself understood!

Tuesday, May 13th

Still dazed from my journey, exhausted by my first few days at work which, although I was given only the simplest tasks, proved the hardest of my whole year because translation was still a constant effort and because I had to become accustomed to the countless details of a new administrative routine, I would find myself, when evening came, in a state of utter loneliness, incapable of taking the least decision and concerned only, once I had gulped down the last insipid mouthful, to climb on top of a 17 bus and watch those nameless streets go by until I reached that room which, once I was inside it, I tried not to see.

In bed, in the dark, I said to myself: "On Saturday it'll all be different, I shall have time to go and look for a room, to find my way about this town, whose resources I have not yet explored."

At midday on October 6th, therefore, on leaving Matthews & Sons, where everyone looked rather more cheerful as the week-end brought its respite (and for my nine fellow-workers the week had, as usual, been a long one, its only meagre incident being my arrival), encouraged by these brighter looks and by the mild clear weather I ventured down Tower Street, to the right, in hopes of finding there some pleasant restaurant.

These were the gloomy housefronts between which the 17 bus sailed away, a tall red rectangle, after I had left it in the morning, gloomy housefronts on which squat capital letters of tarnished gilt sprawled askew, like the chalk writing on the blackboards of primary schools.

I thought I must be quite close to the Old Cathedral, the terminus of this route, and I imagined it to be in front of me, hidden by some tall house, whereas it was on my right.

The streets and squares through which I had passed, the buildings I had seen and even those of which I had only heard had already grouped themselves in my mind to form a vague and quite erroneous picture of the town, by means of which I half unconsciously tried to find my way, having never, as yet, seen any map of the town and being still unable to estimate its real dimensions.

From every door there issued clerks in bowler hats and raincoats; cars drove past in a slow, dense stream; but whereas I expected to see the crowd and the number of shops increase the further I walked, on the contrary I found myself moving into ever more unfrequented regions in which shop windows and signs, already scarce in the neighbourhood of Matthews & Sons, were even fewer and farther between, and where the noise grew increasingly less.

I hurried on, and reached a district where the roadway was unpaved and deserted, where the houses were only two or three stories high, and where my way was blocked by a low wall behind which, at the bottom of a ditch some twenty yards wide, with walls as steep as those of a castle moat, I saw a sheet of water, thick, black and scummy, a peaty ooze, with the same smell I had noticed the first time I breathed the air of the town, on the platform at Hamilton Station, only harsher and more gruesome.

The sky was overcast; I was hungry.

At the sound of my footsteps a man, seated on the top steps of one of the steep iron ladders, turned his face towards me; it was as black as the water.

"Excuse me, Sir; could you tell me the quickest way to get back to the town centre?"

"What did you say?"

He spoke laboriously, as though with distaste; he sat huddled like a lump of earth under a coat, his body bent forward, his legs doubled up, his hands clasping his elbows, which were pressed against his knees at a level with my ankles; the skin of his face, even of his lips, was like thin leather that has long since lost its gloss; he raised his brown and yellow eyes to mine.

"To get to the town centre?"

"What do you mean by the centre?"

All his words were slightly, and as it were sombrely, distorted; but he uttered them so slowly in his deep husky voice, that I had time to identify them one by one.

"Alexandra Place."

It was the first example that occurred to me; I might just as well have told him the Old Cathedral or the Town Hall, neither of which I had ever seen.

"Alexandra Place, I don't know it."

He shook his head slowly to punctuate his words.

"No, really, I don't know; I haven't been that way for years."

"Do you never go out of this district?"

"It's not my own district, you know; I live near the bridge you see over there."

"Is there anywhere to eat near here?"

"I don't know."

"I'm sorry to bother you; I'm a foreigner, I only came here this week."

"You needn't tell me that, Sir, it's quite obvious."

"And over where you live, near the bridge?"

"A foreigner, good Lord! But what are you doing down here? All right, don't go away."

When he stood up I was amazed at his height (he's a whole head taller than I am).

"So you're hungry, Sir! You want some lunch! Well, so do I! Let's get going!"

He burst into that loud laughter that never quite obliterates his sadness, that unpredictable laughter in which even today I can but seldom join.

Wednesday, May 14th

We walked along by the river without looking at it; he kept chinking some coins in his pockets; and as we passed an iron gate he stopped, saying: "That's where I work, a cotton mill, you know; what about you?"

"I work at Matthews & Sons, I look after their correspondence with France."

"What do you mean?"

"I write letters in French."

"So you're a clerk, then. All day on a chair, eh? Very nice. And a Frenchman? Never met a Frenchman before; there can't be many about these parts."

"I can't say; I know nobody yet except the people with whom I work."

A fine drizzle was falling.

"And yourself?"

"What about me?"

"Where do you come from?"

"Me? That's not the same thing; I've been here a long time."

"But before that?"

"From Africa, of course, like the rest of them."

He had stopped in front of a half-open door on either side of which were fastened up advertisements for beer, white enamel plates with Bass's red triangle and Guinness's harp.

"Is this your restaurant?"

"Go in, it'll do you good. We'll go and eat afterwards."

Thus I made my first acquaintance with the chilly atmosphere, the greasy dust of half-empty pubs.

"What'll you have, Mr. Frenchman?"

I knew nothing about Bleston's drinks, their prices or the formulae for ordering them.

"I don't mind."

"Two pints of stout, Miss."

The dark viscous liquid brimming over in tall fluted glasses with handles seemed to me like a distillation of the river water itself.

He paid without leaving me time to protest; he drank his at one gulp, wiping his lips afterwards with the back of his black hand; I took much longer over mine.

As I did not want to be in his debt there was a second round, and as I was very hungry the walls began to sway all round me; I had to stand for a few minutes clutching the brass rim of the counter, watching the rings of foam on the mahogany-coloured linoleum, where each bubble carried a tiny reflection from the windows.

Outside, when we left, everything was streaming already.

He resumed the conversation of his own accord but on a quite different note, a deeper, angrier note, with his eyes fixed on the ground.

"There are many negroes in Bleston, there are many others besides me, particularly when you go farther north, but none of them are really from my country; they nearly all come from Sierra Leone, and they speak their own language amongst themselves—the English don't understand it, but nor do I.

"They live together in big houses with women, and they have gramophones and records; I go to see some of them from time to time, but you see I'm not really quite of the same race."

Through a big window on which the day's menu was painted in white letters I saw, bending over his account-book, a little one-eyed fellow in an apron, who did not get up, when we came in, until we had sat down at one of the three tables, and who then hobbled over to fling down on the stained paper tablecloth between us a bundle of cutlery.

"The usual?"

"The usual, for two."

"Bread... fish... vegetables... vinegar... tea... all right?"

Then he went back to sit behind his cash-desk.

A few minutes later my companion whispered to me, after extracting a last fishbone from his mouth: "Not too bad, eh? Do you want a sweet?"

"What are you having?"

"Me? I don't take anything as a rule; you know, they're not very nice here... So if you're not keen on it either, I think we'd better not bother him."

I felt cold again.

"I'd have liked another cup..."

"You've only to come along to my place; I'll make some tea for you, and it'll be nicer. Come on."

He got up, fastened his raincoat and went to lay a coin on the account-book, remarking: "Hullo, Jack!" to which he got no response.

Outside in the rain two small girls dressed in black scampered away from us, smothering shrill laughter.

"How much do I owe you?"

"Nothing."

"No, really, you're most kind, but although I am a newcomer I probably earn as much as you do."

I pulled a handful of coins from my pocket.

"Of course I know you earn as much as I do."

"In that case…"

"Why won't you accept what I've given you? Are you ashamed because a coloured man has paid for your lunch?"

"Not in the least…"

"Then why are you standing there? I thought you wanted a cup of tea."

He clapped me on the shoulder, encouragingly.

If I followed him although I felt ill at ease and even anxious in his presence, it was from curiosity, to be sure, and also from gratitude for his frankness and generosity, but chiefly because he spoke so slowly that I could understand him, and at the same time so badly that when I talked to him I was no longer ashamed of my horrible pronunciation.

"My place isn't very big, of course, but you'll see it's quite clean."

I looked at the houses around us, detached houses with uncurtained windows on their single upper floors, a few posters here and there on their sides, but no shops.

He twisted the flat, gleaming key between his thumb and his bent forefinger, then I saw the steep stair and the rail that shakes all over when you put your hand on it.

Thursday, May 15th

As I went uneasily into the darkened room, where at first I could make out nothing but the big, rumpled bed, the sour smell of soiled linen met me.

"Take off your raincoat, you can hang it up here; take a chair."

When he pulled down the blanket that hid the window, the light came in like a gust of wind and the twisted folds of the sheets became plaster-white.

"You're not cold? I can light the radiator; see, it heats fairly well. Come close and get dry. I'll put water on to boil; it'll be ready in a moment."

On the floor, almost underneath the washstand, the blue flame of the gas-ring gleamed; on his right, on a small mat, I saw a pair of high-heeled shoes, and in the hanging-cupboard that he had just closed, several dresses.

He straightened the bed, apologising: "She hasn't been here for several days, you see."

"Does 'she' often come?"

"I expect she won't come any more; she must have found work."

Spreading an old newspaper on the table, he laid on it two glasses, some sugar in a white paper bag, two small silver-plated spoons and his earthenware teapot into which he threw in lavish pinches the remains of a tinfoil-covered packet of tea, and then the boiling water.

"D'you like it strong?"

"Fairly."

"It'll be strong. I have no milk."

The liquid he poured out for me looked as black as the beer I had drunk earlier, or as the water in the ditch, full of those floating fragments of dead leaves whence it derived its powerful, bitter tang.

Still standing, he raised his dark right hand, holding the scalding glass in whose transparency a smoky flame gleamed.

"I bid you welcome to my home, Mr. Frenchman, welcome to the magnificent city of Bleston…"

He had meant to say these words in a jovial tone, but the slowness of his utterance gave them a strange solemnity, then suddenly laughter bubbled at the back of his throat as he said "magnificent"; repressed, it trembled through the closing words, then broke out, sarcastic, throbbing with rage, making the windows rattle, and then stopped suddenly as though broken short.

How often, walking along the streets or about my various rooms, I have heard those bitter words of welcome re-echo, whispered in my ears, and even now, when in his absence I think of Horace Buck, I see him first of all striking this attitude, playing this part.

When he had drunk a deep gulp and licked his lips he sat down; clasping his hands round his half-empty glass.

"Shall you stay here long?"

"For one year."

"Pay's good, I hope?"

"About thirty-five pounds a month."

"You're rich, Mr. Frenchman; you've been in Bleston five days and already you're earning far more than I who have been here so many years, far more than many of those who were born here and have never left the place."

His voice grew shriller and older; as I began to drink, he interrupted me by snapping his fingers.

"Wait, I must have a little rum somewhere; that'll warm you up still better. H'm, just a heel-tap."

The last drops trickled from the bottleneck into his glass.

"Pooh, it's not such a bad town; the wind's never as horribly cold as it is on the coast; it may blow mild for you."

He set the bottle on the table, then he sniffed in the fumes of the alcohol.

"Listen; when I arrived here, ten years after landing at Cardiff, I said to myself: I've done with moving about every three months; it's not worth leaving my job and my room merely to find others just like them, with the same rotten weather, and saying goodbye to my mates just as I've begun to know their voices well, merely to say it again just as quickly to the next lot; this is a hard town, but all towns are hard hereabouts; I've got to wait so that one day I can leave for good, take the boat and settle down once for all, with my own shop, in a very different part of the world.

"But whatever I manage to save by living like a tramp, some woman gets it out of me.

"What am I to do with her dresses if she won't come back to fetch them? Another woman wouldn't want them."

If he thus displayed his hatred for the people and streets of Bleston, slowly, framing each word with a margin of silent

26

effort, repeating himself, constantly interrupting himself to ask "you see?", "you follow me?", to which I replied "yes", or "of course" (a detailed reconstruction of our conversation would be pointless), it was because he recognised in me, the newcomer, the stranger, a white man capable of sharing that hatred, and this enhanced its significance, justifying and strengthening it.

He was clutching his cold glass tensely with his right hand; he emptied it with a grimace, then began to stroke it with his fingertips in order to calm himself.

Thus the first man with whom I had had a personal conversation in this town had drawn up this indictment against it, had taken me to witness his misfortune, had requested me to register his complaint, as though I were the delegate of a judge.

I tried, indeed, to be on my guard, to defend myself, but not hard enough; the gigantic insidious sorcery of Bleston overwhelmed and bewitched me, leading me astray, far from my real self, in a smoky wilderness.

Ill at ease in this dismal room, I dared no longer look at his silent face; as I pulled back my cuff to see the time on my watch, he raised himself suddenly as though awakening.

"The pubs will soon be open again; you must come and have a drink with me."

But I could not stay a moment longer doing nothing, waiting in the gathering sullen dusk, and above all I felt I must get away from him, from this negro whom I could not help.

I seemed to dread the contagion of his hatred and wretchedness; and indeed perhaps they had already contaminated me; my eyes were being gradually clouded by the same gloom as his.

I pretended that one of my colleagues had invited me to tea, that I was already late; I even invented an address, asking him whether he could tell me how to get there.

"How should I know? Why do you always begin by refusing? You look down on me. You're sorry to have wasted all this time with me..."

"Another day I shall be glad to; but this is the first time I am going to see these people and I cannot keep them waiting…"

"But if you don't know how to get there…"

"It's near the Town Hall, I believe."

"Then you must take a twenty-seven bus, the one that goes over the bridge."

He walked with me to the bus stop; the rain was lashing down; as I jumped on to the platform he called after me: "Come back and see me! Come back!"

He had not told me his name, and I had not noticed the name of his street.

Friday, May 16th

I climbed to the upper deck of the bus, almost on a level with the roofs of the neighbouring houses, which gradually rose higher, like dripping cliffs of coal crowned with pinnacles of rust.

I asked the conductor: "For the Cathedral, please?"

"Best get off at White Street."

He added something else, but once again I felt like a deaf-mute; he had involuntarily betrayed by a slight frown his surprise at my pronunciation, and his quick slurred speech slid over my ears so that I could not catch his words.

I had stopped short at the name White Street, thinking I must have misunderstood him, that he must be speaking of another street with a similar name, for according to the crude and inaccurate picture I had formed of the town, to go past Matthews & Sons again seemed absurdly out of the way, and I had not time to make him repeat the name, since he had already moved off, shaken by the jolting of the bus, to hand out tickets to the other passengers behind me.

I was forced to accept the obvious fact; we were travelling along Tower Street, we had reached the crossroads and the Vigilant Insurance Company, I could see the door of Matthews &

Sons with its number 62, and the conductor was shouting to me as he went down the stairs, one hand on the rail:

"White Street, Sir, White Street!"

I was back where I had started from at noon.

On the left side of the road I could see the words "Town Hall" on the back of the 27 bus—white on black in the middle of the tall rectangle of wet red metal—dwindle and then disappear, while on the right the words "Old Cathedral" came into sight, growing larger and clearer on the top of a 17 bus travelling in the opposite direction; I leapt into this, furious, feeling I'd been hoaxed.

I could not know that the conductor, hearing me speak of an unspecified Cathedral, had assumed that like most people in Bleston I meant the "new" one (of whose existence I was unaware and which in fact stands barely two hundred yards south of Matthews & Sons) and had directed me thither.

It was nearly six already when I got down in front of the closed side door with its Celtic patterning, in the narrow deserted square above which three black stone towers loomed overpoweringly; the gas lamps were lighting up in the dusky rain.

I walked round the apse without looking at it, and then in a small street, somewhat livelier than its neighbours, where lights still shone in a few junk shops and second-hand booksellers', I discovered a tea room of traditional style, panelled in dark oak, run by some prickly spinsters who offered me, by way of dinner, sardines on toast and tartlets filled with pinkish custard.

Then I came back, through the rainy blackness, to shelter under the arches decorated with a tangle of griffins and wait for the 17 bus, which carried me back to the Anchor; I travelled on it again next morning, Sunday, under a clear sky, having been woken by a gleam of sunshine which was almost warm and which made me long for the country, as far as the other terminus, Deren Square, four rows of villas enclosing a neat sparse lawn.

I walked on straight ahead, whistling, between clipped privet hedges, tiny gardens planted with russet chrysanthemums, and quite pleasant small houses with bow windows on the first-floor, that showed the backs of dressing-tables; I gradually gave up trying to decipher the names, all tinged with the same placid wishful-thinking: "Beau Site", "Blackpool", "My Heaven". I went on between the two rows, which reproduced indefinitely, in a way that could only satisfy a very insensitive eye, some original undoubtedly intended for quite a different landscape, for different vegetation, for a different sky, for solitude, for a background of hills and a screen of great trees.

On the flat horizon, on either side, tall chimneys stood idle.

I walked for nearly two miles past an uninterrupted succession of "retreats" as regular as the divisions on a yard-measure, all silent, with no sign of life save their smoke, frail cosy erections, frail refuges against the dark powers of the town, frail kennels for comfort-loving dogs, built without foundations or reinforcements.

After passing a first crossroads with four shops at the corners, all closed—a grocer's, a cleaner's, a hardware shop and a newsagent-tobacconist's—I hurried on, sick to death of these houses which were individually quite attractive, unable to look at them a moment longer, keeping my eyes fixed on the tiny pebbles embedded in the tar of the roadway or on the sky, now overcast.

It took me more than half an hour to reach, not, as I hoped, the end of this dreariness (the road went on beyond, without visible limits, straight ahead in its sickly-sweet desolation) but a break in it, a round crossing with an open pub, into which I went.

"No, we don't serve lunches, Sir, I'm sorry."

"Can you give me nothing to eat?"

"I can ask my wife to make you a ham sandwich; will that do?"

"Nothing else?"

"No, Sir. Wendy, a ham sandwich for this young man."

"Excuse me, do you know if there's a restaurant near here?"

"I don't think so, Sir. Have you heard speak of a restaurant near here?"

"Oh no, Madame, I haven't. Give me a pint of Guinness, please. Thank you. Where does this street lead to?"

"Which street?"

"This one, in this direction."

"This isn't a street, Sir, it's an avenue, Deren Avenue; it goes as far as Hamilton, you're almost there now."

"Are there houses all the way?"

"Of course, Sir."

"And is Hamilton a large place?"

"Well, of course it's not as big as Bleston, but it's a fair-sized town."

"And beyond that?"

"There are more roads and more towns. You're a stranger I suppose?"

"I wanted to go into the country…"

"There are some nice parks in Hamilton, Queen's Park particularly, isn't that so, Wendy?"

"No, not parks…"

"I see what you mean, real country. That's harder to find round these parts; there are bits of waste land between the towns here and there, but it's rather messed up and spoilt, if you see what I mean. See here; the safest thing, if you've a free weekend, is to take the train at Dudley Station and go out to the hills…"

He spoke too fast, I could no longer follow him; when he realised that I had stopped listening he broke off, and I paid him, with muttered thanks.

I went back the way I had come, between the two rows of identical symmetrical houses.

I felt as if I were not going forward, as if I had never reached the circular crossroads and turned round there, as if I were not only back in the same place but also at the same moment of time, which was going to last indefinitely, which showed no sign of coming to an end; and fatigue and loneliness, like long cold slimy snakes, wound round my breast, crushing it so tightly that my jaws were clenched and my eyes painfully puckered, while overhead the sky grew leaden.

When at last I got away from the dreary suburban mirages and reached Deren Square, which seemed surprisingly lively by contrast, I leapt into a 17 bus which took me as far as the junction of White Street and Tower Street, and there boarded a 27 as far as the Brandy Bridge stop where, the day before, I had taken leave of Horace Buck.

I did not as yet know his name; I did not know that of his street, Iron Street, nor the number of his door, 22; I had not really studied his looks; I could only have described him as a tall negro whose speech was slow and laboured; however, he was the only inhabitant of Bleston who had taken me into his home, and I thought I should be able to find my way to him; but I reckoned without those innumerable small housefronts, narrow streets, blind alleys, and the insidious fall of night, and my own shyness and inability to explain myself in a language still so unfamiliar, and the oddity of my vague question.

"A black man, did you say? What sort of a black man?"

I had gone backwards and forwards, I had wandered uncertainly here and there; then as the sparse, inadequate streetlamps suddenly lit up, their gas jets hissing, each surrounded by a halo of mist like a swarm of white flies with shimmering wings, I discovered that I had come back unawares to that 27 bus stop in Brandy Bridge Street from which I had left to start my quest.

Then I had the feeling that a trap had just closed, and I gave a start as if I had heard it snap.

There was nothing more to be done that night, nothing for it but to go back to the Anchor.

The town had begun to wear me down with its wiles, to stifle my courage; its disease was creeping over me already.

I have never again attempted to escape from it by walking straight ahead, knowing only too well that my strength would fail and the moment of respite lapse long before I could reach the landscape I dreamed of, long before my liberation, before I could be sure of having escaped; for I became aware, that day, that Bleston is not a city bounded by walls or avenues, standing out clearly against a background of fields, but like a lamp in the mist it forms the centre of a halo whose hazy fringes intermingle with those of other towns.

Never yet have I taken the train to get away, to breathe a different air, and this shows how deeply I am contaminated, how heavily my will is doped; and I fear lest, in the four or five months I still have to live here, I shall be incapable of going out to seek the help of different buildings, different horizons, different soil.

I fear that I shall prove unable to break free from the spell of Bleston until those last days of September when my contract with Matthews & Sons comes to an end, those last days of September when—as was decided from the moment I arrived here—I shall leave the place for good.

4

Monday, May 19th

This is where my real research begins; for all the incidents
I have noted hitherto have often recurred to my memory
during the past seven months, vivid and intact, belonging
unmistakably to those first seven clearly differentiated days
which form a quite separate period, a prelude, those days
preceding October 8th, the date on which I first embarked on
the week's round at Matthews & Sons in company with all my
fellow-workers and began to rotate with them, chained to that
grindstone which, on this as on every other Monday morning
at nine, has just resumed its unvarying motion, so that when
I crossed the threshold of 62 White Street I might have been
back in the past, a week ago, a fortnight ago, or even on that
same October 8th, the setting being always the same, varied
only by a decrease of light until January and an increase of
light afterwards, with the same actors in the same attitudes,
so that I should find it hard to specify at what moment some
particular trivial incident occurred, even though this may have
served for a long time as a topic for office chat at meal-times,
on meeting, or on parting (Ardwick's new suit, his first in five
years, Greystone's bronchitis, Slade's mourning for his father's
death, or an unforgettable display of temper by old Matthews
who had burst in with a handful of blank sheets of paper and
torn them into shreds which had fluttered away and settled on
all our desks, or the unexpected visit of his second son, William
Matthews, the firm's London representative, or the breakdown
of the central heating—"Wasn't it nice to see a coal fire in the

grate, Monsieur Revel?") so that in my memory all those weeks, the number of which appals me when I consult my calendar, and each of which dragged by so slowly, seem to be contracted into a single immense week, a dense, compact, confused week, all that is left to me of that long autumn and winter and early spring, that unvarying motion which will not stop until the end of September, since I am not to take a holiday while I am here.

This is where my real research begins; for I will not rest content with this vague abridgement, I will not let myself be cheated of that past which, I well know, is not an empty past, since I can assess the distance that divides me from the man I was when I arrived, not only the extent to which I have been bogged down and bewildered and blinded but also the gains I have made in some spheres, my progress in the knowledge of this town and its inhabitants, of its horror and its moments of beauty; for I must regain control of all those events which I feel swarming within me, falling into shape despite the mist that threatens to obliterate them, I must summon them before me one by one in their right order, so as to rescue them before they have completely foundered in that great morass of slimy dust, I must rescue my own territories foot by foot from the encroaching weeds that disfigure them, from the scummy waters that are rotting them and preventing them from producing anything but this brittle, sooty vegetation.

From the very first I had felt this town to be unfriendly, unpleasant, a treacherous quicksand; but it was during these weeks of routine, as I gradually felt its lymph seeping into my blood, its grip tightening, my present existence growing rudderless, amnesia creeping over me, that I began to harbour that passionate hatred towards it which, I am convinced, was in part a sign of my contamination by it, a kind of personal animosity, since although I am well aware that Bleston is not unique of its kind, that Manchester or Leeds, Newcastle or Sheffield, or Liverpool (which also, I am told, possesses a modern cathedral that is not uninteresting) or else, no doubt, some modern

American town such as Pittsburgh or Detroit, would have had a similar effect on me, it seems to me that Bleston exaggerates certain characteristics of such urban centres, that no other is as cunning or as powerful in its witchcraft.

I had been warned, I defended myself; if I had not put up so much resistance, I should have been incapable of telling this story.

I cannot remember in which of the three restaurants adjacent to Matthews & Sons I lunched on October 8th, whether it was at the Burlington in Tower Street with Slade and Moseley, or with James Jenkins, or else at the White in White Street with Ward and Blythe, or at the Lancaster over the way, with Dalton and Cape, the only restaurant of the three at which I still eat sometimes because they serve beer there, but at all events, after that meal I rebelled and made up my mind to go in quest of less insipid fare which would satisfy my palate as well as my stomach, since one's taste for fine, clean or subtle flavours is blunted and spoiled if one is deprived of them too completely and for too long.

Since we only had a brief hour off at lunchtime, I ate experimental dinners that week and the next, comparing and classifying all the restaurants within a radius of three hundred yards.

I discovered the best of them quite early on, the Sword, on the left side of Grey Street, the first street that crosses Tower Street as you go towards the Town Hall; it was on a first-floor, with green plants in the windows and pleasant waitresses, and the meals were tolerably well cooked. I went back to it the following Thursday, taking as my guest James Jenkins, whose help I had sought in my quest for a new room (I had also appealed to my other colleagues, who had all promised to make enquiries, warning me that I must possess my soul in patience, since it had become very difficult, these last few years, to find lodgings in Bleston, and who may perhaps have kept their word and hunted unsuccessfully in their own neighbourhoods, although I never heard any more about it), James Jenkins with whom I wanted to discuss the problem quietly.

"The best thing is to go through the advertisements in the *Evening News* and then ring up or go and see the places. Would you like me to come with you one day?"

"Thank you so much; I hope that with a good map of the town I'll be able to find my way about. Do you know where I can get one?"

"There's a very good newsagent's a little farther along Tower Street; I know the young lady who serves there. This evening, if you like…"

And that was how I came to meet Ann Bailey.

Tuesday, May 20th

I must try to reconstruct that first meeting, the impression she made on me that day, and therefore to suppress all I have learnt about her and all I have seen of her since then; for several months I thought I might be in love with her, because in those early days, before I had met her sister Rose, she was the only girl in Bleston with whom I had had any conversation.

James Jenkins had already told me her name when he introduced us to one another, that Thursday, October 11th, at about a quarter-past six; I had paid scant attention, and yet it had created a particular link between the two of us; amongst all those Bleston women, those anonymous salesgirls and waitresses, she became somehow different.

I did not look closely at her that day; I noticed neither her heron-grey eyes nor the very long reddish hair which she wore fastened in a knot, and yet, next time we met, I recognised her without a moment's hesitation.

I remember that even then I was aware of the silky texture of her hands, I was struck by the way her fingers moved between the blue and yellow covers of the various maps of Bleston, and the slight shrillness of her voice surprised me.

She watched me from a little distance, still and smiling behind her counter, while I hunted through the maps, unfolding and then refolding them, bewildered by the difficulty of choice among so many, incapable of making up my mind.

As for James, he had turned his back, apparently absorbed in deciphering a series of edifying Biblical quotations hand-painted on cards of various sizes and decorated with a few flowers.

She came up to me: "What do you want exactly? Can I help you?"

Fearful of making howlers in her presence, I became even more inarticulate.

"You see, I would like a map with the…"

The words for *itinéraire* and *trajet* escaped me. She waited quietly.

"You see, the buses… I don't know how you say it…"

She handed me the small sheet bound in red that contains the plan of the municipal bus routes, with all their bifurcations and crossings and the numbers side by side along the same segment, looking like a tangled bundle of string.

"But there aren't the names of all the streets!"

"Oh no, you need another map for that. Would you like a coloured one with an index on the back?"

"Whatever is best, clearest and fullest."

Wednesday, May 21st

I remarked to James Jenkins as I shut the glazed door behind me: "Now we only need an evening paper."

Then I looked up and saw on the opposite pavement, at the corner of Grey Street, the paper-seller in his cloth cap, with his hands in his coat pockets, outlined against the chemist's window, and propped up at the foot of the lighted street-lamp the yellow, black-edged poster headed *Evening News*, on which large letters, clumsily inked, announced some fire or robbery or other disaster.

Six pages out of eight were devoted to "small-ads".

"Well, this will keep me busy this evening! Won't you have dinner with me, Jenkins?"

Alone with him, I recovered my self-confidence and authority.

"My mother's expecting me... and as we have no telephone..."

"Some other evening then, Jenkins: tomorrow?"

He seemed reluctant to refuse; he was afraid of incurring unnecessary expense, since he would not have allowed me to pay for him a second time, and yet he realised how much I disliked eating alone.

"Why don't you come to us instead? Which day suits you best?"

Only later did I appreciate the privilege he was offering me; I am the only one of all his fellow-workers at Matthews & Sons to have been invited into that big house of his and introduced to his mother.

"Look, just now it is absolutely essential for me to find another room, and if I go to your home I shall not have time.

"It is so important for me; I find it rather hard to get used to things here. As soon as I have left the Anchor, as soon as I have settled down somewhere..."

"But you could come to lunch, one Saturday for instance..."

"Yes, of course, that is very kind of you, the day after tomorrow if you like..."

I spoke hurriedly, having suddenly realised to my horror that my first answer must have seemed disdainful.

"That might be a little difficult, but let's settle for Saturday week. Goodbye, Monsieur Revel, and good luck."

I was alone in Tower Street once more, with the prospect of a solitary dinner at the Sword; I was vexed with myself for having pretexted my search for a room, for I felt almost sure that if I had answered him differently he would have asked me to come the next evening or Monday, and as I assumed that I should only have to ring at three or four of the addresses mentioned in the *Evening News* to find a lodging that would suit me, it seemed ridiculous to have refused to postpone my investigations for one day.

James, on the other hand, although somewhat chilled and puzzled by the tone I had assumed, had judged my objections valid, for if he had no direct experience of the kind of difficulties I was about to face, he was sufficiently familiar with the ways of this town to foresee them.

During the following week, when I saw how fruitless were my efforts, I regretted my attitude even more keenly, for I should undoubtedly have preferred to spend at least one of those evenings at some pleasanter, and in the long run more profitable, occupation than this exhausting wild-goose-chase.

Thursday, May 22nd

As soon as I had gulped down my tartlet and wiped my mouth I rushed off to the 17 bus stop at the corner of White Street.

Since, in my anxiety to settle the question of my lodging as quickly as possible, I had put off for more than a week my first entry into the home of one of Bleston's citizens (as for Horace Buck, whose name I did not yet know, his colour and his rebelliousness set him apart, and moreover since I had failed to find his home again the previous Sunday I could not be sure of ever setting foot in it again), I must waste no time now but complete the essential preliminaries as soon as I could.

I felt impatient during the journey back; I kept turning over and unfolding on my knees my two maps and my newspaper, glancing through them although the jolts prevented me from studying any detail carefully; but when I reached my narrow room at the Anchor, where there was no table, a fact which I had deplored ever since my first night there but had forgotten all that day, my narrow, ill-lit room where the thin skimpy curtains over the shutterless windows gave me no protection from the thick blackness of night pressing against the panes, I was seized by a fit of discouragement.

I deposited on the livid green eiderdown the *Evening News*—which in its general layout was just like the copy I have bought this evening from the same paper-seller in front of the chemist's, although every line of the text is different—the red square plan of bus routes, which still lies today, soiled, crumpled and dog-eared, among my other papers on the left corner of my table in this pleasanter room to which I only moved a month later—and that long rectangular booklet the colour of milky tea, the big map, identical with the new clean copy which I have bought since, at the same newsagent's, from the same Ann Bailey, and which I am now turning over between the fingers of my left hand to check my statements and make them more precise; and I sat for a long time on the chair, the one chair, with its upright wooden back, staring at them, smoking the last cigarettes out of a packet of Churchman's, waiting for my strength of mind to come back.

At last I got up and spread everything out on the bed.

Then I saw the town; I who had stumbled mole-like through its muddy passages, I surveyed its whole extent at a glance, like some hovering bird about to pounce.

To be sure, my picture of it was far from perfect; the roof-slates seen from above, the smoking chimneys, the dark bricks, the macadam of the roadways should have spread over it like a great cloak of grey lichen streaked with rust, wrinkled, rugged, foam-flecked like that covering the rocks on the shores of cold seas, while the river, even on the brightest day, would have retained its tarry blackness under sparse gleams, and yet thanks to this picture I had learnt more about the structure of Bleston than an airman by flying over it, if only because of that dotted line denoting its administrative boundary, beyond which the houses are grouped under other names—that egg-shaped out-line with its pointed end towards the north.

Thus I, a mere virus lost amidst its filaments, was able like a scientist armed with his microscope to study this huge cancerous growth, this organism in which the different systems were picked out in appropriately coloured printer's ink:

blue for water notably for the Slee, that stream of pitch that divides the town unequally, the left bank covering twice as much ground as the right, the Slee which makes a wide bend eastward and which is crossed by six bridges—South Bridge, New Bridge, Old Bridge, Brandy Bridge, the only one which I knew by sight then, having watched the 27 bus go over it on the previous Saturday when I first met Horace Buck (whose name I did not yet know), Railway Bridge, over which all the trains for Dudley Station go, and finally Port Bridge, beyond which the river widens and branches out to form the basins between the docks, right up to the north,

black for the railway lines, with Alexandra Place looking like some sinister dark sun in annular eclipse, its three mouths shedding thin sinuous rays along which secondary stations clung like nodules, goods stations hung like pockets,

scarlet for the postal and administrative boundaries, not only the surrounding contour but the network of dotted lines and figures covering the town, indicating the twelve districts, nine on the left bank, three only on the right, and thus clarifying for me the significance of the "7" after Bleston in the address of Matthews & Sons, the "3" in that of the Anchor,

green for the parks, one in each district, except for the three central ones, the fourth with Alexandra Place, the seventh with the Town Hall, Matthews & Sons, the New Cathedral, and the eighth which was Old Bleston with the markets and the Old Cathedral; green, too for the cemeteries, of which the largest, Great Southern Cemetery, in the tenth district to the south-west, alongside the railway lines that run from Hamilton Station, covers as much ground as an average-sized town,

pale pink for the houses, deeper pink for public buildings, particularly in the streets dominated by two great thorough-fares which cross at right angles in the south-west corner of Town Hall Square: Sea Street, running horizontally across the map, which becomes Mountains Street and crosses the Slee by New Bridge: and Continent Street, roughly vertical on the map, which runs obliquely towards Alexandra Place and emerges between the slopes of Hamilton and New Stations as Brown Street, where I got lost on the night of my arrival, and then beyond Dudley Station as Scotland Street.

Friday, May 23rd

I identified the small pink block representing the spot where I was, in the north-eastern quarter, close to the left-hand edge; I traced the route of the 17 bus as far as White Street and that of the 27 bus from there to Brandy Bridge, I picked out the few streets I could remember among those I had already seen, and this revealed to me the extent of my ignorance, the regions with which I was more or less familiar being microscopic in relation to the whole (and if I have gradually succeeded in adding considerably to my knowledge, I have only to look at the big map of Bleston which is identical with the one I then possessed to discover vast zones into which I have never penetrated).

I had a long task deciphering the small classified advertisements in the *Evening News*, where almost every word was replaced by an abbreviation which I only succeeded in translating correctly after several attempts; I had a long and maddening task locating each of the ten addresses I had copied out, for the index of streets was printed on the back of the map and I had to turn it over each time; and finally I had a long and tedious task carefully working out possible ways of reaching them by bus; but when at last I went to bed, late, very late for these parts, I was satisfied, deluding myself that I had solved my problem.

I even wondered whether I had not been too fussy; weren't ten addresses far too many? Considering the modesty of my requirements, wasn't it certain that I should find my future home among the first five or six?

I thought I should need only two or three evenings to make my choice, whereas next day I started off by getting lost, the remote backstreet I was looking for being much farther from the bus stop than I had supposed, one of the crooked backstreets in the sixth district, on the west side, south of the Anchor and just north of the Green Park, close to the Burtons' home, in the district known as Shoemaker's Park because it was built on the site of a large garden *à l'anglaise* laid out about 1860 by a shoemaker who had made a sudden fortune on the Stock Exchange and then lost it all; some backstreet in this district, I've forgotten which.

Having kept neither that copy of the *Evening News* nor the sheet of writing-paper which I had spent so long filling up, I started off by getting lost, in spite of my precautions, in spite of the map I had bought, which was hard to read because of the particularly inadequate lighting in that part of the town and because of the rain, which was falling heavily that night.

Then when at last I discovered the right door I rang and knocked in vain, I got no answer; too weary and disappointed to embark immediately, in the chill wet darkness, on a second attempt, I went back to my narrow room at the Anchor.

5

Monday, May 26th

It is even harder here than in France to go on doing, over the weekend, something you have begun during the working week; the hours seem to belong to a different category.

I was so sick of the rain already, of the low leaden sky and of that climate about which I'd heard so many justified complaints! When I left Matthews & Sons at midday on Saturday, October 13th, and saw the blue sky, the flashes of pale sunlight on the windowpanes, when I felt the mild air, I decided to take advantage of it all.

After lunching by myself at the Lancaster, since Dalton and Cape had gone home for their meal like all the rest, I boarded the 27 bus which took me as far as Brandy Bridge and from there, going past factories and warehouses and railings and under the big railway bridge behind Dudley Station, I followed the left bank of the Slee as far as Birch Park in the 2nd district, one of the more industrialised sections, just beyond Port Bridge, the blind bridge as I call it with its parapets of screwed-on cast iron plates, taller than a man's height—Birch Park, a long rectangle of meagre greenery with clumps of slender trees with quivering foliage, which today is green, like the reflection of rushes on the surface of a ruffled pond, but then was yellow, thinned by the wind at regular intervals, drifting down in showers of planing leaves to light a sodium flare among the clusters of purple asters, a long rectangle skirting the water but divided from it by a high brick wall above which, by standing back a little, on a day as clear as this was, you can see the tops of the

45

cranes and warehouses that stand on the quays of the docks on the farther bank, and the funnels of tugboats: Birch Park, which was so desolate when I revisited it a few months ago, its silver trees barely visible, lightly etched against the façades of sheds topped with huge antennae, but which was overcrowded on the second Saturday in October, overcrowded with men and women huddling together on the benches, clad in raincoats the colour of mongrel dogs, on either side of the walks whose surface was a blend of clay, coal-dust and rubble into which dead leaves and scraps of paper sank, while the harsh cry of a few seagulls sounded shrill above the general hum.

Then, turning west down Birch Street between its serried rows of sordid houses and its high barbed-wire crowned walls, uninterrupted here and there by iron-barred gates and doors of dark corrugated metal, I crossed Scotland Street in which all the houses are shops, I skirted on my left the waste land where the fair is being held this month, and I went under the railway lines that go from New Station to the north, thus passing from the second district into the first, which is wealthier and more spacious.

Birch Street had broadened into Oak Street, which had young ash trees with shrivelled leaves planted along its pavements and newer, pleasanter houses of redder brick, whose windows had small leaded panes and bright fresh curtains.

I skirted on my left the waste land where the fair was held last month, then on my right the rich Jews' cemetery and the big stadium where cricket and football matches are held, and came at last to Oak Park, full of autumn crocuses amid the grass, where children were playing under their nurses' eye, Oak Park, which takes its name from a magnificent oak tree standing alone among elms and planes with tawny foliage like foxes' and bison pelts: I went up to have a closer look at it, while the sun dropped behind the chimneys of the cosy little houses and in the damp air everything took on a crimson haze; its bark seemed made of thick rust or acid-corroded stone, or concrete mingled with coal-dust and lead filings; like the crust that coats old buildings, it seemed to have been deposited by the air of the town.

What a sense of chill and desolation I felt when the keeper in his black, red-braided uniform blew his whistle at me, for I had lingered over-long by the pond, in its cement basin whose cracks were filled in with tar, watching the white, green-splashed ducks swimming about.

I had overstayed the legal hour of sunset, after which nobody may loiter in the parks.

I found a snack bar near the stadium and a bar a little farther on, and while the night grew more deeply violet and two or three stars came out, I walked through the straight quiet streets, where in lighted living-rooms I caught glimpses of meals that grew progressively more modest, until I reached the Anchor.

Tuesday, May 27th

As it was still fine on Sunday I went for a walk in the park in the 3rd district, Lanes Park, which has a small maze and a concrete rockery where chrysanthemums with shaggy fleeces were then in bloom, and afterwards in Green Park in the 6th district, close to the Shoemaker's Park area where I had strayed two days previously; but by evening the sky had turned into a sheet of dirty aluminium.

It took me a whole week to go through my list of rooms; I cannot retrace in detail each of the wearisome treks I made after a hurried meal; they are hopelessly confused in my mind.

I often found the doors shut, and when anybody opened, after an embarrassing interview on the doorstep—embarrassing not only because of my bad accent and the peculiar dialect spoken by my interlocutors, but also, usually, because of their suspicious looks and odd questions—would be informed that I had come too late and the room was already taken.

Only once, I think, during the whole of that week, a woman asked me in, a particularly angular woman, sallow, tight-lipped and hard-eyed, dressed to go out with her hat on her head and a shapeless bag of purple velvet under her arm, who after telling me: "There's no heating, but you can buy an oil stove; you'll be quite free, the only thing I insist on is that you should be in by ten p.m." and other remarks which I failed to follow or which I have forgotten, uttered in the same peremptory tone, showed me into a room without a table, even narrower and colder and more wretchedly furnished than that in which I was living at the Anchor, where I could never get warm.

I had to start all over again, deciphering the *Evening News*, looking up other streets on the map and noting a new set of bus numbers.

But I had learnt my lesson now; since it had proved so hard to make two expeditions in succession, I would pick out one single address each evening in my paper, and since these vacant rooms were snapped up so quickly I would plan my journey in the restaurant, between courses, so as to rush off as soon as possible after the appearance of the advertisement; and I carried out this programme on countless evenings, after leaving Matthews & Sons, while the nights grew darker and colder and rainier (and even when I was not forestalled, the squalor and dreariness of the places made me feel physically sick); the only result being that, as I prowled over the town's surface like a fly across a curtain, I began to grow familiar with the complex network of its transport system, with the main junctions of the channels through which its drab lymph flowed, like beer thinned down with slop-water, its weary crowd of sleepwalkers, their flesh muddily white or mauve, so that little by little I came to feel that my bad luck was due to some malevolent will and that all these offers were so many lies, and I had to struggle increasingly against the impression that all my efforts were foredoomed to failure, that I was going round and round a blank wall, that the doors were sham doors and the people dummies, the whole thing a hoax.

Being constantly reminded of more recent and more obviously significant incidents (such as my meeting with Rose Bailey or with George Burton, or even my eventual discovery of the room in which I am writing today, Wednesday, May 28th) which have begun to form solid clots amidst the haze of those seven months, I need real courage to bypass them and resume my story where I had left off, namely at that visit to the Jenkins' on the third Saturday in October, which I had waited for during a whole week spent in fruitless journeys in search of a room (and once more I feel the weariness of that weary month), waited for impatiently not only because for the first time, at last, a real citizen of Bleston, one born in Bleston and who indeed had never left it, was about to receive me into his home, thus making the first crack in that barrier of negation and mistrust that hemmed me in, that ban of which I had been conscious from the time I arrived, but also because I had already grown fond of this man, who had stepped out of the unfriendly crowd on the very first day and come to me, like a guardian angel with a patient voice, the only voice I could understand among the general babble, and at the same time like a child excitedly greeting the traveller from overseas; because I was already fond of him, and sought out opportunities of talking to him at some length, and above all, possibly, because he had aroused my curiosity about his mother through a few casual allusions made in a humorous tone that only emphasised his reverence for her, enabling one to gauge its depth and solidity.

James had taken me in the firm's black Morris, for which he was responsible, down White Street, across the square where the New Cathedral clock had just struck the twelve strokes that released us from our futile labours, then through Willow Street, alongside Willow Park, where the bare osiers crowd the stream that flows into the Slee after running underground through the whole of the 11th district; their sparse foliage hung like bloodstained pheasant's feathers against the charred bones of their branches. Finally, by way of the farther end of Continent Street, we reached that southern part of the 10th district which, fifty years ago, was the smartest in all Bleston.

On that third Saturday in October I set foot for the first time in that tall dilapidated house standing amidst lime trees and neglected lawns with small patches of kitchen garden here and there, that tall house which was far too big for the two of them but in which they could not possibly have offered me a room, since at that time the rain came into all those that were not in use (and even today the repairs they have at last managed to get done, by dint of saving and scraping, are far from completed). For the first time I saw that oval mahogany table, the three napkins edged with faded lace, the blue and white Chinese cups with their teapot, the clouded glass lamp (unlit, presumably, that day) and the two large copper-plate engravings in their beaded frames (one of a paddle-wheel boat in an Oceanian seascape, the other of some fugitive monarch, cloaked and crowned, rushing through a dense forest full of wolves with luminous eyes).

James sat on my right, watching me with some anxiety, trying to encourage me but wondering if I should stand up to the examination to which his mother, on my left, subjected me (with her eyes of slategrey and pearl, still so keen between lids like scarcely withered wildrose petals, under lashes of soft grey, and with her voice that was so like her son's that I had to make no special effort to understand her, and even more patient than his) during the whole of that meal of which I remember so little that I could not possibly say what we ate nor what Mrs. Jenkins was wearing, although I am sure she had on her ring (indeed she never takes it off); but I am equally sure I never noticed it that day, being entirely preoccupied with making a good impression, since the following week I wondered how I could have failed to notice so curious a detail; that meal of which I remember so little that the whole of our conversation has faded from my mind (we must have talked about France, about my journey, and what I thought of Bleston) except for one remark, Mrs. Jenkins' farewell at the door, inviting me to come back next Saturday, and thus informing me that I had forced my way through one of the cracks in that wall of clouded glass that separated me from the town of Bleston.

Thursday, May 29th

I heard the great gate creak as James closed it behind me, about three o'clock on that Saturday, October 20th, while the metallic sky over Geology Street turned from zinc to pewter.

I went to the nearby bus stop to take a 23, having already discovered that Old Cathedral Square is the terminus for those buses whose numbers begin with 1, Town Hall Square for those beginning with 2, and Alexandra Place for those beginning with 3.

Along Continent Street I passed the fork of Willow Street, then Willow Park, a triangle whose third side consists of Surgery Street and the Royal Hospital with its two domes inspired by those on Wren's Naval College at Greenwich, then on the left came the huge neo-Gothic catafalque of the University, with its belfry; and at last I reached the busy square where a whole herd of red and blue double-decker buses were lining up and moving out in front of the municipal building, which with its ridiculously crenellated black towers looked like one of those lead castle keeps with which our grandparents played at toy soldiers; that square which was obviously the hub of the town's activity, its shopping centre with the three big department stores, Modern Stores at the corner of Mountains Street, Grey's and Philibert's on either side of the opening into Silver Street; with entertainment provided by five big cinemas, the Gaiety next to Grey's, the Royal opposite the Town Hall, and huddled together on the south side the Continental, the Artistic, and finally the News Theatre which shows short films such as cartoons, newsreels and documentaries.

It was the peak rush hour, and the leaden sky was beginning to dissolve into rain over the inhabitants of Bleston who, clad in waterproofs the colour of damp sawdust or wet seaweed, waited for admittance into those sanctuaries where they could watch horses galloping across the screen and women with splendid hair lingering in a passionate kiss.

I felt that Bleston was an unfriendly power, but my happy visit to the Jenkins' home suggested that it might be propitiated; so I went into Philibert's to buy some sort of talisman, some object made in Bleston of Bleston stuff, which I could carry about me as a protective token, a cotton handkerchief which I still possess.

I had not yet been paid by Matthews & Sons, I was living on the few pounds I had been able to bring over from France, and as I was spending a good deal at the Anchor, where I had to settle my bill weekly, I wondered how I should reach the end of the month without borrowing; any expensive purchase was thus out of the question.

I went up from one floor to the next on noisy chromium-plated escalators, under the green glass dome blurred with enormous rainsplashes, until I reached the garden tools department, where sprinklers were whirling with no water on raffia lawns, between counters loaded with hundreds of pottery cats as identical as the houses beyond Deren Square or the Morris cars in the street, or the worn waterproofs of the customers who stopped to finger them curiously as they passed.

Next day, Sunday October 21st, since when it rained every day until the dense fogs came on, I stayed in bed very late, watching the ragged shreds of sky, then in the afternoon I took a 17 bus and went through the mist as far as the Old Cathedral Square, whose old pavements were covered with a film of almost liquid mud.

I was staring up at the two towers over the main façade at the west end, watching them grow flatter as I climbed the four steps, when somebody came out through the left portal, the only one open (its Romanesque pillars are patterned with interlacing scrolls framing oval medallions that represent the Prophets of Ancient Law), and collided with me without seeing me, so that, turning around suddenly, I missed my footing and fell flat on the slippery steps, splashing my face, staining my raincoat a filthy mud-colour; it was a girl, it may have been Rose Bailey; she vanished down a lane between closed shopfronts, while I got up again and tried to dab myself clean with the cotton handkerchief I had bought the day before at Philibert's.

When I had gone through the small dark vestibule, when the door, upholstered in imitation leather with big studs like the seats of very old railway carriages (wisps of tow were escaping through a number of rents), had closed ponderously behind me with creaking hinges, I saw in the dull light from the colourless windows in the nave, among the empty pews and crumbling pillars, a group of little girls of twelve to fifteen in navy blue school uniforms, pigtailed, with beribboned straw hats and black stockings; the three gangling ringleaders, seeing me draw near, broke into strident laughter that echoed under the vault, and were quickly called to order by their teachers.

The windows, to which I paid no special attention on that occasion, seemed barely transparent; candles were burning on a few altars, and the damp air seemed to surround each flame with a feathery halo.

"Now then, girls," whispered the two bespectacled spinsters, prodding their sniggering charges; they all vanished through a small door beside which stood a purple-faced verger who, noticing me in solitary bewilderment in the transept, exhorted me to follow their example for a fee of sixpence.

Muffled footsteps and laughter echoed in the spirals of the new staircase leading to the modern belfry in the middle of the top storey of the square central tower, which is considerably taller than those over the west front.

From up here I glimpsed a general view of the town centre, through the mist which had brought dusk at four o'clock that

October afternoon. I saw the curve of the Slee, the tall spire of the New Cathedral, the battlements of the Town Hall haloed by luminous street signs that flickered off and on, and in the far distance triangular Alexandra Place, with its whistling trains and its sheaf of railway lines; old houses with pointed roofs immediately beneath me, and farther off tall chimneys like tree trunks left standing after lightning has set the forest on fire and the subsequent downpour has half submerged them in a miry flood.

Friday, May 30th

It was Monday evening or Tuesday or even Wednesday, at all events it was at the beginning of that fourth week, that, as I was walking from Matthews & Sons to Town Hall Square, where I intended to take a bus to some remote neighbourhood, seduced by one of those misleading advertisements in the *Evening News*, I stopped in Silver Street, in front of Baron's, the main bookshop in Bleston, half way between Rand's, the stationer where Ann Bailey worked, and Philibert's, where I had bought my cotton handkerchief; behind its heavy trellised blind the shop was brightly lit up, and I suddenly realised to my horror that I had not opened a book since I came to the town four weeks ago, whereas formerly I had been such a voracious reader; and I felt my whole being polluted by that creeping fog, I felt deserted by the man that I had once been, before I landed here, now fading into the immeasurable distance.

So, next day or the day after, or two days after, about six o'clock, on my way from Matthews & Sons towards the Town Hall Square (the days were drawing in and it was almost pitch-dark already), having read on the yellow poster of the man selling the *Evening News* at the corner of Grey Street the words "THE BLESTON MURDER" scrawled in ink in great sinister capital letters (I cannot remember the sordid incident to which they referred, I did not keep the paper) and having seen the same words a few minutes later in Baron's window on the green cover of a Penguin, I immediately decided to buy this book, *The Bleston Murder*, because the suggestiveness of the title—which, as I later discovered, was deliberate—enabled me to enjoy a small private revenge against this town.

But for this I had to wait until Saturday, October 27th, since on workdays Baron's was closed by the time we left Matthews & Sons, and it was just too far from White Street to be visited in the lunch hour; Saturday, 27th October, at about four o'clock, after lunching for the second time with that strange creature, Mrs. Jenkins, whose calm and gentle manner conceals a nature wilful and passionate enough to overthrow any obstacle.

It was on this occasion that I noticed her ring, a gold ring whose stone consists of a glass bubble enclosing a fly in a perfect state of preservation, and on which I complimented her (I can still see her smile: "it was my engagement ring") but without, as yet, daring to ask more about it.

I had to wait until Saturday, October 27th, at about four o'clock (the quicksilver of the sky was mingled with copper filings) before pushing open the glass door on which gilt letters, black-rimmed, proclaimed "Books of All Kinds", and entering the big shop, where a great many people were turning the pages of books and a great many old ladies already choosing Christmas cards, two months in advance (snow-covered cottages, holly and mistletoe, kittens in mittens), where five or six middle-aged shopwalkers, unobtrusive and impeccably dressed, were bending forward, smoothing their hands, answering questions, gliding between the tables, on one of which, devoted to the green Penguin "Crime and Detection" series, I picked up a copy of *The Bleston Murder* by J. C. Hamilton, which I examined and turned over (thus discovering on the back cover, in place of the usual author's portrait, a blank rectangle), just as at this very moment I have been turning over the copy which usually lies on the left-hand corner of my table with my maps of Bleston and other documents—a similar copy, but not the identical one which I then took to the cash desk, where two spotless hands wrapped it in brown paper, tied it up with a thin fibre ribbon stamped with "Baron's, Baron's, Baron's", and stuck on a shiny oval label that said "Come back", after which I thrust it into my pocket and left the shop through a back door opening on to a silent narrow lane cluttered up with metal tubes and steps.

What I hoped to find in the author, this J. C. Hamilton, was not merely an entertainer but, on the strength of his title, an accomplice against the town, a magician familiar with its peculiar perils, who would arm me with spells potent enough to enable me to defy these, and to survive undefeated my year's ordeal in this place, of whose powers of subtle corruption and patient erosion I was not as yet fully aware.

And my expectations were fulfilled, for this book which to the fortunate dwellers in other towns may seem merely a conventional detective story became for me, owing to its intimate portraiture of Bleston, an auxiliary so precious that I can almost say that a new phase of my adventure began at the instant when, back in my room at the Anchor, that odious cubby-hole, that shrine of shabbiness, I read for the first time those opening words which I now know by heart: "The Old Cathedral of Bleston is famous for its great stained-glass window, known as the Murderer's Window…"

II
Portents

I

Monday, June 2nd

I must set down every detail that may help to bring last night's
incident to life again when I re-read what I have written.

I had just heard the clock of All Saints Church strike six (All
Saints, Hallowmas, November 1st, the Feast of Ghosts).

It was a moist spring-like evening, fine and clear; the sky was
still quite blue between ragged clouds, and the watery sun, still
high above the horizon, lit up the fresh greenery of the young
lime trees fluttering in the narrow streets, and the clumps of
wallflower that glowed brown, yellow and purple in all the gardens of the neighbourhood, while their scent contended with the
reek of smoke. This was the 10th district, All Saints, bounded to
the north by All Saints Street (along which I had travelled on a
24 bus), to the west by All Saints Park, to the south by the Great
Southern Cemetery and to the east by the railway lines going
towards Hamilton Station, which like all those in this town are
raised high above the surrounding houses, none of which have
more than one storey.

As I pushed open the gate I saw a long train go past above
the shallow roof, and through the living-room window on my
left I caught sight of Rose arranging a bunch of narcissi on the
table, which was already laid.

Yesterday evening, Sunday, June 1st, at six o'clock, as Ann
Bailey opened the door of 31 All Saints Gardens to me (Ann
with her heron-grey eyes, her fair, almost ginger hair coiled high
on the back of her head, wearing a pink jersey that did not suit
her, a dark green skirt, and her old flat gardening shoes with the

leather cracked over the toes, she exclaimed: "Hullo, Jacques," trying to pronounce the J in French fashion, "come in; I must run upstairs for a minute, I've got something to give back to you."

"Have you?"

"A book you lent me a long time ago, which I'd been rash enough to lend somebody else."

I sat down at the living-room table between Mrs. Bailey on my left, opposite the chimney-piece above which hangs a spherical mirror like the Burtons', and Rose on my right, Rose with her lovely dark hair drawn back like her sister's, but in a far broader sweep, and lit up from behind by the window through which I could see a corner of the hideous façade of the Methodist, or maybe Presbyterian, church (I never found out which, and as the Baileys are Catholics they are not likely to know either), Rose with her violet-irised eyes, like those other irises in bloom now in Willow Park.

"And where has Ann vanished to?" asked Mrs. Bailey as she poured out tea.

"She's gone to fetch a book which she thinks belongs to me."

"If it's a detective story that I haven't read you must let me keep it. Some milk?"

Ann had come in, laughing and breathless, brandishing a green Penguin.

"But you read it long ago, Mother, it's *The Bleston Murder* by J. C. Hamilton."

"What?"

This was the copy I had given up for lost; writing a couple of days ago, I had described my purchase of it last October, and this had impelled me to re-read the book next day in the substitute copy I had unearthed, after months of searching, in a second-hand bookshop—for it had gone out of print meanwhile; this was the original copy, bearing my name, whereas the one that now lies on the left-hand corner of my table, beside the illustrated leaflet about the New Cathedral, the maps of Bleston and the guide, bound in blue, in the series "Our Land and its

Treasures", bears an undecipherable signature; this copy, which had been so much in my thoughts of late, had turned up in the Baileys' house, that house where I am so frequent a visitor, and certainly the last place in which I expected to find it.

When Ann, as she let me in, had mentioned a book, I had tried to remember whether any of mine were missing, but I had never thought of this one.

I knew I had lent it her a long time ago, in December or January, but I felt sure she had returned it.

My face betrayed my amazement so clearly that Rose burst out laughing (reminding me for a moment of those little girls who had made fun of me the first time I had gone into the Old Cathedral) and then stopped in embarrassment.

I tried to smooth things over and justify myself, but as it would have been too long and too hard to explain my true reasons, I began to lie, and to mention things about which I should have kept quiet.

"You looked so funny I couldn't help…"

"It was so long ago you lent it me, six months I should think. One of my cousins took it away one day, with some others; he may have asked my leave, I don't know, I didn't notice, I just let him have it; I didn't realise you valued it so much; and then it went out of my mind."

"It doesn't matter in the least, Ann, really; I have another copy of *The Bleston Murder*."

As I spoke the words I realised that my second sentence, far from confirming the first, contradicted it and emphasised my interest in the book by disclosing the fact that I had felt impelled to buy a second copy, and that my reply, instead of relieving Ann's embarrassment, only increased it, while making my own attitude increasingly incomprehensible; so, with a blush (which probably passed unnoticed in the gathering dusk) I concluded my second sentence thus:

"A present from the author himself" (which was the very opposite of the truth, since it was to that second copy, now lying on the left-hand corner of my table with my other documents, that I owe my acquaintance with George William Burton) "and I shall be glad to let you keep this one."

Tuesday, June 3rd

The impression made by my words was far greater than I had expected.

Ann, sitting opposite me, framed in the doorway, with the last glimmer of sunlight ripening the red gleams in her fair hair that are only latent there in broad daylight, Rose on my right, her features a blur in the darkness, her coiled hair a dark mass against the windowpanes with a shimmering purplish halo like fine metallic smoke (an autumnal moment, that spring evening, but lovelier than the autumn I had lived through seven months ago), Ann and Rose started simultaneously, stared at me with questioning eyes whose colour I could no longer distinguish (how alike they were! when they are seated the difference in their heights disappears, although Ann is as tall as I am whereas Rose's forehead only reaches to my nostrils) and almost with a single voice (Ann's the shriller, Rose's the more velvety) they suddenly exclaimed: "Do you know the author of *The Bleston Murder?*"

Their four elbows on the table, their four hands at shoulder-height, were outspread like cyclamens.

It was my turn to laugh at their astonishment.

"Yes. Why? Do you?"

"No," Ann said, bringing her forefingers together, "at least we don't know. Tell me, Jacques, does he live in Bleston?"

"Yes, not far from here, at the corner of Green Park Terrace and Hatter Street."

"We may have met him, we may know him by his real name without being aware that he wrote *The Bleston Murder*."

Her voice dropped, but retained a tremor of excitement; she closed the fingers of her right hand and began glancing at her nails, which were still gleaming softly in the twilight, like pearls.

"Our cousin Henry lent your book to one of his friends, Richard Tenn; he told me so when he returned it; and if he lent it to him... I don't know if you recall the story?"

"I re-read it quite recently."

"I don't remember much about it, except that a man kills his brother and that the murder takes place in the Old Cathedral..."

"In the *New* Cathedral..."

"Yes, Rose, you're right, but surely there's somebody who dies in the Old Cathedral, or at least who's wounded there, somebody's blood is shed..."

Rose recited, as though quoting: "Blood streaming over the paving stones, in the coloured light cast by the stained-glass window..."

The actual text is more precise: "A dark stain, spreading on the pavement, in the red light projected by the running down of Abel's blood."

The blood of the murderer, when he has been exposed. "So your cousin Henry..."

"Declares that the house in which the two brothers live, the murderer and his victim, corresponds room for room and in every detail of its furnishing with Richard Tenn's house as it was three or four years ago. I must admit that we noticed nothing, which is quite natural, since we only went to Richard's for the first time last year, and haven't often visited him since. And so Henry concluded that the author, J. C. Hamilton, whose real name you know, had taken his friend's house as a model, and must have been a close acquaintance of his. Henry went to see Richard and told him about it; but Richard had never heard of the book, and asked Henry to let him read it."

"Did he recognise his own home?"

"At first he said no, that there were certain resemblances of course but that at Bleston there were so many houses of the same type as his, in which the furniture came from the same shop, and that he did not know any writers of detective stories; then as Henry persisted, he declared that he really didn't see which of his acquaintances could have written this book, and finally asked who had lent it him and whether he had been specially asked by this person to mention it to him."

During the whole of this conversation Mrs. Bailey had sat in silence, in the deepening dusk, but I noticed that when Richard Tenn was mentioned her eyes had opened wider and she grew increasingly attentive, as though there were some danger in Ann's words.

"Will you put on the light, Rose, and draw the curtains."

What had given *The Bleston Murder* its significance for me was the precision with which it described certain aspects of the town, the hold it gave me over Bleston, and I began to wonder whether its relation to the real world was not perhaps even closer, whether the story it tells might not be, to a large extent, literally true, whether George William Burton, not content with writing a detective story, had not himself played the detective by publishing it, assuming for the purpose the pseudonym of J. C. Hamilton; for the two brothers' house, whose actual position in Bleston is left vague, is described with extreme care, with a minuteness that is quite exceptional in a novel of this kind.

And so, as soon as Rose sat down again (the ceiling light shed a bright glare on all the white teacups), while watching Mrs. Bailey in whom I could sense nervous irritation, I tried to find out something about that Richard Tenn who had, in fact, had a brother who had died three years ago in a car accident (the first edition of *The Bleston Murder* came out last year) and therefore I pretended that his name conveyed something to me, that the author had probably mentioned him to me, thus whetting the two girls' curiosity; but is was only on the doorstep at ten o'clock, in the darkness, that Rose (her eyes were on a level with mine as she stood two steps above me, and over her head, a little farther back, I could see Ann's eyes, bright and friendly too) asked me in French: "*Alors, comment s'appelle-t-il?*"

All the good reasons I had for keeping silent vanished at the sound of her voice, of her accent, and I replied: "*Il s'appelle* George William Burton."

She turned to her sister, looking disappointed, and asked her. in English: "Does the name convey anything to you?"

"No, we don't know him."

I hadn't even the courage to ask them to keep it secret, for I did not want to let them guess the seriousness of my suspicions about this Richard Tenn, about the death of his brother, which to them seemed quite natural, as indeed it may be.

They are certain to mention it to their cousin Henry who, in his turn, will speak of it to his friend.

Perhaps this has already happened; perhaps by now he knows the name of the man who, if he is really guilty, has exposed him; how will he answer?

I hope that I am completely mistaken and that in that house, bearing merely a chance resemblance to that of the murderer and his victim, there lives only a very decent fellow mourning the loss of his brother in all sincerity, as Ann and Rose believe (but I'm not so sure about their mother; and as for Cousin Henry, whom I've never met...); I hope that I have not imperilled a dear friend's life.

Then why did I take such a risk, when it would have been so easy, even supposing all this is true, to ensure perfect safety for George Burton behind his protective *nom de plume*, J. C. Hamilton, having neither face nor address, no civil status, no biography and no other works?

Wednesday, June 4th

All Saints Gardens, the Bailey sisters' street, All Saints Church, the Methodist or Presbyterian church of which I could glimpse a corner behind Rose's dark red head, All Saints Park, the whole district of All Saints, all these place-names which I have been turning over in my mind and writing down these last few days remind me that November 1st is a festival, All Saints Day, the feast of the dead; but I could not remember what I had done that Thursday, what had prevented me from spending my leisure in satisfying the urgent wish I had conceived on reading the first sentence of *The Bleston Murder* ("The Old Cathedral of Bleston is famous for its great stained-glass window, known as the Murderer's Window")—the wish to look more closely at that great window, which I had barely noticed on my first visit, being unaware of its subject, which I had not revisited until the following Sunday, my clear memory of the priest's words convinced me of that, but which I should certainly have gone to look at on the Saturday if I had not had to call at Police Headquarters for my identity card, which is dated November 3rd. I could in fact remember no outstanding incident between the last weekend in October and the fire in the following month and had therefore begun to wonder whether All Saints Day had really been a holiday and not a weekday, an ordinary working day at Matthews & Sons, followed in the evening by a journey to look at one of those rooms that degrade and exhaust those who consent to dwell in them.

That is why this evening I questioned James, who told me that of course it had been a holiday, that he had gone with his mother to the Great Southern Cemetery as he did every year, that the weather had been entirely seasonable, far mistier than the year before, the first fog of autumn.

I am amazed and even horrified at the way Bleston people remember the weather; they always know from one year to the next whether more or less rain fell on the same date, as if this were the principal difference between one "first of November" and another, as if nothing had happened in between.

I could never, by myself, have fixed the date of that first autumn fog, the first Bleston fog I had experienced; I should have tended to put it somewhat later owing to the relatively mild weather that followed this harbinger of winter.

I can understand now why I did not go to look at the Window in the Old Cathedral; of course it would have been almost invisible; and if I can remember no outstanding incident it was because I had done nothing and seen almost nothing.

I went for a slow ramble in Lanes Park; there were still a few leaves on the chestnuts, the last of all, shrunken, shrivelled, rusty, their stiff skeletons bulging like mummies' ribs, the last leaves of all eddying slowly through the yellow air and slowly sinking into the mud; and I went to take a 25 bus at Pedlington Street, beside the waste land where the fair was held in March, which took me through Deren Street and then City Street as far as Town Hall Square, where the absurdly crenellated towers faded into invisibility above the lighted street-lamps shrouded in wisps of cotton wool.

This was by no means a dense fog, it was just the first fog of autumn; I could still see the trunks of trees as I walked through Lanes Park, I could still see the walls of houses from the upper deck of the 25 bus passing along City Street, and the luminous signs in Town Hall Square, although blurred and dimmed, were still legible.

If on Saturday, November 3rd, in spite of clear weather, I still did not go to see the Window, it was because the previous day I had received a letter at the Anchor (which rarely happened, for I had asked my family to send my mail to Matthews & Sons until I should have let them know some definite address), a letter in an envelope stamped "Bleston Police Headquarters" (so that the staff at the hotel stared at me with even greater suspicion that day, and began to whisper ridiculous stories about me), a letter which ran as follows (I quote from memory, I threw it away at the time):

Dear Sir,
Please call at your earliest convenience at Bleston Police Headquarters (55 City Street, Bleston 4), Aliens Department, for information.

On November 3rd, therefore, at about 1.30, having lunched by myself at the Sword in Grey Street on leaving the office, I went into that square, newish, six-storey building at the corner of City Street and Museum Place.

I was kept waiting at first, then I was shown into the office of an inspector in navy-blue uniform, very clean and pink-skinned, with close-cropped black hair, his helmet lying peak upwards on the table beside him; in a patient, indulgent voice, as one accustomed to making himself understood by foreigners, to lecturing them gently, he asked me why I had not come to register myself sooner.

"I am only staying temporarily at the Anchor; I was waiting to be settled somewhere."

"You have been at that hotel for a month, Monsieur Revel. Are you going to move soon? Do you know your next address? No? Well then, we shall make you out an identity card with this one; you must come and change it when you've found a lodging that suits you; but don't delay too long next time, please. Have you got an identity photograph? No? I shall keep your passport and your work permit, and you must go to the shop on the other side of the square, they print photographs in an hour (tell them it's for us); when you bring them back here, everything will be ready. You were acting most illegally, my dear man; we'll soon put that right."

I took advantage of this respite to make my way between the blackened Ionic pillars, under the pediment inscribed "Bleston Museum of Fine Arts", into the empty vestibule between the cloakroom, full of unused coat-hangers, and the tiny bookstall, then up the staircase, lighted from a glass ceiling and adorned with an elaborately touched-up moulding of the Elgin Marbles in which the background has been painted bright blue to make the figures stand out; this staircase branches out midway into a way up and a way down, while the two doors on the landing provide a way in and a way out of the series of nine exhibition rooms that surround it:

the first room, Archaeology (two or three Egyptian scarabs, one Greek vase, a fragment of Coptic cloth, a handful of Roman coins, and a number of clumsily-carved tombstones dug up locally, dating from the second or third centuries, almost all the inscriptions on which refer to children), in which was sitting, fast asleep, the custodian, the only living creature I met in the whole building that day;

the second room, eighteenth century dress and furniture;

the next five in which are hung the eighteen pieces of tapestry (together with a few glass cases containing silver and china);

the eighth, nineteenth century painting (a small Constable gouache, a Turner watercolour, a few Pre-Raphaelite canvases, some portraits of businessmen);

the ninth, modern painting (samples of local production).

I did not know that the eighteen woven panels told the story of Theseus; there were no labels on the wall to explain the subject of each; it was only later that I studied them carefully, and I think I had not even read the notice at the entry of Room III which runs roughly as follows:

THE HARREY TAPESTRIES

These eighteen tapestries were ordered from the factory at Beauvais (France) by Lord Harrey at the beginning of the 18th century. His last descendant, who died in 1860, bequeathed them to the municipality of Bleston, which built this museum to house them. The name of the painter who designed the cartoons is unknown.

I am sure I had immediately recognised the theme of the eleventh panel, in the fifth room, opposite you as you go in, on the left of the door into the sixth room, lit from the side by the windows overlooking Museum Street and the low sheds that divide it from the railway lines running towards Hamilton Station: a man with a bull's head being slain by a prince in armour, in a sort of cavern surrounded by complicated walls, to the left of which, up above, on the threshold of a door opening on to the seashore, a girl in a blue dress embroidered with silver, tall, stately and watchful, is pulling with her right hand a thread that unwinds from a spindle held between the thumb and middle finger of her left, a thread that meanders through the mazy passage of the fortress, a thread as thick as an artery engorged with blood, fastened to the dagger which the prince is thrusting into the monster, between its bull neck and its human breast; the same girl appears again on the right, in the distance, at the prow of a vessel speeding with its black sail bellying in the wind, together with the same prince and another girl very like herself but smaller, clad in purple draperies.

But I cannot easily recapture my first impression of the whole amazing thing, which I have studied so much more closely since; the style, indeed, puzzled me somewhat at first, although I am sure I was immediately impressed by the landscapes, particularly by the trees, in the second, third, fourth and fifth panels, which show Theseus approaching Athens and his victories over the four criminals who laid waste his land—Sinis, Sciron, Cercyon and Procrustes—those trees depicted at the four seasons of the year, so obviously inspired by the trees of the Île de France, poplars, aspens and oaks in bud, in full foliage of every shade of green, softly flaming in fantastic splendour, or bare-branched.

Thursday, June 5th

Night was falling when I left the Police Headquarters at the corner of Museum Square and City Street, with everything in order at last and all my papers in my pocket, including the yellow card on which, by now, the Anchor's address has been crossed out and replaced by that of the room in which I am now writing, "37 Copper Street, Bleston 7".

I walked as far as Town Hall Square and, for lack of anything better to do, went into some cinema or other (I don't know what the film was called nor who were the actors) and sat there for a couple of hours while the colourless imagery flowed past my eyes.

On the other hand I remember very clearly my visit to the Murderer's Window in the Old Cathedral the following afternoon, Sunday, November 4th; this stands out with rock-like certainty, and I have rehearsed every detail of it countless times.

I had taken a 17 bus as far as the south portal, and then walked round the side-aisles to go in at the main entrance in the west front, under the two square late-Perpendicular towers with all their sharp ridges, still wet from the morning's rain, glistening in the bright air.

Within, all was quiet; I stood under the organ-loft, in front of the choir screen, through which I could see the glow of an oil lamp in its red glass globe, and I looked up at the circular light in the big window on my right which, as I had already learnt from *The Bleston Murder*, shows Cain killing his brother Abel, Cain dressed like Theseus in a close-fitting cuirass with ribbons floating over his thighs, almost in the same attitude as Theseus at grips with the Minotaur, bending forward like him, his left foot on the breast of his naked victim who lies wounded, prostrate, but lifting his head a little—and yet so unlike Theseus, as he brandishes a tree-trunk with angled roots against the red sky.

I heard a door open; an elderly ecclesiastic in a surplice came up and spoke to me.

The mere fact that I was able to keep up a long conversation with him proves how far my practical knowledge of English had improved in a month's stay; the few words of which I failed to catch the meaning scarcely interfered with my answers.

"You have come to see our window? It's astonishing, isn't it? Bleston is the only town in all England possessing such fine specimens of this period. Is this your first visit to our church?"

"Not exactly. I came here about a fortnight ago, but it was raining; I hardly noticed this window; it was not nearly as bright as today; and then I saw it mentioned in a book…"

"Yes, it's very famous; there is scarcely a work about our country which does not make some allusion to it, and yet here, actually, nobody takes much interest in it; you might have walked about these old streets for months without anyone urging you to go and look at it."

I have never seen this man since, although I have sometimes wanted to, thinking that he might tell me something more about this great spell-binding image, but I can still hear his voice and in particular the disconcerting way in which he pronounced Latin quotations and Hebrew names, and also those sudden waves of passionate feeling amid the quiet course of his friendly talk, giving to such words as "church", "cathedral", "window" or "Bleston" a long-drawn-out reverberation that made his very eyelashes and fingertips quiver with repressed excitement.

"Have you been here long?"

"Just a month."

"You're a student at the University, no doubt?"

"No, unfortunately, I am serving a term with a firm of exporters, Matthews & Sons of sixty-two White Street; I am to spend a whole year with them, and shall not go home until the end of September. I am a Frenchman, as you must have guessed from my wretched pronunciation."

"This stained glass is attributed to French masters."

"Of what period?"

"Mid-sixteenth century. The window was rebuilt at the same time. The large circular light containing the scene of the murder, above the central bay which is broader and lower than the other two, is an unusual feature."

A ray of sunlight flowed through the pool of blood streaming from Abel's wounds and lay on the transept wall on our left in a scarlet stain, which presently faded.

"In the four curvilinear triangles that connect it with the other panels and with the upper edges, you can make out six-petalled flowers that look like flames, flowers with an eye in the middle, which according to some people represent seraphim."

These were partially concealed from us by the thickness of the surrounding stones; to see them in their entirety you have to stand as far back as possible, but then some of the detail is invisible.

With outstretched finger (on his wrist, the white rim of his pearl-buttoned cuff, the black rim of his clerical coat-sleeve, the lace edging of his surplice) he pointed out, in the narrow niche framed by the broken arch that crowns the left bay, the figure of a man, almost naked, against a background of prickly leaves, digging among stones.

"You see Cain, tilling the ground; on the right, offering ears of corn and fruit to the Lord. The smoke rising from his altar has spread all over the sky above him and dropped down again to cover him."

"Is the whole window devoted to Cain?"

"To him and to his descendants."

"Although I was brought up a Roman Catholic I have long ago forgotten the rudimentary Scripture lessons I was given; yet I presume that is Cain standing there in the big central light, underneath the round one depicting the murder..." (Cain with his hands hanging by his sides, his palms stained scarlet, stained with his brother's blood, which seems to stream down like rain in the skies in all the lower pictures.)

"Yes, and there is the Lord appearing to him in the clouds brandishing that thunderbolt, that yellow beam that strikes Cain's forehead, not to destroy him" (that was the hypothesis that had first occurred to me, but conscious of its absurdity I had held my tongue) "but, on the contrary, to make him invulnerable, so that other men should shun him in terror."

Underneath "Cain tilling the ground" was Cain with the brandmark on his forehead, his wife Themech beside him, walking in a sort of desert, with figures fleeing in the distance.

"And who is the mason building a brick wall in the right-hand bay?"

"Still Cain. The artist has followed the text as closely as possible. See the scroll running through the three scenes, with

73

inscriptions which are no longer very legible but can easily be reconstituted. In the centre, *'posuitque Dominus signum'* ("And the Lord set a mark upon Cain", Genesis 4:15), on the left, *'profugus in terra'* ("a fugitive and a vagabond in the earth") from verse 14, and this from verse 17, *'et aedificavit civitatem'* ("and he built a city"), that city which you can see displayed below, taking up the whole width of the window, and for which the artist took as model the city then lying in front of him, the Bleston of those days, which gives great documentary value to this section, since it provides a fairly faithful representation of buildings that no longer exist. Notice these gabled houses: there are still a few of them left, you can see their rooftops through the clear glass window on the other side of the transept; and there is the belfry of the old Town Hall. You recognise the Old Bridge over the Slee" (actually I had never seen it, not yet having walked along that reach of the river) "and the Cathedral in which we now stand, with its three square towers crowned with yellow crescent moons."

They were glittering like golden boats in the flushed sky, struck by one of the last sunbeams of that day and of that year.

"As for the figures in the foreground, they are evidently the people of the city, Cain's descendants; on the left, underneath *'profugus in terra'*, in front of the arcades of the old market-place, sitting at a loom like those used by Bleston weavers at the time, and surrounded by his goats, beside his tent, you see Yabal, ancestor of all those who spin, weave and dye cloth; in the centre, under the scene of Cain's branding, in front of the Cathedral with its crescent moons you see Yubal, ancestor of all musicians" (standing open-mouthed as if he were screaming) "amidst all his sons with wind instruments, organ, trumpet and flute, and his daughters with stringed instruments, harp, viol and lute; on the right, underneath Cain the mason, in front of the river, Tubalcain, ancestor of all metalworkers, with pincers in his left hand, holding a wheel over the anvil."

Bleston, city of weavers and metalworkers, what has become of your musicians?

I hear the hoarse rattle of a lorry.

Friday, June 6th

As I stood in the Old Cathedral that Sunday, November 4th, while daylight ebbed through Cain's Window, the priest's commentary showed me those old stories (which I had thought I knew, through listening to them at Sunday school and repeating them to myself in shortened form) under a wholly unfamiliar aspect.

This great picture, fast fading, had become through his commentary the entry into a mine of mysteries; but what puzzled me more and more was not only its content, but its relation to its surroundings, its situation in this Cathedral and in this whole town which, as I now realised, it portrayed in such precise detail.

"Why is this whole huge window devoted to a reprobate?"

A smile hovered on the priest's face, which was now tinged with a purple glow, a little darker than his garment; he seemed to have been waiting for such a question.

"You must remember that this is a work of the Renaissance. The artist paid tribute to Cain as being the father of all the arts."

Then, after a moment's silence as if to give his remark time to sink into my mind, he continued in a quite different tone, more like that of a schoolmaster on holiday, passing friendly comment on the scenery to a pupil met out of school: "But above all, it was not meant to be looked at by itself. The window behind us, full of uncoloured glass through which you can see the outline of the old gabled houses under the darkening sky, once told the stories of Abel and Seth. We have few details, indeed; no drawings have come down to us; only, thanks to a chronicler's lengthy description of the festivities held when it was put in, we know the subjects of the pictures and their arrangement."

Architecturally, this window is just like the other, divided by two slender pillars into three bays, the central one, broader than the other two, being surmounted by a circular light connected with the upper rim and the capitals by curvilinear triangles, and all filled with plain glass like that in the windows of every house and workshop in Bleston, plain glass deeply grimed and protected by wire netting.

"Up above, in that circular light corresponding to the murder scene on the opposite side of the transept, that empty transparent circle through which you can see those three little twisted chimneys, there were Adam and Eve with Abel as a child; in the right-hand niche, corresponding to the picture of Cain tilling the soil, was Abel keeping his sheep; in the other, corresponding to Cain offering the fruits of the earth, was Abel sacrificing a lamb; below, the burial of Abel, the death of Adam in the centre surrounded by his other sons, and the birth of Seth, the eldest of these, and at the bottom seven old men representing the line of patriarchs from Enoch to Lamech, father of Noah; in place of these, we now see only those blurred housefronts, distorted by refraction, those windows that looked dead, but one of which, in the far corner, has just lit up with a feeble glimmer, and those tiles and rafters which are begrimed, rather than washed, by the sooty rain."

We could hear that rain scratching with its innumerable blunt nails against the great blank wall of glass.

"Why is Cain on the right and Abel on the left? Wasn't the left the side allotted to reprobates?"

Then a light laugh echoed through the nave; I have a mental picture of the tiny quivering flame in its red glass globe hanging in the middle of the choir, behind the organ.

"That's because you are seeing things the wrong way round. These two great windows formed part of a scheme which was never completed, in which every window was to play its part; thus, over the apse we should have seen the Last Judgment."

I discovered that day to my great surprise that the east end of the Old Cathedral is rectangular, like a transept (with a great empty window like Abel's today). I have learnt since, from the guidebook (in the series "Our Land and its Treasures") that this is the case with most English churches.

"The Lord, sitting enthroned in the New Jerusalem, would thus have had the blessed on his right, and Abel on his right, and between them in the little windows of the ambulatory the holy cities—on his right, and hence on our left; and on his left were all the accursed souls and cities since Cain's; come and I'll show you fragments of them."

Outside the rain was falling thicker; within, the red lamp in the sanctuary glowed brighter amid its haloes; a dark blue haze mingled with all the colours of the glass.

"I don't want to take up your time…"

"I have to take evening service at five o'clock, for a dozen worshippers… Until then I'm ready to help anyone who wants to see; you are the only one, I'm at your disposal. We have a great, splendid and famous church which people come from far away to admire, at other times of the year, but in Bleston itself not only are there very few Catholics, but even these seldom come here, as if these arches and windows terrified them. As for the others, they are so superstitious! Even on the greatest festivals, this nave is never crowded, as it used to be so often when our city numbered only ten thousand souls."

His hand, which in the last few minutes had become invisible (I could only see the movement of his white, lace-edged sleeve) was silhouetted against the first of the four small windows which dimly lit the right side of the ambulatory.

"Here is Babel, in very poor shape, alas, for it has been often and badly repaired. Only the unfinished top of the tower is more or less intact, in the middle of a close, tangled network of leads." He sketched its outline with his fingernail. "The two or three topmost storeys, each set back from the one beneath, consist merely of a few pieces of wall standing up in the midst of winches and scaffolding, like fangs snapping at the heavens.

One day when the light is better you'll be able to appreciate the wonderful delicacy with which some of these details are painted. All the lower portion has gone.

"Sodom has suffered almost as much; nothing is left of that upper quarter which showed in the distance Gomorrah and the other Dead Sea cities; but this window has been much more carefully restored.

"The showers of brimstone have just begun to fall; you can see Lot's wife turning into a pillar of salt, all white from her feet, which are rooted to the ground, to her waist, where the folds of her dress are not painted but deeply graven in the glass; she is looking back towards the gate in the brick wall, within which black and yellow flakes are falling thick on the flaming rafters.

"Of Babylon nothing is left but that face, crowned with raven's feathers instead of hair, the face of Nebuchadnezzar turned into a beast, and the last letter of the inscription 'Mene, Tekel, Upharsin' with the finger that has written it."

He pointed it out with his own finger.

"These two fragments were preserved for a long time in a cupboard in the sacristy; my predecessor had them replaced, reconstructing the Window by guesswork."

"And was this last window painted too?"

"It represented Rome."

"Rome?"

"Yes, Rome the Imperial city; opposite it on the other side, on the left of the choir from where we stand, but on the right hand of Christ the Judge in the big east window, was Rome the Papal city, the capital of the Church."

"Is nothing left of it?"

"Absolutely nothing is left of any of the windows on the other side."

The explanations he gave me, far from solving the mystery, only sharpened and deepened it. There was a strange ambiguity about the way these old-time glaziers had set out their subjects, as if wishing to show through their illustration of the official Biblical text that they themselves read something else into it.

Saturday, June 7th

"But why this anomaly? Cain's Window is in perfect preservation."

He answered me in a low voice, as if he still felt the shame of the events he described: "Here is the story; it is a long story, and it goes back to the days when these windows were being made, in the sixteenth century, during England's transition to Protestantism. Feelings ran high in Bleston; there were battles and deaths in the street. This Cathedral, of course, was the stronghold of orthodoxy."

We walked slowly along the darkened transept; on our left the south window displayed its glory like a crimson peacock's tail, the colour fading fast.

"One day the bishop was in his palace (it was destroyed by fire in the early eighteenth century, but you can still see the blocked-up door of the passage that connected it with the sacristy) when he heard the shouts of the angry crowd that had gathered in front of the Cathedral. He put on his vestments and his mitre, took up his crozier and had the central portal opened, convinced no doubt that he would merely have to utter a few words for everything to become calm again, for everyone to go home wondering what had possessed them to join in such a demonstration.

"And indeed, silence greeted his appearance; but he was unable to open his mouth, paralysed by some doubt, some scruple, some sudden dread, overwhelmed by the qualms of an uneasy conscience…

"The crowd interpreted this paralysis as a sign from Heaven and its fury, after a momentary check, broke loose.

"A vast howl of derision swept through the quiet precincts; these madmen laid hands on the Lord Bishop, seized him like a thief by the collar of his cope and dragged him, belabouring him with their fists, on to his throne, to which they fastened him, and then carried him with burlesque ceremony as far as Cain's Window which he himself had ordered a few years before.

"Roaring with laughter they shouted: 'He tried to make our city a city of Cain; this is Cain's Cathedral; let him sleep under his sire's protection!'

"Before his eyes they shattered Abel's window and those of the holy cities with stones."

He spoke with mounting excitement; his last words rang out under the vaulted roof; he looked round, fearful lest he should have disturbed some worshipper at prayer; but the nave was still empty.

Then he resumed his story in the muted tone on which he had begun it, pausing to light the lamps at each pillar.

"When evening fell and the frenzied mob had gone home, the canons of the Cathedral, who had watched the whole scene from one of the galleries, went down to unfasten the bishop; he had gone blind and was moaning softly, and they had to feed him like a small child; he died three years later, without having uttered one word."

A door creaked, and he looked round; an old woman had crept in.

"Once the mad fit had passed, the destroyers regretted their excesses and did all they could to preserve what had been spared; calm was restored, but heresy triumphed; the next bishop was an Anglican."

"But I thought you told me..."

"Yes, our Cathedral is Catholic again. Wait, I have not finished the tale of its misfortunes. We had practically no worshippers in Bleston, in spite of its proximity to Ireland; it was not until the end of the nineteenth century that we began to gain some ground, chiefly, I must admit, among newcomers to the city."

He had switched on all the lights in the nave one after the other; we were back in the transept; the Window, all its transparency gone, seemed a mosaic of gleaming facets of coal.

"Now for a long time there had been a great crack in the tower above our heads, which was a serious matter for the inhabitants of Bleston because it prevented them from ringing the famous bells which for centuries they have held to be the very essence of their city, so much so that they have included them in its coat of arms, and even fancied that its name is derived from them, Bleston, Bells Town.

"Actually there was on this very spot a temple dating from the Roman wars or even from pre-Roman times (some excavation was made under the crypt when the central heating was put in) and as certain late-Medieval texts give the spelling Bellista we must presumably look for the origin of the name in 'Belli Civitas'—city of war.

"Nevertheless on special occasions they could not resist treating themselves to a peal of bells; and so in 1835 one side of the tower collapsed, damaging the ambulatory, where the four windows depicting Babel, Sodom, Babylon and Imperial Rome had hitherto remained intact; it was this accident that destroyed them.

"At this period the city's wealth was increasing prodigiously, and the municipal authorities did not hesitate to undertake the construction of a New Cathedral, the tower of which they were determined to finish before all the rest, so that the bells could be transferred to it with due ceremony. Ever since then they ring every day (you will no doubt have noticed the fullness and richness of their tone, the variety of changes that can be rung on them) and we have been allowed to worship in this venerable and dilapidated building, which we have patiently restored; we even succeeded, two years ago, in installing the latest type of electric carillon, which cannot possibly endanger the solidity of its walls."

He was completely self-possessed again. He was lighting the lamps in the choir; there were now about a dozen people scattered among the pews.

"Have you seen the New Cathedral yet? Of course it's not to be compared with this one."

"If it's a nineteenth century building…"

"Its most interesting feature is our bells; but all the same you should have a look at it, it's rather remarkable, and the people of Bleston are quite proud of it. Excuse me, it is time for me to get ready now."

A choirboy was lighting the candles; I hurried towards the door.

Through a newspaper poster I had discovered J. C. Hamilton's detective story, *The Bleston Murder*; through reading this I had discovered the Murderer's Window, which in its turn had given rise to this conversation with its closing words of advice to visit the New Cathedral. It was as though a trail had been laid for me, at each stage of which I was allowed to see the end of the next stage, a trail which was to lead me hopelessly astray.

Outside as I went down the steps, I looked across the square—once covered with a howling mob, now utterly silent save for the patter of rain—and saw outlined ink-black against the purple sky a set of Chinese characters, raised on bars and edged with glass tubes that reflected a few gleams from the windows of other houses: presumably the sign denoting that restaurant, the Oriental Bamboo, where in the opening pages of *The Bleston Murder* the detective-to-be meets the victim-to-be for the first time, at a table on the first-floor near the window overlooking the façade of the Old Cathedral—famous, as they both know, for its Murderer's Window (a crucial scene, since it is actually his recollection of the way Johnny Winn, that famous cricketer whom his fans had never known to take an interest in art, had scrutinised that Window on the day before his body was discovered in the transept of the New Cathedral, that first leads Barnaby Morton to wonder if all had been well between him and his brother Bernard, if the victim had not, perhaps, been suspicious of his brother's intentions): the Oriental Bamboo, whose existence I had not sought to confirm that first time I crossed the square, on Sunday, November 4th, in the early afternoon, because it seemed to me so unlikely (I did not yet know how closely J. C. Hamilton, alias George Burton, sticks to the truth in his descriptions of the town; through such discoveries I have learnt to trust him implicitly, to take his book as my guide): the Oriental Bamboo, in which I now wanted, as a change from Bleston's appallingly dreary fare, to taste one of those dishes (fried crayfish, duck with pineapple, lychees) which the detective-to-be, Barnaby Morton, enjoyed in silence, while observing the man opposite who had begun to wonder whether his brother were of the race of Cain. But this, for the time being, was out of the question, for it was closed as always on Sundays, and no sound, no ray of light filtered through the iron curtain.

2

Monday, June 9th

The day before yesterday, June 7th, as I set down my recollections of a seven-months-past Sunday, I was plunged
once more into the depressing atmosphere of those November
days, before I had found this room which faces south-west and
which, now that summer is near, is bright even at this late hour.
It was the first time I had devoted a Saturday afternoon to that
auditing of my past experience on which I had been engaged
since the beginning of May; and I shall try in future to avoid
such an infringement of my weekend, for this process of delv-
ing and dredging which now occupies my weekday evenings
with such regularity, is intended to deliver me from the lethargy
which had invaded and blinded me like a turbid flood, from the
gloomy spell under which I lay, and to enable me once again
to behave like a man in possession of his faculties, to avoid the
gravest errors, to ward off the most pressing dangers, in short
to act with effective intelligence; and this is only possible during
weekends, every other day being sacrificed to Matthews & Sons,
being swallowed up by my duties there, and consequently at
weekends my whole attention must be concentrated on the
present moment and must, I hope, become increasingly keen
and prehensile.

But, feeling the pressure of time, I simply had to finish dealing with that priest's remarks about Cain's Window, or rather
with what I could remember of them, for I should have been
quite incapable, even a few days after, of recalling the exact
English words he had used, which were still unfamiliar to

me—words which I have forgotten but whose effect on me is still so powerfully persistent.

About half-past six on Saturday, just as I had reached his last remarks and my departure from the Old Cathedral, I heard a sharp knock at my door, and without waiting for answer in came Lucien Blaise (I knew it must be he, nobody else came to see me in my den, except James Jenkins who never visited me without previous warning and, of course, my landlady, good Mrs. Grosvenor, whose tap was infinitely gentler), Lucien, whom I was not expecting since we had planned to meet an hour later at the Oriental Rose, the Chinese restaurant in Town Hall Square, tucked away between the Royal Cinema and that big popular shop, the Modern Stores; he enquired with a broad smile, as he sank into the leather armchair, whether he wasn't disturbing me, and began to explain with profuse gestures (he is far more of a Meridional than I, more "Gallic") how he'd taken advantage of the sunny afternoon, which is unusual even at this season of the year, to go for a walk along the banks of the Slee, and having recognised my neighbourhood he'd dropped in on the chance of finding me at home.

"Stay quiet for a few moments; I've got to finish this page."

"I ought to follow your example, it's ages since I wrote home."

After three minutes he got up and began to walk up and down the room, casting glances at the pile of papers at my right hand, while I endeavoured to concentrate on the unlit sign over the Oriental Bamboo, as I had seen it for the first time on leaving the Old Cathedral in the rainy dusk of that Sunday, November 4th.

"What a long letter!"

"It's not a letter."

"A detective story, I bet, like *The Bleston Murder*."

"Much simpler than that; I'm writing down what has happened to me here."

"Your memoirs? And have you mentioned me?"

"Not yet; I've only got to the beginning of November."

"You've talked about the Bailey girls, I suppose?"

"Don't tell them, please. Shall we go to the Oriental Bamboo instead of the Oriental Rose?"

"The Oriental Bamboo where, in the opening pages of J. C. Hamilton's novel, Barnaby Burton, no, Barnaby Morton…"

All this was only a prelude; the important conversation started at the corner of Brandy Bridge Street and Alexandra Street, on the upper deck of a 33 bus (Alexandra Place – Pleasance Gardens); it was still broad daylight, only the sky had grown hazier.

"You know, Jacques, as you'd told me you weren't free on Wednesday I rang up the Bailey girls to ask if they wanted to go to the pictures with me, and I called to fetch them after dinner. They talked a lot about you, and told me how oddly you behaved last Saturday when Ann gave you back that copy of *The Bleston Murder* which you'd lent her a long time ago. They looked a bit worried. I told them not to bother their heads about it, that you were like that…"

"I see, you all had a good laugh at my expense."

"They're awfully fond of you, you know."

"I know."

"You see, I'm just what they imagine a Frenchman should be like, but you're a bit different."

"And so then?"

"Did they tell you that some chap they knew slightly lived in a house just like the two brothers' house in the novel?"

"Funny, isn't it?"

"They were awfully excited when you told them you knew J. C. Hamilton's real name."

"I shouldn't have told them that, Lucien; ever since that evening I've felt it was a mistake. Burton let us into his secret because we were foreigners; I'm beginning to wonder if he hadn't some very good reason for concealing his identity on the cover of *The Bleston Murder*."

"I must admit that you were rather…"

"I made a real blunder there, Lucien, and I hope you've done nothing to make it worse."

"If it really was a blunder I don't see how I could have made it worse than it was."

"Lucien, I want to know what else they got you to tell them about George Burton."

"Nothing at all!"

"Liar! I'm sure they asked you if you knew him too, and you said yes, and then they wheedled you into telling them how we got to know him."

"I said it was you who'd taken me there."

"Did you give them his address?"

"No the film started just then."

"And when you came out again, didn't they return to the attack?"

"Here's the Old Cathedral, Jacques; we must get off."

Tuesday, June 10th

The sky was turning pink; shadows were creeping over the out-side of the window, which looked like a great sheet of tar scattered with petals from a nearby orchard; we walked the length of the nave and crossed the square; we went up to the first-floor of the Oriental Bamboo; we sat down at that table which has assumed for us a legendary significance, not only because in the opening pages of *The Bleston Murder* Barnaby Morton the detective meets Johnny Winn there on the eve of his death, but also because it was where George Burton, noticing the green Penguin which I had just bought in a second-hand bookshop, spoke to me for the first time—that table next to the window on the right looking out on the Cathedral, whose sombre façade was hazed over with a rich blood-red glow which grew increasingly mottled until it had become a dark cloudy indigo by the time we had finished our biscuits and drunk our last cups of green tea, under the benevolent reptilian eye of the Chinese waiter pretending to read the *Evening News* in the far corner of the room.

Lucien, who knows my tastes, offered me a Churchman's, and took a long time helping himself to one, extracting his matches from an inner pocket and producing an adequate light; then, at last, after a few puffs, folding his hands and staring at a grain of rice lying on the tablecloth, he began:

"I say, Jacques, about *The Bleston Murder* and the Bailey girls and George Burton…"

The smoke stung his eyes; he laid his cigarette on the glass ashtray.

"The most awkward thing would be if he knew you'd betrayed his secret."

"He'd certainly be disappointed and maybe annoyed."

Lucien was tracing letters on the tablecloth with his toothpick.

"Well, there's absolutely no chance of his discovering it, because they don't know him at all. They thought they might have come across him because of that business of the house being like the two brothers' house, but his name was quite unfamiliar to them and I'm pretty sure they'd never seen him before…"

He snapped the tiny spear with his fingers.

"When we came out of the cinema on Wednesday I saw him and Harriet waiting for their bus and I pointed them out to the Bailey girls. It took me quite a time to get the girls to look at the right couple."

He had begun picking his teeth with the bit of stick he had kept in his right hand.

"I say, Jacques, do you really think that house… all that business… do you know anything more about it than I do? In any case the Bailey girls have nothing to do with it."

"Of course the Bailey girls have nothing to do with it! Whatever are you thinking about it? Let's talk about something else, shall we?"

For one moment I had glimpsed real panic in his eyes; but my last few words restored his smile; he had begun to think about Ann, probably, being an incorrigible breaker of hearts.

He picked up the cigarette which had gone out as it lay on the edge of the ashtray, and I relit it for him, signalling to the waiter meanwhile with my other hand (for it was growing late, and high time we made our way to the Royal Cinema for that mammoth American production in glorious Technicolour, *Tamburlaine the Terrible*, which is still showing there today and which we'd decided to see for a joke, being convinced beforehand of its absurdity), that yellow-skinned, fattish waiter sitting in the far corner of the room, by a sideboard laden with glasses and plates, who was still watching us, his *Evening News* now folded on his lap, with the same half-smile on his lips as on the occasion of that other meal, the memory of which had constantly recurred to me during my present meal and in fact had made me choose this particular place, that other meal which only last Saturday I had decided to describe early this week: my first meal at this table last November, my companion then being not Lucien, who did not arrive in Bleston 'til much later, but James Jenkins whom I had asked by way of return for his hospitality the day following that Sunday when, on leaving the Old Cathedral, after listening to the priest's explanations about Cain's Window, I had seen the Chinese characters outlined against the rainy night sky, and going closer had read on the iron curtain the words "Closed on Sundays", in western lettering, James, who since his mother was expecting him at home, had postponed his acceptance 'til the following evening, Tuesday, November 6th—my first meal beside that Window which was closed then because of the cold, and dark because the days were short, and whose panes were covered on the outside with hundreds of raindrops each holding a minute reflection of the ceiling light with its four pink globes, my first meal, on November 6th, the menu being almost identical with Saturday's, not only because during the whole of these seven months when the three sister restaurants, the Oriental Bamboo, the Oriental Rose in Town Hall Square and the Oriental Pearl in New Cathedral Square, all under the same management and with the same printed menu-cards, had served as my weekly refuge against the overwhelming insipidity of Bleston fare, during those seven months I had more than enough time to run through all their specialities, but chiefly because, with my story in mind, I endeavoured to reconstruct the menu of that first meal on November 6th: soup with eggs, duck with pineapple, and sweet biscuits instead of the lychees which I had first ordered, like Barnaby Morton in the opening pages of *The Bleston Murder*, but which today were "off".

James, who naturally had never set foot in such a place, pleasantly disconcerted by these unfamiliar flavours, congratulated me, with unconscious irony, on knowing my way about the town—that town in which I almost despaired of discovering a lodging somewhat less inhuman than the gloomy hole at the Anchor where I was still living, which I found increasingly oppressive as winter drew near: that town which I was sick to death of exploring in vain, after working hours, wearily and hopelessly wandering through its more sordid districts; and I told him, without of course going into all the details, how I had discovered this pleasant place, and thus I came to mention J. C. Hamilton's novel for the first time.

Wednesday, June 11th

As the name conveyed nothing to him I asked him if he ever happened to read that sort of book, and his eyes—those watchful dog's eyes in which I had not yet learnt to recognise his feline cunning—gleamed as he broke into a laugh in which there was no trace of mockery, it was so frank and simple; he had taken my naïve question as a joke, since he could not imagine anyone having doubts about something so obvious.

I was profoundly disconcerted at the time by his laughter, which I could not interpret, as I did not then know about the huge collection of detective stories which practically fills a whole room in that big house of his, and into which I was subsequently to dip so often in order to occupy my evenings before I had begun to fill them with that research into my own past which I have set down in these pages—a long quest, as the pile of notes on the right-hand corner of my table bears witness, and one which I am pursuing as I write these words.

That great library of detective stories belonging to him or rather to his mother, as he told me a few minutes later (while the plump little Chinese waiter set a plate of round sweet biscuits before us) had been collected by his father up 'til his death from T.B. ten years ago; it provided such an ample store of reading matter that they had scarcely added any recent books, and it did not include *The Bleston Murder*.

"I'm not a specialist like yourself, but it's a rather remarkable book, a clever piece of work; I'm sure it will interest you."

I scarcely had to make any effort in speaking to him and understanding him, whereas I still had great difficulties in my fruitless interviews with landladies, or in asking for some new toilet accessory at the hairdresser's in Grey Street, between the chemist's shop and the Sword restaurant; and even now, whenever dear Mr. Blythe, at whose bald head, broad neck fringed with greying hair, tobacco-stained fingers and tobacco-coloured jacket and collar I stare for nearly forty-four hours a week—when Mr. Blythe mumbles some friendly remark I am forced to ask him to repeat it, or better, to translate it for me.

No, I told James nothing of the story, not even that the table at which we were sitting was the one where the detective meets the future victim, and later on his brother the murderer; I didn't want to spoil his enjoyment of the book by depriving him of the surprise.

As I explained this, he looked at me with his clear, amused eyes.

"You might just as well tell me everything, Monsieur Revel, it wouldn't make much difference."

"Would you forget it?"

"I don't think so, Monsieur Revel."

"You surely wouldn't read a detective story twice, Jenkins?"

And yet hadn't I myself just re-read the opening pages of the one about which we were talking? But only because I considered it as different from other books of its class as James himself was from the mass of his fellow-citizens, and like him a precious guide for a newcomer among the perplexities and misunderstandings of that city.

"I've re-read some of them half a dozen times, Monsieur Revel. How can I explain—they become as it were transparent; through the illusions of the opening chapters you catch a glimpse of the truth which you had vaguely remembered."

I had no need to answer him; I was waiting and watching him; I had seen a new light come into his eyes; I sensed the mental effort, the questioning behind his silence.

He had clasped his fingers, which were longer than Lucien's, with paler, better-kept nails; and his voice was slower and deeper and gentler than Lucien's as he spoke to me in his own language, which as yet only he could make me follow, and with the local accent somehow purified by his reserve and attentiveness, that local accent which is usually so thick and heavy, like the soot that cakes the mortar in Bleston's walls, but which sometimes, especially on women's lips and when touched with a trace of French influence, has a taking lilt.

"A detective story about Bleston," he went on, "yes, you must let me look at that. I was wondering if I knew of any other, but no, I don't think there is such a thing, at least among those we've got at home, and I must admit, Monsieur Revel, that it surprises me considerably."

"Really Jenkins?"

"I've never been out of Bleston, Monsieur Revel."

"Not even to go to the seaside or the hills, or to the Lake District?"

"I've never seen any other town, Monsieur Revel, nor what you call a village, my father went to London to study because the

University, which we passed the other day in Continent Street when I took you to my home, was then only a small engineering school, but my mother has never been in a train and I think she's too old ever to undertake it now. I should like to go for a long journey across the sea, but that's out of the question for the time being; I've neither the time nor the money, and I shouldn't care to go all alone."

With a sad little smile and a quick movement of his right hand, as though to throw a pinch of salt over his shoulder, he dismissed the long-cherished, long-repressed dream—that dream which, to this day, confers such glamour on Lucien and myself, ambassadors from a land beyond the sea, living witnesses to its reality, proofs of its accessibility; then, after nibbling part of his biscuit, he clasped his long fingers once more and stared down again at a corner of the tablecloth.

The Old Cathedral was invisible, for the night was much too dark (on the other side of the windowpane, only drops of water could be seen) and he seemed to be oppressed by its unseen bulk; and yet I am sure I had not spoken of it since we had gone up to the first-floor of the Oriental Bamboo, I had not said a word about the part it plays in Hamilton's novel.

"So you see it's only at the cinema, Monsieur Revel, that I've been able to see anything of other regions and other cities, but I have the feeling that there's something peculiar about this place, something which I've never seen satisfactorily described in any story set elsewhere, a sort of permanent dread.

"You'll think this absurd, no doubt, but although you do know Bleston quite well already, Monsieur Revel, although you've managed to discover restaurants which I'd never have gone into nor even noticed by myself, yet you don't know it in the same way that I do, you're not so used to it.

"You've seen chiefly the best parts of the town so far, the avenues and gardens with their shady trees, but one day you're bound to find your way into those deserted streets where one gets lost; perhaps you've already tasted the bitterness of them, perhaps you've already tried to escape, but in that case you've only just made a beginning, Monsieur Revel; try to understand me—it's hard to explain, it's something that can't be put into words, you'll be losing more than your way.

"I know these streets; I don't know the whole of Bleston, there are districts into which I've never had occasion to go and of which I'm as ignorant as your fellow-countrymen who've never left the Continent; but the streets I'm thinking of now, and there are many of them, are clearly mapped out in my mind; I could find my way through them blindfold unless I had gone crazy there meanwhile.

"You see it's as if all the characters involved in a murder were hidden there; everything is ready; the victim is behind one of the doors, grasping its handle, he's about to go out and turn the corner where his enemy lies in wait with his finger on the trigger; only everything is held in suspense.

"Even at midday the few passers-by hurry, hugging the walls, humming to themselves with lowered heads as if it were black night.

"And then I can only move forward at a crawl, overcome by an ever greater longing for these disasters to break out so that the suspense may be ended and one may at last be able to walk and speak and breathe; and indeed they do sometimes occur, and then there's a big headline in the *Evening News* or the *Bleston Post*; but the suspense is not over; everything is still imminent; for in such a setting nothing can really happen except sordid crimes, and everything else inevitably leads up to them by devious ways, everything else merely serves to conceal them."

Thursday, June 12th

He took a deep breath and then finished his biscuit.

"Do you think such streets are only to be found here, Jenkins?"

"I'd like to hope that nowhere is their power so strong as in this city, which detective writers usually avoid as a setting for their stories, for fear their make-believe may turn into grim earnest, as if they were themselves affected by the dread that hangs in the air; we Bleston folk are said to be superstitious…" he had recovered his smile and his modesty, "living in a city where the Old Cathedral itself…" he could not see it through the rain-spangled panes, but he cast an ironical glance towards it, "is chiefly famous for its Murderer's Window."

How I wish I had noted down his exact words at the time! I cannot check them today; I have to fall back on this rough interpretation.

How I wish I had described, at the time, his expression and the shamefaced gesture with which he seemed to be trying to obliterate the words he had let slip!

I did not tell him that he had practically quoted the opening sentence of *The Bleston Murder*; I don't know if he recalls it now; I even wonder if he noticed it when he read the book.

As he was taking me home that evening in the firm's car—and by home I mean my room at the Anchor, that ill-furnished garret overlooking a small yard paved with clinkers and a tumbledown brick wall beyond, which I had not even attempted to change for a better room since I lived in hope of leaving the hotel next day, and for the same reason had never bothered to change the dim lamp for a brighter one—as he was taking me back to the Anchor that Tuesday evening, November 6th, driving through the damp darkness of Deren Street where the rain had newly ceased, James realised that I was puzzled to see, lit up by our headlights and the blurred glimmer of sparse street-lamps, a whole crowd of children dragging bundles of wood clumsily fastened with ropes, and he explained to me that this was Guy Fawkes' week—in Bleston they celebrate the festival of Guy Fawkes for a week—and that they were preparing bonfires for those puppets made of old clothes stuffed with straw, with features crudely drawn in purple ink or charcoal on oval cardboard faces or pieces of rag that had once been pink or white, puppets such as I had in fact seen that very morning as I walked to the Sword for lunch, being pushed around in doll's prams or even in real cradles and old rickety pushchairs by the grubby urchins of Tower Street and Grey Street, who beset me with shouts of: "A penny for the Guy": effigies of a historical character about whose date and whose crime James could give me no precise information.

The next day but one, Thursday, November 8th, as I walked back on purpose in the pouring rain, I watched them burning smokily at every street corner, sending up tiny flares that fell down and died away almost immediately, to the crackle of squibs and the monotonous rhythm of the chant: "We burn the Guy, we burn the Guy…"—those bonfires of green wood and bits of painted boards which had been spattered with petrol to make them catch fire, and those dangling dummies of damp straw clad in woollen or cotton rags, shod with leather or rubber, sprinkled with gunpowder, all giving out an acrid reek that filled my head and was still clinging to my clothes on the following Saturday, when I went into Baron's bookshop on leaving work, before even having my lunch, to buy there an English Bible in order to look up the passage which the priest had summarised so strangely, quoting the Latin transcriptions on that splendid window that illustrates it.

On Sunday at the Jenkins', James having asked me to lunch in return for the meal I had given him at the Oriental Bamboo, the talk moved quite naturally from this Chinese restaurant and its dishes, the description of which amused my friend's mother considerably, to the Old Cathedral, and to that Window of which neither of them, I noticed, had more than a vague and sketchy knowledge, as though they had not been inside the building for years and could speak of that great stained glass only from hearsay and not from direct contemplation of its flames and its sombre waters.

Then, as I had begun to tell them about my encounter, Mrs. Jenkins, whom I could follow less easily than her son but tolerably well nonetheless, thanks to the similarity of their accents, confirmed the story of the transfer of the bells, and this led me to question her about the New Cathedral, explaining that I had not yet been to see it owing to my dislike of the religious art of that period.

I suddenly realised that for the past few minutes Mrs. Jenkins had ceased to answer or listen to me (James, on the other hand, had become particularly voluble and friendly) and that she had even stopped eating, holding her small right fist clenched a little way above the table and staring down at that fly with iridescent wings imprisoned in the glass bubble on her ring.

A change of topic was enough to disperse the sense of strain; once the meal was over they took me up into the small unfurnished room where the detective stories collected by James' father were stacked in neatly-dusted irregular piles, and they lent me a few of these.

Friday, June 13th

If I were superstitious, like a native of Bleston—Rose or Ann Bailey, James or his mother, or Mrs. Grosvenor—I should no doubt feel uneasy about today's date, although everything seems to have gone quite well so far, the sky is still cloudless, the sun shone into the office and I have just dined pleasantly enough at the Oriental Rose, the Chinese restaurant in Town Hall Square; yet surely the story I am about to tell should serve to avert bad luck (if only I could avert a whole year's bad luck, the bad luck inherent in this town), the story of my second meeting with the man who is, so to speak, the embodiment of my own misfortune, that negro whom I had not seen again since he had entertained me in the early days of October, whose name I did not know and whose face I had practically forgotten (it took me several minutes to recognise him), a meeting which was to have the happiest consequences for me, since it was thanks to this man, from whom I should never have expected help, that I eventually discovered this room in which I can live, this table at which I can write—my second encounter with Horace Buck on Sunday, November 11th, in the evening, a rainy evening like so many others, after I had left the Jenkins' home with my raincoat pockets bulging with the books I had just borrowed from them.

After alighting from a 23 bus in Town Hall Square, feeling at a loose end, I had boarded a 27 which had carried me along Silver Street, Tower Street, Brandy Bridge Street, taking me over the Slee for the first time, as far as Ferns Park in the 5th district, where the trees were leafless but the crumpled russet fronds of bracken covered the grounds like a shaggy bison's fleece, under the grey, curdled, low-lying clouds.

It was while I was staring at the ferns that the darkness and the rain began to fall, implacably taking possession of streets and lanes, driving me back towards the town centre, where I dined very early in the teashop at the top of Mountains Street, opposite the Modern Stores, and then took refuge in a cinema, not the Royal this time but the Gaiety with its mirror-lined lobby.

I was on my way out that Sunday evening, November 11th, after three dreary, drowsy hours spent watching Yvonne de Carlo or some such actress serving bourbon whisky, with a song, to check-shirted horsemen in improbable Arizona saloons, and real horses galloping over rock-studded prairies, it was while I was making my way through the crowd as it dispersed in the rain, in the clammy darkness, under the flickering advertisements for Bovril, Player's, or the *Evening News*, and as the buses one by one splashed their way out of their enclosure, bound for every corner of the town, it was while I was threading my way through that crowd, whose faces were the same colour as the trampled bus tickets on the muddy ground, that I suddenly turned round on hearing somebody call out "hullo", not because I thought I was being addressed (I know now that that voice could have been no one else's, but at that time he was so far from my thoughts, I so little expected to see him again!) but merely out of curiosity, instinctively.

The eyes which had been seeking mine through the crowd, through the darkness, and had clouded over with a look of anxiety and bitter disappointment during the few moments it took me to identify him, lit up again joyfully when I recognised him at last, while the slow, hoarse, harsh voice (whose heavy flattened accent, so unlike mine but just as bad and never improving, I yet found easier to understand than that of the natives of Bleston) said in a tone of relief: "I was wondering if you would want to remember me."

"Why do you say that?"

"I don't know, most people…"

"What d'you mean? I'm not one of these people, I'm a stranger like yourself."

"No, not quite like myself."

"And your girl, the one who wasn't there the day we lunched together?"

"Mary? Oh, she came back."

"That's fine."

"No, not really. She's going off tomorrow, for good this time, bag and baggage. She found a fellow in Hamilton, where she comes from. I think they're going to get married. I haven't even got her with me tonight, she's gone out to supper with some of her friends."

"Maybe she's gone home already."

"Not likely! She stays out 'til all hours of the night with Jessie, Flossie, Minnie and the rest of the gang… Why did you never come back to see me?"

"Well, I'd forgotten your address, and as I don't even know your name…"

"It's Horace, Horace Buck; and yours?"

My trousers were clinging wetly round my ankles as we slipped into the crowded Unicorn, the pub at the corner of Town Hall Square and Continent Street, next to the News Theatre cinema, where the air was thick and a group of men were singing horribly, waggling their heads, and edged our way as far as a dark wooden table in a recess, with six empty glasses on it and a great pool of foam dripping down on to the linoleum, while the wet glitter of the lights reflected in its big bubbles slid imperceptibly forward.

Horace sat taciturn until he had been served, until he had tossed back his beer and wiped his mouth with the back of his dark hand and lit his cigarette, first offering me one (but I had already begun to fill my pipe); then he began to declaim in a gentle, monotonous, elegiac tone:

"It's turning cold outside, really cold too; I don't like it, I don't like the rain; I like night, but I don't like daylight when it's not really daylight. At home I've only got a small gas fire; it's not enough, you know; I wonder what I ought to do."

As the waiter came up to remove our glasses and take our money, Horace ordered two more beers.

"And are you still in the same job?"

"Of course; I've come to Matthews & Sons for a year, and I shall stay there a year."

"And do you like it?"

"I've got to put up with it."

"You're lucky, you know; often people who take a job here find it hard to get used to it; they give it up and look for something else; and they end up with something far worse, but they stay in it a bit longer because they've realised how hard things are. Of course it's probably different in your profession."

The singing had stopped; there was nothing to be heard but a continuous trampling of feet and an occasional hoarse laugh.

"Still in the same digs?"

"Unfortunately."

"A hotel, didn't you say? I'll ask around, you never can tell."

As he called out for two more beers the waiter leaned forward to say reproachfully: "Last drinks, Sir, we're closing."

"Bring us two beers!"

"All right, Sir, stay where you are, I'll bring them at once."

"He hates me; this is the first time I've come here, and yet he hates me. Is it your first time too? Well, if you'd asked him for those beers, do you think he'd have answered you like that, puckering up his eyes as if you'd got a running sore on your face?"

The waiter had come back: he asked me to pay at once, and stood by us to watch us drinking; I felt my face flush, and I was afraid this might hurt Horace's feelings.

He stood up, head erect, and shouted with terrifying contempt: "Don't you see we're through?"

The waiter took fright and made a sign to the barmaid, who hurried out.

"Oh, so she's gone to fetch the Police! Do you think it's going to take the Police to get me out of this joint?"

He spat, and took me by the arm; we went out into the rain, turning up the collars of our coats; people were queuing for the last buses, shivering with cold.

"Isn't it awful, Monsieur? Are things like that in your country? Come to my place; I've still got a bottle of rum; we'll drink it while we wait for Mary to come home."

"But it's… rather a long way to your place."

"Nonsense, it's barely a quarter of an hour's walk. Do *you* think I'm drunk, too?"

"No, but I've a feeling that you soon will be, if we go and drink at your place."

"I'll get drunk much faster if I have the whole bottle to myself."

And so I went back to his room, where he had forgotten to close the window before going out, so that part of the floor was awash.

"Take off your things, take off your shoes, or you'll catch a chill; here are some old slippers. Come on now, drink up! Here's to your good health, Mr. Frenchman! I tell you, I shall have a few days quiet now, without a care in the world, without constantly wondering where she is, what she's been doing, when she's coming in, whether she's going to drop me soon."

"Only a few days?"

"After that I shall fall for somebody else. Women are easy to get for us Africans, easy enough but no good."

He lay down on the bed.

"Will you have lunch with me one of these days? If Mary had stayed she could have cooked for us. But I'll manage, don't you worry. Will Saturday do?"

Then he took up his harmonica and began to play very softly, just to himself, as if I had not been there.

Sitting at his table in front of my half-filled glass, I felt my head beginning to go round, and I dreaded more and more the time when I should have to go out walking in the rain again, walking for over an hour in the rain to get to the Anchor, where I should certainly find the door locked and should have to ring to wake up the porter and get myself let in.

He began to play about far-off voyages along a flat coastline thick with waving grasses, until he leapt up on hearing the key turn in the lock and opened the door to his Mary, of whom I remember only her splendid hair, the colour of ash-bark, streaming with water as she dried it with a towel, his Mary whom next morning he would see off at the station, bound for a happier lot no doubt; I drank off my glass, put on my shoes and raincoat again and said goodbye.

"Don't forget next Saturday!"

"Bon voyage, Mademoiselle!"

Then I plunged into the wet, dark November night, as if into the Slee itself.

3

Monday, June 16th

It is still light, and yet on leaving work I walked up Tower Street, then up Silver Street as far as Town Hall Square to the News Theatre, that narrow strip of a cinema with its scanty screen, its inadequate wooden seats that creak at one's least movement, so close-packed that I have to sit with twisted legs, so airless and hazy with tobacco-smoke, that cinema where it is so chilly in winter; James had introduced me to it (it is the only picture house to which he goes regularly, the only window through which his eager eyes can catch a glimpse of other towns, of the rest of the world), and I had myself acquired a taste for it and become a regular patron, before I took to spending my weekday evenings pursuing and setting down my recollections of the bygone year.

What impelled me to revisit the News Theatre today was the fact that last night, after saying goodbye to Rose and Ann Bailey at their bus stop, while walking with Lucien towards the Town Hall restaurant, where we had a quick and mediocre meal because Lucien had to hurry back to his work at the Grand Hotel (the biggest hotel in Bleston, as its name proudly implies, standing at the corner of City Street and Mayor Street; its restaurant is far too expensive for my means, as is the Prince's opposite it next to the Gaiety Cinema)—while walking towards the Town Hall restaurant, as we passed the News Theatre, whose neon signs were glittering uselessly since it was still broad daylight, since it would still be dully light for nearly two hours, and saw the publicity posters on either side of the mirror-lined lobby where people were queuing at the box office for the programme of cartoons which was being shown for the last time yesterday (they have one every four weeks), I noticed that from today the main film, supported by newsreels and two Mack Sennett comedies, was to be a travelogue, a documentary colour-film about Crete, the home of Phaedra and Ariadne, the isle of the Labyrinth and the Minotaur, whose story is told on the eleventh tapestry in the Museum; I did not guess how far superior, technically, this film would be to most others of its kind which I had hitherto watched in that cinema.

Day must be bright there, shining on the slopes of Mount Ida, along all those high peaks that pierce the sky like slow cries, glittering on the translucent waters at their feet, bathing the whole of that steep, jagged coastline, probing its ravines with long kind sunbeams, that coastline which we followed, after reading the words "A Tour in Crete" and the names of the chief collaborators inscribed against a background of octopuses presumably copied from some ancient pottery, while we sat in darkness, in serried ranks of strangers, ignoring one another, held prisoner under Bleston's spell, staring through the dense, smoky, sooty air at the blurred flickering images on the small, slack, coarsewoven screen.

Day must be bright there, shining over the orange groves and the ragged foliage of banana trees, over irrigation streams, over windmills like great mosquitoes, with twelve sails as slender as twigs opening out into quivering triangles, looking like huge dandelion clocks on straight transparent stems covered with a fine black mesh, opening out in the wind but never scattering; over dazzling white-washed villages between the shoulders of great rocks streaked with rows of olive trees, and beaches perpetually glistening under the salt kiss of the blue water, over the dismantled ramparts of Candia and the esplanade of Knossos where bulls' horns hold sway over the paving stones whose countless cracks are bright with anemones, over the stairways of gypsum or alabaster, over the great urns left lying among the excavations; day must be bright there, even in late December, when we here are doomed to weeks of confinement in airless rooms by the red parching breath of gas fires, to weeks of lamplight-wan, gloomy yellow lamplight, meals by lamplight, work by lamplight, even walks by lamplight—weeks of an almost subterranean existence dominated by murky darkness, with barely a few hours' dun, foggy daylight; day must be bright there, so much brighter during the last days of autumn than it is here today, even on this long June day now drawing to a close without one drop of rain, without one cloud, almost without a trace of fog (only that fundamental pollution of the air, that exudation, that terrible sour noxious breath that Bleston exhales, insidiously stupefying, paralysing and depressing the soul, relentlessly clouding the mind, that iron grip so seldom and so imperceptibly relaxed), even on this long long day, the finest day I have yet seen here, which flung generous sunlight on my desk at Matthews & Sons, and whose last greenish gleams are only now dying away, very gradually, as the moon appears through the light haze over Dew Street where the windows have begun to shine out one by one, one in every house, and where only a few seconds ago I could still see little pigtailed girls in short frocks and black stockings playing on the pavements, without, for once, getting dirty there, for the mud is hard and all the puddles have dried up.

Tuesday, June 17th

I have not yet turned on my light, and yet before coming home, as I left the Sword restaurant in Grey Street, I could not resist turning right down Tower Street, pausing for a moment in front of Baron's bookshop windows (the new Penguins, orange and green, the handbooks about cricket or cookery or gardening, the misleading "How to Make It" series, that encyclopaedia for the handyman, the works on engineering and the *History of Torture Throughout the Ages*), then going along Silver Street as far as Town Hall Square to see once more, in the News Theatre, that film about Crete which I described last night, which will still be showing all this week with its supporting newsreel and the two Mack Sennett comedies, so that if I suddenly felt the need to check something I remembered about it I could go back and see it until the last showing on Sunday, after which the whole programme will change (I have seen the notices: a travelogue about Petra—what is Petra? I shan't go; I shall try to make up for the time I have wasted these two evenings), and then *A Tour in Crete* will become as inaccessible to my sight (at least as long as I stay in Bleston, for even if they do sometimes repeat old films they are unlikely to show the same one in less than four months), as inaccessible as the details and incidents I saw at the crowded fair the day before yesterday, Sunday, June 15th, when Lucien and I walked with Rose and Ann Bailey on the waste ground of the 5th district on the bank of the Slee, near the railway lines that go from Dudley Station towards the north.

Since early morning, probably long before I awoke, a film of cloud like a closed eyelid has hidden the sun, which is going to set a little later than yesterday; the evenings are growing longer, just as the afternoons had grown shorter last November, each encroaching a little further like successive waves of the incoming tide upon the sand, just as the nights had done on those November mornings when I went from the Anchor to the office and the sky was a little darker each time, and the lights were kept on a little longer; a film of cloud, uniformly grey, now hides the blue that was visible yesterday—a blue far less pure and strong, far more remote than the sky shown in that sequence of pictures I have just been watching, the sky above the horns of Knossos and the courtyards carpeted with fine grass, and those encircling stairways upheld, today by columns of cement but formerly, according to the commentators, by pillars carved from the trunks of cedars felled on the nearby slopes of Mount Ida (each pillar set in a base of alabaster and broadening out like an arum up to the capital, which swells out into the curve of a living breast above a slight constriction like that formed by a high narrow girdle) and the platforms adorned with spirals painted sea-colour and with friezes of rams' heads in figures of eight and spotted like the coats of piebald horses or panthers, which lead through many passages and stairways and other courtyards to those apartments where dwelt, over three thousand years ago, the princesses who to the Greeks became Ariadne and Phaedra (shown in such different dress on the Museum tapestries) just as the palace itself became the Labyrinth: princesses with huge eyes and slender waists, according to the statues and paintings of which I have just had a fleeting second glimpse, and with breasts exposed in low-cut, close-fitting bodices, breasts like sensitive peaches, such as I imagine Rose's to be (every lovely face or form irresistibly takes me back to hers) under her high-necked sweater.

Tonight the clouds will prevent me from seeing the new moon rise above the chimneys of Dew Street, where the two little street-lamps are flaring pallidly and people in the houses have turned on the ceiling lights in their narrow living-rooms and bedrooms, behind drawn curtains; and now it's not the fading grey daylight but the orange glow of my lamp that shines on the map of Bleston which I have just spread out on my table, a map similar in every detail to that which I used to spread out on my bed last November, at the Anchor, which I carried about everywhere in my raincoat pocket and which, in my perpetual search for lodgings, I used to unfold every evening during the week—more out of habit than in hope of really finding anything—at the Sword restaurant on leaving work, so as to locate, amidst districts which were usually still quite unknown to me, the approximate position, the street at any rate, of those little houses whose addresses I had just read in the columns of the *Evening News*, and which usually seemed to me, after this cursory examination, so remote and so ill-served by buses that I made no attempt to go and knock at their doors.

True, on this sheet of paper patterned with printers' ink in five colours, the square inches associated in my memory with buildings I have seen, with events and moments of my own experience, have multiplied; an ever-growing portion of it belongs to reality; yet there are still immense gaps in which the inscriptions tell me nothing, the lines call up no image, the streets convey only the vaguest notion of "Bleston streets" with nothing to distinguish them, and as soon as I look at all closely at the sections corresponding to the districts I know, the 7th for instance in which I live and work, which includes Town Hall Square, the Museum, the New Cathedral and Horace Buck's home, or the 10th where Jenkins and the Bailey girls live, I see some name which surprises me, some lane which I have certainly never taken, and I am even uncertain about the appearance of some building marked on the map which I must often have passed without ever noticing it, such as the fire station at the corner of Continent Street and Surgery Street, opposite Willow Park; close to the Royal Hospital and to the ground where the fair was held in January, on the 24 bus route by which I travel every time I go to All Saints Gardens.

Wednesday, June 18th

The grey daylight, which will linger for another two hours before it fades into the slow dusk of a northern midsummer, is still shining on the map of Bleston which has lain spread out on my table ever since last night, undisturbed by good Mrs. Grosvenor while she did her careful cleaning; she is increasingly puzzled and impressed by the mounting pile of papers covered with indecipherable sentences, and by now the sheer bulk of them has convinced her of the serious nature of my mysterious task, which she must assume forms part of my professional duties, and about which she would never dream of questioning me, realising that I could never give her a satisfactory explanation.

The grey daylight shines on the map of this city which is still so unfamiliar, which conceals itself as the folds of a cloak conceal other folds, which shuns scrutiny as though the light scorched it, like a woman whose face one cannot see except by forcibly tearing away her veil: the map which is, so to speak, the city's ironic response to my efforts to see it whole and to take its census, forcing me at each fresh glance to admit the extent of my ignorance: the map over which in my mind other lines are superimposed, with other points of interest, other references, other networks, other systems of distribution—in short, other maps which, though vague and fragmentary at first, are gradually growing fuller and more precise, for instance the imaginary map that shows the route taken by the fair, that miniature mobile town, rather less gloomy than the city itself round which it travels in eight months, staying four weeks in each of the outer districts except for the 12th, in which it would be too close to the big stationary fair in Pleasance Gardens, and always stopping on the same waste lands, as I was informed by James, who is well acquainted with its inhabitants—that miniature town built of boards and canvas covered, as are the bricks of the greater town in whose arteries it circulates, with a thick coat of sooty grime, that miniature town of huts and caravans which I have visited at each of its stopping-places, since three days ago I went into the 5th district, on the bank of the Slee near the railway bridge over the line from Dudley Station to the north, with Rose, who was needlessly worrying over her examination results (her French has improved considerably of late) but who looked more charming than ever on that sunny afternoon, dressed in her close-fitting high-necked sweater, having at last discarded that raincoat, the colour of Bleston's mud and fog, in which hitherto I had always seen her dressed to go out.

I went to the fair in the 5th district with Rose, whom I was trying to reassure, and with Ann and Lucien who were walking together a little ahead, hoping once again to find a safeguard against Sunday's boredom, which even fine weather scarcely alleviates, in its toffee-apples and ice-creams and gingerbreads, its Aunt Sallies and swings and bumper-cars, its Ghost Train and its Giant Wheel and its livelier crowds—above all in its shooting-galleries, the photographic gallery with its magnesium flashes and its proofs left on account (notably that portrait of George and Harriet Burton) and of course the "bear hunt", that tiny theatre in which, against a forest background, a brown, wooden bear with jointed limbs moves amid tropical trees; three lenses, placed on his belly and flanks, are susceptible to the beam of light that the sportsman shoots from his gun (when wounded, the bear rears up and growls and his eyes flash, while the number of hits scored is registered on the glass façade of the booth), the "bear hunt" at which Lucien and I, who are adept, amused ourselves watching the girls' first attempts just as I had amused myself watching Lucien's first attempts last March in the 3rd district near Lanes Park, and Horace Buck had amused himself watching my own first attempts on Sunday, November 17th (he, being far more skilled at the game than we shall ever be, held his gun at arm's length and never missed a shot) in the 9th district, in that other waste land on the bank of the Slee to the north of Old Bridge, from which you can see the three towers of the Old Cathedral above the old houses on the other bank, a fact which I only noticed last Sunday morning when I went back there under that brief shower that washed the sky clear and left it until nightfall so much brighter than even on these other fine June days.

That other waste land was deserted then except for a few cats quarrelling over scraps of fish among the tufts of shaggy grass; it was seven months since the fair had been there and it will stay in the 5th district for another week before returning thither again according to its regular circuit.

Night had almost fallen, that Saturday, November 17th, all the lamps were lit and the Slee, under its blanket of mist, was like a soft peat-bog.

I had just paid my first visit to the house in which I am now living, to that room in which I am now writing while I gaze at the map of Bleston still spread out on my table, in the fading light of dusk, I had been there under the guidance and encouragement of Horace Buck who, on this occasion, proved my saviour, who did not come in himself (at the time I did not understand his caution, but I have realised since then how fully it was justified), who had begged me not to mention him, who has never been inside the house nor even seen good Mrs. Grosvenor, although I only made her acquaintance thanks to his secret help (which had to remain a secret), good Mrs. Grosvenor, whose apprehensions I could only allay by mentioning the name of another woman of whom he had spoken when he gave me this address, 37 Copper Street, Bleston 7, which was to become my own—Mrs. Wilson, a grocer's wife, highly respectable though still youngish, in her thirties, who devotes her leisure hours to mission work, as I have since learnt, and makes a point of being kind to foreigners and coloured people; I suspect her of a special weakness for Horace.

Thursday, June 19th

Mrs. Grosvenor is unaware of the existence of this irrevocably exiled negro who, after taking me to her house, spent the time while our first difficult interview was taking place (her accent was new to me and mine puzzled her; it took us nearly an hour to settle everything and come to an understanding over a cup of tea and biscuits) waiting in his own room, where he was then living by himself, smoking Player's and drinking rum.

And even now, I take care not to mention him to her, since only a couple of days ago while I was breakfasting in her kitchen (she gets up long before I do, and has always finished by the time I come down) she appeared brandishing the *Bleston Post* to read aloud to me, choking with indignation and distress, the account of a murder committed by some negro in the 5th district to the north of the fairground, in one of the small streets lying between the docks and the railway lines that run to Dudley Station.

She wanted to see all those "black devils" as she called them (one of the many terms of horrified abuse that she applies to them, closing her eyes as though shocked by the violence of her own language) sent to the same gallows, the same hell, and could not understand why the Government allowed into the country these barely human creatures whose savage instincts were always ready to break out, a perpetual menace to the virtue of Englishwomen and a source of trouble and strife.

"Mrs. Wilson is very brave to face those dreadful people. Do you know what goes on in Africa, so I'm told, Monsieur Revel? Do you know what they hide behind their quiet-seeming ways? You've probably never seen how their eyes and their teeth gleam when they come out of the pubs where they're admitted. There are many of them in our district, Monsieur Revel; I never dare go out after tea. You be careful!"

On that Saturday, November 17th, when with very little confidence in the success of my undertaking, since James himself, with whom I felt in ever closer affinity, had been unable to unearth a lodging for me, and since among the few people I knew in Bleston at that time Horace Buck was the one from whom I least expected help (I had been touched and surprised when he told me of his discovery, as he let me in, about twenty minutes past twelve, after my morning's work; but how could I have believed in it?)—on that Saturday, November 17th, when with a mixture of timidity and brazenness I had introduced myself to Mrs. Grosvenor, pretending to have heard from Mrs. Wilson, whom I had in fact never seen but from whom, in token of gratitude, I buy tobacco regularly nowadays, and whose name acted as a regular talisman, that she had a front room to let which I hoped would suit me; when I had described my occupation and explained the purpose of my stay here, her first words had been:

"So you're a Frenchman? I'd never have imagined a Frenchman looking like that!"

She still considers me as being of a peculiar species, different from any she has met before, whose habits are incomprehensible, oddly brought up, oddly ignorant of things which she herself considers self-evident, a sort of awkward child who can't be trusted to walk the streets alone, and who nevertheless is actually in contact with that almost fabulous region, the Continent.

I well remember that it took me a little time to realise my good fortune; when Mrs. Grosvenor first showed me into the room I had not immediately understood that I had at last struck gold, that I should be able to settle down, to find a base and a shelter, that I had done with those wearisome and heartbreaking treks from one end of the town to another, with that meticulous, mistrustful, disillusioned scrutiny of the small-ads in the *Evening News* every night after work, in the Sword or some other restaurant, by way of *hors d'oeuvre*, and that I could at last go on to read something else, which I have signally failed to do; that I had done with those freezing Sunday mornings at the Anchor, those horrible evenings spent in semi-darkness, and that at last, after existing for a month in a sort of waiting-room to which some invisible official seemed to have condemned me for the sheer pleasure of humiliating me, I had been made free of the city of Bleston, and I was going to be able to see it at close quarters.

No, my first reaction was that of a disdainful visitor, or a customer who insists on having cases and boxes opened for him although he is already convinced that he will not find what he wants.

It was only gradually, slowly, as I noticed the brightness and neatness of the room, its white ceiling and its fresh curtains and covers (it had been newly decorated), its south-west aspect and the pleasure of having Dew Street outside one's window instead of the sordid housefronts of Copper Street, it was when I realised the convenience of this central district, its easy access to my work, and heard dear Mrs. Grosvenor answering that of course nothing could be simpler than to bring up the table, tomorrow if I liked, that very table on which I am now writing and which was then standing in the living-room on the ground-floor, between the sideboard and the mantelpiece, covered with a lace cloth under a pewter vase filled with branches of apple blossom whose petals were shells—it was only gradually, slowly, with growing astonishment that I realised that here indeed I could live, could stand up to things; I realised it with astonishment and presently, when everything was satisfactorily settled (the rent I pay is modest enough, since it includes cleaning and heating, breakfast and laundry), with immense relief.

I hurried back to Iron Street to tell Horace Buck of the success of his plan; he greeted the news with childish excitement. We had to celebrate, and thus it happened that, in spite of the chilly mist, he took me to the fair for the first time; we travelled by a 27 bus as far as Town Hall Square, then by a 28 over the Slee by Old Bridge, as far as the waste land in the 9th district beside the black water, which I revisited last Sunday morning to revive my memories, where the fair was then stationed and to which it will return next month, and here he introduced me to the "bear hunt", and we lingered long after nightfall, standing by a brazier to eat our meal of fish and chips, hot dogs and milky coffee, before seeking the more effective comfort of pints of Guinness in a pub whose name I forgot to note last Sunday, close to the bus stop, from which we finally took a 28 bus back to Town Hall Square, where the inhabitants of Bleston, cloaked in dirty fog that shimmered in the neon lights, were still queuing up in front of the picture houses.

After saying goodbye to Horace I got into the 26 bus which goes as far as the Docks by way of Alexandra Place and Port Bridge, but which I left at the junction of City Street and Brown Street, taking a 17 (Old Cathedral – Deren Square) on my way back for the last time (with what joy did I remind myself of this!) to sleep in my wretched room at the Anchor.

Friday, June 20th

With what joy did I inform the young woman who stared so glassily behind her oval glasses as she brandished my key at me, perched on her stool just as she had been on my first morning in Bleston, when James Jenkins had brought me, a bewildered and inarticulate stranger, into that musty hall through which I had so often passed since then, with what joy did I inform this wardress of my prison that she might make out my bill for the last time!

With what relief, on the morning of Sunday, November 18th, did I thrust into my one and only suitcase the few articles I had taken out of it, the few articles I had bought in Bleston, the map of Bleston identical with the one now lying folded on the left-hand corner of my table, that map which I had bought from Ann Bailey, the plan of bus routes of which I had not needed to buy a second copy, and that novel by J. C. Hamilton (whose real name I had not yet discovered), *The Bleston Murder*, which was still in my possession that day (for I only lent it to James, I remember quite clearly, the day after our first visit together to Pleasance Gardens), that copy of *The Bleston Murder* which must now still be at the Baileys' house, which their cousin had returned to them (it was Ann who had let him take it, it was to her I had entrusted it; Rose would not have forgotten thus, would not have pretended she had already given it back to me) after lending it to that unknown friend of his, that Richard Tenn whose house, so he told them, bore so strange a resemblance to the house where the two brothers lived, the murderer and his victim—that copy which I had thought lost, identical in text with the one that I possess at present and only, at that time, a trifle cleaner looking.

With what relief did I shut my heavy suitcase, my one and only suitcase, which now lies empty, collecting dust, on top of the wardrobe on my right behind me, and then, after a last glance through the window which, for a change, was streaming with rain, a last glance over the courtyard full of clinkers and the brick wall, after having severed all connection with this place by paying my final debt, with what relief did I make my way here by a 17 bus and then a 27, changing at the junction of Tower Street and White Street outside Matthews & Sons, and walking the last two hundred yards under the rain, now streaming in gentler showers.

With what relief, when Mrs. Grosvenor welcomed me, did I take possession of these few square yards, and set down my suitcase (fortunately not over-wet) on this table, which for a long time only served me for writing a few uninteresting letters home, for reading or for spreading out the map of Bleston comfortably (but that in itself was a major transformation!) and then fill all the wardrobe shelves with my possessions, while Dew Street gradually became visible through the window!

This was already a first awakening; I believe that Horace Buck is well aware of the extent of the service he did me at that time, for his innocent unfathomable gaze implies hidden depths. I believe, even though he cannot express it thus nor even formulate it clearly to himself, that he knows—such is the patient understanding latent under his bursts of anger, his inarticulateness, his poverty of speech and intellect—he knows that he has, so to speak, saved my life, rescued that consciousness in me which, in his own case, is so deeply oppressed, that consciousness which, though sick and soiled, is still alive in me and is now groping its way towards health and daylight.

And thus I escaped, in some measure, from the quicksands of Bleston which would undoubtedly have engulfed me, at any rate as long as I stay here, if I had not had the benefit of his unexpected secret help, of his almost miraculous intervention, for I know that my courage was waning more and more.

When I set off on one of my increasingly infrequent evening explorations of some district which usually proved just as grim and even more remote than that of the Anchor, following one of those misleading advertisements in the *Evening News* which surely somebody, some time, must find rewarding, one of those advertisements in which I had come to believe less and less, not only were my hopes of success dwindling but so was my will to succeed.

I should soon have wholly given up these futile efforts, this pretence of trying; I should gradually have accepted my fate; I should gradually have grown used to my diminished life; I should even have ceased to suffer from it, I should soon have become unconscious of it, like a sleepwalker, a ghost, a mere larva.

My eyes would have succumbed at last to the smoke, the fog, the boredom, to winter and its mud, to all the ugliness and monotony; total blindness would have crept over me unawares; the curse would have been fulfilled; what would have been left of me?

Undoubtedly, if Horace had not urged me to visit this house I should not be writing this now, I should even have forgotten the strange light I had seen gleaming in the Murderer's Window of the Old Cathedral. Nothing more, nothing at all would have happened to me, I feel sure; and on visiting the New Cathedral that Sunday afternoon—for I should have gone there in any case, impelled by a last vestige of the curiosity awakened a fortnight before by what the priest had told me and by Mrs. Jenkins' extraordinary silence and nervous tension when I had alluded to it the following week—I should have been unable to rid myself of the contempt which *The Bleston Murder* had instilled into me, I should have been unable to appreciate the building or to realise that it offered another clue in that puzzling, evasive trail which I had been following for some time and the end of which I have not yet discovered, for it has vanished into the winter's fogs.

When I entered the New Cathedral at last (the rain, which had begun to fall again, was thrumming against all the grimy colourless windows) I stared with amazement at those thick arches that rose halfway up, those bridges bordered with slender balustrades linking the pillars of the nave in pairs, with circular platforms at their centres, and all the balconies along the walls joining and prolonging them; I stared at the extravagant rood screens that crossed at the transept and were floodlit from the windows of the spire above them with greenish light falling vertically, an almost submarine light, very cold and pale, which cast on the limestone pavement, at the very spot where the body is found in the second chapter of J. C. Hamilton's novel, a great cross of shadow, a great X; and I stared at the profuse naturalistic decoration of animals and plants.

That day I did not examine the outside; but on my way out, before plunging into the rain, I stood for a long time under the south porch, staring in the dusk at the grass in the Square, the bare trees, the railings covered with posters in the background where demolition work was going on, and on my left the iron curtain in front of the third Chinese restaurant, the Oriental Pearl, which was closed on Sundays like the other two, and to which I decided to take James.

4

Monday, June 23rd

These last days the sky has been oftener almost blue (and yet how different, still, from that azure which reigns above the esplanades, the horns and courtyards and stairways of the ruined palaces of Crete, according to that documentary which I saw a week ago at the News Theatre and which I went back to see again next day—it is no longer showing today, it has been replaced today by some film about a place whose name, which I've forgotten, conveyed nothing to me) as each day in turn encroached a little further, like successive waves of the incoming tide, stole a few more seconds from the sands of evening; and now, in the week of the solstice, their progress has halted as if they had encountered an obstacle, or had reached the limit of their strength.

In vain they try to break the immemorial interdiction which in our latitudes protects the heart of night, even in midsummer; worn out by their efforts, they will dwindle and grow short of breath, they will fall back like an exhausted army trying to close its ranks; like the waves of the outgoing tide, each in turn will leave a little more of the darkness intact.

The enemy will corrupt these routed troops with ever greater ease, will taint them ever more deeply with its fogs; an ever thicker film will veil that faraway blue which, so briefly, had drawn nearer.

Summer will be short; when I leave at the end of September, when at last I tear myself away from Bleston, from that Circe and her sinister spells, when, set free at last, I shall find it possible to recover my human shape, to wash my eyes clear, the days will have shrunk once more to that pitiful heartbreaking glimmer that I knew when I first walked and sought and strayed and struggled and succumbed and resisted in this town; then they will become those ghosts of days through which I lived, if you can call it living, in November, and they will go on so, mouldering and liquescent as corpses, shrouded like ghosts in mud-soaked winding-sheets, sunk like drowned men in black weeds and banks of slime, as they went on last year until Christmas time.

Oh lovely evening, lovely shimmering sun whose moist velvety gleams still reach me, reflected on the half-open first-floor windows of the dingy little brick houses on the right side of Dew Street, the whole street flushed with an ever deeper rose, steeped in the luminous redness of that fine sky which will go on glowing red for an hour longer above the slate roofs!

And yesterday's lovely afternoon, when I walked in Green Park among clumps of tulips that scarcely swayed, their petals swimming slowly like lazy dazzling fishes in the pearly light, among the lawns strewn with sleeping figures whose heads were hidden by Sunday newspapers, and the walks thronged with women knitting and pushing prams, before I went to have tea with the Burtons (Lucien turned up there a few minutes after me) in their comfortable house at the corner of Green Park Terrace and Hatter Street, where we did not have to put on the light until the end of our game of bridge!

And a lovely afternoon on Saturday (three whole rainless, almost mistless days; how long can it last?) when, as we were all celebrating Rose's success, in Pleasance Gardens, in the open-air café that is set up there in summer in the middle of the zoological section, among the wolves' and foxes' cages and the ragged-winged cranes' enclosure, the duck-ponds and the seals' basins with their white-painted concrete islands, I could see, above the stationary booths of this mammoth fairground, eerily outlined in the faint luminous haze, the tops of the calcined posts of the Scenic Railway, with a few beams still fixed to them like gibbets or like the branch stumps that project from the peeled trunks of trees struck by lightning; and I listened to the noise of the demolition-workers' axes, which the rest of the party probably did not notice, since for them it was drowned by the chatter of voices, the chink of knives on china, the cries of birds and wild beasts; through this medley of sounds I listened to the crash of those ruins at which I had stared so long last week, drawn by some nameless curiosity as soon as I read the news of the disaster on the posters of the *Evening News*.

We were all of us celebrating Rose's success in her French exam, a success which we had all confidently expected, so great was the progress she had made since the day when I had met her for the first time with Ann; all of us, that's to say the Bailey girls, Lucien and myself and also James Jenkins,

(I did not know he would take such an interest in them; I should never have expected him to join in our little celebration; this was the first time in many weeks that I had seen him outside working hours, whereas in the past he had so often invited me to a meal at his home, or offered me the run of his father's library of detective stories; all that had stopped, ever since... that evening, the last Saturday in May, at the fair in the 2nd district, the evening before the day I revealed J. C. Hamilton's real name to the Bailey girls),

the nimble-fingered sunbeams, still frail and pallid, were playing in the red-glinting hair of my Cretan maiden, Rose, my little Phaedra, a figure woven of living gold and silver, even lovelier at certain happy moments, for all her imperfect garments, than the Phaedra of the Harrey Tapestries,

(I restrained myself from drawing near her, from showing too clearly the pleasure I find in looking at her and speaking to her, the increasing interest she inspires in me, an interest that she might easily interpret, if I were not careful, as a sort of passion, which it is not and must not be, an interest which might easily, if I am not careful, become a genuine passion;

fortunately she suspects nothing yet; I think we shall round the cape in safety),

that fine Saturday afternoon when for the first time the scent of roses mingled with the exhalations of the Slee.

A deepening flush over Dew Street, then greenness; the sky is a lake where among thick rushes, the scarcely-misted moon flowers like a pale, downy iris unfolding a single petal.

Tuesday, June 24th

Not one cloud! This is the fourth fine evening in succession, more than I had ever hoped for.

How wily this town is! Endeavouring, by this alleviation of my bondage, to disturb and darken all my knowledge of it, so slowly, so painfully acquired! But far from yielding to these temptations which I know to be ephemeral, or scornfully dismissing all those months of patience, stubbornness and boredom, I shall go on crawling towards remembrance, line by line, page by page, tunnelling my way to light.

Fine summer weather, come to my aid! Or rather, since I am still sunk in the slough of Bleston, and in spite of all this show of sweetness still cut off by a dense wall of fog from the purity of blue sky, of the heavenly sun, of water and earth and even of coal—come to my aid, Summer's pathetic younger brother, Bleston's hireling, you who during these last four days have displayed something so near to splendour and can still comfort me most powerfully with the blood-red, wine-red, fire-red gleams shed on my table from the vast glistening redness outside, against which I see the roofs and chimneys of Dew Street outlined—just as, in the windows of the Old Cathedral, I saw the crescents and towers, the domes and minarets of Cain's town where his descendants wove and forged and silently sang to horn and lute.

Ever since yesterday I have been trying in vain to concentrate all my attention on that Monday, November 19th, when for the first time, after dining in some restaurant or other on leaving Matthews & Sons, where things were already unchanging and I knew every dreary detail of my job, and where nothing has changed since except that the language difficulty has gradually decreased, though of late less and less sharply, I did not take a 17 bus to go back to bed at the Anchor but a 27 bus in the opposite direction to come here.

The fact is that the present (including these last few days) now absorbs my mind so entirely that I have spent a whole evening trying to thrust it aside, and even now I know that I shall only get rid of it by mentioning today's conversation with James Jenkins, which might almost be called a renewal of contact between us.

James, who last Sunday in Pleasance Gardens, in the presence of Rose and Ann and Lucien, had scarcely addressed a word to me (this constraint between us dates quite obviously from that evening we spent together at the fair, when I had caught a distant glimpse of the Burtons and had pointed them out to him, when we had pursued them in vain, and had talked, for the first time for ages, about *The Bleston Murder*, the evening before that visit to the Baileys which I have already described, when the copy of that book which I had lent him in the autumn reappeared, although I was so sure of having lost it that I had gone to great pains to procure another), James Jenkins, who had been unable to bring himself to reply to the few questions I had put to him, came up just as I was leaving for lunch and asked me whether I had seen the programme then showing at the News Theatre, with that documentary, that travelogue about... what was it? I've forgotten already.

I told him no, I had never heard of the place, I asked him if he knew what it was.

"A town, I suppose."

Of course, but what sort of town, dead or alive, sick or healthy, young or old, a source of strength or of weariness? That's the problem.

We shall go and see it together tomorrow, then we shall have dinner at the Oriental Rose, I suppose, and we shall both try, in all sincerity, to behave like the good friends we were a month ago, as if I had not foolishly, by pointing out the author of *The Bleston Murder*, twisted the knife in that strange wound that I had made, or rather reopened, re-infected, when I lent him the book last autumn.

Tomorrow, then, it will probably be late at night, when the slow darkness has completely fallen, too late to write, that I shall return to this room which, when I had first made it my home, had been newly redecorated with this cream-coloured wallpaper, flecked with tiny silver granules, which I scratched with my nails during moments of fearful boredom in midwinter at certain places that I could no doubt identify, tiny silver granules which I have soiled with my fingers or with my rain-soaked clothes, tiny silver granules, dust-encrusted in places but elsewhere more or less intact.

On Monday, November 19th, at this time, it was pitch-dark and the panes of my closed window, against which the rain was no doubt streaming, showed me only the reflected light of my lamp, and if I had been sitting writing where I am now I should have felt against my back, as I did on certain evenings even last month, the unpleasant heat of the gas fire, which is now out.

Already, there lay on my table a map of Bleston just like this one; I had bought it, as I did this one, from Ann Bailey; the plan of the streets is identical on paper, whereas in fact it has undergone certain slight changes; there is nothing here to indicate the buildings that have been begun or finished since last autumn, nor those that have collapsed into rubble or been consumed by fire.

Already, there lay on my table a copy of *The Bleston Murder*, the one that the Baileys have now got, not the copy which I am holding in my left hand at this moment, but with exactly the same words, so that if I open this one at the page I opened the other at that evening, the text before me is identical, and in spite of all that has happened since, the questions I asked myself then still recur to me and still find no answer.

So, within myself, something has endured through these months without either growing or decreasing, certain landmarks have escaped the alluvial work of time, and while I wander, seeking for a meaning to my life, through that waste land that I have become, groping over vast banks of deposit, I suddenly stumble at the edge of a cleft at the bottom of which the original soil is laid bare, and thus I can gauge the thickness of the silt which I must plumb and filter in order to recover my bedrock, my foundations.

The passage before me, in the copy of *The Bleston Murder* which lies open at my left hand, is the same that I re-read on Monday, November 19th, in my original copy when I came back here for the first time after my day's work at Matthews & Sons, the day after my visit to the New Cathedral; it is at the beginning of the second chapter, where the body of the cricketer Johnny Winn is found lying in a pool of blood on the white paving stones, in the wan light of a rainy day, or rather in the wan shadow, in the wan depths of that X-shaped shadow cast by the intersecting screens; that passage about the New Cathedral which I had been anxious to read over again because I had only a confused remembrance of it (surprisingly, since it describes the scene of the crime); it was already overshadowed in my memory by those passages that concern the other Cathedral; the book thus produced an optical illusion which was deliberately intended by the author, as clearly emerged from the remarks he made, long after, to Lucien and myself, an optical illusion which deceived me as it did Rose Bailey.

So much emphasis is laid on Cain's Window that the reader quite naturally associates the idea of murder with what takes place in front of it, and the two corpses, those of the brothers Winn, are so alike, one under the shadowy cross and the other under the splashes of light, that the scene of the fratricide seems merely to prefigure the scene of punishment, and the New Cathedral appears as a diminished reflection of the Old.

I had only a confused remembrance of this passage, now once more open before me, because it is, in a way, self-effacing, strives as it were to efface the New Cathedral by describing it only to enhance by contrast the glory of the Old.

J. C. Hamilton indeed does not spare his sarcasm: "This wretched farce, this make-believe, this empty mimicry of a misunderstood model, this monument of stupidity."

Strange blindness on the part of one so amazingly lucid and keen-witted! For even I, so new to Bleston, had recognised something very far from mere plagiarism in this bizarre edifice, I had been made forcibly aware of a mind of astonishing audacity at work, violently distorting traditional themes, ornaments and metals, achieving thus an imperfect, one might almost say a crippled work of art, but a profoundly imaginative one, instinct with secret seminal force, poignantly striving towards freer and happier creation; "a distorted shadow indeed", as J. C. Hamilton says, but what he failed to see was the rare value of this distortion.

On this point, then, my knowledge of the town surpassed that expressed in his book, which elsewhere is, of course, incomparably wider, with a depth and precision that I have never failed to appreciate; but here I was entering on territory where J. C. Hamilton, who had so well directed me hitherto, could no longer serve as a guide, and I would have to venture alone.

Thursday, June 26th

The clouds gathered again yesterday; as we left Matthews & Sons and drove off in the firm's black Morris to the News Theatre in Town Hall Square to see the documentary film about Petra (supported by the usual newsreels and sketches, more than usually vulgar this time), Petra, that weal left by a city on the cliff-side, with a few columns still glowing white-hot under the

pure Transjordanian sky, amidst the olive trees, if indeed they
are olives, and the scattered stones that the goats' hooves send
flying, among which you can still pick out a sharp-edged moulding, the fragment of a Classical curve or a palm leaf pattern, or
the worn point of an acanthus: Petra, that scar imprinted like
a convict's brandmark on the living surface of the earth; the
implacable clouds gathered again at about six o'clock, suddenly
taking possession of our low skies like a conquering horde of
tall towers, shifting, dishevelled, mossy, frothing, ghostly, their
faraway haughty heads crowned with inaccessible mother-of-
pearl, tossing their grey shrouds and lichens in the wind that
whipped up accomplice clouds of dust and sent the people scur-
rying as though in midwinter, sent the meagre unsmiling men
and women, with eyes like stagnant water never quite free from
the icy film of fear, back to the homes where a precarious peace
awaits them, peace painfully acquired at the cost of relentless
effort, great stubbornness and patience, long attrition, with so
much renounced and rejected, so much buried, besmirched and
betrayed, so many humiliations endured, so many needs unful-
filled, such vital secrets lost, so much forgotten.

And now the rain has begun again and is beating on my panes
with that dull indefatigable noise that wears down, pares down
my courage, the rain whose irony muddles my brain tonight.

Our attempts at conversation were still quite fruitless when
we sat, James and I, near a first-floor window of the Oriental
Rose and watched the clouds racing along like warlike rapacious
ghosts above the absurd crenellations of that gigantic cast iron
toy, the Town Hall, and were robbed of the twilight by them.

Every topic that either of us proposed soon seemed, unfortunately and as it were inevitably, to bring us back to that sore
subject, that forbidden zone, the novel by George Burton (*alias*
J. C. Hamilton); the full extent of the pain it must have given
him and still more his mother when I lent it him a long time
ago, last December I believe, was only revealed to me through
that conversation which we held at the fair in the 2nd district,

on the last evening in May, the eve of that dinner at the Baileys' which fortunately I described in these pages the very next day,

(Oh, how wise I had been that evening, that last Saturday in May, to be apprehensive and mistrustful, to take refuge behind a subterfuge when he told me he wanted to re-read the book; and yet I had only a vague recollection of the insulting terms used by J. C. Hamilton about the New Cathedral, to which I had never really paid attention until, the day before yesterday, I re-read with newly-whetted interest that passage which I had always thought of as one of the least interesting in the book),

that conversation at the fair, and in particular the incontestable alteration in James's attitude towards me ever since then, the more obvious now that, realising that I am aware of it, realising the injustice and the morbid senselessness of it, he tries to conceal it as far as possible, to cancel it.

Last night at the Oriental Rose, every topic seemed to bring us back to that sore subject, and each time I was forced to break off in order to avoid that fatal lodestone; each time a heavy silence, like frosted glass, lay between us.

I feel myself surrounded by a sort of still and silent terror like icy stagnant waters rising irresistibly, as if some net in which I am involved were tightening round me, something unidentifiable taking hideous shape, hanging heavy in the air like those impending murders that haunt the narrow streets of Bleston, of which James had spoken to me, and of whose persistent presence I had myself been so strongly and so frequently aware during my aimless anguished walks through the rain in late autumn and in winter.

Thus when I learnt from the posters of the *Bleston Post* this morning, and again later from those of the *Evening News*, that yesterday, while we were at the News Theatre watching those stones glow like sombre flames under the pure blue sky of the eastern desert, those embers of a Roman city whose remaining ashes have all been scattered by the winds of time, and while we were dining together in the Chinese restaurant in Town

Hall Square, both feeling so embarrassed, so distressed by this embarrassment that emphasised, almost painfully, James's natural shyness—when I learnt that at that very moment a huge shed was burning in the 11th district, on the bank of the Slee between South Bridge and the waste land where the fair was held last December, I could not avoid the impression that those headlines were a personal message to myself and I remembered the flames devouring Athens in the last tapestry in the Museum, and the red sky behind Cain's city in the Old Cathedral window, just as I had remembered them a fortnight earlier when I heard of the disaster at the Scenic Railway in Pleasance Gardens.

Fires have always been frequent in Bleston, but of late they seem to have multiplied: the one at the fair, the one at the Amusements Gallery in Town Hall Square between the Royal Cinema and the Police Station…

All this is merely a nightmare provoked by the narcotic exhalations of the Slee, by my weariness, Bleston's superstitions and the contagious influence of the wretched weather.

Friday, June 27th

The last clouds, like firebrands, like great boughs ablaze during the last stages of a forest fire, fanned and driven by a furious gale, the last clouds roll past above the chimneys and roofs of Dew Street still glistening from recent rain.

It is late, it is past nine o'clock already; I wandered through the narrow streets enjoying the soft light which in November was denied me not only in the evening but even in the morning, since the sun which set at four o'clock did not rise 'til eight and then so slowly, so remotely, with such secrecy.

Oh, if I had realised then, in late November, not only the inadequacy but also the unjust violence of J. C. Hamilton's description of the New Cathedral, above all if I had been aware of the close and vital link between Mrs. Jenkins and that building, if I had been forewarned, of course I should have prudently avoided mentioning *The Bleston Murder* to her son, praising the book to him, lending it to him—to them; but I still had no inkling of why she had stared down, with such fierce intentness, at the fly in its glass bubble on her ring, that Sunday, November 11th, when, without ever having seen the building, I had spoken contemptuously about it; I merely discerned that something was wrong, and began wondering, with amused curiosity, what could be the reason for their strange behaviour.

And so on Saturday, November 24th, I had invited James to lunch with me to try and loosen his tongue.

He is so difficult to handle, so pleasant and discreet but so reserved, always on his guard, almost on the alert, always ready to close up like a shellfish at the slightest disturbance in the water surrounding him; and this has grown so much more marked between us since the beginning of this month, since that old story which I had still not completely understood rose to the surface once again like a reef that re-emerges, sharper and more alluring and more dangerous than ever.

And so on Saturday, November 24th, I had taken James for the first time to the Chinese restaurant in New Cathedral Square, the Oriental Pearl, where I had deliberately chosen a table near the window in the hope that he would speak of his own accord about what he saw through the slight mist, those towers, those porches, that spire which was still comparatively white in places; but throughout the meal, as I might have expected had I known him as well then as I do now, the conversation lingered on other topics, on the films currently showing in the town, I believe (that may have been when he told me that he went to the News Theatre almost every week), or on the novels I was returning to him, so that I was forced to ask him (without disclosing my earlier visit a week before) if it would not bore him to accompany him round the great church.

As he stared attentively at those capitals from which the curious screens spring out like bridges spanning the nave half way up, I asked him in my halting English what they might represent?

"I can't tell you exactly," James replied with a smile that clearly implied that he felt guilty for not knowing the answer.

"I'm not learned enough in zoology to know the names of all those creatures."

He pointed to a cluster of ovals, stars, forms vase-shaped, horn-shaped or spiky.

"Those creatures?"

"Yes, this is the Radiolarians' Capital."

At first I failed to understand this strange word; he had to explain it to me at some length.

"And this one?"

"These are the Echinoderms, starfishes and sea-urchins."

Here my eyes elucidated the unfamiliar terms.

"Does each capital correspond to a particular class?"

"In pairs; a few characteristic and easily recognisable species have been chosen to represent their vast variety. In the nave, the invertebrates…"

"I should like to see the insects."

"At the corners of the transept."

"Is there a flea?"

"Here it is!"

"And a fly?"

"A very fine one, on the other side, in the middle."

"And what comes next?"

"Along this transept, fishes and frogs and the salamander-lizards, snakes, tortoises, and birds; and along the other mammals—with monkeys in the middle."

"And what's left for the choir?"

"The various races of Man are supposed to be represented there, but in my opinion it's the least successful part."

"And what about plants?"

"They are along the side-aisles."

"And minerals?"

"It wasn't easy in those days to find distinctive emblems to represent these. Are you interested in animals?"

"Why do you ask?"

"We have quite a good zoo in Bleston, we might go for a walk there this afternoon if you've no other plans; it's in one of the south-side parks, over the Slee, a sort of big permanent fairground called Pleasance Gardens; there are some very fine birds."

But just as we were about to take the bus the rain began to fall so hard that we postponed our visit to the next weekend, for James (whom I still called Jenkins) was not free on the Sunday; he drove me back here in the black Morris and I came up to my room, thinking of those four pillars around the shadowy cross in the centre of which lay the cricketer Johnny Winn, murdered by his brother, and watched over by tiny monkeys and enormous insects.

5

Monday, June 30th

The wind, warmed by three days of fine weather, stroked my brow, soothing me, exorcising my obsessions, warding off the evil influence of those great buildings that endlessly displayed their dark leprous façades, their excrescences and scabs and the glassy concavities where the sun's pale gold was debased to copper and decaying lead, mitigating the insistent menace of those tall factory chimneys that rose like posts in a prison fence, while I went on foot, after leaving Matthews & Sons, up Tower Street and then up Silver Street to the News Theatre to see the new documentary about Israel and the Dead Sea, those marshy deserts under which the sulphurous ashes of Sodom lie submerged, and that tall rock of salt they call Lot's Wife.

I saw the film alone, just as I went alone yesterday, Sunday—being invited nowhere, and deprived even of Lucien's company since, as on every fourth weekend, he was on duty at his hotel—wandering past the suburban gardens of North Bleston, where prosperous householders took their solitary pleasure trimming their privet hedges; wandering through Oak Park and Birch Park, which were unwontedly thronged and noisy and whose lawns were strewn with sleeping figures half-hidden under Sunday newspapers; seeking consolation here from the quivering green of the fine trees; wandering finally along the banks of the Slee, which glittered like a beetle's shard; and when at last I thought of looking up Horace Buck it was too late—his door was shut.

And then I hung about Town Hall Square in futile exhaustion, staring with inattentive eyes at the stills exhibited in cinema lobbies, unable to make up my mind to go in, and ended the evening stupidly drinking at the Unicorn.

The wind soothed me this evening while I walked up to the News Theatre and the Dead Sea, alone, as I had been yesterday and the day before (spent just as fruitlessly in unrestful leisure), and then while I walked slowly home, alone, from the Oriental Rose where I had dined alone, walked slowly along Silver Street and Tower Street, unmindful that time was passing, that this is the last day of June and that I should have hurried back to explore and set down my lingering memories of those late November days, so as not to increase the seven-months' gap which I have maintained since I began this story, that over-wide gap which I had hoped to reduce, which I must strive to reduce as I go on, and which day by day seems somehow to grow more solid and opaque.

And still, seductively, the wind strokes my eyelids as though to close them, while a menacing bull-headed cloud, horned with moonlight, charges the distant sky.

In that last week of November the most important incident was certainly my meeting Ann Bailey again at the Sword restaurant, where I had gone for lunch (I think it was Monday the 26th); she was sitting alone at a table for two, and I went up and asked in my halting English if I might join her, and she looked up and recognised me and smiled at me.

In my raincoat pocket I had the map of Bleston which I had bought from her the month before, when I was with James Jenkins; it was already dog-eared, stained, tattered at the folds, and since then I have destroyed and replaced it.

We lunched there together, as we were to do next day and almost every weekday for the next three months or more; we started talking, about ourselves and our countries and our jobs, about the reason for her presence there that day, namely the illness of her colleague at the stationer's shop, which meant that she hadn't time to go home for lunch; and so, one thing leading to another, she told me about her sister Rose, who was studying French at the University.

It must have been during the last week in November that one evening, as I came out of one of the cinemas in Town Hall Square, I can't remember if it was the Artistic or the Continental, after seeing a film of which I remember nothing except a sequence about a bullfight, Horace Buck, who was with me (had we met by chance at the cinema, or planned to go there together? I've forgotten) took me for the first time through the narrow doorway with its neon-lit inscription "Amusements", led me for the first time into that narrow room huddled between the Royal Cinema and the Police Station, opposite the Town Hall, which with its electric billiard tables and its Aunt Sallies is like a miniature replica, in the centre of the town, of that great permanent amusement park in Pleasance Gardens, in the 12th district.

And then for the first time I witnessed a scene which was often to be repeated on the same premises (provisionally closed today, owing to an outbreak of fire for which Horace himself may be in part responsible), I watched the big negro take possession with his hands and eyes and his whole bent body of that queer machine gun through which one fires at tiny black aircraft hovering over a city in flames, while amid a clangour of electric bells one's score appears in luminous figures on a painted glass overhead.

But all this is so far away, so blurred; so many problems and possibilities come between; so many things have happened since, which weigh so heavily on my present existence, so many things that I am liable to distort and forget if I postpone writing them down.

Tonight, though, I am tired and it is late…

III

The "Accident"

I

That is why I now feel compelled to interrupt the pattern I had been following for the past month in my narrative, mingling regularly, week by week, notes on current happenings with recollections of last November, a pattern which I had followed ever since that Monday night when I introduced into the middle of pages describing, with scrupulous fidelity, those far-off autumn days, an account of the previous evening, which I had spent at the Baileys' and in the course of which Ann had produced that copy of *The Bleston Murder* which I had lent her so long ago, after first lending it to James—that copy which I had presumed lost because I had forgotten that she had not returned it, and which I had replaced by the copy now lying on the left-hand corner of my table, after hunting endlessly for this out-of-print book in the second-hand shops of Chapel Street, behind the Old Cathedral.

My intractable memory would have yielded only a blurred and patchy picture of that evening at the Baileys' (as I well know from all the inexactitudes and lacunae that I discover when I try to remember it without the help of my notes, and then turn to these for confirmation), if I had not set it down the very next day, Monday, which I should probably not have done if there hadn't been that other reference to J. C. Hamilton's novel the previous evening, Saturday, May 31st, and if I hadn't already betrayed the author's real name, because I should not then have found the book's reappearance so strange and ominous, and I should not have used those particular words.

That is why I now feel compelled to interrupt the pattern I had followed in order to concentrate on salvaging and fixing the chief points I can still remember in that conversation with James at the fair in the 2nd district, on the same subject— *The Bleston Murder* and its author; and the main incidents of that last evening in May, the day before the Baileys' party: our pursuit of the Burtons, our discovery, on the counter of the shooting-gallery, of the photograph which they had forgotten to collect; all these fragmentary recollections which have become increasingly insistent and disturbing, reminding me: "We are important and precious, you can understand nothing without us, and we are slipping from you, soon we shall have faded into that distant past where you find it so hard to recover and distinguish and pinpoint essential details."

It was late, that Saturday, the last evening in May, the sun had set almost half an hour ago, when we reached the waste land in the 2nd district where the fair, with all its bustle and glitter, was still in full swing (it stays open until 11.30, an hour later than all the regular pleasure-grounds), James and I in the firm's black Morris—he has charge of it, keeps it in the garage belonging to his big house, but being a very conscientious fellow only uses it (apart from official journeys) to avoid being dependent on the last bus home after his visits to the fair; these are far more frequent than I should have expected on first acquaintance, judging from his rather prim appearance.

He dared not talk about them to me, uncertain as to what I should think (I'd like to know what else he conceals from me, he's like some magic book of which certain pages open only when a great variety of conditions are fulfilled) so that the first time we went there together I almost fancied I was introducing him to the fair, whereas he was really familiar with its intimate life and personally acquainted with most of the inhabitants of the miniature mobile town.

It was late, that Saturday (we'd had dinner at the Oriental Pearl, the Chinese restaurant in New Cathedral Square), it was half-past eight or later (in the clear dying twilight the velvety moon was rising above the tents) when a young fellow in a blue cap and sweater rushed up and greeted James joyfully with open arms.

"Hullo, there you are, Mr. Jenkins! Come and have a drink with us, you must meet my wife."

"How kind of you, Dylan. This is one of my colleagues from the office, a Frenchman, Mr. Jack Rivel" (he has never succeeded in pronouncing my name correctly, nor have Ann Bailey nor the Burtons; only Rose knows how to say it, only Rose).

"A Frenchie, eh?" He gave a whistle of amused delight. "Oh, Jane will be pleased to meet a Frenchie! You'll have a glass of beer with us, Monsieur? We haven't any wine, you know!"

I remember the interior of the caravan, neat and narrow, with a small table covered with a red-and-pink-checked table-cloth, and an oil lamp swinging from the curved ceiling of varnished wood; I remember the shy young woman who wiped our glasses and served our drinks without uttering a word, while her husband and James talked about the fair's next move into the 5th district, to the waste land on the bank of the Slee near the big railway bridge; the move was to take place a little later than usual this month so as not to interfere with the weekend, when the biggest profits are made.

After drinking a pint of Bass apiece we went along with Dylan Brooks to the Giant Wheel, where he had to help his father, old Tom Brooks; the latter was delighted to see James, and invited us both to take a free ride in one of the yellow-painted cars.

Then slowly, with much jolting and creaking, we rose up among the rods and pale lights as high as a four-storey house, far above the tents and hut-roofs beyond which we could dimly discern (since night had not yet completely swamped the city) the huge mass of the three stations gripping Alexandra Place as though with pincers, far above the bustling chattering crowd as it surged along the sinuous makeshift street, and I suddenly caught sight in the middle of that crowd of George and Harriet Burton, clinging close to one another like young lovers; then we came down slowly, so slowly, and when at last we reached ground level I leapt out, shouting to James to wait for me, and fought my way through the crowd in pursuit of them, then caught a fresh glimpse of them between two heads, at a stand, George holding a gun, taking aim, silhouetted darkly for a moment in a magnesium flash; but when I came panting up to the photographic shooting booth where he had just scored a bull and taken a picture, they had already disappeared.

"How long does it take to develop and print a negative?" I asked the tall, lean middle-aged woman, dressed in black and heavily painted, who stood behind a counter stacked with old cartridge cases. "Half an hour," she replied curtly, proffering a loaded gun which I refused; I went back to James, who had left old Tom Brooks alone, watching his big wheel start on another round.

"I thought I saw two friends."

"And was it not them?"

"I don't know; I couldn't catch up with them; they'll probably come back in half an hour's time to collect their photograph at the shooting-gallery."

But fatigue, as usual, must suddenly have swooped down on Harriet, like a falcon on a leveret, and they left the fair before I could see them again, without bothering to pick up their photograph, which the woman had just laid out in front of her stall when we went past it again (other people were now taking aim, firing, sometimes scoring flashes) but which she refused to sell me, declaring that it was already paid for—refused to let me have a copy, pretexting some regulation or other.

And then I remarked in French, as I looked at George Burton peering down the barrel of his gun with Harriet beside him, caught by the magnesium flash in a tense smile: "I'd have liked to keep this picture of you *en flagrant délit*, J. C. Hamilton!"

I did not think James had paid the least attention to these words uttered to myself in my own language, but the Englishness of the name J. C. Hamilton apparently stood out in the context of foreign sounds, and a little later, as we sat in front of our emptied glasses in one of the little canvas pubs, he asked me: "What's your friend's name?"

"The one at the shooting-gallery? Do you know him?"

He blushed, then ordered two more beers.

"You shouldn't have asked, James. His name is George Burton."

He blushed once more, put down his drink slowly and wiped his lips with his handkerchief.

"The photograph itself didn't remind me of anything; it was just what you said, I thought you'd mentioned his name, and yet it wasn't the one you have just told me."

"I may have called him by another, J. C. Hamilton for instance."

"Yes, that was it, Hamilton, what does that suggest to me? It's the name of a town not far off, the station from which you get to it, and the name of a street too, hut that's not what I'm thinking of; it must be a person. J. C. Hamilton did you say? Yes, those are the initials too; I must have heard the name spoken or read it somewhere…"

"Of course you have, James, on the cover of *The Bleston Murder*, you know, that detective story I lent you a long time ago, last autumn, and which you didn't care for very much."

Wednesday, July 2nd

And now I am actually holding in my hands the negative of that photograph of George Burton which I had failed to buy that last Saturday in May, the dark glossy negative which stridently proclaims itself an embodiment of strange coincidences, since it was only yesterday that, before completing, instead of completing the account of my conversation with James on the day that photograph was taken, I was led to discover it, led blindly from one fairground to the other across the Slee, as though gripped by an unseen hand; and now I cannot look at this negative without a sort of dizzy terror, as being the proof that I have indeed lost myself, that I am the helpless plaything of a secret power.

"*The Bleston Murder*," James had replied, "of course, how could I have forgotten? So that's what the author of *The Bleston Murder* looks like! So that's the face he dared not show on the cover of his book. Would you mind very much if we went back to the shooting-gallery, Jacques?"

"I did not think the book had impressed you so much, James."

"It's a strange book, indeed, a strange book, the only one of its kind where the action takes place in Bleston, for writers seem to avoid our city as if they were afraid of it... I don't remember it very well, I couldn't tell you much about it; perhaps I read it too fast; I shall have to get a copy."

"You won't find that easy, James, the book is out-of-print. I lost the copy I had lent you, and I had to hunt through the second-hand shops to unearth the one I have now."

Most of the booths were putting up their shutters; the woman at the shooting-gallery, who was obviously not one of James's fairground friends, recognised me and angrily snatched off her counter the Burtons' picture, which James was studying.

"Sorry, gentlemen, it's time. You don't want a gun, do you! Well then..."

A few yards farther on he halted, turned back and stared at the booth.

"So that's what he looks like... There's something I seem to remember, something I'd like to check... But after all there's no point, I'm quite sure now... Oh well, it doesn't matter; don't talk to me about that book again; let's get going."

It was all so strange and embarrassing, James was behaving so abnormally that I hurriedly tried to divert the conversation while he took me home in the black Morris; and meanwhile, as I discovered later, a minor fire had broken out in that village of canvas and wood and painted metal which, seemingly nomadic, revolves in its eight-months' orbit, like a planet, round the city centre.

I tried to divert the conversation and asked him the question which for so long had been on the tip of my tongue: "Do tell me James, how do you happen to know so many people at the fair?"

The tension was promptly eased, and he said with a smile: "You wouldn't have expected me to move in those circles, would you, from knowing me at Matthews & Sons? My father had known these people ever since he was a child; my grandfather used to take him amongst them; that was how, when he was quite young, he came to know Tom Brooks from the Giant Wheel, who was about his own age, and I myself was quite young when I came to know his son Dylan. We used to visit them often; when father died I kept on doing so; my mother wouldn't come, but without actually encouraging me she always allowed me to go and gave me my bus fare, for she was glad to have news of these men and women in whom her husband had taken such an interest."

As we drew up in front of my door the clouds were hanging heavy over Dew Street, and a few drops had begun to fall.

Over yonder, in the waste land of the 2nd district, which we had just left, close to that great padlocked box in which lay not only that picture of the Burtons at which James had stared with such passionate curiosity but also the original negative, that scrap of film which has so mysteriously fallen into my hands, towards which I must have been guided during yesterday's ramble—over yonder in that waste land, as we only discovered later on, fire had broken out, damaging a few pieces of painted wood and canvas, but the subsequent downpour had soon extinguished it.

For then, although the lengthening twilights sent their bright surf a little farther each evening into the grim, grimy strand, bad weather reigned for most of the time; I dared not go out without my coat, which was imbued with the city's filth.

And now it is unmistakably summertime, despite all the rain which has been falling for the past four hours.

Yesterday the summer sky was so clear after the storm, so seductive in its obviously transient beauty, that I felt impelled to diverge from my usual route at six o'clock and to call on Horace Buck, who had first, last November, introduced me to the fair—it was then on its present site in the 9th district over the river, Daisy Fields—and then, drawing blank, I made my way to Town Hall Square, where after a solitary meal at the Oriental Rose I took a 29 bus (Town Hall – St. Jude's Gardens; I must go and visit the old streets round St. Jude's some time) and got off after Old Bridge, meaning to try and follow the river (but its banks are thick with houses… From time to time I could glimpse along a street-vista the towers of the Old Cathedral or the huge spire of the other, soaring above the noisome jet-black waters) northward, towards Daisy Fields, where I supposed the fair would already have settled down in its new home, since the move began on Monday.

I walked parallel to the river through unfamiliar streets; I had left my map behind, not having anticipated this urge to explore, and so I was obliged to ask my way of passers-by, who invariably, when I mentioned the fair without specifying Daisy Fields, replied: "It's a long way off", even when I was nearly there; they were all thinking of its last-month's site in the 5th district, which in fact had not been completely vacated yesterday.

I walked towards that waste land in the 9th district, that rent in the fabric of the city, still half-deserted despite a number of caravans and a few booths that had opened by way of foretaste, and the sprinkling of customers who had dropped in by chance, who were prowling round spying out novelties and alterations so as to be able to show off their knowledge next weekend.

Only half the fair was here, and in order to locate the laggard half I went on northward in the thickening twilight as far as the waste land in the 5th district; the last lorries were being loaded, and amongst them I caught sight of a man burning something in his hand; I hurried up, and as he leapt into his truck and drove off noisily, ejecting an unpleasant sepia cloud like a cuttlefish's ink, I identified the object as a photographic film.

There were others on the ground, lying in the short sickly grass, amidst the scraps of paper and old tins that will by now have been swept away; there were about a dozen others, and I picked them up and stared at them for a long time under a newly-lit street-lamp on the other side of the river, near the big railway bridge over which long trains sped shrieking towards Scotland, I turned the glistening things over until I recognised on one of them—the one I am now holding in my left hand— the faces of the two Burtons, George shutting one eye behind the barrel of his gun, which appears as a black or transparent spot according to the angle at which I hold it, and the other eye wide open, almost round, George with his long nose, his high forehead, his thinning hair and his tweed jacket, and Harriet looking worried, wearing her coat (she feels the cold like me); they are there on this small semi-transparent rectangle; I cannot look at it without a sort of terror, I am reluctant to throw it away, and I know I ought to burn it… Is it Bleston's influence that impels me to seek revenge through fire?

Enough of that; it's too late this evening; the rain is still fall- ing behind the dark panes; I've lost track of my thoughts, how could I control my pen?

I shall put back the negative between the pages of the novel.

Friday, July 4th

So many happenings to describe and so many intrusive recent memories have brought me almost to the end of this first week in July, and now I have only this evening left in which to start my record of December, if the seven-months' gap which I have not yet succeeded in narrowing is not to be widened still further; I must start it this evening, in the clear late light as the clouds part in ragged streamers, like an octopus's tentacles disclosing depths of sky on which the red silt will gradually thicken, while below in Dew Street cats stretch themselves on every doorstep, unsmiling faces stare down from every window, and round the puddles left by last night's and this morning's rain, small girls in black or faded frocks play with old kitchen implements, while their brothers swop stamps or drift home from the waste land hugging a football under their arms.

Day was short-lived, that Sunday, December 2nd, for at that season it was still pitch-dark when I left this house to go to the office, pitch-dark with street-lamps gleaming in the fog in empty Dew Street and a light here and there behind some steamy window; day was short-lived and the sun was glowing red through the icy fog when James, who had invited me home, or as he always says to his mother's home, for lunch, introduced me to the big stationary fair in the 12th district.

We had taken a 32 bus in Continent Street, crossing the Slee over South Bridge, as far as the monumental entrance-gates whose two square towers, adorned with grimy stucco, are crowned, like that edifice (temple or mosque?) dominating Cain's city in the Window, with two enormous yellow half-moons fixed to lightning conductors, and are joined by two iron rods bearing an inscription in red-painted letters beaded with electric bulbs then gleaming softly pink: "Pleasance Gardens".

How strange the name sounds—that old French word *plaisance*—as the bus conductors yell it out, with a hateful lewd sneer, sometimes lingering over the last syllable, "pleasaaaance", as if they could not bear to leave it but longed, secretly, to leap off and explore.

Since then I have seen that inscription glittering through the rain in the darkness, above the big folding door which is armoured as if to protect a safe, and only opens on great occasions and for important processions, whereas we, the daily crowd, have to make our way in by one of the six wicket gates on the right (those on the left are for the way out) with their turnstiles and ticket-collectors; only two of these were open just then, at three o'clock that Sunday afternoon, for, as James explained to me, the rush hour had not yet begun.

It was not until I looked up and read, on the big notice board in the middle of the first little square where all the buildings are cafés, that tickets must be handed in on leaving, and then hastily hunted for mine under James's quizzical and sympathetic glance, that I examined the slip of grey cardboard covered with printed lettering:

On one side in tall capitals: "PLEASANCE GARDENS", and then in smaller letters: "Valid for one visitor, Sunday, December 2nd".

And on the other side: "REMEMBER that this garden is intended for recreation, not for disorderly behaviour; please keep your dignity in all circumstances".

This strange injunction might have made me laugh, as it made Lucien laugh the first time he noticed it, if I'd had a French companion with me and if the sun, congealed in fog, had not shed such a gloomy flush on everything; but now, far from making me laugh, it had a chill and sinister ring.

We stopped for a moment in the second square, which was almost deserted, in front of the earthenware-topped table which displayed, on a larger scale and in greater detail, with fresh colours and crude lettering, that green quarter-circle with its apex pointing towards the town centre which I had so often noticed in the lower right-hand corner of the map of Bleston.

There was scarcely anybody in the big, cheap restaurants or in the billiard rooms; avenues, all round, bore black and white arrows directing one to the bear-pit, the stadium, the switch-back, the aviaries, the exit and the monkey-house…

James led the way, looking happy if a trifle lost; we walked in silence past roundabouts with metal aeroplanes and wooden horses, most of them standing still, and past the station for the miniature railway where three children sat shivering in an open truck waiting to start; and past the lake, which was empty because its concrete bottom was being cleaned.

Posters everywhere echoed: "Come back for the New Year, come and see the fireworks"; dusk fell rapidly while along the paths the hum of gathering crowds grew louder, and we watched the melancholy zebras in their heated stables—so rapidly that it was almost dark when we left the reptile-house and went to see the Scenic Railway on which the lighted cars rattled noisily upward and shook the scaffolding, of which today, since the fire, nothing is left but great calcined posts.

Fire is the scourge of Bleston; there was another yesterday, as I have just read on the *Evening News* poster, in the 10th district close to James's home.

On Sunday, December 2nd, when I got back to this room which had been mine for the past week, I sat down at this table and slowly looked through *The Bleston Murder*, presumably in search of some reference to Pleasance Gardens; I had a pencil in my hand and mechanically, opposite a paragraph where I had caught sight of the words "New Cathedral" I drew a tiny picture of a tortoise, promptly wondering why, amongst all the animals I had seen that day, all of which had some representative carved on one of the capitals in that building, I had chosen that particular one.

2

Monday, July 7th

At about eight o'clock this evening I was having dinner by the window of the Oriental Rose, watching the still-bright July sun sink slowly behind the battlements of the Town Hall, after visiting the News Theatre as I always do on Mondays now and seeing the programme of cartoons that is shown there every fourth week; and I said to myself once again:

"No! It was certainly not by chance, it was not instinctively nor inadvertently that I uttered the name of J. C. Hamilton that evening, the day before that Sunday, June 1st, when it cropped up again so unexpectedly and so disturbingly at the Baileys'" (but ah, how sweet and understanding Rose is!) "that I uttered it, quite clearly, in James's presence, that last Saturday in May at the fair in the 2nd district, while I was standing by the shooting-gallery, examining the photograph of Harriet and George Burton which he had just taken and which they had forgotten to collect."

I had not been able to secure that photograph, but now its negative, crumpled and creased, soiled, unusable and unrecognisable, lies between the pages of *The Bleston Murder*.

For yesterday afternoon, as I had decided, in view of the fine weather, to walk to the far end of the 9th district as far as St. Jude's church, which I had never seen, suddenly as I was crossing Old Bridge, tormented by all these baffling problems, these fancies and fears, a crazy notion occurred to me that if I was unwilling to rid myself of this image by burning it I could at least cast it into that black water and thus free myself of its baleful power; and I turned back, obeying this absurd impulse. So instead of crossing over, I began hesitantly and deviously to follow the course of that horrible river glinting in the sunlight, and it was not until I was back in this room and recognised this pile of papers, my raft, that I recovered my wits; and even then not completely, for I opened the book and took out that scrap of film and screwed it up in my fist with instinctive fury.

No, it was certainly not by chance, it was rather through the cunning agency of some mysterious and stubborn will from which I was vainly trying to escape that I had introduced among those French words the name of J. C. Hamilton.

From the summit of the Giant Wheel where I was sitting beside James, as soon as I caught sight of George Burton walking with his wife amongst the crowd, I felt that I should not be able to avoid a meeting, I almost said, a collision, between these two men; how dangerous this might prove I had foreseen for months, ever since I suspected the real identity of the author of *The Bleston Murder*, and particularly since I had been sure of it, since Lucien and I had extracted a confession from him (yes, it was on Sunday, May 18th), when he had laughingly, but nonetheless categorically, enjoined us to keep his secret.

They had so many things in common, in particular the seriousness of their attitude to detective fiction, which made it impossible for me to think of one without thinking of the other, especially since the last talk which Lucien and I had had with George a week before, on Sunday, May 25th, a week after that confession of his which formed an indispensable premise to it, since what he told us that day about his art, although valid, like his comments on other occasions, for all good examples of the type of novel in which he specialises, is pre-eminently applicable to the one which he has signed with that particular pseudonym, J. C. Hamilton, *The Bleston Murder*, which he thus explained for us:

"Any detective story is constructed on two murders" (I cannot remember the exact words nor the order of his sentences in our dialogue, but the fragments that survive in my mind group themselves into a coherent speech) "—any detective story is constructed on two murders of which the first, committed by the criminal, is only the occasion of the second, in which he is the victim of the pure, unpunishable murderer, the detective, who kills him not by one of those despicable means he was himself reduced to using, poison, the knife, a silent shot or the twist of a silk stocking, but by the explosion of truth.

"Oh yes, he is the true executioner" (he spoke with quiet irony, with economy of gesture, throwing back his head with a sudden smile) "and the hangman, the Public Prosecutor, the whole legal apparatus and all the inspectors of Scotland Yard or the Quai des Orfèvres are merely his instruments, and moreover, as you'll have noticed, always to some extent bear him a grudge because he meddles in their business and makes use of them for an end so different from theirs (for they are the guardians of the old order, jeopardised, whereas his purpose is to disturb and probe, to expose and alter things) and eventually, sometimes, double-crosses them, sets himself up as sole judge and robs them of their prey.

"The aim of his whole existence is that tremendous moment in which the power of his explanations, of his disclosure, of the words by which he tears off veils and masks, uttered generally in a tone of grave melancholy as if to soften the terrible, dazzling light they shed, so welcome to those whom it sets free but so cruel, so appalling, so blinding too, the power of his speech actually destroys the criminal, achieves that death that confirms and crowns his work—that moment when reality is transformed and purified by the sole power of his keen and accurate vision.

"A major part of the relations existing between the participants in the drama were maintained only through the errors, ignorances and lies which he abolishes; the actors group themselves in a new pattern from which one member of the former grouping is automatically excluded.

"He cleanses this small fraction of the world from its offence, which was not so much the mere fact that one man has killed another (for there might be such a thing as a pure murder, a kind of rejuvenation sacrifice) but rather the defilement that murder brings with it, the bloodstained shadows that it casts about it, and at the same time that deep-seated, age-old discord which becomes incarnate in the criminal from the moment when, by his act, he revealed its presence, and aroused those vast buried forces which now disturb the hitherto accepted order of things and betray its fragility.

"Thus the first murder" (that of the cricketer Johnny Winn, shot down by his brother in the New Cathedral under the crossed rood screens) "is not merely the immediate cause but also the prefiguration of the second" (that of the murderer Bernard Winn, shot down by Barnaby Morton in the Old Cathedral amidst the crimson stains cast by Cain's Window) "which concludes what it had begun and left in suspense.

"The detective is a true son of the murderer Oedipus, not only because he solves a riddle, but also because he kills the man to whom he owes his title, without whom he would not exist in that capacity (without crimes, without mysterious crimes, what would he be?) because this murder was foretold for him from the day of his birth or, if you prefer, because it is inherent in his nature, through it alone he fulfils himself and attains the highest power."

George must surely be back from London now. I must ring him up and try to see him next weekend.

Tuesday, July 8th

I kept thinking of James during that conversation when, for the first time, George Burton spoke to us not only about the literary interest of his work and the innovations it has contributed to the technique of the novel, but about its essence, about the significance he attaches to its fundamental theme—murder, twofold murder—and thus, incidentally, told us a good deal about himself.

I have even wondered, ever since that evening at the Baileys' on Sunday, June 1st, when for the second time I betrayed that secret which he had begged us to keep, when Ann and Rose told me of the peculiarly close resemblance between the two brothers' house in the book which he signed J. C. Hamilton and the house of their cousin's friend, that friend whose name I have forgotten, who lost his own brother apparently in an accident a few years ago, I have wondered whether he did not intend, for once, to live that detective's role which he merely described under his other pseudonyms.

If during the whole of this conversation I kept thinking of James, it was not merely because of the light it shed on the books he liked but chiefly because the day before, Saturday, May 24th, as I passed through Old Cathedral Square in the late afternoon on my way back from some fruitless errand, I caught sight of him (most unexpectedly, since he had assured me that he had never or at least not for many years, set foot in that venerable building) absorbedly staring at the outside of the Window, one of those two great hieroglyphs that set the mark of the murderer on Bleston's brow, on the brow of that city haunted by murder (as he had so powerfully conveyed to me the first time I spoke to him about J. C. Hamilton's book), so absorbedly staring, with so much hatred in his eyes, that he remained unaware of my presence, and does not know, to this day, that I saw him there.

Their paths crossed, and early this afternoon, at Matthews & Sons (it had been raining almost all day, almost as hard as it rained every day in December; how swiftly this first harbinger of autumn has come upon us!) I saw James come in from lunch, covered with mud, I saw him rummage in the pockets of his raincoat and then rush downstairs again to bring up, a minute later, a soiled copy of *The Bleston Murder* which I identified, when he showed it me with great embarrassment, as the one

I had bought last October at Baron's and inscribed with my name, the one which had been my first guide round the city, which had drawn my attention to the Window and showed me the way to Pleasance Gardens, the copy on which, when I got back from Pleasance Gardens, I had drawn a tiny picture of a tortoise, the copy I had lent to him, James, the next day and then to Ann Bailey, which I had thought lost, which I had had to replace by that second-hand copy which is still lying on the left-hand corner of my table, spotted with ink and inscribed with the name of some stranger, a Scot no doubt, Mac something or other (I can't make it out), the one I had most unexpectedly rediscovered at the Baileys' on the occasion of that memorable and unfortunate supper-party, Sunday, June 1st, and which I had left there, thinking they would keep it as a reminder of myself.

James then felt compelled, by way of apology for himself and for them, to describe in detail the visit he had paid them on Saturday (he sees them more and more frequently, whereas I deliberately neglect them now, I shun Rose with her teasing fragrance and her pretty way of speaking French), that visit during which they had given him the book and related the whole of our conversation about it on June 1st, while he, not to be outdone, informed them how the evening before that, the last Saturday in May, I had chased the author at the fair in the 2nd district, that visit he had paid them last Saturday, the first Saturday in July, while I was sitting like a fool on one of the tiered rows in the stadium near Oak Park, trying to convince Lucien, who had often gone there without me but had begged me to accompany him, that I was as interested in the match as he was.

Finally James remarked (secretive fellow! he's the more baffling because of his apparent extreme, reserved simplicity) that he had just finished re-reading the book and had found in it what he was looking for, that it corresponded to what he remembered and expected.

Oh, I'm only too sure of it! I watched him this afternoon, surreptitiously turning the pages as he sat at his table, with the same look of intense hatred, so unexpected from him, that he had shown towards the Murderer's Window.

Wednesday, July 9th

When I lent him *The Bleston Murder* in December (it was on a Monday morning, I remember, and he was already sitting at his desk in the big room at Matthews & Sons when I got there) the sun had vanished and the rainy season had set in, which was to last until the winter fogs: a far colder, grimmer, grimier, more vicious rain, more depressing and more penetrating than the rain that fell yesterday and went on with brief bright intervals until seven o'clock this evening, when the sky cleared at last while I was dining at the Sword.

The big stores, Grey's, Philibert's, Modern Stores, were getting ready for Christmas, and all the shop windows facing Town Hall Square, Silver Street and Mountains Street were full of real or cardboard fir trees, with their branches sprinkled with cotton wool or sodium borate spangled with electric candles, hung with stars and shiny balls, amidst tufts of holly and bunches of mistletoe, snow-covered cottages with lighted windows, bells, choirboys in embroidered surplices and Elizabethan ruffs gazing heavenward, their hands meekly crossed on their breasts or holding out sheets of music, angels with long wings, and glittering sledges wreathed with bells, loaded with parcels out of which tumbled dolls, toy horses, trailing lingerie, drawn by reindeer or husky dogs and driven by those horrible jolly little men with beards and red faces and twinkling eyes, in boots and furred scarlet coats, bearing bulging sacks.

The swelling hubbub within had for days been punctuated by the rhythmical hammering of the decorators; a crowd of women, some wretchedly poor, queued in their wet raincoats at the Christmas card counter trying to decide on the back of which insipid picture, opposite which smugly bright greeting they would inscribe their names to send to all their friends and neighbours and relations.

Ah, how I hated Bleston in December, and yet this was only the beginning of that long, gloomy, oppressive Cimmerian winter; I still despised the New Cathedral, or rather I forced myself to despise it like the author of *The Bleston Murder*, my guide hitherto, although I had already discerned his blindness on that point.

But try as I would, when I went back there that Saturday, December 8th, intending, I must confess, to strip its tinsel glory from it, to revenge myself for the highly suspect feeling of awe it had aroused in me, to rid myself of that feeling so that I could vent my sarcasms freely and wholeheartedly (and yet I remembered Mrs. Jenkins' silent glance, James's strange reserve) the laughter died away in my throat, ashamed and powerless, in face of that stubborn gleam which I tried to convince myself was a mirage, a will-o'-the-wisp, that barely-whispered message which had penetrated my loneliness and still echoed there gently and insistently amid the growing weight of darkness.

When I had walked a little way into that sombre cavern, that huge whale's skeleton where the dreary rain streamed over the greenish windows, where the shadow cast by the rood screens eclipsed the capitals, where the organist kept repeating the same four bars with the same mistake, terror crept over me as if in a great forest at nightfall in winter.

I went to look once more at the tortoise, which was as huge compared to the living tortoise I had seen the previous Sunday in Pleasance Gardens as was the latter compared to the one I had drawn on my copy of *The Bleston Murder*, and yet small compared to that tortoise which I had determined to go and look at next day, that monstrous, carnivorous tortoise in the third tapestry of the Museum.

Then I wandered idly through the ambulatory, my hands thrust in the pockets of my soaking raincoat, staring down at the paving stones and amusing myself by stepping carefully on my own wet footprints 'til I had formed a pattern which I finally identified as the shape of a fly (I was obsessed by the huge image that James himself had shown me on the Insects' Capital at which I had just been looking, and which had naturally reminded me of the real fly imprisoned in his mother's ring) just as my meanderings brought me to the Lady Chapel, in front of that particularly insipid statue with its grimy plaster, a recent addition no doubt, standing in its stone niche adorned with a sculptured frieze which from a distance seemed to be composed of flowers or ovoids but which, drawing nearer, I recognised as a frieze of flies.

Then, from the stand beside the vestry door, I took from among the pious pamphlets the *Illustrated Account of the New Cathedral, Bleston*, which now lies on the left-hand corner of my table with the guide to Bleston in the series "Our Land and its Treasures" (which I did not then possess), my new copy of J. C. Hamilton's novel, the plan of bus routes I had bought from Ann Bailey in October and the map of the town of which I had bought a second copy shortly before I began to write.

I put the price, two shillings, into the box; I opened the booklet and flicked the pages, but it was already too dark to read a word.

The organist floundered on; the little lamp over his keyboard was the only gleam in the empty nave.

Thursday, July 10th

I forgot to telephone the Burtons this evening; I must remember to do so tomorrow.

When I got back here that Saturday, December 8th, while the rainy darkness thickened outside my window, on which the drops, like thousands of transient, tremulous mirrors, clung for an instant before running down, I examined the booklet I had just bought about the New Cathedral; I found there no comment on the flies, not even a mention of those surrounding the statue of the Virgin. One illustration however fascinated me, a detail from one of the porches I had not yet looked at, on which are carved allegorical representations of the Arts and Sciences: the figure of Botany, in a dress embroidered with ferns, holding in her right hand a huge germinating seed with all its cotyledons wide open, and in her left a handful of fruit; a wreath of flowers and ears of corn frames her face, which I felt that I had seen before, or rather which seemed to me the portrait of a living woman whom I had met recently in this very town, which of course was impossible since the statue had been carved in the latter part of the nineteenth century, so that the model, if indeed she had ever existed and was not merely a dream-figure composed from a score of remembered faces by the sculptor (whose name, E. C. Douglas, is given at the bottom of the right-hand page), the model must have been born over a hundred years ago and must have grown old and died long since.

Time had ravaged the stone, but how much more painfully it would have ravaged the young living flesh that the stone suggested; I pictured the features gradually hardening, the wrinkles gradually appearing and changing the expression, giving it a more sombre tone; and then suddenly, as I imagined the seasons' passage over those deepset eyes with their friendly but secretive look, that broad forehead with the softly modelled temples, that straight slender nose with clearcut nostrils, those delicate somewhat asymmetrical lips, even those long fingers capable of gripping like pincers, I recognised them with no possibility of doubt as the face and hands of Mrs. Jenkins, although I knew she could not be over sixty, Mrs. Jenkins who had retreated into watchful silence when I had spoken lightly of the New Cathedral, staring at her ring as though to gather strength from it, as though to asseverate her attachment; and I felt that it was surely not by coincidence that the glass bubble on that ring enclosed a fly, a real fly which might itself have served as model for those that decorate the Lady Chapel and the Insects' Capital, but by some mysterious connection whose nature and origin I could not determine.

I felt all this, but did not take it seriously; it was only, months later, James's peculiar attitude at the fair and then at the office that made me aware of the deep and intimate nature of this connection.

I recognised these features as those of James's mother, and my impression was confirmed and strengthened when I went next day, Sunday, to look at Botany and her companion figures on the porches; it was in the afternoon, for I had decided a week ago, on the eve of my first visit to Pleasance Gardens, that I would spend Sunday morning revisiting the Museum tapestries.

On this occasion too I was almost alone, for it was barely light even outside in the wet streets, or in the exhibition rooms, where I could hear the trains clattering southward from Hamilton Station; I went, alone, past the sarcophagi of Roman children and the dresses of bygone days with their shrivelled yellow lace, 'til I came to the third panel, and there I gazed once again at the huge tortoise surrounded by the torn shreds of human flesh (one head, upside down, eyes closed, had rolled over between two stones, disturbing scorpions and lizards) in a landscape of rocks and bushes with an acropolis in the background, the enormous tortoise looking, with its bloodstained beak, chequered head, wrinkled neck and round eye, like some great vulture para-lysed in the process of transformation, its feathers all turning into scales of lava, its two great wings folded and coalescing into an imprisoning carapace too heavy to be lifted up by the squat pillars that were once its claws, now firmly earthbound, or those other paws growing from its shoulders through the shell; beside the creature was its slave and accomplice, who caught travellers for its food, the giant Sciron, whose name I did not know until I bought the guide to Bleston at Baron's the following week; I don't need to open it nowadays, for I know by heart the list it gives of the eighteen tapestries in the Harrey collection:

"Childhood of Theseus, slaying of Sinis, slaying of Sciron, slaying of Procrustes, Theseus recognised by his father, slaying of the Pallantides, rape of Helen, rape of Antiope, departure for Crete, slaying of the Minotaur, desertion of Ariadne, death of Aegeus, Theseus crowned king of Athens, decent into Hades, Phaedra and Hippolytus, meeting with Oedipus, exile of Theseus."

Friday, July 11th

I have just telephoned the Burtons, but I only spoke to Doris, the daily woman, who told me that Mr. and Mrs. Burton were out that it was no good asking her questions because she had promised not to talk, and when I asked what time I could ring up tomorrow she retorted curtly that she didn't know, and slammed down the receiver with an air of finality.

I did read in the evening paper that there had been a fire in the 6th district close to their home, in once-fashionable Shoemaker's Park, but surely that cannot be the cause of such an unwonted disturbance in their quiet household.

Meanwhile, pending an answer from them, I must go on with the account I started yesterday of my visit to the Museum that Sunday morning in December, for I feel it plays an important part in my story; I must reconstitute in its broad lines the unsystematic scrutiny by which I slowly grasped the unity of all those scenes, some of which still puzzled me—the eighth and ninth for instance, the rapes of Helen and Antiope, or the seventeenth, the meeting with Oedipus (I am sure that on this occasion I failed to identify the old blind man); I realised however that they were all linked by the figure of Theseus, that they all formed part of his story.

If I had been spared this preliminary work, if I had had at my disposal a catalogue such as the one which has since taught me the names of these men and women and places, the Tapestries would not have played so important a role in my life.

What would I have learnt, in that case, from these few printed lines? Far from helping me to penetrate into the realm to which these Tapestries are the gates, I think they would forever have prevented me from entering it, for even without appreciating their value I should have been satisfied with them, I should have made no further search, perhaps I should never have returned to these museum rooms. But being already involved in exploration of these enigmas when the guidebook came into my hands, I was able to assess its merits as well as its deficiencies and to extract all possible information from it.

As I stood before the panel showing the enormous tortoise I could see on my right, on the next wall of the third room, another giant being slain by the same young man in armour, against a landscape of slender spring trees, elms and birches, their boughs flung wide like whiplashes, trees used as instruments of torture, violently tossing up their ghastly fruits, the quivering sections of human bodies (Sinis used to stop travellers, then bind them to two young tree trunks which he pulled down and let fly like springs to tear the bodies in half lengthwise; in the lower left-hand corner, there's half a head with the eye still shining), with the same acropolis in the background, a little smaller.

I could see on my left, on the same wall beyond the door, inadequately lighted by the window overlooking rainswept Greek Street, another giant with an even more bestial face being slain by the same young man in armour, against a landscape of autumnal oak trees whose thick branches, bent like buttresses, bore the same dreadful clusters, torn human torsos with lolling heads, hanging by their arms, while, underneath, their lower halves stood rooted in earth like strange plants, displaying monstrous wounds (Cercyon used to stop travellers, then bind them to short full-grown trees which he let fly like springs to tear the bodies across) with the same acropolis in the background, a little bigger.

I went on into the fourth room at the corner of Greek Street, and saw on the right of the door by which I had entered another giant, with a face more bestial still, being slain by the same young man in armour, against a landscape of black thickets and grottoes, on one of those strange beds equipped with blades and winches where lay men with mutilated feet and heads (Procrustes used to stop travellers and adjust their height), with the same acropolis in the background, a little bigger still.

Then, on the wall to my left, on the seventh panel, showing the main square of that lofty city, where an old king (Aegeus) sat enthroned (I recognised those Doric and Ionic temples, those palaces and monuments to which each scene had led me closer), I saw the same young man in armour wielding a sword with an elaborately carved hilt to massacre a whole throng; this was the very sword that I had already seen in the first panel in the preceding room being stolen from the old king's belt by a young woman (Aethra) as she escaped with her child in her arms, and that I had next seen, on the right, being offered by her to a boy whose features closely resembled those of the young man in armour; while in the sixth panel, next to the door through which I had just passed, the same sword is shown hanging from the young man's belt, and the old king points at it in amazement with his right hand, while with his left he rejects a phial of poison offered him by a queen (Medea).

Finally, going through the door on the left into the fifth room, I recognised in the eleventh panel—the pivotal scene, the only one whose subject I had positively identified—the same young man in armour slaying the Minotaur with the same elaborately carved sword; the young man, then, must be Theseus and the city represented by the eighteenth century artist must be Athens.

I looked closely at the tall figure of Ariadne standing on the shore in her blue, silver-embroidered dress; I saw her in the upper right-hand corner sailing away with her younger sister (and the same boat, on a larger scale, was depicted on the opposite wall, setting off on its voyage to pay tribute, full of weeping youths and girls, with old King Aegeus standing in tears on the quay, and the Acropolis in the background) and in the next

room, at the corner of Museum Street and Roman Street, I saw
Ariadne lying asleep, forsaken on the shore of a mountainous
island (Naxos) and unaware that behind the rocks a young god
with all his train, riding a chariot drawn by leopards, has landed
from another ship and is approaching.

I was still preoccupied by my discovery of Mrs. Jenkins' face
on the figure of Botany in my booklet about the New Cathedral,
and as at that time I only knew one girl in Bleston, Ann Bailey,
with whom I lunched every weekday at the Sword, my oasis in
those desert months, it was of Ann that the figure of Ariadne
made me think, although I knew that to an unprejudiced mind
there was no very striking likeness.

And then (it had all become clear, save for a few great mysteries; the whole pattern had fallen into shape, save for a few
great lacunae) Theseus became king, took his seat on Aegeus'
throne in the great public square in Athens amidst the temples
and palaces and monuments, and was crowned there; finally, in
the last panel in the sixth room, just before the Pre-Raphaelite
rooms, Theseus, a fugitive from his burning city beyond the seas,
old and white-haired with his golden robe in rags, was shown
lying beside the wreck of his ship, on the shore of an isle (Scyros)
not unlike the isle where he had left Ariadne lying.

Next morning, or the morning after, I returned to James
the book he had lent me, and he told me he would bring back
The Bleston Murder as soon as his mother had finished it: that
he had found it... Oh, what did he say? Something polite and
noncommittal, something like "very strange", only I know those
were not quite his words.

3

Monday, July 14th

It rained almost the whole day yesterday, one downpour after another, thunderclaps and brief bright intervals close on one another's heels, a gleam of copper here and a glint of blue there between the black rainclouds; the days are drawing in, and although the evenings are still light until nine they have begun to dwindle as the afternoons dwindled in December when night fell at three o'clock.

Great sheets of water were toppling down over Town Hall Square when I went to the Grand Hotel to tell Lucien about the news I was expecting to hear without knowing exactly what it would be, just as in a thunderstorm one expects the lightning to strike without knowing exactly where; for weeks the threat of it had loomed, ever since that conversation last May at the Burtons' house in Green Park Terrace, when George had confirmed what we had already suspected for a long time—that he was the author of *The Bleston Murder* (the days were lengthening then, to be sure, yet we'd had to turn on the lights early, for it was cold and wet, a last winter's day lingering on the fringe of that lull which we are still enjoying). We sat for a long time in dreary silence, Lucien and I, before deciding to go to the Gaiety Cinema to see a second-rate Italian film; Lucien was almost as disturbed as I was, though at first he could not understand what it was all about, so excited and incoherent were my explanations; eventually he began to remember things and to grow apprehensive, and his eyes widened, revealing unmistakable terror (calm reliable Lucien, with his Gallic toughness and his

apparent imperviousness to the city's black magic) and of growing entreaty, as if he were begging me to forgive and spare him
(but really it concerns him so little), until I realised that he was
still under a misapprehension, fancying that George Burton was
dead and that the verdict was murder; and then I enlightened
and reassured him, and he resumed his normal expression.

Actually it was Lucien and not I who had dared to challenge
our host that third Sunday in May, and forced him to admit that
he really was that J. C. Hamilton who had refused to have his
photograph printed on the back cover of the Penguin edition of
his book; the admission was made with ill-disguised reluctance,
after a pause, a blank interval to which at the time I attributed
no importance, in my excitement at the prospect of learning the
secret, but which gradually struck me as an essential factor in the
scene, which began to flicker like a warning signal in my mind—a
silence lasting only a few seconds, only one second maybe, but
which in retrospect seems interminable; and then George interrupted it with a sudden burst of laughter as sharp as broken glass.

Lucien and I were irresistibly caught up in his laughter, but
Harriet only smiled; at the time I did not realise how much effort
lay behind her meagre gaiety, how deliberately withdrawn she
was, poor clear-sighted Harriet; I must have noticed it though,
for it strikes me more vividly each time the incident recurs to
my mind.

"Of course," he said, "of course."

He seemed unable to get his breath, to speak naturally; he
gazed at us each in turn with the complacent air of one who has
prepared an elaborate practical joke and when at last it comes
off, revels in his victims' astonishment.

Outside it was almost dark; the trees in Green Park, their
fresh young foliage swaying in the melancholy twilight, were
scarcely visible through the rain.

"You must certainly have wondered how I earn my living.
Well, there you are, chaps, I write whodunits—bestsellers, too,"
and his laugh rang out again, more forced than ever.

"Oh, I see what you're thinking; *The Bleston Murder* is J. C. Hamilton's only book, and I certainly couldn't have supported Harriet on the proceeds of that; my bestsellers are signed Barnaby Rich, and I'm also responsible, with my dear wife's invaluable collaboration, for the prolific and profitable output of Caroline Bay."

Now they were enjoying themselves.

"One day, it must have been ten years ago, dear" (Harriet was passing cigarettes) "our publisher wanted photographs of us for the sake of publicity; and we disguised ourselves for a joke; Barnaby, that's me, had an eyeglass, a hard collar and bow tie and a little moustache."

"And Caroline had a fantastic sleek hairstyle and a few wrinkles."

"We were unrecognisable! As for J. C. Hamilton, you know the big idea: no portrait, a blank frame, the last word in mystery. Mind you don't give me away! You see that if I'm always talking about detective stories, to the point of boring my listeners stiff, I've got some excuse."

Then he went on praising and expounding his art, resuming his lecture at the point where he had left it the previous Sunday, but in quite another tone, for now, by his own admission, he was speaking in his own name, asserting that in the best of such works the novel acquires, as it were, a new dimension, since not only are the characters and their relations transformed under the eye of the reader but so, too, is his knowledge of those relations and of the story itself; the final, definitive aspect of that story, ratified, as he showed us the following week, by the destruction of the culprit, by the pure murder through which the detective attains his supreme self-fulfilment, this final aspect is only revealed after, and through, a number of other aspects, so that the narrative is not merely the projection on a flat surface of a series of events, it rebuilds these as it were spatially, since they appear differently according to the position occupied by the detective or by the narrator...

But my recollection of the things he said two months ago is confused by the news of the "accident" which has just befallen him.

Tuesday, July 15th

That long overdue telephone call to the Burtons which I had endeavoured to make on Friday was scarcely more successful when I repeated it on Saturday evening at about six; once again it was answered by Doris, who normally is never there at the weekend, and who sounded almost as panic-stricken as before.

"Could you call back, Mrs. Burton's rather tired this evening."

"And Mr. Burton?"

I heard the click of the receiver being replaced as if by accident; and I tried a third call on Sunday morning about ten, this time getting Harriet.

"Is that you, Monsieur Revel?"

How thin her voice sounded!

"I'm so sorry about last night; I was beside myself with worry, you know; I was expecting a call from the doctor any moment; thank heaven he's better now, it's all gone off all right, I'm going to see him in an hour's time, and I suppose we've finished with the Police now. Oh, what a grilling they gave me!"

"But what's been happening?"

"Of course, you couldn't know, forgive me, I've just been through two ghastly nights and I'm scarcely awake, let alone tidy… Luckily Doris is here, you know her—our help, who's very kindly staying with me for a few days—I'd be scared to sleep here alone, the house seems so queer now. Doris has just brought me my breakfast; you see how lazy I am…"

"I'll let you eat it in peace then; I'm sure Doris is in the background glaring at the telephone."

"Oh, you've made me laugh, d'you hear? That shows I'm feeling better."

"When may I call you back?"

"Whenever you like, of course, as soon as I get home again. George will probably have been able to talk to me by then; yesterday he could only mutter a few words, I don't even know whether he recognised me. I must tell you all about it; it happened on Friday night, I'd got tea ready and I was waiting for him, and beginning to worry because he was late. It was nearly seven when the telephone bell rang; I thought it must be George calling to tell me he'd got caught somewhere, and I was secretly cursing at him; then I heard a strange voice saying something which I couldn't understand at first and had to have repeated several times: 'This is the Bleston Royal Hospital speaking'; then the voice said in that impersonal but sympathetic tone which makes you fear the worst: 'Are you Mrs. Burton, the wife of George William Burton? I'm sorry to have to tell you that your husband has just had a rather nasty accident; he was knocked down by a car as he was crossing Brown Street; he was brought here straight away, and you can come and see him, Ward 16, bed 7; his injuries don't seem to be serious, but he is still unconscious; they're going to operate tonight.' Of course I asked them to put him in a private ward as soon as possible; and then yesterday, just as I was beginning to breathe again, I had a visit from a Police inspector who asked me all sorts of personal questions, to most of which I couldn't reply, about the company George kept and whether he had any enemies, and so forth. Oh, I was in despair, and today he's sure to go and worry George if he's able to speak, if he's not too feverish; all the sort of things we've described in our books, for which we should have been prepared, they take you by surprise when they happen to you! Doris has gone back to the kitchen, furious with me for chattering like this; her lovely eggs are quite cold."

It was almost seven, she'd said, when she heard the telephone bell ring; so it must have been about half-past six when George Burton was knocked down by that car in Brown Street, while I was quietly eating my evening meal in the Sword, thinking about the Museum tapestries and about my own Ariadne,

Ann, with whom I had lunched there almost every week in December, and who had already told me about her sister Rose; so my own call from the call box at the corner of Dew Street and Tower Street must have been made only a few seconds after the call from the hospital.

Now I understand Doris's panic; she must always have considered her employers' way of life eccentric and their profession scarcely respectable, and have grumbled that no good could come of it.

When I resumed our talk that evening Lucien was standing beside me, holding the receiver, in the cloakroom of the Oriental Rose; we had gone to supper there on leaving the Gaiety.

"He's better, yes, much better; he's been able to take a little food, he's less feverish and he can talk naturally; I was able to stay with him for quite a while; it's as if he'd woken from a bad dream. The inspector came to see him and questioned him chiefly about the accident itself. But he couldn't give any precise information, he only remembers that he was crossing the street, that he saw a car rushing towards him, that he tried to avoid it and then he found himself in a hospital bed. I told him you'd rung up. If you can go to see him he'll certainly be most grateful—not immediately of course, he's very tired, but next week. He'll be in hospital for at least a fortnight; he has a torn ear and a broken shoulder blade and a number of other wounds; he's covered with bandages, and then he's lost a lot of blood. You know, he nearly died; the doctor admitted that he'd suspected a fractured skull, and I guessed as much from the way he spoke yesterday, but thank God there's nothing of the sort, nothing serious; he's just got to lie quiet and take it easy. Do forgive me for bursting into tears like this, it's from relief."

Thursday, July 17th

I stayed longer than I meant to with Harriet Burton last night; it was the first time I had seen her without George, in whose shadow she lives (I feel that Rose may have some of her ways, in a few years' time, when she is married) and we talked about him for a long time, about his injuries and the puzzling "accident" which is presumably a bungled murder, about the investigations and theories of the Police, who seem to have reached an impasse and to have given up trying to solve an enigma which they don't think really important, whereas she, Harriet, has obviously got an idea into her head which she wouldn't tell me and has certainly not told the inspector, but which I can't help thinking must be connected with *The Bleston Murder* and the name J. C. Hamilton, and probably with that person of whom Ann and Rose had spoken, that friend of their cousin's whose name I've forgotten (but I can find it among my papers, for I remember noting it in my account of that supper-party on June 1st) and possibly with that house which, it seems, so closely resembles that of the Winn brothers in the novel.

Yesterday the Press had been silent about the story, but this morning it was on all the placards of the *Bleston Post*, competing for the place of honour with a fire that had just destroyed a garage in the 3rd district between Lanes Park and the Anchor Hotel; and tonight it is in the *Evening News* under an enormous headline:

BROWN STREET MYSTERY

Famous Detective Novelist's Narrow Escape from Death.

One of the most remarkable literary figures in Bleston, G. W. Burton, better known under his pseudonym Barnaby Rich (we need scarcely remind our readers of his many works, *The Blue Crime*, *The Mahogany Ring*, *The House with the Three Elms*, *The Dark Tower*, *Foxes' Lake* and all the other mysteries so cleverly solved by the "little one-eyed detective in a straw hat and white shoes") the husband of the no-less-famous Caroline Bay, was crossing Brown Street at 6.20 p.m. last Friday evening when he was knocked down by a car driving very fast, which had just gone past the red lights without stopping and went on without slowing down, disappearing almost immediately along Trinity Street.

Several witnesses declare that the car suddenly changed its course in order to charge at George Burton. Unfortunately everything happened so quickly, in the confusion of the rush hour, that nobody has been able to provide an exact description of the driver or to remember the number of the car. The Police are making enquiries...

But there is no mention of J. C. Hamilton or his book.

James Jenkins, who had been avoiding me to such an extent that I had not dared ask him on Monday, as I'd intended, to come with me to the film on Palmyra and Baalbek showing at the News Theatre—James Jenkins, who had not spoken to me all week and who now, looking exhausted, came up to me this evening just as we were leaving the office and invited me to his house again next Saturday, that big house to which I had not been for over a month but which I used to visit almost every week in December (it was the only home, apart from Horace Buck's, to which I had access at that time; although I lunched almost every weekday with Ann at the Sword I had not yet met Rose, and I had never been to their home in All Saints Gardens, which I now know so well)—that house in Geology Street which is so much too big, so full of unobtrusive treasures salvaged from the recesses of the nineteenth century, and in which I have not set foot since that last evening in May, when at the fair in the 2nd district we had once again discussed *The Bleston Murder*.

Friday, July 18th

We understand that J. C. Hamilton, author of *The Bleston Murder*, is none other than George William Burton *alias* Barnaby Rich, the recent victim of a mysterious street accident...

So the name is out now: J. C. Hamilton, author of *The Bleston Murder*, that book of which a copy marked with my name was produced to my surprise by Ann Bailey on the last Saturday in May and is now in the hands of the Jenkinses.

I should dearly like to know how James's mother has faced the reappearance of that ghost, for she cannot fail to have noticed its presence, nor can James have failed to strive to conceal it from her; I feel that she sees through all his efforts to avoid her eyes, and that she must have understood merely from his expression (and heaven knows that is altered!) what the whole thing is about, without having to resort to anything so mean as prying—she must have induced an occasion, made confession inevitable, and for all his reserve he must infallibly have disclosed my own part in the affair.

On December 16th, the third Sunday in the month, while a flurry of dirty snow was falling—the first I'd seen that year; it melted before it touched the ground—she had returned that same copy to me, with thanks and judicious compliments which did not prevent me from reading in her gestures and her tone of voice, and more particularly in the glances that she fixed more frequently than usual on the fly in its glass bubble on her ring, as if seeking there encouragement or at least forgiveness, a censure so severe that it implied, for all the efforts of her good sense and her kindness, the deepest mistrust of one who had brought her a phial of poison in the guise of some refreshing drink.

The dirty snowflakes were falling on the other side of the windowpanes, and mingling with the mud and the puddles in the paths of that great uncared-for garden.

I felt myself to be on dangerous ground, as though before a cunningly-guarded castle amidst whose fortifications *The Bleston Murder* had fallen like a bomb, making a great crack which was to prove deeper and more lasting than I would have believed possible, and at the same time setting off all the alarm bells so that if I wanted to move a single step forward I should first have to drug all the sentries, disguise my plans, wait and scheme before creeping in.

And so that day, Sunday, December 16th, I avoided any allusion to the discovery which I had made on the Saturday of the previous week in the illustrated guide to the New Cathedral, and which had grown so much fuller and more precise the next day, Sunday, December 9th, when I had gone to examine the statues on the porches themselves; I now confirmed it by studying Mrs. Jenkins' face, trying to free her forehead, temples and hands from their many fine wrinkles, to give her complexion back its freshness, her cheeks their firmness, her hair its glossy darkness (as for her eyes, they can never have been brighter than now, as she stared at the fly on her ring), in a word to see through her present appearance to what she had been in her youth.

The longer my gaze lingered on her features, the more I observed her attitudes during that meal by lamplight, the more compelling became my impression that all the allegorical figures of the Arts and Sciences on the porches of the New Cathedral were coming to life before my eyes (in the hand grasping the handle of the teapot I recognised that of Astronomy handling her sextant), not that the gestures were literally identical, but those of the statues seemed to fix in emphatic immobility those of the living woman, which were like a first sketch for them, a timid and ephemeral suggestion—or in certain cases, rather the ultimate concentration of them, a perfect epitome within the rhythm of reality.

She is the daughter of the sculptor E. C. Douglas who created most of them, and so, too, of that model whom he had so tenderly, so carefully, so constantly explored and scrutinised, but her relation with the work of art is so intimate that this explanation is inadequate; surely her father had become Pygmalion to her and, from earliest childhood, she had slowly appropriated all that she could of the glances and curves and graces that he had sculptured in stone, and which are thus combined and incarnate in herself.

4

Monday, July 21st

Night is beginning to encroach once more. I have just been
to the News Theatre with Lucien, whom I shall only see
for two more weekends, since his departure is fixed for Sunday,
August 3rd; we saw a documentary about Oxford, where some of
the courts and buildings reminded me of Athens in the Museum
tapestries (next week they're showing the great Canadian lakes
in the series "Splendours of the Commonwealth") and then
Lucien went off to see the Baileys, inviting me to accompany
him; I, like a fool, refused, choosing rather to closet myself with
these blank pages. The air this evening was certainly warmer
than during those last Mondays in May when I took the same
homeward route at the same time, but the light was the same,
the sun hung in the same position over the chimneys in the
misty air.

That Saturday when, almost inadvertently, I pointed out the
author of *The Bleston Murder* to James Jenkins at the fair was a
far longer, finer day, far more confidently serene, than the previous Sunday when that same author, George Burton, had in his
own home, through his talk, revealed to us a little more of that
secret life of which he had disclosed the main mystery the week
before by admitting his identity with J. C. Hamilton, author
of *The Bleston Murder*; on that earlier Sunday it had been still
rainy but yet longer, finer and more confidently serene than the
Sunday before that, May 10th, the second Sunday in the month
(I am tracing the month upstream, back towards winter) when
our dialogue had taken the form of a lecture sparsely interrupted

by our requests for explanation, and for the first time had turned entirely on detective fiction, a topic which, to be sure, we had touched on long before, and which had underlain all our conversations since the beginning, since it was to *The Bleston Murder* that George and I owed our first meeting.

He had watched us the whole of that evening, amused at our reluctance to bring up the name Hamilton, provoking us by furtive allusions, wondering when we would come to it, convinced that we should come to it, seeking to harden himself in that conviction and yet to postpone the moment when he would have at last to give us an answer, and relieved, when we left him, that we had been so close to taking the plunge and yet had not dared to do so, that he could go on playing his game.

Our silence was certainly not due to any fear of offending him by our guess, if it should prove wrong, for he had so often proclaimed his admiration for writers specialising in that branch of literature; it may perhaps have involved a certain unwillingness to look foolish if, by some improbable chance, he had been trying to suggest something wholly different, but the crucial point was that whereas we wanted to get a clear admission we realised that he wished to leave us in uncertainty, not only, as I then thought, because he knew that the prestige inherent in his title as author of *The Bleston Murder* would be greater the better he maintained the mystery surrounding it, but evidently, above all, to ensure his own safety.

The deplorable sequel has shown only too well how right he had been to mistrust us, how fully justified the following Sunday was that hesitant pause before he broke into a laugh, and what a risk he was running; for there's no question that if I had been in the slightest doubt I should never have betrayed the secret of his identity to James Jenkins or to the Bailey girls. Lucien and I were fully conscious, on that earlier Sunday, the second in May, that if we had put the question that was on the tip of our tongues he would still have been too much on his guard, he would have answered us with a ready-made lie which would not have been a real lie, since he would not have expected us to believe him (he would in fact not have answered at all, but forbidden us to question him further on that point), we were conscious that we must still keep silence, that the longer we waited the more he would become our accomplice against himself, the more he would destroy his own defences and despise his own precautions, and the greater would be our chance of learning the truth.

And so we both maintained a heavy silence which our sparse words did not infringe, as we listened to him pointing out that in detective fiction the story goes against the stream, beginning with the crime, the climax of all the dramatic events which the detective has to rediscover gradually, and that this is in many respects more natural than a narrative proceeding without a backward look, where the first day of the story is followed by the second and then by subsequent days in their calendar order, as I myself at that time had been describing my October experiences; in detective fiction the narrative gradually explores events anterior to the event with which it begins, and this, though it may disconcert some readers, is quite natural, since obviously in real life it is only after having met somebody that we take an interest in his previous actions, and only too often it is not until some disaster has struck our lives that we wake up enough to trace its origins.

Thus I myself have striven to rediscover all that could have led me to disclose the real name of J. C. Hamilton to Ann and Rose and hence to their cousins and their cousins' friends, all that could have brought about my treachery—the word is harsh and heavy, but there is no other for it.

Would it seem too harsh and heavy if George had not escaped from death, if I had not been forced to realise my responsibility?

That is why I have gone back to my original act of treachery the previous evening, that last Saturday in May at the fair in the 2nd district, and to that talk between the three of us in the house in Green Park Terrace, searching for anything that might excuse me, that second Sunday in May when the friend of whom we did not yet wish to ask whether he were in fact the author of *The Bleston Murder* pointed out to us that in detective fiction the story goes against the stream, or more exactly that it superimposes two temporal sequences, the days of the enquiry which start at the crime and the days of the drama which lead up to it, and that this is quite natural since in real life one's mental analysis of past events takes place while other events are accumulating.

Thus I myself, while noting whatever seemed to me essential of recent experience and also describing last autumn, have now got as far as that second Sunday in May when he pointed out to us the frequent complexity of things—the detective being often summoned by the victim to protect him from the murder which he apprehends, so that the period of the enquiry starts actually before the crime, starts from the anguished shadow that it casts before it, while the period of the drama may continue after the crime, involving other crimes which echo or underline it, so that any event belonging to the first period may appear, in the inverted perspective of an ulterior moment, as belonging to the second period; all which statements prepared the way for what he wished to tell us the following Sunday, although it was only through that later conversation that I was able to understand their real significance.

Tuesday, July 22nd

In my account of last May I have hitherto described only such incidents as seemed to me to lead directly to my rash and indiscreet disclosure of J. C. Hamilton's real name on the last Saturday of the month, and again on the following day; I have omitted any mention of my visits to the Baileys, of the French conversation lessons which, to my infinite satisfaction, I gave Rose, of my lunches with the Jenkinses or of my walks with Lucien, who is too busy now to wander about with me, since he is leaving in less than a fortnight, but whom at that time I had regularly taken with me to visit any corner of the town that seemed pleasant or interesting.

Thus, on that second Sunday in May, in the early afternoon, before making our way at tea-time to the Burton's house opposite Green Park (which was just beginning to deserve its name, all the branches being tipped with tiny reed-green flames bursting from their buds, while daffodils and narcissi gleamed freshly on the damp lawns) I had taken him to see the Museum in City Street.

Between the light clouds, rays of sunlight, faintly filmed like translucent porcelain, shone through the windows of the three rooms that faced south, and the muslin blinds had been drawn rippling like watered silk when a light breeze stirred their folds.

Lucien listened with amusement as I explained each episode, although I carefully avoided telling him that for me, henceforward, Ariadne represented Ann Bailey, Phaedra was Rose and I myself Theseus, while he was the young prince whom, in the fifteenth panel, the descent into Hades, I guided to the rescue of Pluto's bride, Persephone, queen of the underworld.

On the left of the panel, the two men are standing together before the entry, the cleft in the mountain side; in the middle, they are inside the mountain, in a vaulted hall hung with stalactites and wreathed in smoke, its walls covered with dripping dusky vegetation, where, treading on clusters of faded asphodel, they climb the steps of Pluto's throne amidst astonished demons about to break loose, and endeavour to carry off the girl—Phaedra or Rose?—still glowing with her spring-like colours, crowned and adorned with sparkling gems, and on the right of the panel we behold the failure of their enterprise—both lie in chains in a hell within this hell, a cave in the heart of this cave.

And I identify Lucien, now, not only with that prince, Pirithous (the name made him laugh when I uttered it), but also with another figure, whom I had mistaken for Pirithous before I had bought the Bleston guidebook: the god Dionysos in the twelfth panel, landing on Naxos and catching sight of forsaken Ariadne as he mounts his leopard-drawn chariot.

Lucien was far more ignorant of classical mythology than I had been when I first encountered these great illustrations woven in silk and wool, in silver and gold; only the name of Oedipus, as we stood before the seventeenth panel, suggested old legends to his mind; and as I strove to restore some order to the fragments he delightedly retrieved I came to understand how natural, almost inevitable, was this meeting between the kings of Athens and of Thebes.

Their destinies indeed had much in common; each was brought up in ignorance of his birth and race, far from his native city; each slew the monsters that threatened that city, cleared a road, solved riddles; and each killed his father (Theseus not with the sword but through negligence, which was far more criminal indeed, for Oedipus was ignorant of his victim's identity and the relationship between them, but Aegeus' suicide was due to seeing the black sail which his son ought to have changed, knowing as he did that the sight of it would drive the old man to despair, and which he certainly would have changed but for the presence of that Phaedra, that Rose for whose sake he had forsaken Ariadne, by whom he was hopelessly obsessed and blinded and driven to treachery), and each by this means won a precarious throne, each at last was driven from that throne, each witnessed his city in flames and died far away, powerless to help her.

The name of Oedipus cropped up again a fortnight later in the course of George Burton's remarks about detective fiction— that conversation which really began that Sunday afternoon, the second Sunday in May, when Lucien and I visited him on leaving the Museum, that conversation during which, later, we got him to confess that he was the author of *The Bleston Murder*, the man who hid behind a blank space on the cover of the book, behind the name of J. C. Hamilton: a secret which I could not resist imparting to James Jenkins and then to the

Bailey girls. I made a grave mistake in telling James, since it revived an old wound in his heart and even more in his mother's; I made a far graver mistake in telling the Baileys, for I have an ever-growing fear that the novel may be an exposure of that friend of their cousin's whose house, apparently, is so like the Winn brothers' house in the book, an exposure of a crime he must have thought safely buried, I have an ever-growing fear that this man may have tried to revenge and safeguard himself, and that thus through my indiscretion I may have put George Burton in danger of death (from what he said on Sunday at the hospital, I believe he thinks so too; what I must without fail discover is whether this man, whose name I can surely trace in the account I wrote, the following day, of that disastrous conversation with the Baileys, owns a black Morris), a danger which still threatens him and will do so as long as the truth remains hidden, that danger of death pervading the whole town of Bleston which suddenly struck with concentrated force at him.

And now the whole town is aware of J. C. Hamilton, that name which made its first timid appearance last Friday in a small paragraph in the *Evening News* and which on Saturday was ruthlessly displayed on every front page, with great articles under great headlines naturally echoing the title of the book: "The Bleston Murder", and the whole town knows that J. C. Hamilton is George Burton, who would surely not now be lying on a hospital bed if he had not met me, George who had expressly bidden us to keep his secret, and whom I have nearly killed through negligence.

Wednesday, July 23rd

When we went to see him in his ward at the Royal Hospital about four o'clock last Saturday, as we had promised Harriet, I had in my jacket pocket the copy of the *Bleston Post* which I had just bought in Town Hall Square, on the corner by the

Grand Hotel, on my way to fetch Lucien after lunching with the Jenkinses (the first time for so long; how strained they both seemed!), that copy of the *Bleston Post* whose headlines shouted in a derisive misleading echo of his title: THE BLESTON MURDER; he saw this as soon as we entered, tried to sit up and struggle free of his pillows to point at it, then burst into that broken-glass laugh of his which stopped suddenly, for it obviously hurt him; then he sank back exhausted, moaning softly to himself, with a smile of contempt, "The Bleston Murder!" tossing his head about as though to shake off a nightmare.

While Lucien went to find the nurse I stayed watching him, waiting for the moment when his eyes would at last meet mine, when he would lift up his head and speak to me, when this strange fit would pass, and I became increasingly absorbed in following the buzzing flight of a huge fly which had just come in through the open window overlooking Willow Park with its crowded walks and its spreading green. It was a fine day for these parts, warm and sultry; lately, although the evenings have been inexorably drawing in, it has been increasingly warm and sultry; the air seems to have thickened, condensed into a leaden mist that coats my window, blurring the view of Dew Street.

I kept my eyes fixed on that great fly, that hairy metallic blue-bottle as it flew in narrowing circles round George Burton's head, settled on the white bandage, then walked over his forehead, sucking the drops of sweat with its tiny proboscis (he had closed his eyes; he was wearily waving his uninjured hand to drive it away), and I dared not go closer nor do anything, when to my relief I heard the door open; and the woman who came in with Lucien told us we had better leave him now and come back next day when he was calmer.

On Sunday, Harriet, sitting at his bedside on the white chair, gave us a friendly welcome to the bleak room which still smelt faintly of ether, although the window was wide open on account of the persistent fine weather, the sun being veiled only by a few slow-drifting wisps of white cloud.

He seemed rested; he was sitting up, leaning against piled pillows, and he started talking to us with all his old kindly irony, making no reference to our unfortunate visit the previous day; but there was an unfamiliar gentleness in his tone, a highly deliberate gentleness as though he knew all our misdeeds and had forgiven them all, as though something within him were ceaselessly whispering: "I don't bear you any grudge; I nearly died, but please believe me, I don't bear you a grudge for it; you see, I'm treating you just as I used to."

He told his own version of the "accident" (he used the word, but what he said to us only confirmed our fears, contradicted the euphemism), for it was not true that he remembered nothing about it; that was what he had told the Police and the newspapers had repeated it, but, faithful to the ideas he had expressed when talking about detectives two months ago, he had wished to keep something essential back for himself so as to solve the problem alone, so as to confound and punish the criminal, not with his own hands but with his own voice, declaring (to test us no doubt, to see how far we could follow a hint): "You let your fancy rip, you make up stories, you're fool enough to write books, you amuse your readers with descriptions of anguish and murder, of corpses and narrow escapes from violent death; and then things happen, the ball you'd thrown for fun, after bouncing on a lot of walls, comes back and hits you; it was probably only an accident after all, although you can understand how I should enjoy really being involved in a mystery like one of my leading characters; the driver had had rather too much to drink, that was all, that explained his wild stare, the fury I could sense in him as he charged at me, the distorted features on that face that I glimpsed for less than a second (was it from terror of the very accident that he saw he could not avoid, or from crazy determination and hatred?), so distorted indeed that I could not recognise them if I met the man in normal circumstances; he must have escaped in a panic; perhaps he's forgotten everything already; most likely he'll never turn up again with his black Morris…"

None of the papers had specified the make of the car; this was a completely fresh piece of evidence; how did it happen that he alone had recognised it, when he'd had so much less time than the other witnesses?

Of course it may be that the whole scene engraved itself on his mind with exceptional precision, but may not the real answer be that he's on the track of somebody, some suspect who he knows owns a black Morris?

What I simply must discover is whether that friend of the Baileys' cousin, whose name I haven't yet looked up in my notes, comes under that heading; but how could I ask them without immediately arousing suspicions which may turn out to be absurd, without disturbing them and making a fool of myself?

That is why I refused to go with Lucien to visit them on leaving the hospital; I wanted to think things over; I walked about for a long time, and lost my way among the depressing streets of the 11th district, until I found myself by the banks of the fetid Slee.

"Was it a black Morris, then?" I had asked George Burton, and he'd replied: "Oh, of course I couldn't be absolutely sure."

I should dearly have liked to make a clean breast of the whole thing—how I had betrayed him, had proved unworthy of his trust, had imperilled his life by disclosing the real name of J. C. Hamilton to the Bailey girls at supper on Sunday, June 1st (and the evening before to James, while we were standing by the shooting-gallery examining that photograph, the soiled and crumpled negative of which now lies between the pages of my copy of *The Bleston Murder*), although if my suspicions were justified he had the strongest reasons for keeping that name a secret.

But how could I put the case without being certain? Where could I start, in that jumble of apprehensions and suppositions, if I were to avoid misunderstandings? How could I fail to appear ridiculous if by any chance he were not on the same trail as I, and, since mine might prove to be a false trail, why risk misleading him? And finally, how could I tell him about Rose, whom he does not know and to whom I have never referred to in his presence, about Rose and Ann, and the part I assume they have played in the affair—a wholly innocent one, since I had never told them, nor James, that it was a secret.

How could I do all this, seeing him so weary, sensing Harriet's anxiety?

Soon, after a few moment's silence, the nurse came into the room with a smile intended to tell us that our visit had lasted long enough.

Thursday, July 24th

I was thinking about James the whole time, while we were saying goodbye, while I was promising to return next Sunday at the same time (but without Lucien, who is leaving Bleston in eleven days and will be on duty for the last time at his hotel).

It is even sultrier than yesterday; I almost long for rain; my hands are sticking to my paper and my shirt to my back; while I was coming home the heavy air was acrid with lingering smoke, as if I were pursued by the smell of burning from the tyre warehouse in the 1st district (in this evening's paper the report of the fire has quite ousted the story of George Burton's accident).

I was thinking about James during the whole of our visit to the hospital on Sunday, about James and his mother (her ghost seemed to be present, staring at the glass bubble on her ring), not only because there had been talk of a black Morris, but also because of that buzzing fly the day before, and chiefly because, during my lunch with them, the first for so long, during that meal which should have brought reconciliation but which was still so painfully tense (she was making superhuman efforts to be friendly, James sat silent most of the time, casting an occasional pathetic glance at me as though appealing for help and forgiveness), just before our first unsuccessful visit to the hospital, they had asked me for news of George with the strangest insistence.

It was no doubt because they were ashamed of having displayed in front of me such peculiar hatred for a man who was now on his sickbed; it was no doubt because they had welcomed the news of the "accident" as though it avenged them for the searing wound inflicted on them by certain pages of *The Bleston Murder*, which seemed to violate and disfigure the things they held most dear: a wound which had gradually healed, but which I had reopened and probed deeper by my tactlessness, my treacherous indiscretion; and because they were ashamed of their hatred and of their pleasure, and ashamed that I, a friend of J. C. Hamilton's, should have witnessed their passionate attachment and their close relationship to the New Cathedral, which is at the bottom of it all; and they now regret having let me discover it while they watched my progress with a friendly eye last autumn, amused at my resourceful curiosity, gradually relaxing their defences because my perseverance flattered them, during those weeks of rain and fog, those blind diminished days round about Christmas, such as that fourth Saturday in December when, after taking James to lunch at the Oriental Pearl I had paused with him in front of the porches where the statues of the Arts and Sciences stood, streaming with rain, and I had watched him watching me; to my casual remark, "What an amazing likeness!" he had merely replied, "Yes, isn't it?" and then gone on to suggest a visit to the cinema to warm ourselves; which had proved to me that he had perfectly well understood me, that I was on the right track and that he encouraged my researches.

In those dark days of late autumn I had begun to feel at home in this room, which had already become my refuge, and at this table which served me as a rampart against Bleston; I had not yet begun to write at it, but I could spread out that map of Bleston which I have since destroyed and on which I had already superimposed that other map which nobody has ever printed, where the two Cathedrals appear as the two poles of an immense magnet which disturbs the trajectory of all human atoms in its neighbourhood, according to the stuff they are made of and the energy with which they are charged—James Jenkins and his mother for instance, on the one hand, and on the other J. C. Hamilton whose real name I had not yet discovered.

I was by then on excellent terms with kind Mrs. Grosvenor, to whom I had lent *The Bleston Murder*, and who, having got over her initial mistrust, used to hold forth to me at great length every evening; and every evening I understood her a little better. On Christmas Eve, as she was invited out to a neighbour's, she prepared a small private feast for me (a glass of sherry, a slice of pudding, a plateful of cold meat) which I discovered when I came in after walking for hours in the rain, while the bells of the New Cathedral harried me with a full peal; I had been into every church that I passed in my wanderings, regardless of denomination, and everywhere I had heard the same hymns, and guessed at the same sad worried minds behind the apparently cheerful faces of the worshippers; and everywhere I felt that here was only the shadow of a festival, the ghost of a dead festival; this very consciousness excluded me from that shadow, from that simulacrum, and soon, unable to bear the curious glances that denounced me as a dangerous intruder and the stifling atmosphere, I was forced out again to face the driving sheets of dark rain and the relentless hammering of the bells.

Next day, the darkest day of the whole year, Mrs. Grosvenor was expecting guests, and I had been obliged to escape, at the risk of offending her somewhat; I had roamed all alone through some of the most sordid streets in Bleston, creeping along like a starveling cat under the ceaseless downpour, past the lighted windows (where was daylight at that season?) of homes where parents were playing with their children, where presents had just been handed out, where the wax from the tiny coloured candles was slowly trickling down the fir tree branches; here and there I caught sight of other solitary prowlers like myself, excluded like myself from all rejoicings, even the most elementary, since the pubs were officially closed until eight o'clock, and at last I came back to this neighbourhood to see if Horace were

at home; I went up, although his window was dark, hoping that
he might be sleeping as he often does on a Sunday afternoon;
I heard the sound of laughter from the neighbouring rooms;
I knocked and called, but in vain.

Friday, July 25th

On Christmas Day then, on that horrible Christmas Day (how
can I help loathing you, Bleston?) I came back here to change
because I was soaked, then I set off again along the streets as far
as Town Hall Square and went into the Amusements Arcade;
and there I saw him, Horace Buck, with his eye glued to the
sights of the big machine gun, doggedly firing at the painted
aircraft circling in the glass sky above the painted image of a
town in flames; I saw him suddenly shake the machine indig-
nantly (I heard the rattle of flimsy metal) and glance furtively
at the old woman who was replacing the usual cashier; then he
recognised me and burst out laughing, and took me by the arm
to lead me outside.

He was whispering, in the rain: "I think I've mucked up that
gun…" When the bells began to ring again; then, fists clenched,
teeth clenched, looking askance with his yellowish negro's eyes,
he started muttering: "Their bells and their Father Christmas,
and all their choirboys with eyes turned up and folded hands."
when the clangour stopped; it had not been the real bells of
Bleston, those of the New Cathedral, but merely those of the
Town Hall clock tower, striking seven and reminding us that
we were hungry.

All the restaurants on the Square were closed (it was
Christmas), as were those near the two Cathedrals (lights gleaming in the windows, wafts of organ music from some service,
deserted lanes outside; it was Christmas); I did not want to come
back and beg a little food from Mrs. Grosvenor, whose offer to
leave me some I had already refused that morning (anyhow she
must be at her cousin's by now, it was Christmas); so I went with

Horace into the confusion of his room, but the cupboard was bare (there were three cigarettes on the table, which he thrust into his pocket before turning out the light) and we went out again into the cold dark rain, and back to Town Hall Square which we had left just over an hour before (we'd had to walk; there was only one bus every half hour; it was Christmas), where the lengthening queues outside the big cinemas were crawling jerkily forward; as the pubs had opened at last we were able to comfort ourselves with a pint of Guinness apiece.

Then we walked along City Street and Brown Street as far as Alexandra Place, because I felt sure that there at least we should find something to eat at the buffet of one of the stations.

We went up the slope into Hamilton Station; the dank hall was full of a swarming crowd of people from the outskirts on their way home; we pushed open the glass door of the refreshment-room, where not only were all the tables occupied but a number of travellers were standing with their piled suit-cases beside the scanty coal fire, waiting for an empty seat.

At half-past nine, when our turn came at last, when at last we managed to sit down (we had stood beside the embers, drying our clothes and drinking a cup of tea) we ate our meagre meal rapidly under the impatient eyes of those who wanted our places, and as we were still rather hungry and it was clearly impossible to go on eating here, we went down the slope again, across Brown Street and into New Station; but when we reached the glass door of the refreshment room we saw that the last customers were being turned out, and the woman in charge, as she locked up, informed us that we were too late, for the last train, presumably ours, was leaving in five minutes.

So, still hurrying, we went under the insidious grimy rain, along the busy glistening pavements, to try our luck for the last time at the third apex of the triangle, Dudley Station, where we were served fairly quickly; but when we emerged, our hunger satisfied at last, we saw that it was after half-past ten, and consequently all the pubs were shut and there would be no bus home since, as we knew, all night services had been suspended (it was Christmas).

We crossed Alexandra Place and went down Brown Street and then City Street, and found ourselves once more in Town Hall Square, where there were no more queues, not a soul, not a car in sight, the cinema lights were out and there was nothing to be seen but the glimmering haloes round the street-lamps in the dense rain.

We passed alongside the wooden shutters of Prince's restaurant, the entrance door of the Gaiety, the darkened windows of Grey's behind their thick-mesh iron curtain, where figures and trees could be dimly glimpsed amidst a glitter of tinsel.

We turned down into Silver Street, which was certainly the shortest way, but Horace who, in daylight, might have guided me, was half asleep; he tottered along, mumbling to himself, letting himself be led like a great child or a big brown bear, and I did not know this part of Bleston well enough to find my way through it except along the main streets.

He suddenly halted to tell me that we ought to have spent the holiday, since this was a holiday, at Pleasance Gardens, and then as an afterthought declared that as it was Christmas Pleasance Gardens would certainly have been closed, like last year (the words were blurred as they issued slowly from his thick lips; overhead the pallid flame of the gas jet was hissing amidst a swarm of raindrops) but that on New Year's Day it would be open and we ought to go there.

We started off again along Tower Street, then into Dew Street; we stopped in front of this house, drenched and weary, confusedly formulating a plan for New Year's Eve, most of which we agreed to spend in the negroes' tavern near New Station, where we should be able to drink and dance, he told me, if I didn't mind drinking and dancing with bastards who made fun of him because he came from a different region from theirs, and where we might meet some girls, where he might maybe find one who'd be willing to come and live with him for a while.

Two days later, Thursday, December 27th, as I was having lunch in the restaurant in Grey Street, looking out for Ann Bailey, I saw her come in with a girl who was slighter and prettier than herself, obviously her sister, that Rose of whom I had already heard her speak, and whom she introduced to me as they sat down at my table, explaining that Rose was a student, that being on vacation she had spent the morning nosing about the bookshops before calling for Ann at the stationer's, and that I might speak French to her, since that was her main subject at the University.

For the first time since I had come to Bleston I had a chance to talk to somebody in my own language; how grateful I was to Ann for allowing me this relief, for smiling patiently at me during the whole of that conversation of which she understood nothing! For I still knew very little English, I only understood what was said to me as though through a haze, I felt that every syllable I uttered sounded wrong, and my interlocutors had to pass over my blunders, to disentangle my meaning through a chaotic jumble of mistakes; my vocabulary was so scanty that I was constantly obliged to distort the meaning of words to make myself understood.

I promptly sought to repeat this revivifying experience, and invited the two girls, in two languages, to come with me to watch the fireworks at Pleasance Gardens on the following Saturday.

When I got home that evening Mrs. Grosvenor asked me if I could lend her another novel, and returned *The Bleston Murder* which I had already mentioned to Ann, which I had promised to lend her as soon as I could, and which I took to her next day: that copy marked with my name, which I subsequently assumed to be lost and which I replaced by another, and which I did not see again until five months later, on Sunday, June 1st.

5

Monday, July 28th

The sinking sun fills my room with rosy light and shines on my table as it did that evening when I sat down for the first time before that ream of paper bought the previous day from Ann Bailey and still sealed in the wrappings which I tore apart, that evening when I held in my hands the first of these blank white pages, lifted it to look through it at the watermark, then laid it down before me, dazzling in the sunlight.

I had barely taken time for an evening meal; it was about seven; and now it's eight o'clock and I have been to the News Theatre to see a film on the Canadian Lakes; next Monday, as on every fourth week, the programme will consist entirely of cartoons.

That first white page dazzled me in the sunlight as I tried out my fountain pen, spilt a drop of ink in the top left-hand corner and wrote in the top right-hand corner the figure 1 with a ring round it to protect it from the confusion of future sentences.

For, during the whole of May, the clue to my behaviour is not only the fact that I had those conversations with George Burton (who must have gone home by now) but also that I used to spend every weekday evening writing, and consequently had far less time to see Ann and Rose, or James Jenkins outside office hours, or Lucien, or Horace.

The sun, glowing ever redder, is still shining on the left-hand corner of my table, the sun which during so many gloomy weeks, so many weeks of dense rain, of dirty half-snow, of frozen fog, had been practically invisible, had merely from time to time given a hint of its distant presence in a rift between the clouds, an area of misty light between dark masses, the sun which had at last reappeared as a lovely pale circle against the blurred milky blue of the sky, a lovely pale circle over which smoke wreaths passed without distorting it, and which when it touched the edge of a cloud spread out long beams that rose and fell at the wind's touch, shifted and floated over one another like veils and then dwindled and vanished, the sun which had at last succeeded, in the late morning of the first of May, in casting on my desk at Matthews & Sons a patch of bright light that glowed on the typewritten figures on the page I held in my hands so that each of them seemed to be surrounded by minute smokeless white flames, imparting no heat to the paper but scorching my eyes so that I had to close them for coolness, and then saw behind closed eyelids the typewritten figures still burning, no longer surrounded by fire but written in fire against a background of violet blackness, like the last letter in the inscription Mene, Tekel, Upharsin in the fragment of glass representing Babylon in the Old Cathedral—the sun now disappearing behind the chimneys of the small houses in Copper Street.

I have before me now that first page, dated Thursday, May 1st, the whole of which I wrote by the light of that setting sun, three months ago; it was lying at the bottom of the pile which has slowly accumulated in front of me since that time and to which, in a few moments, I shall add the page I am now covering with words; and I read my opening sentence: "Suddenly there were a lot of lights", the letters of which dazzled my eyes when I closed them and appeared written in green flames against a dark red background, and then reappeared, black as dead embers on the page, when I reopened my eyes; those embers are lying before me once again.

The sun had shifted from my table; it had sunk behind the chimneys of the house at the corner of Dew Street, and I wrote the second sentence: "And then I was in the town: my year's stay, more than half of which has now elapsed, began at that moment", plunging deeper and deeper into those October days, into that first night, "while I gradually struggled free of drowsiness, sitting there alone in the corner of the compartment, facing the engine", just as I plunge into it again as I read and copy the words, re-awakening "beside the dark windowpane covered on the outside with raindrops".

The rope of words that uncoils down through the sheaf of papers and connects me directly with that moment on the first of May when I began to plait it, that rope of words is like Ariadne's thread, because I am in a labyrinth, because I am writing in order to find my way about in it, all these lines being the marks with which I blaze the trail: the labyrinth of my days in Bleston, incomparably more bewildering than that of the Cretan palace, since it grows and alters even while I explore it.

I shall restore that first page, dated May 1st, to its place under the pile of pages that followed it, on that table covered with the same articles and documents that lay there on the first of May.

I carried on next day, then gradually every weekday evening since, closeting myself with my researches, which I certainly never thought to find so arduous nor so slow, having imagined then that by the end of July I should long since have finished not only my account of last autumn but also that of winter, and of spring up to the end of April; and the following day, Saturday, I spent alone, as I had spent those early October days I was about to describe, because Lucien was on duty at his hotel (as he was yesterday and the day before, for the last time, since he's leaving Bleston on Sunday). I wandered alone about Alexandra Place, from one station to the other, eating my lunch in the buffet at Hamilton Street, drinking pint after pint of beer, and then walking aimlessly along the river bank 'til the rainy evening fell.

Tuesday, July 29th

I did not expect, then, that so many things would happen to interrupt my undertaking, that enigmas and obscurities would grow so complex, so manifold, so dense, that I should find myself so intimately involved in the attempted murder of George Burton; my investigation of this has for the past week made no progress, since, obsessed by my writing, torn by conflicting problems, uncertain how to set about things, I had not yet tried to hunt out that friend of the Baileys' cousin, Richard Tenn, whom I have such good cause to suspect and whose name I rediscovered in these pages; my investigation has made no progress, since, the day before yesterday, when I went to the hospital, I found that George had visitors whom I did not know, and this made the conversation somewhat difficult, particularly as they spoke very fast, their accents were unfamiliar to me, and they made no effort to help me understand them, so that I withdrew after a few…

Wednesday, July 30th

They came here together yesterday evening, Rose and Lucien; I had just begun to write when I heard them knock.

They looked so happy, both of them; she was so lovely in her white linen hat, my Rose whom I had failed to hold or to love, whom I had failed, through lack of courage, to wrest from Bleston, Rose against whom I had guarded myself so carefully, whom I had avoided lately, of whom I was fonder than I could have believed, whom I had flung into his arms myself, through my own reticence and blindness, because I had closeted myself in this room, never suspecting that things would go so far, never noticing that things were growing serious, because I would not have believed it possible.

They looked so happy, both of them; they laughed at my amazement, while I was forced to clench my fists (I'd never have believed it of myself) so as not to burst into angry tears.

As soon as I saw them, before they had even opened their lips, before she had uttered, with that sweet frank smile, the horrible word "engaged", those horrible sentences "you're our best friend; we wanted you to be the first to know" (spoken in French with that delicious tremulous accent and that self-conscious grammatical correctness *"nous avons voulu que vous fussiez prévenu le premier"*) "and besides, we owe it all to you", a mere look at them told me what had happened, and I felt as though I were on fire, tottering as if the ground had opened up beneath me, gasping for breath as if a whirlwind had carried me away, and my heart shrivelled up like a scorched thing.

And I felt at the same time that all these pages had crumbled to dust.

What is the good, now, of pursuing this immense, absurd attempt to see things clearly, which has only served to ruin me more utterly? What is the good of pursuing this futile, dangerous work of exploration and analysis, of trying to mend the broken thread? What is the good of reviving my pain by thinking of that evening when I went out with Rose— my Rose who should have been my Rose, of whom I could have made my own Rose, who was never false to me because I had never declared my love, Rose whom I have lost out of blindness and cowardice, out of hatred for this city whose sinister spells I was trying to exorcise, Rose whom I have lost because of the horrible power of Bleston, its creeping, insidious, soporific fumes, the acrid wafts from all its smouldering mysterious fires?

Only yesterday, in the 2nd district, fire broke out in an oil depot close to the waste land where the fair was held in May.

What is the good of rediscovering that evening at the end of December when I had taken her, Rose (oh, I cannot write her name without an ache in my heart! I want her to be happy, I bear Lucien no grudge, I cannot spoil their happiness, but how I long for him to be gone!) to Pleasance Gardens to see the New Year fireworks, with her sister Ann who, sitting on my right on the tiered seat, grasped my wrist and dug her fingernails into my skin at each of the explosions that set that sham city ablaze in the foggy night?

From time to time you could hear the animals howling in their nearby cages.

What is the good of rediscovering that negroes' tavern where Horace took me on New Year's Eve, where I drank with him as I had never drunk before in Bleston nor since, and where he met the girl with whom he is now sharing his room—what is the good?

I want a drink; it's not half-past ten yet; I can go out and drink.

IV

The Two Sisters

I

Monday, August 4th

I've begun again; I've resumed my old habits; it's the only thing to do.

On leaving Matthews & Sons I went to the News Theatre to see the programme of cartoons that is shown there every fourth week.

Once again I'm all alone in Bleston, with no one of my race or speaking my tongue, for although there are most probably other Frenchmen in this city beside myself, sitting alone in their rooms or trying to find one another as they walk through Town Hall Square in the rush hour or go to the News Theatre week by week, they have failed to pick me out, or I them.

The only one of them all that I had met or recognised was Lucien, who has robbed me of Rose, who has served his term here, who went off yesterday, fortunately for me, for him, for Rose, because I could not have gone on much longer playing the part of faithful friend, consumed as I was by this horrible ludicrous jealousy; because I felt my mask about to crack every minute and venomous words accumulating in my heart, ready to break all the barriers with which I tried to restrain them; because I could hardly conceal my vile longing to part them, to destroy their naïve trust in one another, that happiness from which I am shut out, that happiness which is based on my misfortune, on my blindness and my folly.

He went off yesterday at last, as I shall go in a couple of months (I begin to see the end of my exile glimmering through the eight remaining weeks); I went with him and Rose to Hamilton Station.

How I envied them for being free to weep, while I must restrain my black, bitter, grimy tears!

How I strove to avoid looking at Rose, who suddenly seemed a stranger to this town, released from it!

I had never truly loved her, I was never able to love her truly, I had kept myself from loving her, what right had I over her? Only this anguish…

I saw him to his train, with Rose, whom I then had to take back to her home in All Saints, comforting her although she was so happy, talking to her about Lucien, saying nice things about Lucien although I could hardly bring myself to utter his name; and she asked me to go in with her and have dinner with her, which was so much beyond my strength that despite the distance, in order to calm my nerves and allay by exhaustion the muttering tumult within me, I came home on foot through the squalid streets owned by the University in the 6th district, to the east of the railway bridges over which Lucien's train had just passed.

After skirting the porches of the New Cathedral I set off by a zigzag route through old Bleston, because I knew I should find a teashop open there, while the sky turned green above the three towers of late-Perpendicular style and the unlighted sign of the Oriental Bamboo, while dusk darkened slowly, even more slowly than this evening, so slowly that when I got home I undressed without turning on the light, by the watery glimmer from the window.

Then, unable to sleep, I got up to switch on the lamp and took up once again the pile of pages lying on this table, resumed my reading of them where I had left off on Thursday and went on with it nearly the whole night.

That's why I feel stiff and aching now, and can hardly keep my eyes open nor form my letters.

I had reached the account written on Monday, June 2nd of the conversation I had had the previous evening with the Baileys about *The Bleston Murder*; Lucien had been absent, but his absence was very different from that which started yesterday, since he was still in Bleston, at his hotel, so that one could go and see him whenever one wanted, tomorrow or the next day, and could be sure that he would come some time to knock at one's door, whereas now he is going farther and farther away, fortunately for him, fortunately for me, for now I need no longer be afraid of meeting him.

I had reached the account of that conversation during which nobody mentioned his name nor asked for news of him, but in which nevertheless he was present in everybody's mind, although I was unaware of it, in the mind of Mrs. Bailey who distrusted him, I knew, and whom he only won over slowly (she has given her consent to the engagement, but she too must be glad that he has gone, prudently anxious for this sudden love to be tested by separation), in the mind of Ann who was becoming increasingly attached to him now that she felt me drifting away from her, and above all in that of Rose, whom I had kept myself from loving but whom I wanted to attract.

Because of that sleeplessness which has left me so weary this evening, because of my emotional agitation, because of the loneliness to which Lucien's departure has condemned me, and which is far deeper than I could have imagined only a week ago, I resumed my reading of these notes (such a pile of them already, and this evening I've started adding to it again) at my account of the conversation on Sunday, June 1st, at the Baileys', which is most probably at the bottom of the attempted murder of George Burton, that conversation during which I disclosed for the second time, although I was well aware of the gravity of my act, the real name of J. C. Hamilton, that name which since then has been shouted at every street corner in Bleston.

All this made me blind, and Rose and Lucien drew close to one another without my knowledge.

Last night, then, I read that account which I had written myself, but which appeared to me more and more like the scrupulous work of another to whom I had confided only a portion of my secrets, through lack of time, through incapacity to distinguish as yet what was important, and also, I must admit, through a desire to deceive that other, to deceive myself.

For although these pages reminded me of many details which my memory had let slip or had distorted, it is nonetheless true that I still possessed, that I still possess certain pieces of evidence which I had not set down, no doubt mostly because they were then lurking in shadow, from which subsequent events have dragged them.

This feeling of inadequacy grew almost unbearable as, reading through the night, I came to the events of early November, to my second visit to the Old Cathedral, because that scene is intimately linked to the conversation at the Baileys' by another which also took place on Sunday, June 1st, in the afternoon, and which I had entirely omitted to describe, although, or possibly because, it provides a partial explanation of my behaviour that evening.

Tuesday, August 5th

I must restore that missing link, and since the recollection of it has recurred so clearly to me I must fix it in these pages before it fades or is submerged again under the pressure of other waves of events and memories.

It was a few hours before I went to the Baileys'.

The previous evening I had been with James Jenkins to the fair in the 2nd district; from the top of the Giant Wheel I had caught sight of George Burton with Harriet in the crowd; then, in front of the photographic shooting-gallery, while we examined the print which they had forgotten to collect, I had already betrayed his name, the real name of J. C. Hamilton.

A few days earlier, I had already described my first visit to the Old Cathedral in October, when I had failed to notice the Window, and when I had gone up into the tower, after having fallen flat in the mud at the feet of a girl who had then run away.

In order the better to reconstruct and describe my November visit, which I intended to write down next day, never anticipating what would happen at dinner that evening, I had gone back in the afternoon of June 1st, crossed that Cathedral Square which was once filled with a howling mob, and entered the left portal, between the prophets, through the little black lobby, reeking of dust and always damp even in the mildest weather; I had once again pushed the creaking door, padded with imitation leather.

I had never seen so clear a light in the nave, which was now silent and deserted; I spent a long time wandering round the pillars, as if I were waiting for somebody, with the guide to Bleston in my hand like a missal, before going to sit down in a pew in the transept to gaze at the Fratricide's Window, through which the sun was streaming, to gaze at Cain, so stalwart in his cuirass, and at the head of Abel lying so white in its pool of blood; I tried to elucidate its expression, but in vain, since the tiny piece of glass was too far off and, for once, was gleaming too brightly.

The effort strained my eyes, so that the leaden lines began to quiver and dissolve, the red blood began to stream thickly down from Abel's wounds to Cain's red tunic in the light below, where the Almighty brands him on the forehead.

The red blood went on streaming down like a slow downpour through the red sky above the city, behind Yabal's looms, behind Yubal's orchestra, behind the forge of Tubalcain, then it spilled out from the Window over the walls and paving stones, even over the pews, even over my hands, most of all over my hands which were covered and steeped in thick luminous redness, like a murderer's hands, as if I were condemned to murder, my hands in the centre of the pool of blood, my hands in the centre of the bloodstain spilled from the scene above, amidst the silence.

For I was all alone, the organ over the choir screen was silent, and everything was taking place in silence—ploughing, building, fratricide; the looms wove in silence, the hammers forged in silence, the musicians mimed their sounds in silence; and then suddenly I heard, above all those fettered words, above the concert of blows and brass and lamentations that was frozen into stillness in that Window, I heard the grating sound of a Police car suddenly stopping, and the screech of its siren as it drove off again; and that brief scream seemed an inevitable part of the streets of that city of dark glass.

Then I got up, and went to look through the vestry door, where there was only another priest reading his breviary, who could not possibly be any help to me; and when I went back to my seat (the sunbeams had shifted slightly) I reopened the guide to Bleston and re-read the description of the Window; and through those printed lines, through their very inadequacy, through the feeling of the difference that lay between those words and my conversation with the priest last November, I was able to reconstruct the latter with considerable precision.

But while, in the very heart of spring, that autumn day which I was trying to describe took firmer shape, there came into my mind another, rather earlier day, which I had retrieved from the shadows a few days before: the day of my first visit in October, a gloomier, rainy day, and particularly that scene on the slippery steps in front of the left portal, when I had sprawled so ridiculously in the mud in front of a girl who had suddenly emerged and who, I felt increasingly sure, must have been Rose Bailey; and I felt increasingly afraid that she might remember something of that deplorable encounter, that she might have identified me, even if only subconsciously, with that loathsome mud-stained figure, as pitiful as an epileptic in his trance, so repellent that she had instinctively taken flight; and I could not bear the thought, and felt impelled to counteract it by some word or action which would enhance my prestige in her eyes.

That was why, in our conversation that evening, when I saw her excitement at the mention of J. C. Hamilton's book, I could not let slip this chance of showing off before her, and I contrived, it's clear to me now, to have my secret dragged from me; and I was well aware that I was endangering George Burton's life (and therefore felt compelled to set down next day all that I had said), but I disregarded this, I turned murderer for the sake of Rose, whom I did not want to love, Rose who is out of my reach, who thinks only of her Lucien, Rose whom I failed to love because of Bleston and my struggle against Bleston, because of this writing of mine, this exhausting, absorbing quest which has taken up almost all my evenings ever since the beginning of May, ever since I declared war on Bleston and determined to break free of it.

It was at the end of April; Lucien was still undecided between the two sisters; I had a clear field, but I was too befogged, too paralysed to will or wish—embarrassed, moreover, by my feelings towards Ann, who had once been so indispensable to me, to whom I had almost declared my love, and from whom I had surreptitiously drifted.

It was at the end of April; not the last day of all, not the 30th, that Wednesday (the day before May 1st when I began to describe my arrival), that Wednesday when I went to Rand's the stationer's to buy these blank sheets of paper which, ever since, I have been covering with words.

How persistently Ann gazed at me from behind her counter, wondering at my new purchase, and obviously waiting for some explanation which I could in any case not have offered her, because it would have been too difficult, too complicated! But she guessed at my distress and said nothing, and I merely gave her a smile.

It was on the day before that last day of April, it was on the Tuesday when I got back here and saw the brand new cover of the map of Bleston that I had bought from Ann the previous day, Monday, lying on the table beside this copy of *The Bleston Murder*, this guidebook, this bus plan and this illustrated booklet about the New Cathedral—but without the pile of blank sheets and the pile of scribbled sheets that are there now.

Then I realised the senselessness of my action on Sunday, when I had burnt the old map which I had inevitably had to replace.

Then I decided to write in order to get things straight, to cure myself, to explain to myself what had happened to me in this hateful town, to offer some resistance to its evil spell, to shake myself awake from the torpor it instilled into me with all its rain, its bricks, its dirty children, its lifeless districts, its river and its stations, its sheds and its parks, in order not to become like those sleepwalkers who passed me in its streets, in order that the grime of Bleston should not seep into my blood, into my bones, into the crystalline lenses of my eyes; I decided to erect around me this rampart of written lines, feeling how deeply tainted I must already be to have come to such a stupid pass and to be so distressed about it, feeling how completely Bleston had outwitted my pitiful vigilance and how, in a few months of loathsome caresses, its slow poison had oozed into my brain.

Wednesday, August 6th

It was at the end of April, on a Monday, on leaving Matthews & Sons, in the Tower Street stationer's where Ann was all alone when I went in with James, just as on that first occasion in October which I began describing a few days later, so much like that earlier occasion that when I asked her for a map of Bleston she began to laugh, thinking I was affectionately teasing her by mimicking our first meeting, so that I had to convince her that I really did need a new map just like the one I had bought six months earlier, and had to lie to her since I could not tell her that I had burnt the old one, deliberately, in what now seemed to be an act of folly of which I was ashamed, which I wanted to forget.

And if I told her a lie it was not only for fear of seeming ridiculous, but in an attempt to confuse and blot out the incident in my own memory.

But the very next day, as soon as I got home and saw the map in its brand new cover, I realised that all my efforts, all my lies in that direction were vain, since the thing I was trying to play down, to disguise, to cloak with ordinariness, was here flung in my face in all its obvious absurdity, since this new map which I had been lucky enough to procure, exactly similar to what the other had been when I had bought it rather more than six months previously in the same shop, from the same Ann, with the same James Jenkins by my side, this new map which I had hoped would replace the other, would be indistinguishable from the other, would be the other for me, this new map—insolently new, never unfolded, never lugged around in a wet raincoat pocket—far from disguising the disappearance of the other only emphasised it.

I realised that the thing I had done during the night of the last Sunday in April, that profoundly irrational act, was obviously not going to let itself be submerged or extinguished, that through the new map I should always see the old map burning, and that this torment would persist so long as I should not have clarified a little the alteration I had undergone in this evil city, shaken off the cloak of ash that had settled on my life, washed the film of mud that masked my skin and come into daylight again.

I had lied to Ann in the stationer's shop; I had pretended to have lost the old map, which was not a very heinous lie apparently but which distressed me horribly because through the actual falsehood of these words I discerned the profound falsehood of my attitude towards her.

It was at the end of April; many things had changed between us three since that October day when James, who barely knew her then, had taken me into the shop and introduced me to her.

I had often seen her since; I had done my best to attract her; I had come to need her badly by the beginning of the winter, but now for a number of weeks my interest in her had been transferred to her sister, while I tried to behave with her as if nothing had altered, namely—and here the lie was blatant—as if nothing had happened, as if I had never tried to read more than friendship in her eyes.

It was at the end of April, a little over three months ago; it was the last Monday in April; I bought a map of Bleston to replace the one I had burnt the night before with great secrecy, almost with great ceremony, in a long interval of unreason, the last Sunday in April.

I had left Lucien, the seducer, Lucien Blaise, the bride-groom-to-be, Lucien Blaise to whom I had been systematically showing the town, bit by bit, glad to act as guide where I had for so long, so miserably, wandered on my own—helping, protect-ing and initiating him, thus laying the foundations for my own discomfiture—Lucien Blaise with whom I had spent a boring afternoon in Pleasance Gardens, boring because of the rain and because we had drunk too much the night before at the Burtons' and gone to bed too late; I had left Lucien after dining with him at the Town Hall restaurant.

The sky had cleared; twilight was not quite ended; people were queuing in front of the cinemas, with water still dripping from the hems of their raincoats.

I felt an impulse to walk home along the pavements, shiny and mud splashed like riding-boots; I went down Silver Street between the big shops, Grey's and Philibert's; behind the barred windows I visualised the spring dresses and sports clothes amongst great sprays of artificial flowers.

I turned right, then left, then right again, moving towards the towers of the Old Cathedral, of which I had caught a distant glimpse round some corner, glowing purple against the dark-ening greenish sky; and soon I halted, having lost my bearings, at a narrow crossroads where I had never been before (and yet this was the part of the town I knew best), the crossing of Sale Street and Guard Street; it lay deserted under the rising moon, quickly clouded over, under the weight of the darkening sky while I began to feel the cold creep up my legs and belly and weariness struck me in the back.

I went towards the lights of a pub which I made out in the distance among rows of unlit windows. Inside, it was chaos: steam and froth, old women, snatches of hummed song, soot-grimed hats.

I sat down at a round table covered with beery puddles, on which, after putting down pint after pint, I unfolded the map of Bleston which was lying in my raincoat pocket that last Sunday in April, the old map of Bleston which I had bought from Ann in October, soiled, worn at the creases: almost indecipherable in some places; the thick beer soaked into it in widening patches that crept from one district to another while I looked up the street I was in, Sale Street, much farther south than I had fancied, a much longer trek home; I felt all eyes scanning me furtively as I wiped the wet map hurriedly with my handkerchief before folding it and replacing it in my pocket next to my wallet, in which there was hardly any money—just enough to buy me one last glass of beer.

Thursday, August 7th

It was at the end of April, the last Sunday in April, late at night, and the rain was falling again.

I came up here, clinging to the stair-rail, and as the room felt very cold I lit the gas fire; the blue flames, shrilly whistling, transformed the fretted tubes of fireproof clay into a net of live embers. After I had taken off my soaking shoes and put them to dry on either side of the fire, I crouched there for a long while, motionless, without thinking of taking off my clothes, warming myself at that red glow in the heart of darkness.

I had not switched on the light; I could make out the bulb overhead by the curved gleam of reflected light, and behind me I could hear the patter of innumerable, indefatigable tiny drops against the windowpane.

Then I picked up the map of Bleston, unfolded it, held it outstretched in both hands against the firelight; through the steam that rose from it as from my garments, I could make out the pattern of the streets; then it darkened in patches, exuding a smell of smoke (the stuff of my trousers, over my knees, was scorching hot) and suddenly broke into a hem of tiny flames, which grew bigger as they spread over the whole screen, devouring it, tearing it (I felt the hot blast of the gas fire on my face) into two fragments, which shrivelled into a brittle black film (I watched the six-pointed star that marks the prison vanish) until there were only the two corners between my fingers, and these I put in my ashtray on a tiny pyre of spent matches so that they too might be consumed.

I had a dream that Sunday night, after destroying the image of this city, this old map which I was forced to replace next day, since I could not find my way about the little streets without it.

After turning off the gas, undressing in the darkness, where the three rain-lashed windowpanes could barely be made out above the bars of my bed, and the reek of burning still hung in the chilly air, I dreamed that I was having dinner at the Burtons' with Lucien, as I had done the evening before, and that Doris brought us each, for a sweet, a copy of *The Bleston Murder* soaked in rum; and that George told her to put out the light.

Then I dreamed that on each of our plates, in the darkness, the seven letters of the word Bleston grew luminous, that the rum began to flame gently, that the flames spread to the author's name, J. C. Hamilton, which glowed fierily as we all held our breaths; and then it all faded.

That last Saturday in April was the first occasion on which I had taken Lucien to dinner at the Burtons'; it was the first time he had met Harriet, and he was horribly afraid of behaving incongruously in that beautifully-furnished dining-room, since his profession made him disproportionately conscious of questions of etiquette.

He was afraid of speaking incorrectly, too, for he had only been two months in Bleston and could still not express himself fluently except in very colloquial English.

But if he practically never spoke a word during the whole meal, it was chiefly on account of the setting George had staged in order to puzzle us, and above all the two copies of *The Bleston Murder* laid side by side on the little table in their lobby opposite the coat rack, so that we should notice them as soon as we came in, and at which we could not help staring while he was introducing us to Harriet, so that she remarked to Lucien: "You've read it, I suppose?"

And George burst out laughing, revelling in our embarrassment, and told her on our behalf: "Of course! Jacques has lent it him. Did you think I'd invited illiterate guests?"

Then after the usual chat about French cooking and laments about the various restaurants in the town, after a discussion of the Oriental Bamboo where George had met the pair of us, we worked our way round to the question he had obliged us to ask ourselves, without managing to put it outright, so promptly and easily did he dodge any insinuation that was too precise.

"Do you know who J. C. Hamilton is?"

"I think I do."

"He must know Bleston very well."

"He's obviously lived here for some time."

"Do you suppose he's written other books?"

"Yes, he's clearly an experienced writer."

"But then why this particular pseudonym for one book?"

"No doubt it represents a different intention; I'm willing to bet that what he writes under other names is quite different."

He was certainly enjoying himself that Saturday, April 26th, was George Burton—from whom, a few weeks later, we were to force a confession and then to betray it: who has so narrowly escaped death: who is out of hospital now, and whom I saw again, last Saturday, in that same house at the corner of Green Park Terrace and Hatter Street, sitting, a pale convalescent, in that first-floor room whose window overlooks the trees, now wearing their full greenery; the window was shut against the driving rain that day, that horrible day of humiliation and rage and of frantic efforts to conceal these, the day of my rival's well-deserved triumph.

It was only for a few moments, fortunately, that I saw George Burton again that Saturday, August 2nd, in the early afternoon (and this time I was the one who could not speak); Lucien was there, quite unaware of the tempest he had let loose within me, Rose was there—Lucien had brought her with him on this goodbye visit, after lunching with her in the big dining-room of his hotel, no longer as a member of the staff since he had served his term—and they went off together he and Rose, on foot under the rain along Hatter Street and Diggers Street towards All Saints, to help with the preparations for that evening's party, and he had his arm round Rose, kissing and caressing her.

Friday, August 8th

Rose, whom I saw again in the evening of that horrible sultry Saturday (storm-clouds were gathering again) amidst all sorts of guests crammed together in the Baileys' little living-room bedecked with white flowers; she was wearing an unbecoming dress of mauve tulle, evidently borrowed for the occasion since she had had no time to make herself one,

Rose, who was perched on the edge of the table, which had been pushed into a corner and loaded with great rich cakes laid out on a white cloth; she sat there joking in pidgin French with her student friends while Mrs. Bailey kept severe watch over everything, particularly over Lucien's slightest word or gesture, and Ann, with a fixed lifeless smile, mechanically muttering names to which I paid no attention, introduced me to her friends and relations—to that Cousin Henry who had been mentioned in this very room at that supper-party on June 1st (then James Jenkins came in with his mother, and we went up together to speak to them), and finally to Richard Tenn, that very Richard Tenn whose house was described in *The Bleston Murder*, she told me (but I certainly had no desire to talk about George Burton and his "accident" at this engagement-party) and who proved to be a pleasant, travelled young man; in my anxiety to find out more about him I refused a kind offer from James and his mother to take me home, a long way out of their way, in the firm's black Morris; and then I overheard Richard Tenn telling a lady that he hadn't got his car with him, it was being repaired and would not be ready for several days,

Rose, who gave me such an appealing glance, as though she understood me, as though she was sorry about something (but her pity and sympathy in no way affected her joy), while she reminded me that I was invited to lunch with them next day in the big dining-room at the Grand Hotel (which I should probably have forgotten), as I said goodbye to her before rushing off after Richard Tenn, who had just left; I caught him up at the 24 bus stop in All Saints Street, under the railway bridge, just as he was mounting the bus (it was moving off and the conductor helped me climb on); I recognised the back of his head above one of the seats on the upper deck; I followed him when he got off at Town Hall Square, the terminus, and took a 27 along Silver Street (behind the darkened barred windows of Grey's and Philibert's the mannequins still sat chatting silently in their deck chairs), then along Tower Street past Matthews & Sons, along Chorley Street close to Horace Buck's house, across the Slee over Brandy Bridge (the first big raindrops flattened themselves against the windows), then beside the waste land in the 5th district, where the fair was held in June and where in early July I discovered the negative of the Burtons' photograph, now deserted under the steamy rain (this evening's paper tells of a fire in a furniture factory close by); he got off the 27 just before Ferns Park, the terminus, in a region of identical small houses, and began to run because of the rain; he was soon two hundred yards ahead of me, as though trying to escape from me, and went into his house, slamming the gate; I couldn't see which gate, or which of those three darkened houses (his room must look out the other way, for no light went on), well-to-do houses with garages—that house of which the interior is so exactly described, it seems, by J. C. Hamilton, that murderer's house, of which I couldn't be sure of the number, somewhere near No. 216 Lichen Street,

Rose, with whom I lunched next day in the big dining-room of the Grand Hotel, in company with Lucien of course—Lucien, whom all the waiters were congratulating, Lucien for whom I hailed a taxi, Lucien for whom I bought a ticket to London while they kissed each other goodbye (the sun shone through the blurred window and glinted in the puffs of steam that rose from the engine), Lucien whom we finally settled in his compartment,

Rose, who stood beside me wringing her handkerchief in her hand as she watched the train draw out,

Rose whom I saw to her doorstep (I couldn't bear to go in),

Rose who depends on me to talk to her of Lucien, to hear her talk of Lucien,

Rose who has changed so much since I first knew her, since those days in late December, since the fireworks in Pleasance Gardens, since our meals at the Sword in January, when she was the only person in the town who could talk a little French to me, since those days of thick yellow fog when you could scarcely see your own hand at midday,

Rose who has changed so much during these seven months, seven months spent feeding and growing, studying, meeting people, seven months' resistance against Bleston, crowned with the adventure of this sudden violent, straightforward passion, this betrothal to a foreigner, and my own guarded and secretive affection,

Rose, whose body has gained poise, whose voice and accent and knowledge of our tongue have deepened, whose skin and hair have brightened, whose dress has grown harmonious (except for that horrible borrowed frock on that horrible Saturday), while the same seven months have left Ann, her elder sister, far less changed, almost as I remember her in those early January days when, at the Sword, she gave me a calendar for the

New Year, saying that I'd have left her, I'd have left this frightful town before all the days inscribed on it had passed, that calendar which I put into the guidebook to Bleston which I bought at Baron's about that time, and which serves as bookmark for the page about the Tapestries—Ann, whom I was imperceptibly deserting for the sake of Rose,

Rose, who should have guessed my feelings better, who should have ensnared me,

Rose, whom I must now give up completely, for whom I must remain just a faithful patient friend, a comforter, a guardian (God, don't let her ring at my bell quite yet!) because I don't want her to be hurt,

Rose, my Persephone, my Phaedra, my Rose blossoming in this marshland, amongst its creeping miasmas—not my Rose, alas, but only Rose, out-of-reach Rose, elusive, reserved, lively, simple-hearted, tender and cruel Rose.

2

Monday, August 11th

I have used the last inch of daylight to finish re-reading my account of the second week in June, written two months ago at this very table.

The day before yesterday I read through the pages dated Monday and Tuesday, telling my conversation with Lucien on the evening of the 7th, first here, then in a 33 bus, then on the first-floor of the Oriental Bamboo, near one of the windows overlooking the façade of the Old Cathedral, when we discussed my betrayal and the way Lucien had crowned that betrayal by pointing out George Burton to the Bailey girls after I had already told them his name, all of which had so disturbed me that despite all my efforts to clear my vision from the turbid fog of Bleston I had grown even blinder.

I grew even blinder after that "accident" in Brown Street, which I took to be the direct result of my imprudent tactlessness, imagining that the culprit must be that friend of their cousin's whose house, so I'm told, is so like that of the Winn brothers in the novel—Richard Tenn, furiously resentful at having been found out; although, probably, that betrayal at the Baileys' on June 1st harmed nobody but myself, whereas that of the previous evening at the fair, in front of the shooting-gallery… But how can I believe such a thing of James, kind gentle James?

Nobody but myself can have suffered from Sunday's betrayal, since Richard Tenn's black Morris, as I discovered last night, is not black at all but grey, and the one point on which all the witnesses are agreed is that the car which ran George down in Brown Street was a black one.

This evening then, after watching a documentary on San Francisco at the News Theatre and dining at the Oriental Rose, sitting once more at my table I went on reading the notes I had written in the second week in June, which dip suddenly back into November after dealing with my talk with Lucien on the Saturday, and make no mention of Sunday, June 8th, or of the other talk I had then, this time with James Jenkins, whose attitude towards me was so changed, and in the Museum this time, a talk about the Tapestries; I only remembered it while reading, because of the obvious influence it had had on the structure of my account, on the way it jumped from the last dinner in that Chinese restaurant to the first, seven months earlier, through the intermediary of that unchanging figure, the waiter—the little plump yellow-skinned waiter with the unvarying half-smile on his lips.

I used the last inch of daylight to read the pages about that dinner at the Oriental Bamboo with James, nine months ago, when we had already discussed J. C. Hamilton and his book, the pages about Guy Fawkes' Day, those about Mrs. Jenkins' strange behaviour when the New Cathedral was mentioned, and finally those about my second meeting with Horace Buck, all the sheets of paper on which I had scribbled during the second week in June; then I rose to turn on the light, for night, which encroaches a little more each evening, had already almost fallen, and then, only then, I began to write.

Tuesday, August 12th

On the afternoon of Sunday, June 1st, while preparing the account of my discovery of the Murderer's Window in November, I had gone back to look at the Old Cathedral once more; on the Monday and Tuesday I had described that conversation at the Baileys' during which, for the second time in two days, I had betrayed the name of J. C. Hamilton; and when, after this interruption, I resumed my account of last autumn's happenings, I remembered that it was before going to look for that Window described in the opening sentence of *The Bleston Murder* that I had paid my first visit to the Museum, had stood for the first time before the Harrey Tapestries; it had been the previous day, while waiting for the photographer to develop those little portraits of myself required for the Police register, one copy of which I still possess, duly stamped and stuck on to the alien's identity card which they gave me that day.

It was the effort required to describe this visit which aroused my longing to re-examine those splendid woven panels, although I had seen them again not so long ago, barely a month before, on Sunday, May 11th, with Lucien, before going to tea with the Burtons: a longing which I could not have satisfied on Saturday, June 7th, because I wanted to come back here as quickly as possible to finish my account of the week I was dealing with, including the priest's comments on Cain's Window in the Old Cathedral: a longing which proved quite opportune on the Sunday, since James and I, at the Bombay restaurant in City Street, did not know what to say to one another; we did not want to talk about the fair, nor about *The Bleston Murder*, nor the New Cathedral, all topics which obsessed both of us, which put so painful a barrier between us; so that it was almost a relief for him when I asked him if it would bore him to come with me to the Museum, which was close by; he knew it already, of course, but he had not been there for a long time, so he told me; and there, once again, he surprised me by his penetration, pointing out an essential aspect of the tapestries which had escaped me, namely that they nearly all represent not single incidents but actions of some duration, so that a single panel comprises several scenes in succession; thus the same figure appears two or three times in No. 15, "The descent into Hades" (Theseus and Pirithous on the left, in front of the cleft leading into the underworld, Theseus and Pirithous in the centre, climbing up

the steps of the throne to carry off Persephone, and the same
Theseus and Pirithous on the right, chained, in a cave within
that cave) and furthermore, which is even more striking, the
same figure appears in incidents obviously several years apart, as
in No. 1, "Childhood of Theseus", which had hitherto puzzled
me (on the left, in the middle of the city square which reappears,
on a larger scale, in No. 6, "Theseus recognised by his father",
No. 7, "Theseus slaying the Pallantides", and No. 14, "Theseus
King of Athens", we see Aegeus seated on the throne while by
his side stands Medea driving out a woman with veiled face and
naked breast who runs towards an old man seated in a grotto on
the right, to whom she is holding out the infant she carries in one
arm, while with her free hand she trails a long girdle of which
one end still lies at the feet of the king; the old man on the right
is looking not at her but at an adolescent Theseus who seems
to be taking leave of him and of the woman, thanking them,
binding on the long girdle to which is fastened the dagger which
is to be his inseparable weapon, with which he will slay Sinis,
Sciron, Cercyon, Procrustes, the Pallantides and the Minotaur—
the brilliant, ornate, unmistakable dagger at which Aegeus, in
No. 6, points with such amazement, convinced that the young
stranger to whom he was about to offer a poisoned drink on
Medea's advice is his long-lost son: the dagger which thus saves
Theseus' life and which eventually brings him to the throne),

No. 1, "The Childhood of Theseus", which had hitherto
baffled me most of all, but of which James Jenkins offered me
the first satisfactory commentary, analysing the whole thing
into its three principal moments (first, Aegeus taking a new
wife, and the repudiated queen fleeing with her child; then,
these two taking refuge with Pittheus; finally, the infant, grown
to young manhood, leaving his guardian and his mother, who
arms him with that murderous weapon once stolen for his
sake, that dagger which is the proof of his identity, of his birth),
explaining the real significance of that female figure whose
flight represents not a single moment but a whole long story,

a growth and a slow alteration—the figure of Aethra, whose flight spans whole years.

James Jenkins, who is an incomparable expert on certain of Bleston's secrets, pointed out this essential aspect of the Tapestries which had escaped me, reading them out to me, explaining them almost all, to the very last: Theseus in exile dying at Scyros while the city of Athens is seen in flames in the distance. Then we went out again on to the damp pavements of the Square, kissed by the mild June sun as it broke through clouds after the rain, and once again we had nothing to say to one another, nowhere to go together, and we felt so ill at ease that he suddenly pretexted anxiety about his mother's health; and so we went along City Street to the 23 bus stop in Town Hall Square, since he had not brought the firm's black Morris that day; and so we passed in front of the Amusements Arcade, between the Police Station and the Royal Cinema; it was closed, even more definitely than on other Sundays, since the iron blind bore a small handwritten notice saying it would reopen on June 16th;

and so I asked James if he knew why it was closed for so long, and he replied that of course he didn't, but he thought he remembered hearing something about a fire, though perhaps he was imagining this through hearing so much talk about the fire at the fairground in the 5th district, where he had been the day before, where one of the booths had been destroyed on the last evening in May,

all of which he started telling me almost against his will, obviously vexed with me for obliging him, by my question, to broach a subject—the fair—which he had hitherto succeeded in avoiding, but which was tormenting him; the more so that, presumably, he had gone back to the shooting-gallery to look once again at George Burton's self-portrait, the negative of which I picked up on that very fairground in early July; he was so obviously vexed with me indeed that when a 23 bus arrived he left me almost without saying goodbye.

Wednesday, August 13th

Now I knew one person who frequented the Amusements Arcade and could certainly tell me what had happened— Horace Buck, whom I'd met there on that horrible Christmas Day (for although it is closed on Sundays it stays open on public holidays) and whom I had not seen for over a month, not since that Saturday in April when I had taken Lucien to visit him, the same Saturday that Lucien and I had lunched in the Chinese restaurant opposite the Old Cathedral, where we had met George Burton; and I was anxious for news of Horace Buck.

He greeted me at first with his usual torrent of quaint, plaintive abuse, accusing me of having dropped him—although actually my visit must have disturbed him, for he was with Katie, who was putting on her little black shoes again when I came in; then he offered me a great glass of rum as usual.

"The Amusements Arcade? Not open yet? Oh, it happened several weeks ago… yes, a small fire; there was a sort of game of skittles, you know, a set of stuffed dummies with wooden heads all in a row, a parson in a dog-collar, a policeman in a helmet, a judge in a wig, a professor in a square cap, a Salvation Army lass in a bonnet, a peer in a coronet, an old lady in a flowered hat; you hit them with balls stuffed with sawdust and knock them over backwards onto the floor; well, it was all that junk that burned, sawdust and old rags and old wooden heads—you can guess how easily it caught; that was all, but as the fire had made an awful mess of the wall behind and the ceiling above, they decided to clean up the whole place and give it a coat of paint, and about time too! It was really filthy."

"And does nobody know how the fire started?"

"Why, Monsieur, what with their machines that don't work, and go out of order as soon as you touch them, and blow up in your hands as soon as you're starting to win a bit, the wonder is that it didn't all catch fire sooner; it may have been a fag-end chucked on to one of those heaps of paper lying about on the floor, there may even have been a new box of matches thrown away by mistake... You know, whoever did it, even if he did it on purpose (I don't mean really intentionally, but when he saw the first puff of smoke rising and the sawdust beginning to glow red round it, instead of putting out the fire he just let it be, you see what I mean?) I'd like to congratulate him, because now maybe it won't be quite so scruffy when it reopens."

I hadn't seen him since Saturday, April 19th, when I had taken Lucien to supper there (Katie had gone out for some reason but had left a meal ready) and Lucien, who had been very keen to meet this queer character of whom he'd often heard me speak, did not find him at all amusing when they actually met, but rather terrifying; he was overcome with a sort of instinctive dread, of unease, aversion and mistrust, in spite of all his efforts and all Horace's efforts too—poor Horace being equally mistrustful, uneasy, stiff and shame-faced and unable to conceal his antipathy, his secret resentment and disappointment.

I had not seen him since Saturday, April 19th, when the three of us had sat in weary, bored silence, eating our oranges, watching one another, while I sought in vain for something to say that would ease the situation, that would disperse the harsh prickly fog that thickened between them irremediably; and then we had all three gone, as planned, to the fair, which struck me as drearier, gloomier, more futile than ever before or since: the fair of which they were both so fond, but which could not bridge the gap between them, under the murky sky, laden with damp coal-dust, that cold spring night; it was in the north-west then in the 1st district, between Oak Park and the smart Jewish quarter; I know it was April 19th because it was the same day at lunchtime that George Burton invited Lucien and myself to visit him a week later, the last Saturday in April, the eve of that Sunday when, sick to death of my own degradation, I burned the map of Bleston.

It was that day, Saturday, April 19th, just as Lucien and I had finished our sweet biscuits and drunk our last cup of green tea in the first-floor room of the Oriental Bamboo, at the same table close to the window overlooking the front of the Old Cathedral, watched by the same plump yellow-skinned waiter who sat in the far corner wearing the same half-smile as on the occasion of that dinner in November with James, when we'd talked about *The Bleston Murder*; or that other dinner in June with Lucien, when we'd talked about J. C. Hamilton and the Bailey girls; or that lunchtime in winter, the date of which I shall find if I go on hunting, when I had met George Burton for the first time, when he had spoken to me on noticing the copy of his book, the second-hand Penguin I had just bought, lying beside me; or that lunch last Saturday with Rose (oh, why did she come so soon to torture me?) when we talked about nothing but her Lucien; it was that day, Saturday, April 19th, as we finished our meal and got up to leave, that this man, George Burton, who has so narrowly escaped death and is not yet quite recovered, this man whom we had not yet thought of as J. C. Hamilton, George Burton in his full health and spirits, George Burton in all his splendour came into the room, came up to us, and burst out laughing as he saw on our tablecloth the copy of *The Bleston Murder* which now lies on the left-hand corner of my table—the book of which we did not yet know that he was the author—the copy which I had brought for Lucien and which lay beside his plate as it had lain beside mine on that earlier occasion; he burst into a great sudden shout of laughter.

That was the day on which he began to set the stage to bamboozle us still further, Lucien and myself—Lucien who is free and happy, and myself, Lucien the bridegroom-to-be, the lover, the beloved, and myself, Lucien who is in the best of health and spirits, who writes long letters to his Rose, who wants nothing but his Rose, and myself.

Thursday, August 14th

Rose, why did you come so soon to torture me, to reopen that wound which was beginning to heal, which must heal, which is healing but so slowly, so painfully, because of you?

Rose, why did you bring me that half-day of torment, on Saturday, with your smile, your beauty, your happiness, your delicious way of speaking French, the pleasure your presence gave me and which I could no longer accept?

Why did you condemn me to renewed renunciation?

Every time I looked at you my eyes could not help dwelling on, seeking out the curves of your body under your summer dress.

Why did you come and take me by surprise as I was leaving Matthews & Sons, to ask if I would lunch with you and keep you company on a few errands?

Why, oh why, did you accept when I offered to take you to the fair in the 11th district?

I knew only too well that in the end you would forsake me, leaving me even more desolate than before.

Why, when it was Ann that I wanted to see, for she would have been gentle, would have comforted me—Ann that I needed to see, that I needed to talk to, so as to find out what her feelings for me still were, whether she could possibly forgive me—why did you come and tell me that Ann was not at home, that she was having lunch with some friend, you didn't know who, that she had suggested your going with her but that you hadn't even listened, choosing rather to seek me out in order to hear whether I'd had any news of Lucien?

No, I'd none! What did I care about Lucien now that he had got away from Bleston, taking with him your promise, and would later come back to take the whole of you, your flesh and your voice?

Why did you come to read me the first letters you'd had from him, with those repeated vows of affection and the tale of his successful journey?

Why did you come to blind me once again to Ann's beauty, less dazzling than your own and thus fitter for me, who am unworthy of you, that graver beauty from which yours had once before distracted me?

I should like to grasp those two days, that Saturday and Sunday, to transcribe them completely, spread them out on paper in order to read them, in order that they may become transparent in the light of all the phosphorescences I have dredged up from past months—those two days, the only days of my week that I have really lived, the others being consumed by dusty toil at Matthews & Sons and the necessary drudgery of my writing—in order to understand them, to understand myself, before it's too late, before things have taken their course without my will.

I feel all around me the threads of the warp flooding into the weft; soon tiny hands will be caught up in the cloth and I myself, imprisoned within the loom, unable to find the lever to move in order to change the pattern.

It is dark night already; it is already Thursday; tomorrow, Friday, is all I have left of the escaping week to bring up to the surface those events of last January which lie sleeping seven months deep, as those of October had been when I fished them up and related them in May; I had hoped to reduce the seven months' gap, but I have barely been able to prevent if from widening, so many shadows and consequences, so many accidents and ghosts have come between—while the stream, seven months deep, has grown ever more turbid under the stress of my agitation.

I must be finished with these two days by tonight, and I will not go to bed before having reached that point on the Sunday when I went to bed, before having written: "And so I went to bed" (the time is running on; if I don't sleep enough tonight, I shall pay for it tomorrow night); and so I cannot linger in description of that painful talk with Rose, that painful meal at the Oriental Bamboo, that painful expedition in search of a scarf which we found at last in Bleston's smartest shop, Minton's in City Street, that painful visit to the Museum as we made our way back to Town Hall Square ("Won't you show me your beloved tapestries?", but how could I tell her about Phaedra and Ariadne? and yet she was so delightful, so intelligent, so attentive and ready to love them!), that painful walk round the fair in the 11th district, while the Slee glittered in the lovely summer sunshine, that goodbye, that last smile from her as she climbed on to a 24 bus to go back to All Saints Gardens; nor tell how I got drunk pub-crawling with Horace Buck, whose Katie was neglecting him increasingly, nor how I sat late into the night re-reading what I had written on the first two days of the second week in June about my talk with Lucien (the inevitable Lucien) at the Oriental Bamboo on the preceding Saturday.

And so I must come without delay (the time is running on) to the Sunday afternoon, when I was in the house in Green Park Terrace, where Harriet was smiling again, in the first-floor room where the sun came in through the open window together with the smell of the trees and the murmur from the crowds swarming along the walks, sprawling on the lawns, slumped on the benches, where the sun lay in pools of shifting light on the sheets, and George, sitting up quietly and seemingly recovered, said to me:

"It's all over; I've had a narrow shave; I shall be careful from now on when I cross the streets."

We were joking about it as we had tea, when his gaze suddenly began to follow a fly wheeling about in the sunbeams, to follow it so attentively that he fell silent, as did Harriet soon after, and then I myself, so that nothing could be heard but the buzz of the fly and that of the Sunday crowd in the park, with the sough of the wind in the tall pines, and then suddenly he sat erect, overturning his tray and his cup so that the little spoon tinkled to the ground and the spilt tea made a great dripping stain on the white sheet; then he fell back against his pillow, panting, twisting his head right and left with his eyes half closed and his hands over his face as though to protect it, plaintively murmuring to Harriet who had quickly risen and bent over him:

"Can't you drive it away?"

While I stood still holding my cup of tea she chased the fly, trying to crush it, finally driving it out through the window, which she then closed so that we no longer heard the buzz of the fly nor that of the crowd in the park nor the wind in the great pines, nothing but George's breathing which grew steadier as he calmed down.

"Sorry about that."

"Would you like another cup of tea?"

"I'll be going now."

"No, Jacques, wait a minute longer, come close to me, I want to ask you a question. They say it was an accident, I told you it was an accident, but don't you really think, Jacques, as I do, that it may have been something else? What do you know about it, Jacques? I can see in your eyes that you don't want to answer."

"Whatever are you thinking of? What could I know? What could I be hiding from you? I wasn't in Brown Street on Friday, July 11th, at half-past six; I saw nothing; I've been trying to find things out, I still am…"

"You've been trying to find things out?"

"Without success; there's probably nothing to be found out."

"Jacques, I've been watching you ever since that day. Why won't you trust me? Believe me, whatever you may have done you needn't be afraid…"

"What are you trying to make me say? If anybody knows what happened that day it must be you, surely, Barnaby Morton…"

"Don't say that!"

"You've guessed everything, of course… Please forgive me."

"Calm yourself, Jacques, what's the matter? I've guessed nothing yet, I have only my suspicions, my unfounded fancies. Why won't you help me? Don't you find the game amusing? But why d'you look like that? Of course it was only an accident;

everyone said so, I said so… Now forgive me; don't let's talk about it; oh, I'm feeling rather tired now. Glad to have seen you, Jacques. Any news of Lucien? I was so touched by his visit. The girl seems delightful; Bailey, did you say? And haven't you found one for yourself? Come back and see us soon."

I am sure he meant that Richard Tenn whom I too had thought of as guilty, but that's impossible since Tenn's Morris is grey, as I discovered that very evening (I was bent on getting things clear); I prowled about Lichen Street, in that horrible 5th district, near those three somewhat larger and more comfortable houses—I didn't yet know which of the three was the right one—amongst all those cramped dwellings with wretched little gardens; I prowled about there for hours 'til night fell, waiting for him to come home or go out, and at last I saw him drive up in his car, which is indubitably grey and not black; he got out of it with several women; I was able to look closely at it by the light of the street-lamp opposite, while he opened his gate and his garage; I wasn't afraid of being noticed or recognised because he had obviously not taken the least notice of me at the Baileys' party the week before. It's a car just like the one belonging to Matthews & Sons, which James drives and looks after, except that it is grey, with some old scratches (perhaps George knew that this Richard had a Morris but was not sure of the colour?), grey (but that doesn't settle the question, it doesn't free me from responsibility, since James… Oh, but I cannot believe that James…), grey.

Then I came home, and I went to bed.

Friday, August 15th

I went to lunch by myself in that restaurant in Grey Street where I used to lunch every weekday with Ann at the beginning of the winter, right up to the middle of February, all through the thick fogs—Ann, who helped me so much to endure Bleston, in the days when Rose was only her charming little sister; I went to the stationer's after work to see her, but there were a crowd of customers, so that I had to wait beside James, who had come in close on my heels, until each of them had been served with notebooks or pencils or maps of Bleston.

"Well, Jacques," she said to me, "shall we see you tomorrow evening?"

I had forgotten the invitation that Rose had given me on Saturday, amid all the tumultuous feelings she had aroused in me.

So then I shall see them both together; we shall still talk about nothing but Lucien's letters, and I shall still be unable to speak to Ann of my loneliness and my need.

I could not snatch a single moment's private conversation with her, because James never left our side but came with us as far as the 24 bus stop on Town Hall Square, where the rain began falling on to the asphalt which had been soaking up heat all of that sultry day, and the air was full of the smells from factories and restaurant kitchens and the trains leaving or nearing Hamilton Station, and all the crowded traffic.

O Bleston, city of smoke, when we passed by the chemist's shop I read on the poster of the *Evening News* that a paint-store had been on fire close to the prison, in the 9th district; Bleston, how dark and implacable and noisome are your flames!

The light, now, is what it was at three o'clock on a January afternoon (we kept the lights on all day then at Matthews & Sons); I stare at the grey sky and the rain beating against my windows, as dark as the melting snow was then; the colour has gone out of things; on my table I can only make out the pages as paler rectangles and the written lines as faint streaks at which I must peer closely to read them; I can't go on without my lamp.

O my Ann, the Ann I knew in January, Ann who was so close to me then, whom I forsook for Rose, so furtively, trying to efface all that had been between us, to pretend there had never been anything but friendship between us, Ann whom I shall see tomorrow but in vain, since I shall never reach her with my cry of distress, my prayer for help which she might grant if only my folly has not driven her from me irreparably, if my wretched cunning has not been too ironically successful, Ann to whom I so long to speak today, after leaving her question unanswered for more than three months, to whom I so long to explain why, at the end of April, I bought from her a second map of Bleston and this ream of paper on which I am still scribbling.

I shall not sit writing much longer tonight in the yellow lamplight, by the blue rain-lashed window, listening to the distant rumble of thunder, for I feel drowsiness overtaking me, numbing my hand as it struggles on, my sticky sweating hand.

Ann with whom I lunched every weekday at the Sword, even on Saturdays sometimes, such as that first Saturday in January when Rose was there too, since her term had not begun, Rose who led me through the fog and the first flakes of dirty Bleston snow to see the University, its laboratories and its library and its Natural History Museum with stuffed animals and wretched drooping flowers in labelled glass vases.

This is the scattered flotsam of that first weekend in January, all that I can salvage without long research, without the research I should undertake but which will be henceforward increasingly difficult, as the silt of time thickens; but may these fragments at least not be swept away by the waves!

Ann, I had asked you to bring me back *The Bleston Murder*, and you apologised, saying that your mother was still reading it, to which of course I replied that it didn't matter; you never returned it, although you claimed to have done so until that Sunday, June 1st, when I saw it in your hands once more, and was so upset by this; Ann, I have tried to call you up amidst the January fogs (I can hardly see you) but my voice is buried under the melting snow falling on to the innumerable streams of that great fen, Bleston, snow, storm, but my voice fades away, stifled by the storm, Oh Ann...

I sat for a long time without writing, with my eyes closed, and if I still linger here, at this table, before this sheet of paper, beside this window to which the melting snow and the January fogs once clung, it is because I am reluctant to admit that any attempt to pursue this exploration is vain tonight, and that I must drag my pen from the page over which it is crawling, must rise and undress, put out my light and sleep.

3

Monday, August 18th

On leaving Matthews & Sons I went past the Burlington restaurant, past the chemist's, past the man selling the *Evening
News*, past Rand's Stationery, Ann's shop, which always closes
early on Mondays; I went along Silver Street as far as Town Hall
Square; I threaded my way through the crowd coming out of
Grey's and Philibert's; I went past the Police Station, past the
Amusements Arcade, where Horace Buck had started a fire in
mid-May, reopened and more or less redecorated since June
16th with a fresh game of skittles, fresh puppets' heads (already
a trifle shabby) but the same old worn-out apparatus, guns and
billiards and "bear hunts"; I went past the Royal Cinema and
the Chinese restaurant, the Oriental Rose; I threaded my way
through the crowd coming out of Modern Stores; I went into
the News Theatre to see the film about the ruins of Rome (next
week Athens, last week San Francisco) and there, as the screen
displayed the Italian sky, the azure sky of Crete reappeared
before my eyes; behind the Roman stones and paintings there
reappeared those of Minos' Palace, all the images that I had
seen there on Monday, June 16th, all those images and that
blueness that had been so refreshing and revivifying that I had
gone back to see them again next day, all those images which
I had described on my return (I re-read the description only last
night) so as to make sure of recovering them: the courtyards
carpeted with fine grass surrounded by stairs of gypsum and
alabaster, the bulls' horns on the esplanade, the pavements in
whose countless cracks anemones grow, under the deep clear

dome of the sky, unclouded and unstreaked, the azure of the Cretan sky reviving unaltered in the azure of the Roman sky, above the Imperial ruins enclosed within the living town, the Renaissance town and the Baroque town.

The days are drawing in now, the weather is breaking up, but there will still be many bright hours before I go, bright hours such as I was unable to enjoy in October, when I felt crushed by the unfamiliar desolation on which they shone.

On leaving Matthews & Sons I went, as I do every Monday now, to the News Theatre, then, crossing Town Hall Square in the gathering darkness, I dined in the first-floor room of the Oriental Rose, from which I watched the last red gleams fading behind the ridiculous crenellated towers of the municipal building; I took a 27 bus as far as the Chorley Street stop; I turned on my light as soon as I came in here and I finished reading what I had written during the third week in June: the afternoon of Sunday, June 15th, spent at the fair in the 5th district with Lucien, Ann and Rose, where I had seen yet again, on the counter of the photographic shooting-gallery, the portrait of George and Harriet Burton (but I was careful to avoid drawing my companions' attention to it, dreading any conversation on that subject): the evening of Saturday, November 17th, spent at the fair in the 9th district with Horace Buck: my discovery of this room, thanks to him, that same afternoon, and my removal here next day, followed by my first visit to the New Cathedral on Sunday afternoon.

But I read no account of the visit I had paid alone to Pleasance Gardens on Saturday, June 14th, because I had written none, probably through shamefaced unwillingness to admit my own feelings.

If I had not felt deeply involved, responsible, should I have gone to that great stationary fairground for the sole purpose of staring at the ruins of the Giant Wheel which had blazed away there a few nights earlier—for that sole purpose, since I went into none of the booths, wandered nowhere, never set foot in the precincts of the Zoo? Should I have determined to see for myself what damage had been done as soon as I saw on the *Evening News* poster: "Fire at Pleasance Gardens"? Should I have read the article so eagerly, and felt such relief on reading that there had been no victim?

I had just learnt, a few days earlier, of the fire which had destroyed one of the booths at the fair during the night of May 31st – June 1st, and of the tiny one which had defaced the Amusements Arcade in mid-May; I felt the conflagration growing, spreading over the town; I felt it with intensive vindictive satisfaction; I have felt it ever since, welcoming the news of each new fire in any quarter of the town.

I read no account of that expedition to Pleasance Gardens, so closely linked in my mind not only to my destruction of the map of Bleston but also to another, earlier act of destruction which prefigured it—a tiny, apparently insignificant destruction which recurred forcibly to my mind as I left the enclosure and handed in my ticket.

Tuesday, August 19th

As we wandered, Lucien and I, amidst the crowd, which thinned out the farther we advanced between the wretched wild beasts' pens, away from the huge entrance gate with its towers of dirty stucco surmounted by half-moons of yellow painted iron, one Sunday in April, I noticed on the ground, in some remote alley, one of those rectangles of grey perforated cardboard inscribed on one side "Pleasance Gardens" and on the other "remember…" etc., one of those permits which have to be handed in on leaving (the poor wretch who lost this one must have had to pay a heavy fine); I picked it up and examined it, and saw that it was dated for the previous day or the day before that, I can't remember which.

In a remote, unfrequented alley I lit a match and set fire to the card, explaining to puzzled Lucien: "It had escaped its fellows' fate, but things are all square now."

This must have been one Sunday in April, for it was the previous day, at the Royal Cinema, during the afternoon (and therefore, of course, a Saturday) that we had decided to go there, while we sat half-heartedly watching a picture called *The Red Nights of Rome*.

In those days I went far oftener to see films, although I saw them blurred through the foggy atmosphere of Bleston, since they at least provided me with a topic of conversation and a butt for sarcasm; I was at a loose end all April, not being as yet absorbed by my present task, not standing as yet upon the solid ground which, page by page, grows firmer and helps me grow firmer, but sinking deeper daily into the mire, nearing the level of complete absorption and asphyxia, drifting daily further from Ann and yet afraid to draw nearer to Rose, upheld only by my hatred, that hatred which I needed to salvage and strengthen by some act, my hatred which sought relief in that minute act of destruction, which gained some relief when I burned the map of Bleston, and for which I now provide relief, laboriously and unremittingly, by my writing.

This film was a sort of *Quo Vadis*, a giant production in Technicolour with martyrs, wild beasts, bathing beauties, and of course with huge flames devouring cardboard dwellings, shedding the red glow of destruction on the clouds; and last night, in the News Theatre, it intruded surreptitiously between the blue of the flawless Italian sky evoked for us by the camera and the identical blue of the Cretan sky; and while the arcades of the Colosseum were displayed before us, not only did I glimpse among them the bulls of Knossos charging, but furthermore, between the bright splendour of their vanished newness, the splendour of their inaugural day, and their present decay, held in check by restoration, I glimpsed the red glow of destruction reflected in the clouds, the glare from the fires of the last sacrificial games and the invasions; it intruded surreptitiously last night, in the News Theatre, beneath that blue of the sky shown on the screen, that blue which, to be sure, first recalled a definite moment of the recent past when the operators, in Italy or in Crete, had caught it on their film, but which, above all, sent one back to a far more distant, more extensive past, almost effacing the later moment in the spectators' minds, that blue which sent us back to the period when these monuments were cities and not ruins, the blue of that sky which proclaimed its permanence, its continuity with the sky that spread, pure, beneficent and immense, when these palaces and these temples were new.

On Saturday afternoon in April, at the Royal Cinema, Lucien and I sat half-heartedly watching that long ridiculous picture, with its patently artificial red clouds, obviously manufactured on purpose to be shown at a huge profit to thousands of sleepy spectators like ourselves, those sham red clouds, as red as the glass sky above Cain's city in the Old Cathedral, the product of a wicked speculation on the besotted condition of all those who, like ourselves, were caught in the tolls of such gigantic insidious crawling towns as Bleston; but also, as I began to realise yesterday at the News Theatre while their crimson glow pervaded my vision, these make-believe red clouds were mirrors, poor crude mirrors, dim and tarnished, blurred and dulled, through which, nevertheless, there reached us the reflected glare of a whole series of fires, the long-drawn out intermittent red glare of ancient times, the shrieks, the smoke, the crackle of flames, which separated that city whose ruins lie on the Palatine from the Roman palaces still standing.

That Saturday afternoon in April, we had gone to the Royal Cinema with the express purpose of having a laugh, and to be sure we found ample matter for mockery in that shocking idiotic film, *The Red Nights of Rome*; yet we somehow felt through all its bogus trickery something else, the power of fire, the lure of fire, so that I can remember when I came out into Town Hall Square its brick walls seemed to me like painted sets on flimsy canvas that could easily be set ablaze; it must have been Saturday, April 12th, for that was the day I had taken Lucien for the first time to lunch in the first-floor room of the Oriental

Bamboo, opposite the Old Cathedral—a week before Saturday, April 19th, when George Burton met us there and invited us to visit him the following Saturday, and thus a fortnight before that last Saturday in April when, at his home, he had intrigued us so by displaying those two copies of *The Bleston Murder*, fifteen days before that Sunday night when I burned the map of the town, so that next day I had to buy a new one from Ann (Ann whom I thought I no longer loved, whom I tried to convince that I had never loved her, which was surely impossible, which I hope was impossible); fifteen days before that Sunday night when I burned the map of the town, a fresh copy of which I found two days later, Tuesday, on my table, so new, so loudly proclaiming the other's destruction that on the Wednesday I went and bought from Ann, without being able or willing to tell her why, these sheets of paper on which I began to write these notes on May 1st; it was Saturday afternoon, April 12th, after taking Lucien for the first time to lunch in the Chinese restaurant opposite the Old Cathedral, at the very table beside the window where one day last winter I had made the acquaintance of George William Burton, and where during dinner one November evening I had mentioned *The Bleston Murder* for the first time to James Jenkins.

While we were eating our meal at the Oriental Bamboo, that second Saturday in April, Lucien asked me who was that George Burton to whom I had introduced him the week before as we came out of a different cinema, and I told him as much as I knew—how I had met him in that very place about two months earlier, how he had come to sit at this table, how the conversation had turned on a book I had laid beside me, *The Bleston Murder* by J. C. Hamilton, of which I had just bought a second-hand copy, a book which had been my guide in the early days of my stay here, and thanks to which I had discovered this very restaurant: a book which I could lend Lucien if he liked; in fact I brought it along to give him in Pleasance Gardens next day, that's to say Sunday, April 13th, and he returned it to me the following Saturday, April 19th, at this same table where George Burton saw him again, this same table where one evening in June, Lucien and I talked about J. C. Hamilton and the Bailey girls, about Rose to whom he is now engaged, Rose with whom I had dinner at this very table ten days ago, and Ann with whom I should be so happy to have a meal one of these days at this same table, because I feel that this is where I could most easily tell her about the writing that I began because I had burned the map of Bleston I'd bought from her so long ago, in October, the first time I saw her, because I had burned the map of Bleston—an action prefigured by my destruction of the Pleasance Gardens ticket one Sunday in April, the second Sunday in April, April 13th, since it was the day before that, Saturday, April 12th, that Lucien and I had been to the Royal Cinema to see *The Red Nights of Rome* and talked about *The Bleston Murder* in the Chinese restaurant opposite the Old Cathedral under the benevolent reptilian eye of the plump yellow-skinned waiter.

Wednesday, August 20th

That Saturday, April 12th, as we had time to kill between the end of our lunch at the Oriental Bamboo and the next programme at the Royal Cinema at half-past three, we went on foot, in spite of the rain, as far as Town Hall Square, passing the New Cathedral which Lucien had not yet seen (it was only just over a month since his arrival in Bleston and our first meeting); and so when I went back by myself into that great chilly nave four days ago, last Saturday, August 16th, after lunching by myself at the Oriental Pearl at the corner of White Street, my thoughts full of Ann Bailey whom I was to meet that evening, only in Rose's presence so that I knew I should not have a single moment alone with her, my thoughts full of Ann, of Rose, and hence of Lucien, I remembered my visit with him in April, not so much what we had done or seen inside as the look of the Square that rainy day as we crossed it, particularly the look of the concrete framework for Bleston's big new store; four days ago the sun was shining on its appalling façade, almost completed, behind palings on which I read the announcement of its opening in just under three months' time, in early November, when I shall have gone: a ten-storey building, not quite as tall as the spire but rising high above the nave and henceforward dwarfing everything else in the Square, a fact which I had not noticed in April because then there was only its delicate skeleton soaring up in the grey air like a great musical promise, now immured and lost, ten storeys of counters and cash desks and storerooms, a new commercial pole intruding into the life of all Bleston's inhabitants, distorting the entire city, bringing busy traffic into the neighbouring streets, depriving Town Hall Square of its monopoly as shopping centre for the poorer districts, so that Saturday expeditions will take quite a different course.

Four days ago, on August 16th, that sunlit façade so loudly proclaiming its newness made me almost forget the older building which I had meant to visit once again, and which I entered only for a few moments, unable to concentrate on anything, on the flies round the Virgin's statue or the crossed screens or the great tortoise on the Reptiles' Capital, because I could not help seeing through the tall colourless windows that huge wall of gleaming bricks, too sure a proof of the evil city's vitality, a token of change cancelling all hope of genuine change, that façade that seemed to tell me:

"You'd be glad of my death, Jacques Revel, but see this new hydra-head of mine, how strong it is, how hard to strike off; on this vast carapace all the embers you can collect will leave but the tiniest scorch-mark! I am Bleston, Jacques Revel; I endure, I am tenacious; and if some of my houses fall down, don't let that persuade you that I myself am crumbling into ruins, that I'm ready to make way for that other city of your feeble dreams, those dreams that through my power have grown so thin, so obscure, so formless and impotent—maybe you fancied last April that the framework hidden within these walls foreshadowed that dream-city? But my cells reproduce themselves, my wounds heal; I do not change, I do not die, I endure, my permanence swallows up all attempted innovation; this new first sign of my contamination by that imaginary city which my enemies contrast with me, although they can never describe it; no, no, this is the present face of an old, though not an ancient, city, a city that some call doomed; look at me, Jacques Revel, nothing has made me retreat, look at my newness, you who hate me so violently, you who were banking on my decrepitude, who reckoned the time 'til I should decay and abdicate, you who in your dreams scattered my ashes to the winds, you must start your reckoning afresh, and not even from today, but from the time when I shall be rid of you, vermin, since the great store at which you're already gazing which already overpowers you and overwhelms you, will not be finished until then; no hope, Jacques Revel, all the might is on my side, haven't you experienced it enough yet? You nearly brought about the death of your accomplice George Burton; you lost your love Rose through your own fault, and through your own fault your longed-for Ann has forgotten you; give it up, wretched little Jacques Revel, give up your attempt to awaken and to escape your doom of dust and attrition; go to sleep, close those aching eyes, give it up, sleep."

It only increased my hatred and strengthened my resolve to carry on, and I remembered the fine lines of the framework now enclosed in that horrible sheath of bricks, as I'd seen it in April in the rain behind the great palings, covered with ironical posters urging me to escape: "Go by Air", "See Europe", as if one could possibly escape; behind those great palings already covered with rain-soaked travel posters in April, which had aroused our rancour and our sarcasm as we passed, Lucien and I, on our way from the Oriental Bamboo to the Royal Cinema, through New Cathedral Square—new posters on the top of old posters, several layers of posters glimpsed through the rents in the most recent ones.

Thursday, August 21st

Last Saturday, August 16th, five days ago, as I had time to kill between leaving the New Cathedral and visiting the Baileys at six, and felt a great need to calm my nerves so as to take advantage of any opportunity of speaking to Ann that evening (which I failed to do), I went on foot as far as All Saints, through Mountains Street, Town Hall Square, Continent Street where I stopped to shelter from the first shower of the afternoon in the University buildings, now empty of students for the whole summer, where Rose had taken me in January when I scarcely knew her and she was merely the younger sister of the girl with whom I lunched every weekday at the Sword; I went back to the University last Saturday, August 16th, to look at all those stuffed, dried or pickled animals, classed on the same principles as those carved on the capitals of the New Cathedral by E. C. Douglas, Mrs. Jenkins' father, and his assistants.

I went back to the Natural History Museum in the University buildings, where amongst the diptera in the case containing the species Muscidae I gazed at a fly just like the one on Mrs. Jenkins' ring, just like the one that tormented George Burton; and then I went down to the basement, to the geological department, amongst dioramas crudely representing the Bleston landscape with its flora and fauna back through the ages until Roman times, amongst the maps which with their contrasting colours denoting different periods reminded me of the torn posters on the palings outside the new building in New Cathedral Square. And here again, in the geological department, I was reminded of Mrs. Jenkins, because of the statue representing that science on the porch of the New Cathedral through which I had so lately passed, with its face turned to the ground, its eyes fixed with that expression that I know only too well, not on a ring, but on a fossil in her hand, a stone bearing the imprint of a great insect; I was reminded of Mrs. Jenkins and her son, in their great house on Geology Street, into which Continent Street leads directly, that great house where a whole room is given up to the detective stories collected by James's father, and where the garage houses the black Morris belonging to Matthews & Sons; I was reminded of Mrs. Jenkins and James, and that "accident" in Brown Street on July 11th, and that conversation at the fair on the last evening in May, and that supper-party at the Baileys' next day at which I had refused to take back my copy of *The Bleston Murder* which Ann had just discovered, and which she lent to James a few weeks later. Consequently, instead of relaxing, my nerves grew more on edge.

I left the Museum when it closed at five o'clock, and went out in fine rain, autumnal rain already, to resume my journey along Continent Street (thinking about Ann, placing all my hopes in Ann, trying to forget for the moment all my resentment and suspicion, all my investigations, all the labours that had filled my weekday evenings, but in vain since on my left I could see the Royal Hospital which George Burton had left so lately) and then along Surgery Street as far as All Saints Street, with All Saints Gardens on the left.

And so I came late, with a mind more than ever in turmoil, to ring at your door; you opened it, Rose, with a smile against which I had thought myself better forearmed, and then started telling me about the letters you had just received from Lucien (who would have thought him such a ready writer?) and as you showed me into the living-room, all aglow with the wet evening light, you told me that Ann had not come home yet (how I longed for you to tell me where she was, with whom she was, or at least that she should tell me herself when she came in, wearing a smile as heartbreaking as your own, a smile that aroused my worst fears—but I should probably not have known the name), Ann to whom I could not speak, because of you, Ann with whom I could not even fix a definite date that evening for our meal at the Chinese restaurant opposite the Old Cathedral, that meal at which everything would be explained and forgiven, because you were still there and I could not speak of it in front of you, because you still disturb me too intensely, Rose, because all through the meal I was captivated by your face, from which I wanted to be free, as much as by hers, by hers, of which I long to be captive, because I kept on discovering her behind you, recognising that whatever I had seen in your face was more profoundly present in hers.

Oh Rose, take pity on me, stand aside; because of your smile, I could not ask Ann to see me on Sunday, to postpone anything that might prevent her from listening to me, and when I hurried to your home four days ago, in the early afternoon, desperately anxious to lose no time, it was you, again, who opened the door to me, welcoming me happily, overwhelming me with kind attentions, and you who told me with a smile that Ann had gone out again; and it is because you must stand aside, must no longer come between us, Rose, that I could not ask you to pass my message on to her.

Friday, August 22nd

Ann, I was unable to speak to you on Saturday; I was unable to see you on Sunday; on Monday when I passed your stationer's shop on my way to the News Theatre to see the film about the ruins of Rome it had closed early, as usual; and next day, Tuesday, on leaving Matthews & Sons, as James was walking my way—James, more secretive than ever, but far less worried and self-conscious, as though he had begun to forget some terrible and unsuccessful deed—I let him go on in front, I watched him push that door through which I wanted to enter, I waited for him to leave, standing on the opposite pavement beside the man selling the *Evening News*, but you drew down your iron blind, you went out with him through the inside of the building, you walked away together towards Silver Street, and I did not attempt to follow you.

And so it was not until Wednesday, the day before yesterday, Ann, that I was able to get hold of you, after watching James drive away in the black Morris and pass your shop door without stopping, and that I asked you to lunch with me tomorrow, Saturday.

You seemed surprised, Ann, but pleasantly so; as I watched your face in the shadow above your counter I thought I saw there not your salesgirl's smile but a sort of relief, as if a long ridiculous quarrel were coming to an end; and it was I who went with you this evening, once the iron blind was drawn, along Tower Street and Silver Street as far as the 24 bus stop in Town Hall Square, but you said nothing all the way, as if you had lost the habit of being alone with me, as if you could no longer remember the words you used with me in January, and I feel as if those January fogs were still clinging round you, thicker than ever, mingling with the smoke from all the fires of the last few weeks.

Tomorrow, Ann, in the first-floor room of the Oriental Bamboo, at the table by the window overlooking the front of the Old Cathedral, I hope, that fateful table of the opening scene of *The Bleston Murder*, under the eye of the yellow-skinned *genius loci*, I shall be able to speak of my loneliness and of my need of you, to explain my silence and the strange vagaries of my behaviour, to rend the veil that divides us so cruelly, once again to touch your deepest springs of feeling, to recover that miraculous intimacy with you which I had felt for an instant amid the January fogs, in that season of supreme dereliction when one could not see one's own hands in the street by the lamplight that was kept burning at noon, that miraculous intimacy experienced for an instant amongst the bleak trees of Willow Park, and earlier amongst the bleak apparatus of the Dental School, opposite the Royal Hospital and the Fire Station, at the corner of Continent Street and Surgery Street.

Then I used to lunch with you every weekday at the Sword in Grey Street; I used to walk there as fast as I could, from Matthews & Sons; you were such a bright light amidst my darkness!

My Ann, the Ann I knew in January, it was about that time of year, in mid-January, that you must have let your cousin take away that copy of *The Bleston Murder* which I had lent you and which you have now lent to James Jenkins; it was then that you forgot having (casually and automatically, I suppose) allowed him to borrow it, and told me with slight surprise at my persistence that you'd returned it to me long ago; looking for it at home for form's sake and of course not finding it; it was then that I must have begun to believe you.

The January fogs bemused your mind, as they did mine—those yellow insinuating fogs, those acrid icy fogs that still linger between us today, but which we shall succeed in piercing, as we succeeded then.

I remember, it was while I was crossing the Square, past the barely visible New Cathedral, that a stabbing pain began to tease my jaw; it was while I was crossing that Square, unable to see the sides when I stood in the centre; there was as yet no sign of the great store now nearing completion, nothing rose above the poster-covered palings, not even that tall well-proportioned framework that stood there in April and that is now so deeply buried and concealed under the slime and silt, the inertia and opacity of Bleston.

I remember I began to walk very fast to calm my nerves, going round and round through the streets in the harsh yellow fog, under the spluttering gas lamps like swarms of white flies, hunting for a chemist's shop to buy some sedative, and finally, after a long, devious, futile journey, after passing so many that were uncompromisingly closed (it was a Sunday) I ended up at the one at the corner of Tower Street and Grey Street, opposite Rand's Stationery, in front of which every weekday evening stands the man selling the *Evening News*.

I got no sleep all that night, and next day I must have asked James as soon as I arrived at Matthews & Sons to give me the address of a dentist, and he advised me to get free treatment at the Dental School of the University, opposite the Royal Hospital.

I remember, old Matthews immediately gave me permission to stay away the rest of the morning, asking no questions but with a look of insulting pity; and I was taken into that huge ward where stood five rows of dentists' chairs, twenty in a row, with their apparatus buzzing; there, a few days later, I saw you, Ann, and surprised on your face that look of terror and shame, that secret aspect of yourself, that distressed bewilderment which usually you conceal so well.

Ann, my Ann, how indeed can I have tried to make myself believe that I never really loved you?

4

Monday, August 25th

It is only a temporary setback, Ann, an unfortunate postponement; it's nothing more; the words of your language suddenly
failed me, I was so upset at finding the iron blind drawn; but
I shall wait for the Oriental Bamboo to reopen, and I'll bring
you to that table by the window overlooking the front of the Old
Cathedral and then at last I shall be able to satisfy the expecta-
tion I read, so deeply disappointed, in your eyes.

It is only a temporary setback, and I think I shall be able to
explain it to you too; it's merely an unimportant postponement,
and has altered nothing in my life, which is growing ever more
orderly and must grow ever more orderly, so that I may be
as calm as possible when I renew my approach to you; it is a
mere postponement which distresses me, of course, but in no
way discourages me, and which did not prevent me, when I got
home on Saturday night, from settling down to read over what
I wrote in June, starting with that fourth week which I have
just this minute finished reading (the lengthening of the days,
the deepening blue of the skies, the afternoon spent in Pleasance
Gardens celebrating Rose's success in her French examination,
the travelogue about Petra, and my visit in November to the
New Cathedral with James Jenkins). And what I wrote in
June seems so remote now, separated from the present by such
deep differences, for then the weather was growing brighter
whereas now rain and darkness are gaining the mastery; then,
I imagined I had ceased to love you, Ann, and thought only
of Rose, but tried not to let her see it (you see that, in spite

of all appearances, in the depths of my heart I was faithful to you, my Ann), in those far-off days of early June, separated from the present by such profound alterations—for, since those lovely evenings when I marvelled at the tawny, furry gleams of moist sunlight reflected on the walls of Dew Street from half-open windows, Bleston has struck a murderous blow at George Burton (and only my affection prevents me, I fear, from accusing James Jenkins); since that afternoon when I walked in Green Park amongst beds of tulips that are now filled with dahlias and chrysanthemums, my eyes have been painfully opened by Rose's engagement to Lucien, who has now left us—so painfully opened, my Ann, that they could not but turn for balm and succour to you, who sustained them so profoundly of old, they could not but strive to see you again, those poor weak eyes of mine, reddened and horribly irritated by all the smoke that assails them in this town.

It is only an unimportant postponement, Ann, which did not prevent me from settling down quite calmly to read what I'd written in the fourth week in June, this evening after a meal in the Oriental Rose, from which I watched the last shreds of daylight crumble and dissolve beyond the absurd crenellated towers of the municipal building on the other side of the Square, where the buses were lighting up and the street-lamps glowed, already woolly with fog; I had dined there after going to the News Theatre, as I so often did on Mondays, and as I had done that Wednesday, June 25th, when James and I had tried to celebrate our reconciliation, the first signs of healing of that wound of his which I had so sharply reopened that last Saturday in May when I had pointed out "J. C. Hamilton", that wound which had rankled so painfully when he re-read my copy of *The Bleston Murder*, the same copy that he had read last autumn, the copy I had lent you, Ann, which I saw at your house on June 1st, the copy I had given you hoping you would keep it, but which you had passed on to James without, of course, suspecting the result of your action (that's one of the things

I wanted to explain to you on Saturday, Ann, and that I shall have to explain to you when the Chinese restaurant reopens and when this whole business has become clearer and more definite in my mind), that wound which, after its alarming inflammation at the time of what surely cannot be called an "accident" pure and simple, seems today, most unexpectedly, to have healed like the wounds of the victim, George William Burton.

It is only a postponement, the importance of which I tend to overestimate, thus playing into the hands of Bleston, which is trying to keep me from you (I recognise its wiles!), from you who must become Ariadne for me once again; and so I felt it essential this evening to leave my habits unchanged, to settle down quite calmly to finish reading what I had written in the fourth week in June, quite calmly, having dined at the Oriental Rose after seeing, at the News Theatre, the ruins of Athens enclosed within a living city just as, a week ago, I had seen those of Imperial Rome—after tasting this evening that fabulous elixir, Ariadne, which streamed over the stones from the heights of the pure blue sky, that elixir which I recognised, since the wool and silk, the silver and gold of the Museum tapestries are deeply impregnated with it.

Tuesday, August 26th

The beam of the projector shone through our cigarette smoke and our dense Bleston breath like a shaft of pale sunlight through shifting clouds, and displayed upon the tremulous coarsewoven screen those dazzling pillars, like blocks of rock salt, not quite white but softly veined as though with mineral blood, their sharp flutings eroded by wind and by the rare violent rain, the angles of those temples older than those of the Forum, the remains of that tall city which is so profoundly akin to that imagined by the eighteenth century artist as the scene of Theseus' exploits although identical to it in no detail, and

the corners of present-day houses or public buildings which
the photographers had not managed to exclude, dating at the
very earliest from the middle of the nineteenth century and
thus far more recent than the Baroque churches and palaces
of the Papal city.

In the blue sky that linked the two epochs, the blue sky that
turned ruby-red and then iridescent towards the close of the
brief film, revealing a distant prospect of islands, mountains
and bays, I seemed to recognise the sky of Rome; between the
newer streets and the ancient pediments and capitals, I felt the
intervening presence of the Roman Empire, as expressed particularly by the inscription over a certain gateway: "Here ends
the city of Theseus, here begins the city of Hadrian."

But if last week's picture influenced my impression of
today's, the latter in turn transformed the former retrospec-
tively: Flavian's Amphitheatre, the Baths of Caracalla, the
Pantheon and the Palatine ruins appeared to me through their
Athenian echo (the New Agora, the Temple of Zeus, the Great
Library) as the source of some gigantic resonance, just as a flame
encircled by mirrors is multiplied into countless images of itself,
casting back its heat and increasing the incandescence.

Other images intruded in my vision of Rome, not only
those that flowed before my eyes, but the parallel images of
other ruins further from the glowing centre—notably those
of the travelogue on Petra which I had seen here with James
Jenkins on June 25th, Petra, that weal left by a city on the
Transjordanian cliff-side, like a block of rippling red silk (the
graded seats of an amphitheatre, a few tombs, the pillars of the
Treasure House), that scar imprinted like a convict's brandmark on the living tissue of the land (and while we marvelled
at those marble caves, a hangar was ablaze in the 9th district,
as I learnt next day from the *Evening News*); other images
intruded, those of the ruins of Petra, those of the temple at
Baalbek which I had seen here a little later, those of the paved
square at Timgad, near Aurès, in some story about a holiday in

North Africa (two lovers were seen kissing lengthily in one of the thermae, in that delicious dry heat that we might go and enjoy together some day, if you will help me to come back to you, if you will become my Ariadne once more—faraway Ann, Ann whom I can scarcely make out through blurred eyes, and to whom I was unable to speak on Saturday; but that was only an unimportant postponement; you are prepared to listen to me; you are waiting with your patience, your indulgence, your inexhaustible forgiveness; the two lovers were seen kissing lengthily in one of the thermae, while the other tourists sedately walked the paved streets, examined the Triumphal Arch, the gates, the mosaics and the market place), the images of Timgad in some second-rate French film showing at the Continental with subtitles to help not only such spectators as those who were wholly ignorant of our language, but also those who had a smattering of it, such as yourself, Ann, enabling them to perform in reverse the arduous task of translation which I now achieve a little less painfully, a little more naturally each day, but which at that time, round about Easter, was still a torment, although I coped with it far better than that cunning rascal Lucien, in spite of his greater aptitude, that naïve slyboots Lucien, that innocent seducer who's far away from Bleston now, peacefully enjoying the beauty of summer in his native land, sure of his prey, of lovely vibrant Rose, whom I must not see for many weeks because her eyes still trouble my mind and prevent me from meeting yours: the images of Timgad in a second-rate French film that we'd been to see at the Continental, Lucien and I, that same evening that George Burton caught sight of us on the way out and spoke to me, and I introduced my companion to him, and he took us both for a drink in the bar of the Unicorn, at the corner of Town Hall Square and Continent Street, next to the News Theatre (where I went only occasionally in those days); at first he spoke French to us, with a strong English accent, and then, after stumbling over a word, he changed over to English (while we answered with a strong French accent), trying to articulate very clearly so that we might understand easily, selecting Gallicisms and flattening the lilt of his sentences for us, just as under the influence of local speech we have felt our own gradually lose their flatness. It was one evening in early April, about a week before that conversation at the Oriental Bamboo (the Chinese restaurant which we found locked against us on Saturday, Ann, so that I was unable to speak to you; unbeknown to me it had fallen victim to those sinister fires which I myself had started, which had sped through the town but which the town had transformed and turned against me), about a week before that conversation between Lucien and myself in the first-floor room, at that table by the window overlooking the towers of the Old Cathedral, during the course of which he had questioned me about this man George Burton with whom we had drunk at the Unicorn, and I had told him all I then knew, I had talked about *The Bleston Murder* although I did not yet realise that George Burton was its real author—about a week before that conversation and about a fortnight before the second meeting between George Burton and Lucien at that very table to which I could not bring you on Saturday, Ann, that very table on which lay, that day, the copy of. J. C. Hamilton's novel which is now at my left hand; it was in early April around Easter time, when the grass in Easter Park in the northern part of the 9th district was ablaze with daffodils, and when your counter in Rand's Stationery, like all the stationers' shops in Bleston, displayed a variety of greetings cards, beribboned and bespangled, adorned with chicks and rabbits and bells, when every confectioner's window was full of imitation eggs in every sort of sweetstuff, in anticipation of that Easter Sunday which for me was exactly like all other Sundays except for the long merciless clangour of bells from the New and the Old Cathedral, which hounded me during long hours of weary wandering through the rain.

Wednesday, August 27th

Into my vision of Rome (I see it through a screen of murky fires, acrid and clamorous, a swelling red tide of devastation), of Imperial Rome whose window has vanished, other images intruded, as though Rome were the centre of some gigantic resonance; not only the images of Athens that flowed before my eyes, such as the Gate and the Library of Hadrian ("Here ends the city of Theseus"), not only the parallel images of Petra, Baalbek and Timgad, all against a background of dazzling sky and sand, but also the infinitely less luminous images, tinged with dank anguish, of those small sarcophagi, as mournful as some cluster of dead rushes where a quivering animal huddles in the deathly grip of winter, those coffins of children who died of fever and cold far from their great native city, amidst the evil winds and yellow fogs, beside marshlands haunted by the thin whine of insects, children who died of boredom and terror and longing for the warm bright day,

the mournful images of those sarcophagi, white or grey, decorated with crude portraits, with round heads and three or four folds suggesting the tunic, and clumsily carved brief inscriptions giving the name and age of the small corpse laid within; those sarcophagi discovered in the region of the New Cathedral and of Matthews & Sons when the foundations of great buildings were being laid there, and which now form the principal feature of the first room in the Museum,

and the image of the painted plaster model in the last of those dioramas which hang in the basement of the University buildings beside cases of fossils and samples of rock, and which aim at conveying to the spectator the whole geological evolution of the region from age to age; this painted plaster model represents Bleston, Bellista, Belli Civitas, in the second century A.D., a fortified square surrounded by forests and marshes, with its little thermae, its Temple of War on the very site (as shown in adjoining plans) of the choir of the Old Cathedral, and the central cross of its grid of paved streets on the very site of the south-eastern corner of Town Hall Square, at the junction of Sea Street and Continent Street, a few yards from where I now sat in a creaking seat at the News Theatre watching the blue of the sky and the golden glow on white stones that were once painted, above the quiet green of the aloes,

into my vision of Rome there intruded not only the images of conquered Athens, of Petra, Baalbek and Timgad, but also that of Bleston, that city of doom and oblivion, the ancient town of Bleston, Bellista, Belli Civitas, cause of my misery, hounding me relentlessly, that hydra, that octopus with spreading tentacles, that squid disgorging its black ink over us so as to make us unrecognisable to one another and even to ourselves, Ann, Bleston the sorceress, my bitter enemy, who has divided us for so long and strives with all her spells to keep us still apart, raising between us that wall of fog and ashes, lowering between us that iron curtain that confronted us on Saturday, driving back against me the flames which I had foolishly expected to destroy itself, making you deaf and making me dumb, clouding my sight with blood, dazing my heart with its treacheries.

And at the same moment I saw the town itself in a new light, as though the wall alongside which I have been groping ever since my arrival, here and there less opaque, had suddenly grown thinner, disclosing forgotten depths, so that my shrinking courage returned and I felt once again, thanks to this unfamiliar light, capable of defying the town and protecting myself from it, of resisting it more strongly until the time comes, at the end of September, for me to leave it, snatching you, I hope, from its turbid depths and leading you to those lands where you can feel the closeness of the stars through the clear warm sky; I felt capable once more of foiling Bleston's wiles and of coming near you, of seeing you and making you hear me, Ann, you for whom all these words are written, towards whom these lines flow like waves to an island, since the writing that I began at that very moment of my year when I was most indifferent to you, most oblivious of your beauty, of your kindness, has now turned into a letter addressed to you, a letter which you'll be able to read in its entirety when I shall at last have reached you and caught you and when you'll have adopted my own language, Ann, my Ariadne. Your image haunted me in the News Theatre the day before yesterday; I thought only of you, sought only you through all those visions and reflections, Rome with her crown of cities all ravaged, crumbling, calcined under the contagious influence of barbarism and the fatal decay at their centre, Petra, Baalbek, Timgad and that Belli Civitas, Bleston of so many centuries ago.

Oh Ann, my Ariadne, I imagined you walking under the Athenian sky that merged into the sky of Crete, your true homeland, and your feet, which I have never seen bared, which were shod on Saturday in shabby shoes with worn heels and cotton stockings the colour of the pavements of Tower Street, I imagined your feet stepping naked and steeped in sunlight over fine roads paved with marble pebbles, over fresh grass and sand, behind the bases of the portico of the Erechtheion, which in my fancy leads not into a temple but into one of those palaces in the Museum tapestries surrounding the square where Theseus is crowned—stepping behind those bases full of coiled scales like those of some old captive serpent turned oracle—stepping in such freedom and beauty that my shrinking courage was restored, Ann, my Ariadne, still so terribly remote, whose island I seek through rains that grow denser daily and nightly, my courage was restored and I was able to deny the importance of Saturday's setback, of my inability to speak to you save in meaningless commonplaces to which you responded only with a puzzled and slightly anxious smile, so utterly disconcerted was I when we reached the parvis of the Old Cathedral and I saw the iron curtain lowered in front of the Chinese restaurant.

Thursday, August 28th

I was troubled enough already, my heart throbbing, full of uncertainties and fears when I left Matthews & Sons at midday and went to fetch you at the stationer's shop as we had arranged, carrying this manuscript in my briefcase, intending not to read it to you as yet but to show it you, to help me explain why for the last few months I have been closeted in my room every weekday evening, to make it easier for me to answer the question you silently asked me at the end of April, just when I was most indifferent to you, when I had bought from you these sheets of blank paper which I was now bringing back to you scored over with the long furrow of writing I am still tracing.

My mind was in turmoil as I wondered where to begin disentangling my skein of requests and reasons, feeling sure that everything would be easier when we were sitting in the first-floor room of the Oriental Bamboo, if possible at the table beside the window overlooking the towers of the Old Cathedral, where so many encounters had already taken place under the eye of the plump Chinese waiter; my mind was in turmoil as I pushed open the glazed door and you greeted me from behind your counter, and above all when James came up to us, smiling as if the drama in which he is the leading actor had never taken place, he who a few weeks before looked so distraught, smiling now as if George Burton had never been wounded.

The latter, whom I saw next day, Sunday, has now recovered; and he too must have learnt that Richard Tenn, whom we suspected, is innocent of his "accident" (if indeed it was Tenn whom he suspected; we have never uttered his name), for he told me, with his characteristic laugh, that he had made up a whole long story about the incident, imagining that he had escaped from an attempt at murder, and even that he had discovered the culprit, playing for once the part of the detective, the hero of all his writings, but that on further investigation the whole elaborate construction had crumbled to pieces, such were the wild fancies bred by his professional habit.

When I saw James's face behind the window, when you greeted him so charmingly, I wondered, with throbbing heart and mind in turmoil, whether he was once again to come with us, to come between us, and I only breathed a little when he took leave of us both, as if he knew that we were to have lunch together, when you closed the door and led me out by the back entrance.

If I scarcely spoke a word to you in the bus, it was because I was afraid of being too precipitate and thus committing some irreparable blunder, because my heart was throbbing and my mind in turmoil, because I was waiting for more favourable conditions before beginning my difficult explanation.

And so you must see why it was, Ann, that when we got off in Old Cathedral Square and I saw, through the rain which had just begun to fall, that the iron curtain was lowered over the door of the Oriental Bamboo, this seemingly insignificant circumstance brought on a sort of vertigo, made me almost despair of ever reaching you, made me feel immediately that I should never be able, that day, to tell you of my misery or even to speak as I'd have liked about what I have written, which you will read before long, I'm quite sure, and which will tell you of the bitter enmity this city bears me, of its responsibility for Saturday's setback, will make you see the full irony of that closed door and of the answer I got, in your presence, from the workman in plaster-stained overalls of whom I enquired what had happened (we could hear his mates still at work inside): "Why, the whole thing nearly burned down, but don't worry about the owners, the insurance company's paid up."

You must see why this lowered iron curtain immediately made me feel that everything had gone wrong for today, that all my efforts to put things right would be in vain, as soon became only too obvious, unfortunately, Ann; we trudged a long way in the rain before finding another restaurant, up near White Street, since in my agitation I had forgotten the existence of the tearoom near the second-hand bookshops in Chapel Street, behind the great blank window of the apse where the Last Judgment ought to have stood; we trudged a long way without my being able to speak a word, while I watched your face which gradually, to my great distress, revealed boredom and irritation and fatigue, and at last, since you were exhausted and I dared not make any further suggestions, we went into the nearest third-rate café (which was absurd since a few minutes more would have brought us to New Cathedral Square and the Oriental Pearl), a café inferior to those patronised by my colleagues at Matthews & Sons, including James (they wonder why I go to the Sword, which is so much dearer and farther off, the Sword where I used to meet you every weekday at the beginning of winter, Ann); we trudged a long way in the rain and then at last went into an underground eating-place which was ill-lit, ill-ventilated, noisy and overcrowded.

Friday, August 29th

If only we had been left to ourselves at our table next to the ceaselessly-banging kitchen door, you could have helped me to regain my self-control; but a man came up, with his bowler in his hand and an umbrella hung over his arm, bowed, pulled out a chair and sat down without waiting for our reply, which could only have been consent; then he pulled out of his pocket the *Bleston Post*, which he partially unfolded to read during the long waits between courses, and every time I raised my voice, amid the hubbub of that reeking place, so that you might hear me, he would look up from his paper and start listening to us, probably because my accent struck him as queer.

We could not stop there after finishing our ice-cream; we could not go for a walk in some park because it was raining too hard; we could not take refuge in some cinema because you had told me you'd have to leave me early to meet somebody else at three o'clock.

There was nothing else to do but drink a glass of beer in a corner of the nearest pub, and there I told you that I wanted you to meet those friends of mine of whom I had already spoken, the Burtons, to whom Lucien had introduced Rose at the Royal Hospital, in the room overlooking Willow Park, George Burton the famous writer, and wise, enchanting Harriet, whose pictures had been in all the papers at the time of that "accident" in Brown Street which was actually, though I could not tell you about that yet, an attempt at murder, a crime which had fortunately failed, committed in a moment of insensate rage by that apparently sedate and highly sensitive friend of ours to whom we owe our acquaintance, Ann, since it was he who took me for the first time into your stationer's shop and introduced us to one another, James Jenkins, your devoted admirer, Ann, of whose qualities you are well aware but who conceals under that reserve and that courtesy a dangerous fury that burst forth, through my imprudence, that day, through my imprudence and your own, Ann, since it was you who lent him for the second, fatal, time at the beginning of July, the copy of *The Bleston Murder* marked with my name which I had thought lost, which I had seen again at your house on the evening of Sunday, June 1st, to my great surprise, and which I had then given you to keep, a dangerous fury that burst forth through our joint imprudence on that Friday, July 11th, in that "accident" in Brown Street.

I told you that I should like you to meet George Burton, the famous writer, author of *The Bleston Murder* under the pseudonym J. C. Hamilton and of so many other detective stories under those of Barnaby Rich and Caroline Bay, George Burton and kind, enchanting Harriet; I told them, when I called on them on Sunday in their house overlooking Green Park, that I should bring you to visit them; and in that pub in White Street where we had taken refuge from the rain after the fiasco of our lunch together, you told me that you couldn't manage the next day, Sunday, as I had suggested, but you yourself proposed the following Sunday, the day after tomorrow, and invited me to lunch at your home first, where I shall still be unable to speak to you because of the presence of Rose.

Then you got up suddenly, looked at your watch, drained your glass and asked me to go with you as far as the stop for the 27 bus in Tower Street; and here, as we waited in the shelter, you looked at me more closely and said, noticing my uneasiness: "What's the matter, Jacques? You seem distressed; have I done anything to upset you?"

I let you go, trying to smile, and merely saying: "No, of course not; I'll explain it all later."

When I was alone I felt tears mingle with the raindrops on my cheeks as if I had parted with you forever.

And yet it was only an unimportant setback, Ann, for though you were so remote from me during those few wretched hours, I shall be able to speak to you some time, somewhere; for I have rediscovered those few instants that bind you to me forever, through the densest darkest fogs of winter I can see the shining secret look you gave me when you recognised me in that great ward on the first-floor of the Dental School, at the corner of Continent Street and Surgery Street, close to Willow Park where the trees were black and naked then, and touched with fleeting rays of sunlight through the thick mist, that look you gave me in the great ward with its five buzzing rows of blood-stained instruments of torture, to which I had come for the second time and where I had just left the white-enamelled movable chair, identical with the one in which I saw you sitting, open-mouthed, terror in your eyes, trying to master yourself while a young man in a spotless overall ground away at your incisor, that pathetic effort to smile at me, that look you gave me from the furthest depths of that terrified childhood within yourself which you could no longer control, taken unawares, that look which nobody but myself has seen, which was meant for nobody but myself, and which made me for evermore the confidant of that part of yourself which never peeps out when you are in full health.

I had seen you at lunch in the Sword, but when I waited for you in Continent Street I learnt to know your face for the first time.

For a few moments we went into Willow Park, which was like a lonely wood at that time of year; dusk was rapidly falling; I took your head between my hands and for a long time I stroked your brows with my thumbs as though to banish your pain without daring to go further because in a sort of tenuous dream I had begun to hear Rose's voice whispering, speaking such delicious French, the only person who spoke French to me in those days, Rose's voice had begun whispering to me, leading me astray from you.

5

Sunday, August 31st

Now that everything has crumbled about me I have nothing left but this pitiful accumulation of futile phrases, like the ruins of an unfinished building, the partial cause of my downfall, incapable of sheltering me against the torrential sulphurous rain, against the surging pitchy waters that lap with a low booming sound, against the perpetual assault of that rumbling, sneering laughter that spreads from house to house and runs round my own wallpaper.

This is the deplorable end of my attempt to struggle; nothing is now left me, contemptible thing that I am, but to acknowledge my defeat, my undeniable and irremediable defeat, without the slightest hope of revenge, as though I were already dead: my defeat and your incontestable power, horrible amorphous town that I detest, the disproportion of our strengths.

The crowning cruelty, the ultimate irony by which you set your seal on this final blow, was to choose Rose as innocent executioner; it was Rose who came to tell me with a smile on her lips and Lucien's latest letter in her hand, yesterday at noon as I was leaving Matthews & Sons, that James and Ann were engaged.

Then, wholly crushed, I barely had the strength to tell her that I should not go to lunch with them today, muttering some pretext to leave her, and telephone the Burtons to say that we should not come this afternoon.

I should have liked to burn out my eyes which had only served to deceive me, my eyes and all these pages I have written…

A fresh wave of horrible laughter breaks about me.

V
Farewell

I

Monday, September 1st

All last night I lay on my bed unable to sleep, like the night before, unable to take off my clothes after that endless empty day between, those long hours of aimless wandering in a circle like a sleepwalker, lonely, dazed and dizzy and cold, as though harried by a swarm of dirty white gadflies, their wings dripping with Slee water—dejected and humiliated, enduring my extreme punishment and my impotence, all night, unable to sleep, without a moment's respite from the tormenting breath of the creature that seemed to hover a few inches above me on enormous fly's wings, a monstrous tortoise with scales of cast iron and brick, horned like a bull, its muzzle stained with smoky blood; I could not even take off my heavy shoes, but lay shivering in the chilly small hours, feeling myself tossed and trailed in the viscous scummy waters of the stagnant lake that feeds the Slee; and a carapace of pitch on my garments, a mask of pitch on my face, gauntlets of pitch on my hands which seemed paralysed, riveted into this hell within my hell: my hands which in vain tried to clasp the head of Ann glimpsed between waves of dense mist, a swaying phosphorescent head with staring terrified eyes, not a lash quivering, its features frozen like a moonlit marble image on a tombstone; I lay thus all night, without a single minute's respite, hastening to the muttering of my days in Bleston as they swirled round me like a sulphurous snowstorm, all those spring days, those autumn days, particularly that Monday in November which I described at the end of June, the day of my second meeting with that

Ariadne who had given me the map of the city which I burned at the end of April, and all the bygone days of summer, all the days at the onset of winter which I had already tried to control with that long chain of sentences the forging of which had worn me out and ruined me, that long chain of sentences now left unfinished, dangling in mid-air; I listened to the mutter of all those days in March and February which I had not yet tackled, the big two months' gap in the very middle of my recension, the mutter of that Sunday in early April when I had shown Lucien the fragments of Sodom in the Old Cathedral window, that Saturday in late January when heavy flakes were falling from the low yellow sky and melting before they touched the pavement, while I went from one bookshop to another, from Baron's to Lind's in Continent Street, looking for *The Bleston Murder* and always being told it was out of print; I lay all night listening to the swirling of my days in Bleston, listening to the swirling of the streets of Bleston as they poured like glaciers round my bed, piling up into immense moraines of rusty blood-stained scrap iron; I lay all night listening to the days and the streets as they swirled round me, and the laughter echoing from house to house, from age to age, right back to other cities and other ages, as far back as those cryptogamous forests of the Carboniferous era, now turned to coal and buried deep under the nearby regions, those palms and tree-ferns swaying above a floor of humus thick with carrion and mineral ore, trodden by reptiles; I lay thus all night.

Then in the freezing dawn the surge died down, the frothing lake that my sheets had become grew smoother and solidified, while the muttering voices echoed with increasing clarity, reiterating the word "blind", not tauntingly but as a lamentation; then the layer of pitch enclosing me like a knight's or an insect's armour, like a madman's straitjacket, thinned and split into innumerable scales that grew glassily transparent and resonant.

Then gradually in the freer air I was able to begin moving my fingers, I was able to wrench them one by one from the invisible claws that had gripped them so close all night; then I was able to raise my hands, painfully, creakingly, as if my body had been the stump of a tree and my arms two branches being torn off, leaving a ragged splintery wound oozing sap; then I was able to roll over on to my side and let my feet in their heavy shoes drop to the ground, I was able to stagger to the washbasin and stare in the glass, as daylight brightened, at my ashen, tense, haggard face, feeling in the middle of my forehead a stabbing cauterising pain; I was able to splash my face so that drops of water ran over my cheeks and clothes like pebbles over a slope of withered grass, to light the gas fire for the first time in six months, to undress and wash, to take out of my wardrobe and put on clean linen, this suit and these shoes, a fresh belt and tie, rejecting everything that I had slept in all night; I was able to sit down at this table as I am sitting now; I was able to look through the window, of which darkness has now made a mirror, and see the watery morning sun shining on the panes of glass on the right side of Dew Street, sliding over the bricks of Copper Street; and I seemed to hear a murmur coming from those bricks, like the murmur that seemed to reach me from the wheels and footsteps in the neighbouring streets, and from the sleepers lying behind drawn curtains in their bedrooms, a murmur strangely like the muttering that had gone on all night, which was the same voice as the muttering voice, the same voice which had never fallen silent but which now spoke in a different tone, with a different message; then I was able to write on a blank page these three words which did not come out of my own mind but which I read through my window, inscribed on the brick wall to my left on the other side of Copper Street, clearly outlined in the crisp light, these three words which I felt resumed all the message of those murmuring voices, and which I merely recorded:

"We are quits."

Tuesday, September 2nd

I know that the story which had been unfolding ever since I first came here has now reached its end, that the pattern is complete, now that this has happened without my knowledge, in despite of me and yet by means of me, making me suffer almost to the point of death and turning me into the ghost that I now am—now that Ann and James have come together, Ann who had loved me, who had watched my glances in the heart of winter and seen them slowly turn away from her, Ann whom I was wearily striving to reach again, my only hope in my distress, to whom I called but could not make her hear me, and James, whom I had come to believe guilty of attempted murder, guilty of George Burton's wounds, which is doubtless another illusion, another of your tricks to bewilder me, Bleston, another pitfall laid so that you might mock at me; Ann and James have come together, just as did Rose and Lucien a month ago.

The pattern is complete, and I am left out of it; and when on Saturday I came back here and saw all these pages piled up, scored with lines of writing, this accumulation of sentences like the ruins of an unfinished building, the partial cause of my downfall, I was overcome with a wild longing to burn them completely one after the other, meticulously, without leaving one scrap, carefully pulverising all their ashes; and this, it might have seemed, would have closed that other circle starting from that April evening when I destroyed your map, Bleston, in this same room;—a wild longing inspired by you, Bleston, as like some possessing demon you crept into my soul, hoping with your relentless irony to use me as your instrument against myself, completing your revenge on me for the insult, the wound I had dealt you, a wild longing to burn all these pages, all these sentences; and yet this would have been a false ending, Bleston, for as I now know by experience I should have had to go back through those flames, day after day, to try and recover a few fragments of this writing, most of which they would have removed from my reach without wholly destroying it, I know that by experience, Bleston, without preventing it from haunting me.

It was the number of these pages, of these sentences, which saved them and saved me, it was the time I'd have needed; it was the weight of hours spent that allowed me to preserve intact this great pile of pages, on which I have begun to accumulate new ones, this chain of sentences to which I am now adding fresh links; it was the number, the time, the weight which allowed me not to obey the insidious persistent counsellor, to wait for the voice to grow weary or to alter, to wait motionless like a man sheltering prone behind a slope in the thick of the bombardment, still dazed by the hailstorm of your sarcasm, streets of Bleston, that had assailed me as I crept between your carious jaws, with a remorseless noise like a drill which the passers-by seemed not to hear but which went on echoing inside and outside my head, so that in the call box I could scarcely make out Harriet Burton's voice as she answered me:

"But what a pity you can't come, dear Jacques, we should have been so delighted to meet your friend; her sister was quite charming; you must bring her to see us another time—do come next Sunday."

A few minutes before I had scarcely been able to make out the far harder voice of Mrs. Bailey: "But what a pity! Rose has just told me; do come next Sunday."

Rose, sweet Rose, was in high spirits on Saturday when I met her in Tower Street outside Matthews & Sons, delighted at having just received a letter from Lucien which she showed me; I was happy to see her, in spite of my vexation, little suspecting, when we began to speak of James, that she was to be the unwitting messenger of my doom.

"He often comes to see us," she said, "he talks about you and about that mysterious mother of his of course, that charming old lady who's sometimes so strangely silent that she almost frightened me when he took us to see her in their great half-empty house."

"Mightn't one sometimes believe them guilty of something—don't take me literally, it's just a flight of fancy, a manner of speaking—do tell me, Rose, mightn't one sometimes believe them guilty of some secret crime, a murder or something of the sort, which they've successfully concealed?"

"What a thing to think about your friends!" She burst out laughing in the sunshine. "I hope your morbid imaginings have no sort of foundation, or else I'd really be terrified to think what sort of a hornets' nest we'd all be in! You know, Ann and James have at last made up their minds to get engaged; I'm so happy for her sake. Don't say a thing about it to them, though, it's not official yet; I trust your discretion."

I plunged down the streets, hurrying aimlessly as though goaded by an aching jaw, going round and round, caught in a great trap which had just closed over me, while the houses seemed to grate together like grindstones, splashing me with a shower of cold sparks; and as I skirted Lanes Park, where the grass was strewn with couples, a swarm of flies began to buzz in my sweating head and I tried to drive them off with the gestures of a drowning man struggling to part the weeds.

I went to eat a sandwich at the buffet in Hamilton Station; I went to get out of Sunday's invitations at a call box in Alexandra Place; and stooping under the hailstorm of your sarcasms, windows of Bleston irrevocably closed against me, I slowly made my way towards this room, this table, this pile of pages, this chain of sentences, the partial cause of my downfall.

Wednesday, September 3rd

Now three days' effort and perseverance, three days' writing stand between me and those terrible moments.

I was able to resume my reading, and for the past two hours I have been back in those first days of July, as I deciphered the long succession of lines I wrote then, which subsist as intact evidence of those days: the lines that tell of my evening with James at the fair in the 2nd district, on the last Saturday in May, when I had betrayed to him, before betraying it to Ann and Rose, the real name of "J. C. Hamilton", and when I had shown him George Burton's face on the self-portrait taken at the photographic shooting-gallery, which George had forgotten to collect; the lines that tell of that Wednesday evening, July 2nd, during which I had gone alone to the deserted fairground in the 5th district and had picked up the negative of that portrait, which I still possess; and finally the lines that tell of that short Sunday afternoon, December 1st, when James—the same inescapable James—had taken me for the first time to Pleasance Gardens.

I had forgotten one temptation, the trace of which I have come across during my study of these archives, under the date of Thursday, July 3rd: my impulse to burn that negative which I had discovered the evening before, that piece of film showing George's face peering down the barrel of his gun, and Harriet's face anxious despite her smile, as if she had some apprehension of the "accident"; I had forgotten that other attempt of yours, city of Bleston, to fool me, to use me as your instrument in your revenge against myself, the more deeply to involve me in your revenge against George Burton, the more cruelly to crush me under the sense of my complicity, of my responsibility in this business which, even if your Police and your Judges declare that they can find no trace of attempted murder, must surely be far more than a mere "accident", and remains the crux of that bad dream which you set in motion in order to ruin me and confound me and make mock of me, since all the illusions which you have used to lead me astray are as much a part of your real being as those aspects of yourself which you acknowledge.

I had touched you to the quick, Bleston; and your revenge was so deliberately, so meticulously prepared and executed! It's clear, at last, that I have in fact succeeded in wounding you, that my writing has seared you, since it's clear that I have narrowly escaped from destroying these pages thanks to which all this is clear at last, all this is safeguarded from your oblivion—just as George Burton narrowly escaped from death in Brown Street and, earlier, the negative of his likeness had narrowly escaped from fire.

And so I thank you, Bleston, for taking such cruel and blatant revenge on me; I shall have gone from you in less than a month, but I shall still be prince over you since, by acknowledging my defeat, I have managed to survive (as you secretly wished me to) the fate you had in store for me, I have not been engulfed; and now, having endured the ordeal of your fury, I have become invulnerable, like a ghost; I have won from you this offer of a pact, which I accept.

Thursday, September 4th

In the entry dated Thursday, July 3rd, which I was reading yesterday I noted an important gap, due no doubt to the lateness of the hour at which I reached the passage where this incident should be inserted, but also, more deeply, to the fact that I had not yet seen its connection with the fragment of experience that I was then endeavouring to establish.

As I was walking roughly parallel to the Slee, from Daisy Fields where the fair was partially set up, towards the waste land in the 5th district which it had just left, I came to one of the corners of the hexagonal wall of the Prison, and I went out of my way to walk round that dangerous place, skirting in the dusk the high rampart whose ridge bristles with broken glass, that place lies like a sort of hole within your living tissue, Bleston, a hole in which, like an amoeba in its vacuole, you gather together those bodies that you have not assimilated, unable to cast them out because your own limits are undefined, a place that lies like a threat in your very heart, your reproach, Bleston, and your safeguard, a six-pointed star with the penitentiary building in its centre, the image of which, like a black snow-crystal, had appeared to me when I burned your effigy, at the end of April, like a sort of negative of the gleaming mark imprinted on Cain's forehead.

I did not suspect then, on July 3rd, that I should trace back time through the weeks, up to the period when my hatred for you had begun to flare up so violently in my head that I had to find some way of externalising its flames, the period when I had not yet begun to write, when I bowed helplessly, lay prostrate, sank down ever deeper under your hypnotic Lethean terror, so that I had at all costs to strike some spark in the midst of that gloom that gathered more quickly despite the lengthening days; and then further back towards winter, almost as far back as that Sunday when I had shown Lucien, in the near darkness of the Old Cathedral, the famous Murderer's Window, after taking him for the first time to the fair in the 3rd district, near the Anchor.

Before leaving you, Bleston, as has been settled, when my year's service with Matthews & Sons comes to an end on the last Tuesday of this month, I shall have to go back and gaze at that magical hieroglyph of glass; I shall have to acquire the closest possible knowledge of you, in these numbered days, to visit for instance the old streets lying beyond the Slee, southeast of the Prison, at the tip of the 9th district, around St. Jude's Church, which has some old glass in it, and a few half-timbered houses, an inn decorated with grotesques and a small synagogue, the stronghold of the poor Jews I suppose, which I had decided to go and see, which I never went to see, having forgotten my decision, hating you so, terrible town, you who after depriving me of Rose have cut me off from Ann so completely that my jealousy of James almost fades away before the shame I feel, terrible town, you who mocked me so cruelly but whose sarcasms seem so strangely to have turned into entreaties, Bleston, from whom I was separated by a wall which your own blows, relentlessly aimed at me, brought down; I must acquire the closest possible knowledge of you to fulfil my part in this pact between us, whose conditions are gradually growing clearer to me.

Friday, September 5th

As I sat at this table, on Monday, as motionless as some very ancient funereal monument standing weatherworn amidst ploughland and sands, staring at the brief message I had just transcribed, meticulously shaping each letter with trembling hand, like a clumsy child toiling at its copybook, this brief message which I had seen written on the bricks of Bleston, in the soothing, purifying light of early morning, I heard a tap at my door.

It was Mrs. Grosvenor with my "morning cup of tea"; the machinery of a working day was starting up again.

My colleagues asked me when I went into the office: "What's happened to you, Monsieur Revel?"

It was the first time they had shown any interest in me, after spending so many hours in the same room almost daily for the past eleven months; but I was incapable of replying.

James, who has not yet said a word to me about his engagement, and to whom I have not said a word about it, James who does not know that I have heard of it from Rose, came to lunch with me at the Sword today, showing all his old charm and friendliness, even exaggerating his attentions as though I were a convalescent; he told me that he was to take his fortnight's holiday (like all the staff except myself who am bound to serve a full year) on September 15th when Blythe returns from his; but that once again he would have to spend it at home on account of his mother's health, and of some major repairs needed to the roof of their big house.

As I came back here, not only on Monday but each evening since, each of these last few light evenings (dusk was gathering before I reached the house, and now cloudy night has fallen behind my windowpane), as I came straight back after dining at the Sword, without deviating by way of Grey Street, Tower Street and Dew Street, for I dreaded their mockery, I seemed to hear a deafening cry of lamentation rise from your bricks, Bleston, from the glowing ember at the heart of each of them longing to convert its matrix into clear glass, and I seem to read the same entreaty, the same stifled desire in all the vacant eyes that passed by:

"When shall our strength be set free? When shall we see our velvet spread out, our metals gleaming? When shall we be cleansed, and you too, Jacques Revel?"

Great city, gripping my heart between your pitiless teeth, whatever spark you may strike from me, and through me from yourself, will remain ineluctably feeble and futile until others arise to echo and reinforce it; and so all that I can do during these numbered days is to try and complete my exploratory description, the basis for a future interpretation, to try and fill in as best I can the gaps in this exploratory description which, like some son of Cain's, I compose, I forge, I weave, starting from the time of that mimic murder when I burnt your map, from that declaration of war, my entry into your war, Belli Civitas, Bellista, Bleston: for instance the long gap preceding that day in March when I briefly expounded to Lucien on the great Window in the Old Cathedral, and beginning with those early February days which I remember only dimly, the coldest time of the year, when often in the morning, if there weren't a dense fog, the puddles on the pavements were all frozen over and long yellowish wax-like icicles hung from many burst drainpipes, that coldest time of my year, when I went through the second-hand bookshops in Chapel Street assiduously hunting for a fresh copy of J. C. Hamilton's novel, which was out-of-print,

when Ann, who is now engaged to James, used to meet me every weekday for lunch at the Sword—Ann, that Ariadne who loved me in those days, from whom I was gradually drifting, whom I forsook, whom I hurt, even before she suspected my faithlessness, by the indifference I showed her; for I realise, I admit that I wanted to get rid of her, to obliterate all that had been between us, and for once I succeeded only too well in my wretched undertaking, thanks to your cruel irony, Bleston,

Ann whose name I cannot write without a pang of jealousy, of course, but above all without a shudder of shame at my meanness, my vileness, my folly and blindness, without that sense of frozen isolation which ghosts must experience,

Ann who does not yet know that I am aware of my doom, and who, having forgotten how close we were to one another last winter, cannot suspect what suffering her engagement brings me,

Ann whom I shall see the day after tomorrow, in love and blissfully happy, for sure; I shall have to keep calm and betray nothing of my knowledge nor of my anguish when I see her, with her mother and Rose, at their home in All Saints Gardens, I shall not be able to say anything to her;

Ann to whom I shall never, now, be able to explain my misfortune until I have gone away from Bleston, until my departure has formed the last link in that long network of sentences enclosing the whole of my year, which I shall make her read then to show her all my weakness and all my desire, to disclose my reasons to her at last,

Ann whom I shall have to introduce to the Burtons, but not in the way they expect and I had hoped, not in the way that Lucien introduced Rose, but forced, on the contrary, to disillusion them, to stress the fact that nothing of the sort exists between us,

Ann whose grey eyes which looked so kindly at me last winter now haunt me, now are closed to me, those eyes to which, despite all our estrangement, something bitter like the mist of those days still binds me indissolubly.

2

Monday, September 8th

This evening, at the News Theatre, instead of Athens I beheld Bombay, the Hindu city—its quays and avenues, its temples and its squalor: Bombay, that name printed in thick black lettering on hundreds of cases full of tea unloaded daily at the port in north-west Bleston, for the shreds of leaf at the bottom of this white cup which Mrs. Grosvenor has just brought me are not the produce of this soil, of the fields that lay here before these houses were built, of that Slee valley depicted in the University's diorama, any more than are the Ionic capitals, now soot-begrimed, on the façade behind which the story of Theseus is illustrated: forms which came from Athens by way of Rome and then France, altering at every stage, and probably from farther away than Athens; these shreds of leaf have now diffused their aroma and their restorative principle in that autumn-coloured liquid which I have just been drinking, after reading that vain letter of entreaty which I had begun to write on August 25th, that letter to Ann Bailey which will not reach her until my departure has set a full stop not only to this writing, but to the experience of which it forms a part; this autumn-coloured beverage, this aid to vigilance and survival; and while I watched this film, you yourself, Bleston, appeared to me as one of the sources of an immense resonance, a smoke-dimmed resonance of darkness and cold.

On leaving Matthews & Sons, resuming my old habits, I went to the News Theatre; I dined, however, not at the Oriental Rose but at the Bombay in City Street, a little beyond Museum

Square, and when I got back here I did not go on reading what I had written in July, but turned instead to the passage at the end of August that described my visit to the cinema on Monday 25th, my vision of other towns seen through the picture of Athens, of ancient Bleston seen through the parallel images of Imperial Rome, of Petra, Baalbek, and Timgad, even of Crete, the real homeland of my Ariadne, of Ann in whom I still placed all my hope then, that passage at the end of August relating the deplorable fiasco on that Saturday when I had found the green-painted iron curtain down in front of the Chinese restaurant opposite the Old Cathedral, my inability to speak to her, that deplorable fiasco which I strove to convince myself was not irreparable in spite of all the accumulated portents and symptoms, that it was only a postponement—whereas really everything was ruined, I had missed my last chance, and it was with James, as I see only too clearly now, that she had her date at three o'clock and that she was to lunch next day; that passage which finally leads down into the dense fog of the last days in January, those dark misty days when she loved me (and of all my memories these are surely the most painful),

that vain letter of entreaty to Ann Bailey which shall reach her later, so that she may read it in its context, so that she may know how I really loved her in spite of everything, and how I miss her now, so that she may know how mean, calculating, blind and bitter I was, so that she may recognise me and recognise herself, so that she may understand certain aspects of my behaviour which surprised and even distressed her, notably my silence on August 23rd, the involuntary culmination of the silence I had kept towards her for so long, ever since that day at the end of April when I had not replied to her unspoken question about the paper on which I am still writing, certain aspects of my behaviour and thereby of her own, of others' behaviour, of my manoeuvres, my stubbornness, my defeat and my survival, so that through the eyes of these two sisters you yourself, Bleston, may begin to interpret this interpretation of yourself which I have begun and which I shall carry on 'til I leave, striving to abide faithfully by the rules of that obscure pact to which I could not but subscribe, striving to satisfy that dormant, muzzled, buried desire within you, aroused by the wound I dealt you, that desire for death and for deliverance, for light and for fire;

so that through the eyes of these two sisters, Bleston, thanks to this writing which will remain after I have gone, and then gradually by contagion through other patient eyes, you will be caught in the net I have woven, and will pursue this study of yourself, you will build up your slow recovery, strengthen the surest of your dreams, and gather together your host of sparks, so that my silent words may begin to echo through all your rafters, so that your own silent words may at last achieve passionate utterance, Bleston, you who in the depths of your heart long, as much as I do, for your death.

Tuesday, September 9th

While I was reading the pages I had written during the second week in July, just before the "accident" in Brown Street, I felt my mind awhirl with a storm like that now raging against my windows in the darkness, harried with suspicions of that lover of Ann Bailey's, tormented by the question of guilt which I cannot yet solve, and by certain old buried feelings that came to light within me.

When I saw the iron curtain down in front of the Chinese restaurant opposite the Old Cathedral on August 23rd, I did not even need to hear the workman's comment before saying to myself: "This was not what I intended, I am hoist with my own petard," sure that there must have been a fire, started by the very flame which had burnt the map of Bleston, I had burnt the map of Bleston in this room, that flame, denatured, corrupted and contaminated by its long journey through your veins, which you had succeeded in taming and turning against me, to perfect that revenge which you had so effectively begun by implicating me in the attempted murder of your other enemy George Burton, in the "accident" in Brown Street, the attempted murder of which you are guilty, Bleston, whatever instrument you made use of, and in which I should retain my share of complicity even if James were not involved in it.

You had amplified my slender resentment against George Burton for his failure to appreciate the New Cathedral, to which the Jenkinses had introduced me, you had made it reverberate until it filled my mind, and you succeeded in making me crush and disfigure his image, since you could not make me destroy it by fire as I had destroyed yours—that image, that now unusable negative which I inserted on July 6th in the passage of *The Bleston Murder* which sarcastically described the vast building inside which, at the central point of the shadowy X, at the junction of the rood screens, the body of the cricketer Johnny Winn, murdered by his brother, is discovered by the detective Barnaby Morton; I looked at that negative, before closing the book, with satisfaction and relief, not only because I had preserved it, but also because I had reduced it to this state, and I heard myself whispering to the author that message which I have since received from yourself, prodigiously amplified:

"We are quits."

Then the sharp, low, penetrating alien voice faded away, that evil voice of yours, Bleston, and I felt nothing but my old friendship for the man who, a few days later, was to be wounded, that J. C. Hamilton whose name I had already twice betrayed, that name which was shortly to be shouted at all your street corners, Bleston, on the headlines of your newspapers, during that month of July when, quite unconcerned, I saw James's visits to the Baileys grow more and more frequent, when I saw this without seeing it, because I had eyes only for Rose, and those eyes were already blurred by the smoke of that imminent abortive murder, that "accident" in Brown Street which was about to happen.

Wednesday, September 10th

I walked through your streets, Bleston, with my eyes veiled by scaly lids, which I have now begun to lift but which are constantly liable to close again, through my fatigue and inattention and your undying cunning.

In me and all around me, in yourself, Bleston, lie hidden countless sources of mist, so that while I stare at the objects in my room I cannot see them properly; huge obstacles seem to separate me from them, even from this sheet of white paper on which I write, from the very sentence I am writing.

In order to diminish this distance from my own reality I must plunge back into my winter, set out a relief map of myself so as to trace the pattern of shadows cast by my days over one another, forward and backward to the present moment; and if I am now free to tackle this task during the few weeks I still have to live here, it is because, to my grief, Ann and James have come together like Lucien and Rose, and it is too late for me to make fresh plans for my time here; I have outlived myself.

I see you now, Bleston streets, I see your walls and your inscriptions and your faces; in the depths of your seemingly vacant stares I see the gleam of a precious raw material from which I can make gold; but how deep I must plunge to reach it, what efforts I must make to secure and collect all that dust!

During the misty days at the beginning of the week, after that cruel weekend, yesterday and the day before, when I found it hard to defend myself against the tide of ancient horror that rose afresh as I read, I cried in despair: "Have we not concluded a pact, city of Bleston? Was that yet another trick, that momentary respite granted to a tortured victim so as to add disappointment to his agony? Have you not taken enough from me to complete your vengeance?"

But now, on this lovely evening, surely one of the last real summer evenings, you seem to speak as my accomplice against yourself: "Do you imagine, puny alchemist, that you can so quickly, so easily free yourself, free me from my vast powers of darkness, from that monstrous lethargy which corrodes your resolution and which, if you ignore it, will ruin you the more completely?"

I need all your patience, Bleston, to hurry on; I need all your prudence, lest my haste should make our task miscarry.

I must plunge back into my winter to reduce the great gap still yawning in my story, plunge back into that obscure period preceding that Sunday at the end of March when I repeated to Lucien, in the Old Cathedral, some of the explanations of Cain's Window given me a long time ago by a priest whom I never saw again; I must plunge back into those days when I thought more and more about Rose and drifted further and further from Ann, in those days before I knew that J. C. Hamilton was George Burton's pseudonym, but when I already felt a close connection between *The Bleston Murder* and that man who had invited me to his home, where I had already dined one Saturday after roaming the streets all afternoon with Horace Buck, waiting in the rain for the pubs to open and then watching him get drunk by himself because I wanted to make a good impression on that unknown woman, Harriet, to whom I was to be introduced that evening—one Saturday when Lucien must have been on duty at his hotel since, in those days, it was with him that I used to go out whenever we were both free together.

We talked about my country, that Saturday, March 22nd, on my first visit to that house in Green Park Terrace, my country to which they had been together and to which they intended to return in August, a plan which of course was never fulfilled owing to the "accident", owing to myself, owing to your animosity, Bleston; we talked in French a little, which was a great relief for me because I still found it hard to express myself in your language; and when they asked me about you, Bleston, you to whom I was already bound by terrible bonds of hatred and curiosity, when I uttered my justified complaints, we managed to laugh at you together, the three of us, finding great pleasure and comfort in the game of subtle insults at which George shone particularly, with his sudden shouts of laughter, venting his spleen on the New Cathedral, which reminded me of *The Bleston Murder* and of Mrs. Jenkins whom I had often visited during the previous weeks; I dared not speak in its defence, I have never dared speak in its defence in front of him.

Thursday, September 11th

I had already noticed, that Saturday, March 22nd, the first time I entered the living-room with the windows overlooking Green Park (invisible then in the rainy night) the spherical looking-glass which gave a concentrated reflection of the whole room; there was one like it at the Baileys', and last Sunday, while beyond the windows, in the afternoon sun, the swaying crests of pines and firs looked greener from their proximity to the yellowing foliage of the other trees, that looking-glass showed me the image of Ann, who had herself told me, the day before, in James's presence, of her engagement, and whom I had managed to congratulate—the image of Ann, seen from the back, quite tiny, as if she was already far away from me, as if the sea already lay between us, the image of Ann moving farther and farther away from me, in that looking-glass room from which I was excluded because Ann's hand, holding up before my eyes the new copy of the new edition of *The Bleston Murder* which she had bought at Baron's the previous day so as to secure a dedication, prevented me from seeing myself reflected there; we had just come in, and Harriet had left us alone together for a moment while she went to fetch George, who was hard at work on his next book.

It was the previous day, last Saturday, September 6th, on leaving Matthews & Sons, that James had come up to me self-consciously, knowing only too well what he was going to tell me, what cruel news he would have to confirm with that smile that covers up his secret rages, and yet obliged to feign ignorance—it was the previous day that he had taken me in the black Morris to the stationer's to collect Ann, then to the Sword restaurant where the farce of the announcement took place, where I forced myself to seem delighted, and reminded Ann that we were both expected at the Burtons' next day; then, leaving them, I had roamed about the streets, driven by an anguish as sharp as raging toothache, exacerbated by the tension I had needed to maintain and intensify my mask; I had roamed about the streets and then called on Horace Buck, who was also alone once more, once more on the lookout for a woman, and we had ended the evening by visiting one pub after another, drinking one beer after another; at last I had come slowly home by a very devious route, peering through curtain chinks at scenes of family life.

I experienced a bitter happiness on Sunday on finding myself alone with her at the home of my victorious rival's enemy; I savoured this meagre revenge; but when I saw her in the glass moving farther and farther away from me of her own accord I realised the injustice of making even the slightest attempt to part her from her companion, and knew that their two images must be brought together even in this tiny contracted room.

That was why when George came in, looking well and cheerful as if nothing had happened to him, as if the Brown Street "accident" had only been a bad dream, after congratulating him on his perfect recovery and introducing Ann I immediately told him about James, her fiancé, without hinting of course that I suspected that very James of being responsible for, or rather instrumental in, that "accident", in a fit of furious resentment and anguished folly provoked by that raw wound which I had myself irritated and which today seems completely healed, I immediately told him about James who, I declared, was most anxious to meet him; consequently I was urged to bring James to dinner along with us next Sunday. I passed on the message next day at the office, cautiously, expecting to meet with a refusal, but on the contrary, after a long hesitation, James accepted the invitation.

It was not until all these preliminaries had been dealt with that I asked George Burton to tell us about his work.

"Is it a new J. C. Hamilton?"

"No, there won't be another *Bleston Murder*."

"Barnaby Rich then, or Caroline Bay?"

"No, this is something quite different, I shall have to find a new name."

Then he signed Ann's copy of his book, in the new Penguin edition, which I had not yet examined; at first glance it's just like its predecessor, but the back cover bears not a blank space but a mediocre photograph above a statement to the effect that J. C. Hamilton's identity is no longer a secret, that *The Bleston Murder* is by a local author, George Burton, *alias* Barnaby Rich, ten of whose novels have just been reprinted simultaneously by Penguin, and that curiously enough the event that caused the press to unmask the author was a mysterious accident still suspected in some quarters of being an attempted murder; the solution of which enigma no doubt awaits a detective as skilled as Barnaby Morton.

He signed Ann's copy of *The Bleston Murder*, in the new Penguin edition which I saw next day on show in Baron's window, between a *History of Corporal Punishment Through the Ages* and a *New Handbook of Cricket*. I saw it there next day on my way from Matthews & Sons to Town Hall Square to see the film about Bombay, and the day after that, last Tuesday, I bought myself a fresh copy, my third, at the same time as one of Barnaby Rich's ten novels picked at random; this third copy, boasting the author's real name and face, now lies on the left-hand corner of my table beside the old copy which I bought last winter in one of the second-hand bookshops in Chapel Street to replace the first one of all, on which I had written my name, which had served to guide me during the first months, which I had thought lost because Ann had assured me she had not got it at home, which I saw once more in her possession on June 1st and which her fiance, James Jenkins, now has.

Friday, September 12th

Twilight still allows me to see through my window the brick wall on the farther side of Copper Street, over which the moon is rising; and meanwhile I have switched on the light overhead, which shines on this blank page I am covering, this mirror, this trap to catch you, Bleston; and on the three rectangular images on the backs of three books, three portraits of the same man masked to varying degrees, the completely blank portrait on the old edition of *The Bleston Murder*, where the whole face has vanished behind its make-up, the second in which it is possible to recognise under the disguise of Barnaby Rich the familiar features of the author, and finally the latest, on the new edition of J. C. Hamilton's novel, the photograph for which George Burton has posed as George Burton, where the mask is less apparent but is still there, a particularly deceptive mask since it pretends not to be a mask, since one might imagine oneself to be looking at the man's own face at last—these three portraits serve as a kind of alphabet by means of which I can picture his different expressions and attitudes, just as, far more fully, the statues of the Arts and Sciences on the porches of the New Cathedral do in the case of Mrs. Jenkins, an incomplete alphabet of which I know one letter is missing, a keyboard of which I know one note is missing, a Tarot pack of which I know one card is missing, since the back of the next book will obviously display a new photograph corresponding to the new name, a new mask, whether deliberate or involuntary, a calculated disguise or an unposed snapshot, a new map which will help me to unmask the blank map, the blank rectangle on the old edition of *The Bleston Murder*, the blank map which itself unmasks the blank, mute, deceitful, secretive element in the others, a new document which will help me to reconstitute, behind the final result of his camouflage, the face of the man himself as he puts on his mask.

As for the blank sheet of paper on which I am writing, it too is a thick mask of paint, like the blank rectangle on the back of the book in front of me, the book I bought in midwinter in a second-hand bookshop in Chapel Street; but a mirror lies beneath the thick layer of paint that I am scratching with my pen as though with a knife, that I am burning away as though with a blowpipe, and gradually, through the cracks that my words make, my own face is revealed in its coating of thick grime, my own face being gradually cleansed by my misfortunes and my stubbornness, and yours behind it, Bleston, your face ravaged with inner conflict; and yours will shine through more and more clearly, until nothing can be seen of me but the glitter of eyes and teeth, while yours is consumed at last in an amplified incandescence.

Last night, in a dream, I was standing in New Cathedral Square, which I had crossed last Sunday on my way back from the Burtons' after taking Ann home to All Saints Gardens, passing Willow Park with its yellowing leaves; I stood in that square where, on Sunday, I had read on a long streamer stretched at first-floor level across the new store, now almost completed and freed of its palings: "Opening in November, Special Bargain Sale". I was standing in that square in the midst of a huge terrified crowd; we stared with our thousands of eyes at the grey spire, the towers, the porches, no longer motionless as a stone building should be but appallingly alive and breathing; we stared at the nave, which seemed to expand and contract like a thorax, its buttresses parting and closing in like ribs, and which with every breath thus taken grew bigger; we stared at those walls which had broken their moorings and were sweeping towards us like huge waves, which drove us back against the almost-completed shop, so that we battered the doors begging to be let in for shelter; then suddenly these walls rose up and turned back like the flaps of a tent opening, and we found ourselves—the whole crowd and all the buildings round the square—within the New Cathedral, which still on went breathing and growing, where all the animals on the capitals had come to life, and the rood screens multiplied like the rungs of a ladder, and the windows were no longer colourless but painted with changing scenes larger than life-size in front of towns, and then the windows and walls moved away and grew dark and slowly vanished behind the mist that was thickening, the whole crowd and all the buildings round the square now stood under the shadowy X in the transept, beneath an enormous fly made of enamel and gold, its eyes of coal, its wings of quivering glass slowly opening and closing, and meanwhile the New Cathedral itself was replaced by a completely new building which I could not describe because I only caught a glimpse of it, I only saw one of its doors, and only the handle and the crack of that, through the thickening fog.

Before retreating from myself once more into the folds of sleep I must spare a few moments and a few lines for that evening in midwinter, a month or a little over a month before my first visit to the Burtons, that evening when for the first time I went to dinner with the Baileys, when for the first time, while I looked at Ann sitting on my right, I raised my eyes towards the spherical mirror above the chimney-piece where the gas fire burned with a hissing noise (outside, melting snow was falling in the dense darkness); I raised my eyes towards the spherical mirror and caught there a smiling look from Rose, who in that contracted living-room had taken Ann's place on my right; at that time, Lucien Blaise had not yet come to Bleston, and I did not know George Burton, although I think I had noticed him sitting alone at a table in the first-floor room in the Oriental Bamboo, without suspecting any link between that distinguished-looking man who had clearly taken not the slightest notice of me that day, and the book I was hunting for; at that time I hated you, Bleston, I hated you bitterly already.

3

Monday, September 15th

Yesterday, Sunday, September 14th, in the late afternoon, I crossed New Cathedral Square on my way to the big house in Geology Street, where James was expecting me—we had arranged to pick up Ann in the Morris and go together to the Burtons'—James, whose holidays have begun, whose desk beside mine at Matthews & Sons was empty today, James whom I suspected for so long of being the instrument of Bleston's vengeance in the Brown Street "accident", but whom I now believe to be innocent, at least in a literal and legal sense. I crossed the empty Square, where cloudy night was falling on the empty New Cathedral and the almost-completed new store, so that I could scarcely see the long banner, already somewhat bedraggled, with its announcement of the opening in November, lit up by feeble projectors; yesterday, Sunday, September 14th, in the late afternoon, I felt once more in the depth of my being that terror, that dismay, that depression which I had experienced a month previously, in front of the same façade in broad sunlight; I heard a diminished echo of the stern, thunderous voice with which you had uttered that pitiless speech that I recorded during the following week, the third week in August, and which I have just re-read, your snarling, self-satisfied, authoritarian voice, which has not yet been stilled but through which there sounds now pleading for me, a different, far deeper voice, a voice of lamentation awakened by the flames I lit, the wound I inflicted on you, Bleston, the voice of your inner conflict, to which I now act as echo, having been forced by your inevitable victory to abandon my private quarrel, the voice of your longing for death and deliverance, to which I am striving to give utterance, according to the pact between us.

On leaving Matthews & Sons, I went to the News Theatre to see the film about New Zealand; then, crossing Town Hall Square over which night was falling, I went to dine in the first-floor room of the Oriental Rose, from which I watched the last green lights fade behind the ridiculous crenellated towers of the civic building.

Certain fragments of the older text I have been reading mingle naturally with the words I write this evening: "The days are drawing in now, the weather is breaking up, but there will still be many bright hours before I go, bright hours such as I was unable to enjoy in October, when I felt crushed by the unfamiliar desolation on which they shone", certain expressions of that old self which return to haunt me, tinged with another light, as if their meaning had ripened, as if the lines I wrote then were merely the prefiguration of this evening's lines, for if the days were shortening then, they are shortening far faster now, and the fine days still left me before I leave will be increasingly precious, increasingly dazzling by contrast with the darkness, the mist, the lashing rain that now hold sway, until the imminent new October which I shall not be here to see.

Throughout August, each Monday, before settling down to write I finished reading what I had written during the corresponding week in June, and now, following the same pattern, I have been reading my July pages, only not on Mondays now but on Tuesdays, since on September 1st I was still dazed by the violence of the blow you had struck me, Bleston, and last week I was exhausted by the strain of keeping up appearances, of disclosing nothing of my knowledge or my agony when I visited the Burtons and the Baileys; then I sought a bitter consolation in that long cry of entreaty sent up, from the wilderness into which I was wandering, towards Ann who could not hear it, and this evening I have been studying what I wrote the week

before that, the third week in August; thus I have traced back
the course of the month, week by week, in my reading, just as
in my writing in July I traced back the course of May, in August
I traced back April, and now, following the same pattern, I am
tracing back March, because the events which happen to us shed
light progressively on what has led up to them.

Tuesday, September 16th

I now know that the car which, on Friday, July 11th, at half-past
six, in Brown Street, suddenly swerved and rushed headlong at
George Burton was not Richard Tenn's; and I now believe that
it was not Matthews & Sons' black Morris, that the driver was
not James, as up 'til Sunday evening I had feared, but another
man, some man whom I don't know, whom I have probably
never seen, who has probably never heard of me, another man
in another black Morris; and yet this does not in the least mean
that the affair was a mere "accident", and my responsibility is
in no wise diminished by the fact that the chain of interme-
diaries is longer and more complicated than I had previously
imagined, and perhaps impossible to reconstitute with any
certainty; I believe now that you made use of another man,
Bleston, to revenge yourself on J. C. Hamilton, to strike at me
through him, to taunt me and ruin me, to stifle me in the dense
smoke of conjecture and remorse rising from this enigmatic
incident as from the sulphurous mouth of a volcano; but this
acquitted James only on the legal and literal plane, because
the confession he made me, far from reducing to nothing my
suspicions about him, confirms them to a large extent, shows
me exactly how far they were justified and that it only needed
a slightly different arrangement of circumstances for James to
have played in actual fact the part I had so long attributed to
him, in that scene which he could not have described to me thus
on Sunday evening if he had experienced it otherwise than in
a dream, just as it only needed a minute difference in speed

for George Burton to have died instead of getting away with a few weeks in hospital.

We were driving back from Green Park Terrace in the black Morris; we had dropped Ann in front of 31 All Saints Gardens; we had passed under the railway bridge, under the lines that run from Hamilton Station towards the south, on which I shall travel on the last Tuesday of this month; we were going along Surgery Street, past the waste land in the 10th district where the last lights were going out in the fairground, the shutters going up over the last booths, the last pleasure-seekers leaving with their raincoat collars turned up in the cold wet night, when James slowed down and stopped at the side of the almost deserted pavement, and turning towards me in the darkness, spoke through the purring of his engine and the patter of raindrops, in praise of George Burton and his kindness; then, staring once more at the road before him, a blur through the beating windscreen wipers, he went on:

"I had a strange dream about him, the very evening on which he had his accident.

"I was in Brown Street in the rush hour; I was holding this steering wheel as I am now, but I was not in control of my driving, my arms were paralysed, I was charging into the middle of the crowd of people who fled in panic before me, and I saw a man crossing in the distance ahead of me, a man whom I knew I shouldn't be able to avoid, who stopped in front of me and suddenly looked at me as if he were aiming a gun at me, closing one eye, a man whom I recognised, whom I was sure I had seen before.

"Suddenly he disappeared; then I was able to move again, I got control of my car and managed to turn down a street on the right.

"As soon as I woke up I realised that the face in my nightmare was that of George Burton in the photograph he had taken of himself at the fair that evening when you hurried after him, and when you told me that he was the author of *The Bleston Murder*.

"When I read, the week after, in the newspapers that he had been knocked down by a car on Friday at 6.20 p.m. in Brown Street I had a moment of horrible anguish, wondering whether what I had taken for a dream might not be reality, whether in a moment of madness I could have committed the crime; and I only managed to reassure myself after meticulously reconstituting my actions between six and seven that evening, and confirming that it was practically impossible for me to have been in Brown Street at the time of the accident."

Wednesday, September 17th

He started off again, and we drove along Surgery Street and Continent Street, away from that fairground where I had spent the previous evening, a dark, damp, cold but not rainy evening, with Horace Buck who had talked unceasingly to me about his latest girl and his possible departure, while I thought about Ann and James and their engagement, which is to be officially celebrated next Saturday in the house in All Saints Gardens, quite close by, and about the visit to the Burtons' which we were all three to pay next day.

James Jenkins did not speak another word 'til we reached Town Hall Square, where the cinemas were closing, and there, still without looking at me, he asked: "Was it you that I saw yesterday waiting for a twenty-four bus?" Then he added without a transition: "I'd never have believed George Burton to be so fair; from his photograph I'd imagined him a very dark man, darker than yourself; almost like a negro."

I realise that the link between these two apparently disconnected remarks was that "very dark man", that man much darker than myself, that negro, Horace Buck, who had been standing beside me the previous evening waiting for the 24 bus to take us to the fairground in the 10th district (where James had stopped the black Morris to tell me his dream), Horace Buck with whom he had seen me in March, at the fairground which was then in the 3rd district alongside Lanes Park, a day or two after the day when I had taken Lucien there for the first time and had met James himself there for the first time; I know that the two remarks were closely connected to one another and to the dream about the "accident" in Brown Street by that negro, Horace Buck, whom he could not have failed to see the previous evening when he saw me, and with whom I had been wandering round the fair in March, under the drizzling rain, when I saw James himself there for the second time in a couple of days, to my amazement, since I had as yet no inkling of his relations with the little travelling town or its people, of that whole aspect of his personality; Horace Buck, in whose company he had been shocked to see me, I remember clearly, when I met him, for the second time in a couple of days, amidst those booths and caravans, that collection of boards and canvas and corrugated iron, and that wet crowd: Horace Buck, whom I had then introduced to him, and to whose offer of a drink he had been unable to reply, but turning away with a look of horror and unsurmountable disgust on his face had hurriedly left us.

James had never mentioned the scene to me again, whereas Horace, deeply humiliated, had often alluded to it sarcastically during our monotonous conversations; but it's clear that his recollection of it fostered his secret resentment towards me, that resentment born of his reading of *The Bleston Murder* and above all of the pain I had given his mother by lending her the book; and indeed, in his dream, the victim of his criminal attempt had not only worn George Burton's face but also borne a certain likeness to Horace; he had sought to strike at both of them, and through them at myself too, as being the link between them, just as in the real "accident" in Brown Street Bleston had sought revenge not on J. C. Hamilton alone, but on myself too.

Thursday, September 18th

How could I have made James understand, then, that what bound me to this negro was the fact that I recognised in him my own black hatred towards you, Bleston, just as intense, my own black hatred which you have succeeded in making incandescent by the violence of your repeated blows, in transmuting into an equally passionate destructive attachment? How could I have made James understand this? I knew that I could not explain it even to Lucien, who was surprised at our friendship, wondering whatever we could find to talk about, whereas we had that inexhaustible theme for complaints and abuse, we had you, Bleston, to feed our monotonous conversations broken by long pauses; I knew that I could not even succeed in explaining it to Lucien, who has always been too much of an outsider in Bleston to appreciate the real merits of his future brother-in-law James Jenkins.

It has rained every day this week, it rains harder as each day grows shorter, it was raining on Saturday when I left Matthews & Sons and went to Old Cathedral Square, where I found that the Oriental Bamboo was still closed, that it would not reopen until Saturday next, the day after tomorrow, and then went on to lunch by myself at the Oriental Rose in Town Hall Square; I watched the buses filing past under the rain, the queues forming in front of the cinemas under the rain, the minute hand of the clock on the ridiculous crenellated tower in the centre of the civic building reach the highest point in the clock face and then move jerkily downwards, under the rain; I watched the blanket of clouds grow paler and split to reveal a glimpse of distant milky blue, and then saw the sheen of sunlight on the asphalt.

Then, as the afternoon grew ever brighter, I went to revisit Oak Park, in the 1st district to the north-east, to look once more at the great oak with its rusty bark, looking like the oaks in the fourth of the Museum tapestries; its tawny leaves were eddying in the surrounding walks and carpeting the lawns and puddles;

I went to revisit Birch Park in the 2nd district, alongside the Slee, hidden by a wall above which you can glimpse the funnels of tugboats and the tops of cranes, I went to look once more at the silver birch branches, visible again through their shimmering foliage of pale moist gold; then I slowly walked upstream along the black, bubbling river, while the sky grew overcast again and the sun dropped lower, and when I reached Horace Buck's house in Iron Street it was dusk already and it was raining again, a light rain which did not prevent us from going out, eating in a snack bar in Continent Street and then travelling by a 24 bus as far as the fair in the 10th district, where we drank pint after pint of beer to keep out the unexpected chill; then we came back on foot through the wet deserted streets, while behind the darkened windows I seemed to hear the murmur of all your sleeping inhabitants, Bleston, who long for your death as much as I do, from their very depth of their bones, under their carapace of fatigue and resigned acceptancy.

Great clouds were sailing over Dew Street when I woke up, late, on Sunday; the pale shifting sunbeams lit up transitory gleams in the windows of City Street as I made my way to the Bombay for a solitary lunch, and on the façades of Dudley Station and New Station while I was waiting for a 31 bus in the middle of Alexandra Place; they shimmered on the black swirling Slee as I crossed Brandy Bridge on my way to Ferns Park, where I carried on my farewell walk through your gardens, Bleston, in the russet underwood on which the first great glistening raindrops were falling, while women turned up their hoods.

Then I made my way under a downpour past great silent factories, under great smokeless chimneys, past great closed iron gates and grilles, as far as the muddy walks of Easter Park, where beds of withered flowers were shedding their rotting petals and their crumpled leaves.

I had to change when I got home; but the rain had stopped, and under a low, darkening, dust-coloured sky I walked southwards to that big house in Geology Street where James expected me, the Jenkins' big house in which I had not set foot since July; I walked by way of Tower Street and White Street, crossing New Cathedral Square and then skirting Willow Park, slowly, watchfully, trying to catch every word you whispered to me, Bleston, as I passed in the gathering darkness.

Friday, September 19th

The black Morris was standing in the neglected garden; I got in beside James, while in the lighted doorway, above the three dilapidated steps, his mother waved goodbye with her right hand, on which glittered the glass bubble that contained the fly; and we drove off to fetch Ann at 31 All Saints Gardens, where Rose let us in, Rose who, while her sister got ready, delightedly read me extracts from Lucien's latest letter, promising to come back and see her at Christmas; then we drove off with Ann to dinner at the Burtons'.

What mattered was not so much the conversation, in which James, after a few moments' awkwardness, overcame his shyness, his apprehension, the last traces of his former violent aversion, and thanks to the encouraging and stimulating presence of his fiancée, displayed more charm and far more brilliance than I had ever seen in him; what mattered was that here, in the house of that enemy who had tormented his dreams, the spherical mirror above the fireplace, where coal was once again burning in the grate, reflected the double image of the engaged couple between the faces of the married couple who were welcoming us, the images of Ann and James, and my own too, close to the edge, a tiny image framed in a tiny curved doorway, the images of Ann and James together, as I shall see them tomorrow night reflected in the spherical mirror above the fireplace at the Baileys', amidst the excited crush of their engagement party.

I shall go and see George once more, a couple of days before I leave, on Sunday, September 28th; and this will bring to a close the long dialogue that has gone on between us since that moment in the coldest part of the year, at the heart of winter, in the middle of those few days of clear bright cold, of white hoarfrost in the morning on the roofs of Dew Street and hard puddles in the streets and along the park walks, that dialogue that started between us on Saturday, February 15th, in the first-floor room of the Oriental Bamboo, at the table described in the opening pages of *The Bleston Murder*, where the detective-to-be, Barnaby Morton, has lunch with the victim-to-be, the cricketer Johnny Winn, at that table close to the window overlooking the façade of your Old Cathedral, Bleston, with your famous Murderer's Window (the façade which that day was glistening under its thin glassy carapace of ice, while the late-Gothic towers stood out against a sky the colour of soapy water), overlooking the Romanesque porches with their kings and prophets, above the steps where I fell flat a very long time ago in front of a girl who was probably Rose Bailey, that table at which I so much longed, last month, to sit alone with Ann, that table to which I shall take them both, I hope, Ann and her fiancé James Jenkins, as I suggested last Sunday while we were driving back from Green Park Terrace to All Saints Gardens.

On that Saturday, February 15th, I had laid beside my plate, on the cloth, the copy of *The Bleston Murder* which I had at last unearthed in one of the second-hand bookshops in Chapel Street and which now lies on my left underneath the latest edition, the one with the real name and photograph; and I realise clearly today that it was for this reason that he came to sit opposite me, that he was on the lookout for the slightest pretext to start a conversation with this stranger who was reading his favourite of all his books, but he succeeded admirably in concealing this and in making our encounter seem entirely a matter of chance.

His first words had been a conventional enquiry whether the seat were free; then he had looked at the menu and ordered a chop suey, and unfolded his paper, which he had begun to read as he ate, observing me discreetly meanwhile.

He folded the paper and thrust it into the pocket of his tweed jacket, and then laid his hands on the edge of the table behind his empty plate; the plump yellow-skinned waiter came up between us asking if we wanted anything more; and each of us in turn, myself first, replied: "An almond cake and some more tea."

When the plump, yellow-skinned little waiter came back, with the same half-smile on his lips, there was only one teapot on his tray, a pot for two; and the man sitting opposite me, the other side of the fateful table, the man whom I did not yet know to be George Burton, whom I did not suspect of being that J. C. Hamilton whose name was displayed on the cover of the book I had laid beside me, this man poured tea into both our cups, bending forward to say in a friendly manner: "He thought we were together."

From that moment our thoughts began to impel each other on, like toothed gearwheels; we talked about my country, which we knew, and about you, Bleston, of course, deploring the poor quality of the food provided by most of your restaurants; and for the first time I heard that grating laugh of his which brought such wonderful relief to my obscure hatred.

From that midwinter conversation, held under the benevolent reptilian eye of the yellow *genius loci*, there has grown up a huge scaffolding of living branches, spreading, meeting, overshadowing one another, crossing one another, joining, conflicting, and leading up to the present moment, from which I scan it; all this week I have explored it in my writing, recognising at different levels a whole series of footholds by means of which, this evening, my straining memory has climbed down to reach that ground of long ago.

4

Monday, September 22nd

What I had written during the second week in June struck me as surprisingly inadequate when I re-read it on Monday, August 11th, after seeing a documentary about San Francisco at the News Theatre which I have not mentioned because I scarcely remember it, and after dining at the Oriental Rose; it struck me as inadequate because, for one thing, I had failed to record my last visit to the Museum tapestries the previous Sunday, June 8th, with James Jenkins; it struck me as inadequate when I re-read it on Monday, August 11th, before starting to write the set of pages that I have been re-reading this equinoctial evening, after seeing at the News Theatre that mediocre documentary about Sicily which, despite the poor quality of its colours and images, fleetingly recalled the azure sky of Crete, that blue heaven which is now receding ever farther above your streets, Bleston, above your parks and chimneys, your people and your animals, your slow murders and your slow decay, and which will go on receding farther behind the mists and rains of your autumn, after this final weekend of summer weather, these two last days of fickle flaming sunshine.

It was late this evening, after dining at the Oriental Rose, that I began to read this set of pages, written during the second week in August; and I read it hurriedly, whereas I should have pored over every sentence so as to discover how much I had changed in my vision of events and people and things; I read it too hurriedly because it was already late, after my meal at the Oriental Rose, and because it is late in our year together, Bleston, because I have

302

only nine days left before leaving your walls of cast iron and rain and smouldering embers, less than nine evenings to finish this record, to try and fill its most important gaps, to try and fulfil that clause in our pact, which I must do if I am to survive.

And these pages written during the second week in August are inadequate too, because for one thing I failed to lay stress on my last visit to the Museum tapestries with Rose, the previous Saturday, during which we'd had that brief talk of which a few words recurred to me just now while, against the blue Mediterranean sky so feebly displayed on the screen of the News Theatre, there arose in my mind's eye visions of Crete, Athens, Rome and many other lands, other cities, other ages, that brief talk of which a few words recurred to me two days ago while I examined those Tapestries yet once more, after gazing yet once more at the Window in the Old Cathedral—that visit on Saturday, August 9th, with Rose, who had been astonished when I told her (intending to puzzle her, to deceive her, to revenge myself for all the pain she innocently inflicted on me that terrible afternoon) that what I sought for in those panels was an understanding of the origins of Bleston (adding to myself: and consequently of my own misery); Rose had been astonished, though not in the way I expected, and had replied that there were many far more ancient things in Bleston. I have re-read them inadequately, too, this evening, those pages written during the second week in August, before starting to complete them inadequately, before starting to write this last section which will be dated the fourth week in September, the last complete week I shall have spent here, Bleston, amongst your mirages and murmurs, your gloomy unrest, your exudations that nightly grow harsher and chillier, this set of pages which will inevitably be inadequate and incomplete, because, for one thing, I shall not succeed in saying all I should like to about my last visit to the Museum tapestries (which will certainly be the last of our year together) the day before yesterday, Saturday, September 20th, before coming back here to change and then going on to

All Saints Gardens for the party given to celebrate Ann Bailey's engagement.

Tuesday, September 23rd

What I had in my memory yesterday while I was writing, apart from the experiences of that evening (my visit to the cinema, my meal at the Oriental Rose) and the experiences of the previous day and particularly the day before that, Saturday (the Baileys' party, my last visit to the Museum tapestries and to Cain's Window, and my lunch at the Oriental Bamboo, now reopened) was not a clear, insistent picture of the previous week's events with an increasingly dim perspective of earlier events, going back day by day into the past; no, while I was writing yesterday the recollection that stood out against the dark blurred background of our whole year together, Bleston, the recollection that conditioned all my words and that alone can explain them, is of that period in August during which I had written the pages I had been reading, and the earlier periods which these described, fragments of April, January and June, and through the latter one fragment of November, in fact a whole series of bands of varying brightness separated by broad zones of shadow, like the beams into which the brightness of an incandescent body is broken up on the black screen of a spectroscope, a whole series of resonances of varying intensity separated by broad intervals of silence, like the harmonics into which the timbre of a sound is broken up.

Those bands of memory still persist this evening, but while I was reading the pages written during the fourth week in July, other periods in our year together, Bleston, came into the foreground: that two-month-old fragment of time when I wrote them (those inadequate pages, all marked and coloured by the sudden public disclosure of J. C. Hamilton's real name, and by my tergiversations about Rose when I did not know that Lucien had already won her)—that fragment of July coming to light within the zone of darkness between those fragments of June and August remembered yesterday, making them yield an unfamiliar sound, itself growing richer by association with them, growing clearer and more accurate; and then the fragment of December around that atrocious Christmas Day, which came to light within the zone of darkness between the fragments of January and November remembered yesterday; and in the same way, between the fragments of April and June there came to light that period in May during which George Burton, in his talk about detective fiction, had begun to give me certain hints about the labyrinth of time and memory which helped me considerably to find my way through our year together, Bleston, our year which will be up in a week, since by this time next Tuesday I shall be far away from you already, from your horrible oppressive and exhausting tyranny—that period in May during which I had taken Lucien to see the Museum tapestries.

These are the periods which have come into the foreground this evening, slipping between those remembered yesterday like the fingers of clasped hands; and into the only interval left intact, between the fragments of April and January—according to the complex order which has gradually imposed itself on me in my narrative, according to the incomplete pattern which it has now assumed, the gaps in which I must fill as best I can in the few days left to me—I must insert the second week in March.

But first I must use these last moments before sleep overtakes me to add a few lines about those flies whose buzz echoed once again through the pages I was reading today and yesterday (the fly that tormented George Burton in hospital on Saturday, July 19th, and the one that tormented him at home in Green Park Terrace on Sunday, August 10th), those flies that belong to you, Bleston, that are an inseparable part of you.

For it might seem at a first glance that you are made up only of stones and men, and that animals have no share in your being, but if one considers the caged beasts in the Pleasance Gardens Zoo, the last remaining cart-horses and the processions bound for the slaughterhouses in the 11th district, the innumerable cats and all the vermin, one is forcibly made aware that these too have become an organic part of your system, and that alive or dead, spectacular or parasitic, meat or carrion, they incarnate certain of your powers.

Wednesday, September 24th

It was in the City Street restaurant, to which I returned for lunch on Sunday, that I had spoken for the first time on Saturday, March 8th, to Lucien Blaise, whom I had already noticed a week previously in a snack bar in Alexandra Place because he was so obviously a Frenchman. I had spotted him as soon as I came in, and I'd gone to sit at the same table, where he had laid down a book on which I could make out, upside down, the French title and the name of an English author familiar to lovers of detective fiction; and when I saw him pull a packet of *Gauloises* from his pocket I could resist no longer, but started a conversation, first in English (and what a pleasure it was to hear him speak with an even stronger accent than mine!) and soon, of course, in French (and what a pleasure it was to be able to use my own language familiarly, without having to make an effort in order to be understood, as was necessary at that time with Rose, and still more with George Burton), and I learnt that he had just begun a five-months' term as barman at the Grand Hotel, opposite Prince's restaurant, at the corner of Town Hall Square, across which we soon went together for a drink at the Unicorn, next to the News Theatre.

We spent the whole of that afternoon wandering together through your streets, Bleston, and next day we met again to visit Pleasance Gardens with the Bailey sisters, who promptly adopted him.

Thus each day, evoking other days like harmonics, transforms the appearance of the past, and while certain periods come into the light others, formerly illuminated, tend to grow dim, and to lie silent and unknown until with the passage of time fresh echoes come to awaken them.

Thus the sequence of former days is only restored to us through a whole host of other days, constantly changing, and every event calls up an echo from other, earlier events which caused it or explain it or correspond to it, every monument, every object, every image sending us back to other periods which we must reawaken in order to recover the lost secret of their power for good or evil, other periods often remote and forgotten, whose density and distance are to be measured not by weeks or months but by centuries, standing out against the dark blurred background of our whole history, far beyond the limits of our year together, Bleston, other periods and other cities far beyond your frontiers, like those that came into my mind's eye on Saturday while I was looking at the Museum tapestries, those great illustrative panels woven of wool and silk, of silver and gold which have so often provided me with terms of reference for understanding you, Bleston, whose trees have enabled me to discover some of your trees, whose seasons have revealed your seasons, and which have been such weighty factors in my destiny, those links forged in France in the eighteenth century through which there has come down to me—to us, Bleston—a very ancient legend transmitted through the culture of Rome, by a Greek of the Roman Empire, Plutarch ("Here ends the city of Theseus, here begins the city of Hadrian"), a legend that first took shape in the days of Athens' glory, and through which a whole long story of earlier days was handed down, perpetuating the name of Minos and recalling an arrangement of reality which was both fundamental and highly recondite.

Every monument, every image sends us back to other periods and to other cities, such as those which are associated with Cain's Window, that major symbol which decided the pattern of my whole life during our year together, Bleston, Cain's Window in that Cathedral of which Rose was clearly thinking when she spoke of "much more ancient things", those pieces of glass cut and joined together in sixteenth century France, whose historic themes arouse harmonic echoes in those of the Museum tapestries and are interlaced with these like the fingers of clasped hands, the Window of Cain who founded the first city—that great enigma which I had revisited on Saturday to renew my strength in its light, after lunching with Ann and James in the first-floor room of the Oriental Bamboo, now reopened, at that table next to the window overlooking the dark façade, that crucial table, the scene of so many encounters under the benevolent reptilian eye of the plump Chinese waiter with the unvarying half-smile on his lips.

At the News Theatre on Monday night, while I was watching that poor documentary about Sicily, the two series of cities and periods portrayed in those two great hieroglyphs of yours, Bleston, were interwoven in my mind's eye, those two series of cities and periods which still live on here painfully, stifled, mutilated, falsified, pursuing within you Bleston, within each one of your inhabitants, within each of your street corners, in darkness, their wars and misunderstandings, those two series of traditions, of translations, interwoven against the blue Sicilian sky behind which I sensed the dawning of a miraculous glow, the red of your innermost fires set free at last, a red beyond all colour, of which the most majestic conflagrations offer only a remote, impure prefiguration.

Thursday, September 25th

At the house in All Saints Gardens, last Saturday, I was present like a ghost at the little party in honour of Ann and James's engagement, unable to join in, and remembering that other party, the one on August 2nd.

I wandered like a ghost on Sunday afternoon under a bright sky with shifting cloud, after calling at Hamilton Station to find out the exact time of my train next Tuesday morning, six days from now, and then revisiting the Anchor; I carried on my farewell tour of your gardens, Bleston, walking under the rust-coloured trees of Lanes Park and the dark trees of Green Park, past the chrysanthemums of the great cemetery in the south and those of All Saints Park, and then among the misty reed-beds of Willow Park.

Like a ghost, choosing a different way back each evening from the Sword restaurant after work, making ever wider and more complex detours, walking more and more slowly, I stare through the night, which grows ever darker and colder, and the ever finer and denser rain, at the faces that stand out in the wan light of your street-lamps against the glistening blackness of your pavements and housefronts, the faces hurrying home-wards muttering or chattering; and when I pass beside them a few scraps of their talk reach me, and I clutch them like precious ore, although most of the time so terribly impenetrable to me, Bleston, that I feel far better able to interpret the sign I read between those two bricks on a cracked wall; that is the message by means of which I can erode your carapace, Bleston, that slow relentless flame issuing from your own innards and which gradually will arouse reflections and echoes in the eyes of these passers-by, gaining strength from such resonance; I stare, through the night's tapestry of fine rain, at all those faces, doomed to share your misfortune until their death, Bleston, all those faces which the rain will destroy before it can turn once again into a blessing, before these slow fires have transformed their sand to glass.

There was a crack between two bricks on a streaming wall, and I drank from it a mouthful of tears mingled with such strong venom that I have doubtless hastened my own decrepitude, that torments await me, and my face will be marked with a leprous star; but it was the draught of ghosts, the elixir of immortality, its bitter taste left me no doubt of that.

All of a sudden the weariness mounting for months, your weariness, Bleston, has overpowered me, swathing my bones like the folds of a wet shroud, and I have been standing motionless a long time gazing through my own reflection in the window at the countless drops of water, minute spherical mirrors, dropping indefatigably in Dew Street; and yet there are only a few moments left me to finish this week's pages, since the Burtons, called away to London for the weekend, have written to ask me to dinner with them for the last time tomorrow evening instead of Sunday, there are only a few moments left me to recall that week in February after which I ceased to meet Ann at the Sword for lunch, the other assistant at Rand's having recovered, that week in February when George Burton, during our second conversation in the first-floor room of the Oriental Bamboo, at that table beside the window overlooking the façade of your Old Cathedral, announced that he would invite me to dinner in his home in Green Park Terrace as soon as his wife was back, that sinister period in February of which I should like not to think, but which on the contrary I ought to pick out from among the tangle of my winter memories with strong supple pincers of language, which I ought to keep firmly before my eyes, that period in February during which I longed so impatiently for the moment when I'd have done with Matthews & Sons, when I should leave you, Bleston, that moment of my deliverance which seemed immensely remote, when the train would start to move, carrying me far away from your face and your loathsome breath: the morning of September 30th, which I longed for so impatiently during those sinister days in February that I could not resist prowling about ever more frequently near Alexandra Place and going ever more frequently into Hamilton Station to watch the trains leaving amidst clouds of chilly steam.

5

Tuesday, September 30th

In the corner of my carriage, facing the engine, next to the grey pane covered outside with drops of rain through which I have just watched them going away after saying goodbye to me—Ann and Rose Bailey, James Jenkins and even Horace Buck—I have only a few moments left, Bleston, before the long minute hand stands upright on the clock face, before the train starts, carrying me far away from you, only a few moments to sketch out the pages that I could not write last night as I should have liked because it was far too late, and I could no longer struggle against sleep, after I had finished re-reading the sentences set down at the end of July and in early August, before and after Lucien's engagement and departure, re-reading those sentences as I had not succeeded in doing during the weekend as I should have liked, that weekend during which I had not even been able to visit the old church of St. Jude's on the other side of the Slee, that weekend too crammed with expeditions and goodbye visits which I haven't time to set down in detail because the long minute hand is rising higher and higher on the clock face that I can see on the platform, that platform of Hamilton Station at which I had gazed on Saturday, March 1st, as on all my free days in that period of our year together, Bleston, at which I gazed from the hall, summoning with all my hatred the distant moment of my deliverance, that moment of our separation, Bleston which is now come,

on Saturday, March 1st, before going into a snack bar in Alexandra Place to warm myself with a cup of tea, where I saw a young man with a suitcase who had evidently just arrived and who looked so obviously a Frenchman that I could not resist accosting him when I met him a week later in a restaurant in City Street, that young man whose name was Lucien Blaise;

there are only a few moments left me, Bleston, to recall for the last time the big room at Matthews & Sons in which I shall never set foot again, where all the staff were foregathered for the last time, Blythe, Greystone, Ward, Dalton, Cape, Slade, Moseley, Ardwick, and even James Jenkins, whose holiday was over;

and I haven't even time to set down something that happened on the evening of February 29th, something that seemed very important and that I shall forget as I move farther away from you, Bleston, as you lie dying, Bleston, whose dying embers I have fanned, for now the long minute hand stands upright and my departure closes this last sentence.

· A WORD ON THE WORDS ·

The mid-century Mancunian-Parisian ancestry of this work has determined our font selections: three typefaces from Linotype, whose chief manufacturing works were situated at the Linotype & Machinery complex in Altrincham, just south of Manchester, from 1899 until the 1980s.

Main body text is set in Granjon, a rather misnamed yet elegant typeface constructed by master printer George W. Jones, in derivation of a face cut by Claude Garamond—originally displayed in a 1554 publication from the Parisian printer Jacques Dupuys. The contemporary design was engineered at the L&M factory in the mid-1920s by the taciturn and brilliant Harry Smith—a draughtsman recognised for his unique sensitivity to letter spacing.

Titles are composed in Méridien, a font developed by Adrian Frutiger from 1953—the year of Butor's escape from Manchester. The type was initially cut for Deberny & Peignot in Paris and later digitised by Linotype.

Egyptienne is utilised on the cover spread. Created in 1956—the year in which *L'Emploi du temps* was first published—and chosen in allusion to Butor's employ as a teacher in Egypt, directly prior to his unfortunate sojourn in Manchester.